CLASSIC TALES FOR

Halloween

First published in 2010 by Miles Kelly Publishing Ltd
Harding's Barn, Bardfield End Green, Thaxted, Essex, CM6 3PX, UK

This edition printed 2016

2 4 6 8 10 9 7 5 3 1

Publishing Director Belinda Gallagher
Creative Director Jo Cowan
Senior Designer Simon Lee
Junior Designer Kayleigh Allen
Cover Designer Rob Hale
Image Manager Liberty Newton
Production Elizabeth Collins, Caroline Kelly
Reprographics Stephan Davis, Jennifer Cozens,
Anthony Cambray, Thom Allaway
Assets Lorraine King

ISBN 978-1-78617-152-8

Printed in China

British Library Cataloguing-in-Publication Data
A catalogue record for this book is available from the British Library

ACKNOWLEDGEMENTS

The publishers would like to thank the following artists
who have contributed to this book:
Cover: Zdenko Basic and Manuel Sumberac/The Bright Agency
Martin Angel, Vanessa Card, Jon Davis/Linden Artists Ltd, Mike White/Temple Rogers,
Peter Dennis/Linda Rogers Associates, Richard Hook/Linden Artists Ltd, Eric Rowe/Linden Artists Ltd,
Mike Saunders, Colin Sullivan/Beehive Illustration, Gwen Tourret/B L Kearley, Rudi Vizi
All other artwork from the Miles Kelly Artwork Bank

All photographs are from:
Corel, digitalSTOCK, digitalvision, Dreamstime.com, Fotolia.com, iStockphoto.com,
John Foxx, PhotoAlto, PhotoDisc, PhotoEssentials, PhotoPro, Stockbyte

Every effort has been made to acknowledge the source and copyright holder of each picture.
Miles Kelly Publishing apologises for any unintentional errors or omissions.

Made with paper from a sustainable forest

www.mileskelly.net

CLASSIC TALES FOR
Halloween

Compiled by Vic Parker

Miles
KeLLy

Contents

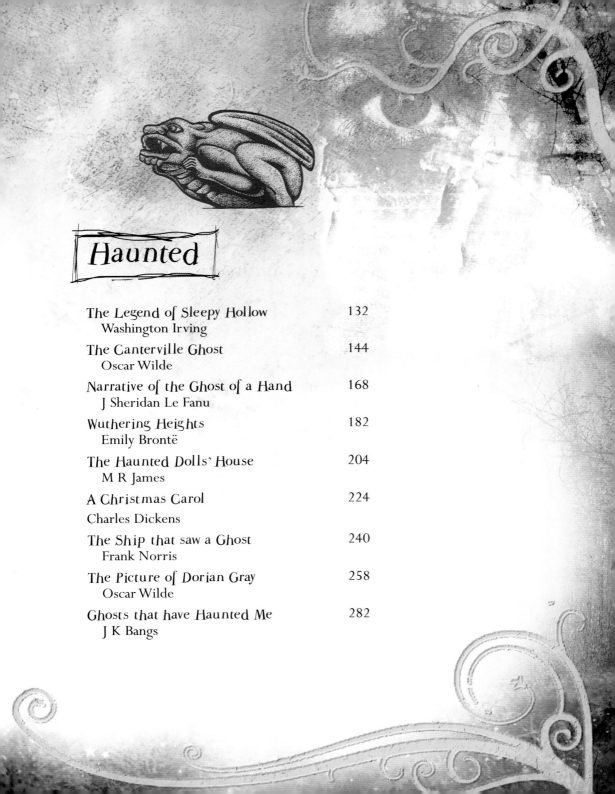

Haunted

Cursed Creatures

The Doomed and the Dead

Foreword

This book is filled with creepy stories to chill you, thrill you and send shivers down your spine. They are some of the very best from a rich tradition of terrifying tales that dates back to Christmas Eve 1764. It was then that the first ever 'horror' novel was published, *The Castle of Otranto* by Horace Walpole. This was an eerie tale of ghosts, family curses, and macabre goings-on, set in a foreign land during medieval times – an era when everyone believed in the supernatural and lived in fear of many superstitions. *The Castle of Otranto* captivated the imagination of eighteenth century readers and began a public craze for many more.

Through the Victorian era (1837–1901), families and friends loved nothing better than to gather round the parlour fire on dark evenings to listen to a sinister and spooky story.

Spiritualism also became fashionable, and many Victorians dabbled in attempts to contact the dead. Victorian authors transformed Gothic horror-writing by developing it in exciting directions. For instance, they did away with remote locations and past times, bringing horrors to their readers' front doors.

In 1918, Virginia Woolf wrote an article for the *Times Literary Supplement* exploring just what it is about ghost stories that makes them so irresistible. She decided that, "It is pleasant to be afraid when we are conscious that we are in no kind of danger…" So, settle back and enjoy these haunting tales, safe in the knowledge that there's no such thing as ghosts… or is there?

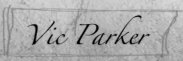

Vic Parker

From the Grave

Many people will testify that 'dead and buried' certainly does not mean 'gone forever'. In these stories, the dearly-departed simply refuse to take death lying down...

The Body Snatcher

1884

EXTRACT

Robert Louis Stevenson

In his young days, Fettes studied medicine in the schools of Edinburgh. He had talent of a kind, the talent that picks up swiftly what it hears and readily retails it for its own. He worked little at home; but he was civil, attentive, and intelligent in the presence of his masters. They soon picked him out as a lad who listened closely and remembered well; nay, strange as it seemed to me when I first heard it, he was in those days well favoured and pleased by his exterior. There was, at this period, a certain extramural teacher of anatomy, whom I shall here designate by the letter K——. His name was subsequently too well-known. The man who bore it skulked through the streets of Edinburgh in disguise, while the mob that applauded at the execution of Burke called loudly for the blood of his employer. But Mr K—— was then at the top of his

vogue; he enjoyed a popularity due partly to his own talent and address, partly to the incapacity of his rival, the university professor. The students, at least, swore by his name, and Fettes believed himself, and was believed by others, to have laid the foundations of success when he had acquired the favour of this meteorically famous man. Mr K—— was a *bon vivant* as well as an accomplished teacher; he liked a sly allusion no less than a careful preparation. In both capacities Fettes enjoyed and deserved his notice, and by the second year of his attendance he held the half-regular position of second demonstrator or sub-assistant in his class.

In this capacity, the charge of the theatre and lecturer room devolved in particular upon his shoulders. He had to answer for the cleanliness of the premises and the conduct of the other students, and it was a part of his duty to supply, receive, and divide the various subjects. It was with a view to this last – at that time very delicate – affair that he was lodged by Mr K—— in the same wynd, and at last in the same building, with the dissecting rooms. Here, after a night of turbulent pleasures, his hand still tottering, his sight still misty and confused, he would be called out of bed in the black hours before the winter dawn by the unclean and desperate interlopers who supplied the table. He would open the door to these men, since infamous throughout the land. He would help them with their tragic burden, pay them their sordid price, and remain alone when they were gone with the unfriendly relics of humanity. From such a scene he would return to snatch another hour or two of

slumber, to repair the abuses of the night and refresh himself for the labours of the day.

Few lads could have been more insensible to the impressions of a life thus passed among the ensigns of mortality. His mind was closed against all general considerations. He was incapable of interest in the fate and fortunes of another, the slave of his own desires and low ambitions. Cold, light, and selfish in the last resort, he had that modicum of prudence, miscalled morality, which keeps a man from inconvenient drunkenness or punishable theft. He coveted, besides, a measure of consideration from his masters and his fellow-pupils, and he had no desire to fail conspicuously in the external parts of life. Thus he made it his pleasure to gain some distinction in his studies, and day after day rendered unimpeachable eye-service to his employer, Mr K——. For his day of work he indemnified himself by nights of roaring, blackguardly enjoyment; and when that balance had been struck, the organ that he called his conscience declared itself content.

The supply of subjects was a continual trouble to him as well as to his master. In that large and busy class, the raw material of the anatomists kept perpetually running out; and the business thus rendered necessary was not only unpleasant in itself, but threatened dangerous consequences to all who were concerned. It was the policy of Mr K—— to ask no questions in his dealings with the trade. "They bring the body, and we pay the price," he used to say, dwelling on the alliteration – "*quid pro quo*." And again, and somewhat

profanely, "Ask no questions," he would tell his assistants, "for conscience's sake." There was no understanding that the subjects were provided by the crime of murder. Had that idea been broached to him in words, he would have recoiled in horror; but the lightness of his speech upon so grave a matter was, in itself, an offence against good manners, and a temptation to the men with whom he dealt. Fettes, for instance, had often remarked to himself upon the singular freshness of the bodies. He had been struck again and again by the hangdog, abominable looks of the ruffians who came to him before the dawn; and, putting things together clearly in his private thoughts, he perhaps attributed a meaning too immoral and too categorical to the unguarded counsels of his master. He understood his duty, in short, to have three branches: to take what was brought, to pay the price, and to avert the eye from any evidence of crime.

One November morning this policy of silence was put sharply to the test. He had been awake all night with racking toothache – pacing his room like a caged beast or throwing himself in fury on his bed – and had fallen at last into that profound, uneasy slumber that so often follows on a night of pain, when he was awakened by the

third or fourth angry repetition of the concerted signal. There was a thin, bright moonshine; it was bitter cold, windy, and frosty; the town had not yet awakened, but an indefinable stir already preluded the noise and business of the day. The ghouls had come later than usual, and they seemed more than usually eager to be gone. Fettes, sick with sleep, lighted them upstairs. He heard their grumbling Irish voices through a dream; as they stripped the sack from their sad merchandise he leaned dozing, with his shoulder propped against the wall. He had to shake himself to find the men their money. As he did so his eyes lighted on the dead face. He started; he took two steps nearer, with the candle raised.

"God Almighty!" he cried. "That is Jane Galbraith!" The men answered nothing, but they shuffled nearer towards the door.

"I know her, I tell you," he continued. "She was alive and hearty yesterday. It's impossible she can be dead; it's impossible you should have got this body fairly."

"Sure, sir, you're mistaken entirely," said one of the men.

But the other looked Fettes darkly in the eyes, and demanded the money on the spot.

It was impossible to misconceive the threat or to exaggerate the danger. The lad's heart failed him. He stammered some excuses, counted out the sum, and saw his hateful visitors depart. No sooner were they gone than he hastened to confirm his doubts. By a dozen unquestionable marks he identified the girl he had jested with the day before. He saw, with horror, marks upon her body that might well betoken violence. A panic seized him, and he took refuge in his room. There he reflected at length over the discovery that he had made; considered soberly the bearing of Mr K——'s instructions, and the danger to himself of interference in so serious a business, and at last, in sore perplexity, determined to wait for the advice of his immediate superior, the class assistant.

This was a young doctor, Wolfe Macfarlane, a high favourite among all the reckless students, clever, dissipated, and unscrupulous to the last degree. He had travelled and studied abroad. His manners were agreeable and a little forward. He  was an authority on the stage, skilful on the ice or the links with skate or golf club; he dressed with nice audacity, and, to put the finishing touch upon his glory, he kept a gig and a strong, trotting horse. With Fettes he was on terms of intimacy; indeed, their relative positions called for some community of life; and when subjects were scarce the pair would drive far into the country in Macfarlane's gig, visit and desecrate some lonely graveyard, and return before dawn with their booty to the door of the dissecting-room.

On that particular morning Macfarlane arrived somewhat earlier than his wont. Fettes heard him, and met him on the stairs, told him his story, and showed him the cause of his

alarm. Macfarlane examined the marks on her body.

"Yes," he said with a nod, "it looks fishy."

"Well, what should I do?" asked Fettes.

"Do?" repeated the other. "Do you want to do anything? Least said soonest mended, I should say."

"Someone else might recognize her," objected Fettes. "She was as well known as the Castle Rock."

"We'll hope not," said Macfarlane, "and if anybody does – well, you didn't, don't you see, and there's an end. The fact is, this has been going on too long. Stir up the mud, and you'll get K— into the most unholy trouble; you'll be in a shocking box yourself. So will I, if you come to that. I should like to know how any one of us would look, or what the devil we should have to say for ourselves in any Christian witness box. For me, you know there's one thing certain – that, practically speaking, all our subjects have been murdered."

"Macfarlane!" cried Fettes.

"Come now!" sneered the other. "As if you hadn't suspected it yourself!"

"Suspecting is one thing—"

"And proof another. Yes, I know; and I'm as sorry as you are *this* should have come here," tapping the body with his cane. "The next best thing for me is not to recognize it; and," he added coolly, "I don't. You may, if you please. I don't dictate, but I think a man of the world would do as I do; and I may add, I fancy that is what K— would look for at our hands. The question is, why did he choose us two for his assistants? And I

answer, because he didn't want old wives."

This was the tone of all others to affect the mind of a lad like Fettes. He agreed to imitate Macfarlane. The body of the unfortunate girl was duly dissected, and no one remarked or appeared to recognize her.

One afternoon, when his day's work was over, Fettes dropped into a popular tavern and found Macfarlane sitting with a stranger. This was a small man, very pale and dark, with coal-black eyes. The cut of his features gave a promise of intellect and refinement which was but feebly realized in his manners; for he proved, upon a nearer acquaintance, coarse, vulgar, and stupid. He exercised, however, a very remarkable control over Macfarlane; issued orders like the Great Bashaw; became inflamed at the least discussion or delay, and commented rudely on the servility with which he was obeyed. This most offensive person took a fancy to Fettes on the spot, plied him with drinks, and honoured him with unusual confidences on his past career. If a tenth part of what he confessed were true, he was a very loathsome rogue; and the lad's vanity was tickled by the attention of so experienced a man.

"I'm a pretty bad fellow myself," the stranger remarked, "but Macfarlane is the boy — Toddy Macfarlane, I call him. Toddy, order your friend another glass." Or it might be, "Toddy, you jump up and shut the door." "Toddy hates me," he said again. "Oh, yes, Toddy, you do!"

"Don't you call me that confounded name," growled Macfarlane.

"Hear him! Did you ever see the lads play knife? He would like to do that all over my body," remarked the stranger.

"We medicals have a better way than that," said Fettes. "When we dislike a dead friend of ours, we dissect him."

Macfarlane looked up sharply, as though this jest was scarcely to his mind.

The afternoon passed. Gray, for that was the stranger's name, invited Fettes to join them at dinner, ordered a feast so sumptuous that the tavern was thrown in commotion, and when all was done commanded Macfarlane to settle the bill. It was late before they separated; the man Gray was incapably drunk. Macfarlane, sobered by his fury, chewed the cud of the money he had been forced to squander and the slights he had been obliged to swallow. Fettes, with various liquors singing in his head, returned home with devious footsteps and a mind entirely in abeyance. Next day Macfarlane was absent from the class, and Fettes smiled to himself as he imagined him still squiring the intolerable Gray from tavern to tavern. As soon as the hour of liberty had struck he posted from place to place in quest of his last night's companions. He could find them, however, nowhere; so returned early to his rooms, went early to bed, and slept the sleep of the just.

At four in the morning he was awakened by the well-known signal. Descending to the door, he was filled with astonishment to find Macfarlane with his gig, and in the gig

one of those long and ghastly packages with which he was so
well acquainted.

"What?" he cried. "Have you been out alone?"

But Macfarlane silenced him roughly,
bidding him turn to business. When they had
got the body upstairs and laid it on the table,
Macfarlane made at first as if he were going
away. Then he paused and seemed to hesitate;
and then, "You had better look at the face,"
said he, in tones of some constraint. "You had
better," he repeated, as Fettes only stared at
him in wonder.

"But where and how and when did you come by it?" cried
the other.

"Look at the face," was the only answer.

Fettes was staggered; strange doubts assailed him. He
looked from the young doctor to the body, and then back
again. At last, with a start, he did as he was bidden. He had
almost expected the sight that met his eyes, and yet the shock
was cruel. To see, fixed in the rigidity of death and naked on
that coarse layer of sackcloth, the man whom he had left well
clad and full of meat and sin upon the threshold of a tavern,
awoke, even in the thoughtless Fettes, some of the terrors of
the conscience. It was a *cras tibi* which re-echoed in his soul,
that two whom he had known should have come to lie upon
these icy tables. Yet these were only secondary thoughts. His
first concern regarded Wolfe. Unprepared for a challenge so

momentous, he knew not how to look his comrade in the face. He durst not meet his eye, and he had neither words nor voice at his command.

It was Macfarlane himself who made the first advance. He came up quietly behind and laid his hand gently but firmly on the other's shoulder.

"Richardson," said he, "may have the head."

Now Richardson was a student who had long been anxious for that portion of the human subject to dissect. There was no answer, and the murderer resumed: "Talking of business, you must pay me; your accounts, you see, must tally."

Fettes found a voice, the ghost of his own: "Pay you!" he cried. "Pay you for that?"

"Why, yes, of course you must. By all means and on every possible account, you must," returned the other. "I dare not give it for nothing, you dare not take it for nothing; it would compromise us both. This is another case like Jane Galbraith's. The more things are wrong the more we must act as if all were right. Where does old K— keep his money?"

"There," answered Fettes hoarsely, pointing to a cupboard in the corner.

"Give me the key, then," said the other, calmly, holding out his hand.

There was an instant's hesitation, and the die was cast. Macfarlane could not suppress a nervous twitch, as he felt the

key between his fingers. He opened the cupboard, brought out pen and ink and a paper book that stood in one compartment, and separated from the funds in a drawer a sum suitable to the occasion.

"Now, look here," he said, "there is the payment made – first proof of your good faith; first step to your security. You have now to clinch it by a second. Enter the payment in your book, and then you for your part may defy the devil."

The next few seconds were for Fettes an agony of thought; but in balancing his terrors it was the most immediate that triumphed. Any future difficulty seemed almost welcome if he could avoid a present quarrel with Macfarlane. He set down the candle which he had been carrying all this time, and with a steady hand entered the date, the nature, and the amount of the transaction.

"And now," said Macfarlane, "it's only fair that you should pocket the lucre. I've had my share already. By the by, when a man of the world falls into a bit of luck, has a few shillings extra in his pocket – I'm ashamed to speak of it, but there's a rule of conduct in the case. No treating, no purchase of expensive class books, no squaring of old debts; borrow, don't lend."

"Macfarlane," began Fettes, still somewhat hoarsely, "I have put my neck in a halter to oblige you."

"To oblige me?" cried Wolfe. "Oh, come! You did, as near as I can see the matter, what you downright had to do in self-defence. Suppose I got into trouble, where would you be? This second little matter flows clearly from the first. Mr Gray is the

continuation of Miss Galbraith. You can't begin and then stop. If you begin, you must keep on beginning; that's the truth. No rest for the wicked."

A horrible sense of blackness and the treachery of fate seized hold upon the soul of the unhappy student.

"My God!" he cried, "But what have *I* done? And when did *I* begin? To be made a class assistant – in the name of reason, where's the harm in that? Service wanted the position; Service might have got it. Would *he* have been where *I* am now?"

"My dear fellow," said Macfarlane. "What a boy you are! What harm *has* come to you? What harm *can* come to you if you hold your tongue? Why, man, do you know what this life is? There are two squads of us – the lions, and the lambs. If you're a lamb, you'll come to lie upon these tables like Gray or Jane Galbraith; if you're a lion, you'll live and drive a horse like me, like K——, like all the world with any wit or courage. You're staggered at the first. But look at K——! My dear fellow, you're clever, you have pluck. I like you, and K—— likes you. You were born to lead the hunt; and I tell you, on my honour and my experience of life, three days from now you'll laugh at all these scarecrows like a high-school boy at a farce."

And with that Macfarlane took his departure, and drove off up the wynd in his gig to get under cover before daylight. Fettes was thus left alone with his regrets. He saw the miserable peril in which he stood involved. He saw, with inexpressible dismay, that there was no limit to his weakness, and that, from concession to concession, he had fallen from the

arbiter of Macfarlane's destiny to his paid and helpless accomplice. He would have given the world to have been a little braver at the time, but it did not occur to him that he might still be brave. The secret of Jane Galbraith and the cursed entry in the day book closed his mouth.

Hours passed; the class began to arrive; the members of the unhappy Gray were dealt out to one and to another, and received without remark. Richardson was made happy with the head; and before the hour of freedom rang Fettes trembled with exultation to perceive how far they had already gone towards safety. For two days he continued to watch, with increasing joy, the dreadful process of disguise. On the third day Macfarlane made his appearance. He had been ill, he said; but he made up for lost time by the energy with which he directed the students. To Richardson in particular he extended the most valuable assistance and advice, and that student, encouraged by the praise of the demonstrator, burned high with ambitious hopes, and saw the medal already in his grasp.

Before the week was out Macfarlane's prophecy had been fulfilled. Fettes had outlived his terrors and had forgotten his baseness. He began to plume himself upon his courage, and had so arranged the story in his mind that he could look back on these events with an unhealthy pride. Of his accomplice he saw but little. They met, of course, in the business of the class; they received their orders together from Mr K——. At times they had a word in private, and Macfarlane was from first to last particularly kind and jovial. But it was plain that he

avoided any reference to their common secret; and even when
Fettes whispered to him that he had cast in his lot with the
lions and forsworn the lambs, he only signed to him to hold his
peace. At length an occasion arose which threw the pair once
more into a closer union. Mr K— was again short of subjects;
pupils were eager, and it was a part of this teacher's
pretensions to be always well supplied. At the same time there
came the news of a burial in the rustic graveyard of Glencorse.
Time has little changed the place in question. It stood then, as
now, upon a crossroad, out of call of human habitations, and
buried fathom deep in the foliage of six cedar trees. The cries of
the sheep upon the neighbouring hills, the streamlets upon
either hand – one loudly singing among pebbles, the other
dripping furtively from pond to pond – the stir of the wind in
mountainous old flowering chestnuts, and once in seven days
the voice of the bell and the old tunes of the choir master, were
the only sounds that disturbed the silence around the rural
church. The Resurrection Man – to use a by-name of the period
– was not to be deterred by any of the sanctities of customary
piety. It was part of his trade to despise and desecrate the scrolls
and trumpets of old tombs, the paths worn by the feet of
worshippers and mourners, and the offerings and the
inscriptions of bereaved affection. To rustic neighbourhoods,
where love is more than commonly tenacious, and where some
bonds of blood or fellowship unite the entire society of a parish,
the body snatcher, far from being repelled by natural respect,
was attracted by the ease and safety of the task. To bodies that

had been laid in earth, in joyful expectation of a far different awakening, there came that hasty, lamp-lit, terror-haunted resurrection of the spade and mattock. The coffin was forced, the burial robes torn, and the melancholy relics, clad in sackcloth, after being rattled for hours on moonless byways, were at length exposed to uttermost indignities before a class of gaping boys.

Somewhat as two vultures may swoop upon a dying lamb, Fettes and Macfarlane were to be let loose upon a grave in that green and quiet resting place. The wife of a farmer, a woman who had lived for sixty years, and been known for nothing but good butter and a godly conversation, was to be rooted from her grave at midnight and carried, dead and naked, to that far-away city that she had always honoured with her Sunday's best; the place beside her family was to be empty till the crack of doom; her innocent and almost venerable members to be exposed to that last curiosity of the anatomist.

Late one afternoon the pair set forth, well wrapped in cloaks and furnished with a formidable bottle. It rained without remission – a cold, dense, lashing rain. Now and again there blew a puff of wind, but these sheets of falling water kept it down. Bottle and all, it was a sad and silent drive as far as Penicuik, where they were to spend the evening. They stopped once, to hide their implements in a thick bush not far from the churchyard, and once again at the Fisher's Tryst, to have a toast before the kitchen fire and vary their nips of whisky with a glass of ale. When they reached their journey's

end the gig was housed, the horse was fed and comforted, and the two young doctors in a private room sat down to the best dinner and the best wine the house afforded. The lights, the fire, the beating rain upon the window, the cold, incongruous work that lay before them, added zest to their enjoyment of the meal. With every glass their cordiality increased. Soon Macfarlane handed a little pile of gold to his companion.

"A compliment," he said. "Between friends these little accommodations ought to fly like pipe-lights."

Fettes pocketed the money, and applauded the sentiment to the echo. "You are a philosopher," he cried. "I was an ass till I knew you. You and K— between you, by the Lord Harry! But you'll make a man of me."

"Of course we shall," applauded Macfarlane. "A man? I tell you, it required a man to back me up the other morning. There are some big, brawling, forty-year-old cowards who would have turned sick at the look of the thing; but not you – you kept your head. I watched you."

"Well, and why not?" Fettes thus vaunted himself.

"It was no affair of mine. There was nothing to gain on the one side but disturbance, and on the other I could count on your gratitude, don't you see?" And he slapped his pocket till the gold pieces rang.

Macfarlane somehow felt a certain touch of alarm at these unpleasant words. He may have regretted that he had taught his young companion so successfully, but he had no time to interfere, for the other noisily continued in this boastful strain.

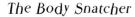

"The great thing is not to be afraid. Now, between you and me, I don't want to hang – that's practical; but for all cant, Macfarlane, I was born with a contempt. Hell, God, devil, right, wrong, sin, crime, and all that old gallery of curiosities – they may frighten boys, but men of the world, like you and me, despise them. Here's to the memory of Gray!"

It was by this time growing somewhat late. The gig, according to order, was brought round to the door with both lamps brightly shining, and the young men had to pay their bill and take the road. They announced that they were bound for Peebles, and drove in that direction till they were clear of the last houses of the town; then, extinguishing the lamps, returned upon their course, and followed a by-road toward Glencorse. There was no sound but that of their own passage, and the incessant, strident pouring of the rain. It was pitch dark; here and there a white gate or a white stone in the wall guided them for a short space across the night; but for the most part it was at a foot pace, and almost groping, that they picked their way through that resonant blackness to their solemn and isolated destination. In the sunken woods that traverse the neighbourhood of the burying

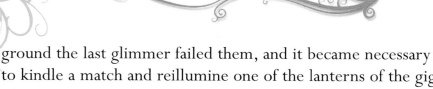

ground the last glimmer failed them, and it became necessary to kindle a match and reillumine one of the lanterns of the gig. Thus, under the dripping trees, and environed by huge and moving shadows, they reached the scene of their unhallowed labours.

They were both experienced in such affairs, and powerful with the spade; and they had scarce been twenty minutes at their task before they were rewarded by a dull rattle on the coffin lid. At the same moment Macfarlane, having hurt his hand upon a stone, flung it carelessly above his head. The grave, in which they now stood almost to the shoulders, was close to the edge of the plateau of the graveyard; and the gig lamp had been propped – the better to illuminate their labours – against a tree, and on the immediate verge of the steep bank descending to the stream. Chance had taken a sure aim with the stone. Then came a clang of broken glass; night fell upon them; sounds alternately dull and ringing announced the bounding of the lantern down the bank, and its occasional collision with the trees. A stone or two, which it had dislodged in its descent, rattled behind it into the profundities of the glen; and then silence, like night, resumed its sway; and they might bend their hearing to its utmost pitch, but naught was to be heard except the rain, now marching to the wind, now steadily falling over miles of open country.

They were so nearly at an end of their abhorred task that they judged it wiser to complete it in the dark. The coffin was exhumed and broken open; the body inserted in the dripping

sack and carried between them to the gig; one
mounted to keep it in its place, and the other,
taking the horse by the mouth, groped along
by wall and bush until they reached the
wider road by the Fisher's Tryst. Here was a
faint, diffused radiancy, which they hailed
like daylight; by that they pushed the horse to
a good pace and began to rattle most merrily
in the direction of the town.

They had both been wetted to the skin during their
operations, and now, as the gig jumped among the deep ruts,
the thing that stood propped between them fell now upon the
one and now upon the other. At every repetition of the horrid
contact each instinctively repelled it with the greater haste;
and the process, natural although it was, began to tell upon the
nerves of the companions. Macfarlane made some ill-favoured
jest about the farmer's wife, but it came hollowly from his
lips, and was allowed to drop in silence. Still their unnatural
burden bumped from side to side; and now the head would be
laid, as if in confidence, upon their shoulders, and now the
drenching sackcloth would flap icily about their faces. A
creeping chill began to possess the soul of Fettes. He peered at
the bundle, and it seemed somehow larger than at first. All
over the countryside, and from every degree of distance, the
farm dogs accompanied their passage with tragic ululations;
and it grew and grew upon his mind that some unnatural
miracle had been accomplished, that some nameless change

had befallen the dead body, and that it was in fear of their unholy burden that the dogs were howling.

"For God's sake," said he, making a great effort to arrive at speech, "for God's sake, let's have a light!"

Seemingly Macfarlane was affected in the same direction; for, though he made no reply, he stopped the horse, passed the reins to his companion, got down, and proceeded to kindle the remaining lamp. They had by that time got no farther than the crossroad down to Auchenclinny. The rain still poured, as though Noah's flood were returning, and it was no easy matter to make a light in such a world of wet and darkness. When at last the flickering blue flame had been transferred to the wick and began to expand and clarify, and shed a wide circle of misty brightness round the gig, it became possible for the two young men to see each other and the thing they had along with them. The rain had moulded the rough sacking to the outlines of the body underneath; the head was distinct from the trunk, the shoulders plainly modelled; something at once spectral and human riveted their eyes upon the ghastly comrade of their drive.

For some time Macfarlane stood motionless, holding up the lamp. A nameless dread was swathed, like a wet sheet, about the body, and tightened the white skin upon the face of Fettes; a fear that was meaningless, a horror of what could not be, kept mounting to his brain. Another beat of the watch, and he had spoken. But his comrade forestalled him.

"That is not a woman," said Macfarlane, in a hushed voice.

"It was a woman when we put her in," whispered Fettes.

"Hold that lamp," said the other. "I must see her face."

And as Fettes took the lamp his companion untied the fastenings of the sack and drew down the cover from the head. The light fell very clear upon the dark, well-moulded features and smooth-shaven cheeks of a too familiar countenance, often beheld in dreams of both of these young men. A wild yell rang up into the night; each leapt from his own side into the roadway; the lamp fell, broke and was extinguished; and the horse, terrified by this unusual commotion, bounded and went off towards Edinburgh at a gallop, bearing along with it, sole occupant of the gig, the body of the long-dead and long-dissected Gray.

The Legend of Don Munio Sancho de Hinojosa

1832

Washington Irving

In the cloisters of the ancient Benedictine convent of San Domingo, at Silos, in Castile, are the mouldering yet magnificent monuments of the once powerful and chivalrous family of Hinojosa. Among these reclines the marble figure of a knight, in complete armour, with the hands pressed together, as if in prayer. On one side of his tomb is sculptured, in relief, a band of Christian cavaliers capturing a cavalcade of male and female Moors; on the other side, the same cavaliers are represented kneeling before an altar. The tomb, like most of the neighbouring monuments, is almost in ruins, and the sculpture is nearly unintelligible, excepting to the keen eye of the antiquary. The story connected with the sepulchre, however, is still preserved in the old Spanish chronicles, and is to the following purport:

In old times, several hundred years ago, there was a noble Castilian cavalier named Don Munio Sancho de Hinojosa, lord of a border castle, which had stood the brunt of many a Moorish foray. He had seventy horsemen as his household troops, all of the ancient Castilian proof; stark warriors, hard riders, and men of iron; with these he scoured the Moorish lands, and made his name terrible throughout the borders. His castle hall was covered with banners, scimitars, and Moslem helmets, the trophies of his prowess. Don Munio was, moreover, a keen huntsman, and rejoiced in hounds of all kinds, steeds for the chase, and hawks for the towering sport of falconry. When not engaged in warfare, his delight was to beat up the neighbouring forests; and scarcely ever did he ride forth without hound and horn, a boar-spear in his hand, or a hawk upon his fist, and an attendant train of huntsmen.

His wife, Dona Maria Palacin, was of a gentle and timid nature, little fitted to be the spouse of so hardy and adventurous a knight; and many a tear did the poor lady shed when he sallied forth upon his daring enterprises.

As this doughty cavalier was one day hunting, he stationed himself in a thicket, on the borders of a green glade of the forest, and dispersed his followers to rouse the game, and drive it towards his stand. He had not been here long when a cavalcade of Moors, of both sexes, came pranking over the forest lawn. They were unarmed, and magnificently dressed in robes of tissue and embroidery, rich shawls of India, bracelets and anklets of gold and jewels that sparkled in the sun.

At the head of this gay cavalcade rode a youthful cavalier, superior to the rest in dignity and loftiness of demeanour, and in splendour of attire; beside him was a damsel, whose veil, blown aside by the breeze, displayed a face of surpassing beauty, yet beaming with tenderness and joy.

Don Munio thanked his stars for sending him such a prize, and exulted at the thought of bearing home to his wife the glittering spoils of these infidels. Putting his hunting-horn to his lips, he gave a blast that rang through the forest. His huntsmen came running from all quarters, and the

astonished Moors were surrounded and made captives.

The beautiful Moor wrung her hands in despair, and her female attendants uttered the most piercing cries. The young Moorish cavalier alone retained self-possession. He inquired the name of the Christian knight who commanded this troop of horsemen. When told that it was Don Munio Sancho de Hinojosa, his countenance lighted up. Approaching that cavalier, and kissing his hand, "Don Munio Sancho," said he, "I have heard of your fame as a true and valiant knight, terrible in arms, but schooled in the noble virtues of chivalry. Such do I trust to find you. In me you behold Abadil, son of a Moorish lord. I am on the way to celebrate my nuptials with this lady; chance has thrown us in your power, but I confide in your magnanimity. Take all our treasure and jewels; demand what ransom you think proper for our persons, but suffer us not to be insulted nor dishonoured."

When the good knight heard this appeal and beheld the beauty of the youthful pair, his heart was touched with tenderness and courtesy. "God forbid," said he, "that I should disturb such happy nuptials. My prisoners in troth shall ye be, for fifteen days, and immured within my castle, where I claim, as conqueror, the right of celebrating your espousals."

So saying, he dispatched one of his fleetest horsemen in advance, to notify Dona Maria

Palacin of the coming of this bridal party; while he and his huntsmen escorted the cavalcade – not as captors, but as a guard of honour. As they drew near to the castle, the banners were hung out, and the trumpets sounded from the battlements; and on their nearer approach, the drawbridge was lowered, and Dona Maria came forth to meet them, attended by her ladies and knights, her pages and her minstrels. She took the young bride, Allifra, in her arms, kissed her with the tenderness of a sister, and conducted her into the castle. In the meantime, Don Munio sent forth missives in every direction, and had viands and dainties of all kinds collected from the country round; and the wedding of the Moorish lovers was celebrated with all possible state and festivity. For fifteen days, the castle was given up to joy and revelry. There were tiltings and jousts at the ring, and bull-fights, and banquets, and dances to the sound of minstrelsy. When the fifteen days were at an end, he made the bride and bridegroom magnificent presents, and conducted them and their attendants safely beyond the borders. Such, in old times, were the courtesy and generosity of a Spanish cavalier.

Several years after this event, the king of Castile

summoned his nobles to assist him in a campaign against the Moors. Don Munio Sancho was among the first to answer to the call, with seventy horsemen, all staunch and well-tried warriors. His wife, Dona Maria hung about his neck. "Alas, my lord!" exclaimed she, "how often wilt thou tempt thy fate, and when will thy thirst for glory be appeased?"

"One battle more," replied Don Munio, "one battle more, for the honour of Castile, and I here make a vow, that when this is over, I will lay by my sword, and repair with my cavaliers in pilgrimage to the sepulchre of our Lord at Jerusalem." The cavaliers all joined with him in the vow, and Dona Maria felt in some degree soothed in spirit. Still, she saw with a heavy heart the departure of her husband, and watched his banner with wistful eyes, until it disappeared among the trees of the forest.

The king of Castile led his army to the plains of Salmanara, where they encountered the Moorish host, near to Ucles. The battle was long and bloody; the Christians repeatedly wavered, and were as often rallied by the energy of their commanders. Don Munio was covered with wounds, but refused to leave the field. The Christians at length gave way, and the king was hard pressed, and in danger of being captured.

Don Munio called upon his cavaliers to follow him to the rescue. "Now is the time," cried he, "to prove your loyalty. Fall to, like brave men! We fight for the true faith, and if we lose our lives here, we gain a better life hereafter."

Rushing with his men between the king and his pursuers,

they checked the latter in their career, and gave time for their monarch to escape; but they fell victims to their loyalty. They all fought to the last gasp. Don Munio was singled out by a powerful Moorish knight, but having been wounded in the right arm, he fought to disadvantage, and was slain. The battle being over, the Moor paused to possess himself of the spoils of this redoubtable Christian warrior. When he unlaced the helmet, however, and beheld the countenance of Don Munio, he gave a great cry, and smote his breast. "Woe is me!" cried he, "I have slain my benefactor! The flower of knightly virtue! The most magnanimous of cavaliers!"

While the battle had been raging on the plain of Salmanara, Dona Maria Palacin remained in her castle, a prey to the keenest anxiety. Her eyes were ever fixed on the road that led from the country of the Moors, and often she asked the watchman of the tower, "What seest thou?"

One evening, at the shadowy hour of twilight, the warden sounded his horn. "I see," cried he, "a numerous train winding up the valley. There are mingled Moors and Christians. The banner of my lord is in the advance. Joyful tidings!" exclaimed the old steward: "my lord returns in triumph, and brings captives!" Then the castle courts rang with shouts of joy; and the standard was displayed, and the trumpets were sounded, and the drawbridge was lowered, and Dona Maria went forth with her ladies, and her knights, and her pages, and her minstrels, to welcome her lord from the wars. But as the train

drew nigh, she beheld a sumptuous bier, covered with black velvet, and on it lay a warrior, as if taking his repose. He lay in his armour, with his helmet on his head, and his sword in his hand, as one who had never been conquered, and around the bier were the shields of the house of Hinojosa.

A number of Moorish cavaliers attended the bier, with emblems of mourning and with dejected countenances; and their leader cast himself at the feet of Dona Maria, and hid his face in his hands. She beheld in him the gallant Abadil, whom she had once welcomed with his bride to her castle; but who now came with the body of her lord, whom he had unknowingly slain in battle!

The sepulchre erected in the cloisters of the convent of San Domingo was achieved at the expense of the Moor Abadil, as a feeble testimony of his grief for the death of the good knight Don Munio, and his reverence for his memory. The tender and faithful Dona Maria soon followed her lord to the tomb. On one of the stones of a small arch, beside his sepulchre, is the following simple inscription: '*Hic jacet Maria Palacin, uxor Munonis Sancij De Finojosa*': 'Here lies Maria Palacin, wife of Munio Sancho de Hinojosa.'

The legend of Don Munio Sancho does not conclude with his death. On the same day on which the battle took place on the plain of Salmanara, a chaplain of the Holy Temple at Jerusalem, while standing at the outer gate, beheld a train of Christian cavaliers advancing, as if in pilgrimage. The chaplain was a native of Spain, and as the pilgrims approached, he knew the foremost to be Don Munio Sancho de Hinojosa, with whom he had been well acquainted in former times. Hastening to the patriarch, he told him of the honourable rank of the pilgrims at the gate. The patriarch, therefore, went forth with a grand procession of priests and monks, and received the pilgrims with all due honour. There were seventy cavaliers, beside their leader, all stark and lofty warriors. Some carried their helmets in their hands, and their faces were deadly pale.

They greeted no one, nor looked either to the right or to the left, but the procession went its way nearer and nearer.

At last the soldiers began to enter the chapel, and kneeling before the sepulchre of our Saviour, said their prayers in silence. When they had concluded, they rose as if to depart, and the patriarch and his attendants advanced to speak to them, but they were no more to be seen. Everyone marvelled at what could be the meaning of this prodigy. The patriarch carefully noted down the day, and sent to Castile to learn tidings of Don Munio Sancho de Hinojosa. He received for reply, that on the very day specified that worthy knight, with seventy of his followers, had been slain in battle. These, therefore, must have been the blessed spirits of those Christian warriors, come to fulfil their vow of a pilgrimage to the Holy Sepulchre at Jerusalem. Such was Castilian faith, in the olden time, which kept its word, even beyond the grave.

If anyone should doubt of the miraculous apparition of these phantom knights, let him consult the *History of the Kings of Castile and Leon*, by the learned and pious Fray Prudencio de Sandoval, bishop of Pamplona, where he will find it recorded in the *History of King Don Alonzo VI*, on the hundred and second page. It is too precious a legend to be lightly abandoned to the doubter.

The Fall of the House of Usher

1839

extract

Edgar Allan Poe

One evening, having informed me abruptly that the lady Madeline was no more, he stated his intention of preserving her corpse for a fortnight (previous to its final interment) in one of the numerous vaults within the main walls of the building. The worldly reason, however, assigned for this singular proceeding, was one which I did not feel at liberty to dispute. The brother had been led to his resolution by consideration of the unusual character of the malady of the deceased, of certain eager inquiries on the part of her medical men, and of the remote situation of the burialground of the family. When I called to mind the sinister countenance of the person whom I met upon the staircase on the day of my arrival at the house, I had no desire to oppose what I regarded as at best but a harmless, and by no means an unnatural, precaution.

At the request of Usher, I personally aided him in the arrangements for the temporary entombment. The body having been encoffined, we two alone bore it to its rest. The vault in which we placed it (and which had been so long unopened that our torches, half smothered in its oppressive atmosphere, gave us little opportunity for investigation) was small, damp, and entirely without means of admission for light; lying, at great depth, immediately beneath that portion of the building in which was my own sleeping apartment. It had been used, apparently, in remote feudal times, for the worst purposes of a dungeon, and in later days as a place of deposit for gun powder, or some other highly combustible substance, as a portion of its floor, and the whole interior of a long archway through which we reached it, was carefully sheathed with copper. The door of massive iron, had been also similarly protected. Its immense weight caused an unusually sharp grating sound as it moved upon its hinges.

Having deposited our mournful burden upon trestles within this region of horror, we partially turned aside the yet unscrewed lid of the coffin, and looked upon the face of the tenant.

A striking similitude between the brother and sister now first arrested my attention; and Usher, divining perhaps my thoughts, murmured out some few words from which I learned that the deceased and himself had been twins, and that sympathies of a scarcely intelligible nature had always existed between them. Our glances, however, rested not long upon the dead – for we could not regard her unawed. The disease which had thus entombed the lady in the maturity of youth, had left, as usual in all maladies of a strictly cataleptical character, the mockery of a faint blush upon the bosom and the face, and that suspiciously lingering smile upon the lip which is so terrible in death. We replaced and screwed down the lid and, having secured the door of iron, made our way with toil into the scarcely less gloomy apartments of the upper portion of the house.

And now, some days of bitter grief having elapsed, an observable change came over the features of the mental disorder of my friend. His ordinary manner had vanished. His ordinary occupations were neglected or forgotten. He roamed from chamber to chamber with hurried, unequal, and objectless step. The pallor of his countenance had assumed, if possible, a more ghastly hue – but the luminousness of his eye had utterly gone out. The once occasional huskiness of his tone was heard no more; and a tremulous quaver, as if of extreme terror, habitually characterized his utterance. There were times, indeed, when I thought his unceasingly agitated mind was labouring with some oppressive secret, to divulge which he struggled for the necessary courage. At times, again, I was obliged to resolve all into the mere inexplicable vagaries of madness, for I beheld him gazing upon vacancy for long hours, in an attitude of the profoundest attention, as if listening to some imaginary sound. It was no wonder that his

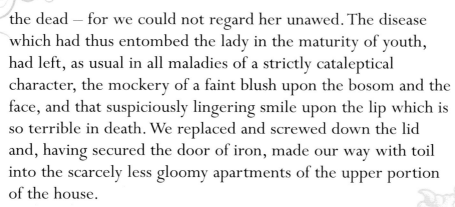

condition terrified — that it infected me. I felt creeping upon me, by slow yet certain degrees, the wild influences of his own fantastic yet impressive superstitions.

It was, especially, upon retiring to bed late in the night of the seventh or eighth day after the placing of the Lady Madeline within the dungeon, that I experienced the full power of such feelings. Sleep came not near my couch — while the hours waned and waned away. I struggled to reason off the nervousness which had dominion over me. I endeavoured to believe that much, if not all of what I felt, was due to the bewildering influence of the gloomy furniture of the room — of the dark and  tattered draperies, which, tortured into motion by the breath of a rising tempest, swayed fitfully to and fro upon the walls, and rustled uneasily about the decorations of the bed. But my efforts were fruitless. An irrepressible tremour gradually pervaded my frame; and, at length, there sat upon my very heart an incubus of utterly causeless alarm. Shaking this off with a gasp and a struggle, I uplifted myself upon the pillows, and, peering earnestly within the intense darkness of the chamber, harkened — I know not why, except that an instinctive spirit prompted me — to certain low and indefinite sounds which came through the pauses of the storm at long intervals, I knew not whence. Overpowered by an intense sentiment of horror, unaccountable

yet unendurable, I threw on my clothes with haste (for I felt that I should sleep no more during the night), and endeavoured to arouse myself from the pitiable condition into which I had fallen, by pacing rapidly to and fro through the apartment.

I had taken but few turns in this manner, when a light step on an adjoining staircase arrested my attention. I presently recognized it as that of Usher. In an instant afterward he rapped with a gentle touch at my door, and entered, bearing a lamp. His countenance was, as usual, cadaverously wan – but, moreover, there was a species of mad hilarity in his eyes – an evidently restrained hysteria in his whole demeanour. His air appalled me – but anything was preferable to the solitude which I had so long endured, and I even welcomed his presence as a relief.

"And you have not seen it?" he said abruptly, after having stared about him for some moments in silence – "You have not then seen it? But, stay! You shall." Thus speaking, and having carefully shaded his lamp, he hurried to one of the casements, and threw it freely open to the storm.

The impetuous fury of the entering gust nearly lifted us from our feet. It was, indeed, a tempestuous yet sternly beautiful night, and one wildly singular in its terror and its beauty. A whirlwind had apparently collected its force in our vicinity; for there were frequent and violent alterations in the direction of the wind; and the exceeding density of the clouds (which hung so low as to press upon the turrets of the house) did not prevent our perceiving the lifelike velocity with which

they flew careering from all points against each other, without passing away into the distance. I say that even their exceeding density did not prevent our perceiving this – yet we had no glimpse of the moon or stars, nor was there any flashing forth of the lightning. But the under-surfaces of the huge masses of agitated vapour, as well as all terrestrial objects immediately around us, were glowing in the unnatural light of a faintly luminous and distinctly visible gaseous exhalation which hung about and enshrouded the mansion.

"You must not – you shall not behold this!" said I, shudderingly, to Usher, as I led him, with a gentle violence, from the window to a seat. "These appearances, which bewilder you are merely electrical phenomena, not uncommon – or it may be that they have their ghastly origin in the rank miasma of the tarn. Let us close this casement – the air is chilling and dangerous to your frame. Here is one of your favourite romances. I will read, and you shall listen – and so we will pass away this terrible night together."

The antique volume which I had taken up was the *Mad Trist* of Sir Launcelot Canning; but I had called it a favourite of Usher's more in sad jest than in earnest; for, in truth, there is little in its uncouth and unimaginative prolixity which could have had interest for the lofty and spiritual ideality of my friend. It was, however, the only book immediately at hand; and I indulged a vague hope that the excitement which now agitated the hypochondriac, might find relief (for the history of mental disorder is full of similar anomalies) even in the

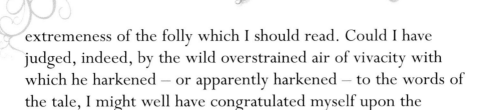

extremeness of the folly which I should read. Could I have judged, indeed, by the wild overstrained air of vivacity with which he harkened – or apparently harkened – to the words of the tale, I might well have congratulated myself upon the success of my design.

I had arrived at that well-known portion of the story where Ethelred, the hero of the Trist, having sought in vain for peaceable admission into the dwelling of the hermit, proceeds to make good an entrance by force. Here, it will be remembered, the words of the narrative run thus:

"And Ethelred, who was by nature of a doughty heart, and who was now mighty withal on account of the powerfulness of the wine which he had drunken, waited no longer to hold parley with the hermit – who in sooth was of an obstinate and maliceful turn, but, feeling the rain upon his shoulders and fearing the rising of the tempest, uplifted his mace outright and, with blows, made quickly room in the plankings of the door for his gauntleted hand; and now pulling therewith sturdily, he so cracked and ripped and tore all asunder, that the noise of the dry and hollow-sounding wood alarummed and reverberated throughout the forest."

At the termination of this sentence I started, and for a moment, paused; for it appeared to me (although I at once concluded that my excited fancy had deceived me) – it appeared to me that, from some very remote portion of the mansion, there came, indistinctly, to my ears, what might have been, in its exact similarity of character, the echo (but a stifled

and dull one certainly) of the very cracking and ripping sound which Sir Launcelot had so particularly described. It was, beyond doubt, the coincidence alone which had arrested my attention; for, amid the rattling of the sashes of the casements and the ordinary commingled noises of the still increasing storm, the sound in itself had nothing which should have interested or disturbed me. I continued the story:

"But the good champion Ethelred, now entering within the door, was sore enraged and amazed to perceive no signal of the maliceful hermit; but, in the stead thereof, a dragon of a scaly and prodigious demeanour, and of a fiery tongue, which sate in guard before a palace of gold with a floor of silver; and upon the wall there hung a shield of shining brass with this legend enwritten:

    Who entereth herein, a conqueror hath bin;
    Who slayeth the dragon, the shield he shall win;

And Ethelred uplifted his mace and struck upon the head of the dragon, which fell before him, and gave up his pesty breath with a shriek so horrid and harsh and withal so piercing, that Ethelred had fain to close his ears with his hands against the dreadful noise of it, the like whereof was never before heard."

Here again I paused abruptly, and now with a feeling of wild amazement – for there could be no doubt whatever that, in this instance, I did actually hear (although from what direction it proceeded I found it impossible to say) a low and

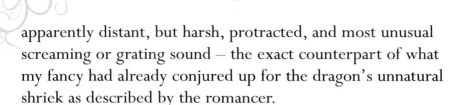

apparently distant, but harsh, protracted, and most unusual screaming or grating sound – the exact counterpart of what my fancy had already conjured up for the dragon's unnatural shriek as described by the romancer.

Oppressed, as I certainly was, upon the occurrence of this second and most extraordinary coincidence, by a thousand conflicting sensations, in which wonder and extreme terror were predominant, I still retained sufficient presence of mind to avoid exciting, by any observation, the sensitive nervousness of my companion. I was by no means certain that he had noticed the sounds in question; although, assuredly, a strange alteration had, during the last few minutes, taken place in his demeanour. From a position fronting my own, he had gradually brought round his chair, so as to sit with his face to the door of the chamber; and thus I could but partially perceive his features, although I saw that his lips trembled as if he were murmuring inaudibly. His head had dropped upon his breast – yet I knew that he was not asleep from the wide and rigid opening of the eye as I caught a glance of it in profile. The motion of his body, too, was at variance with this idea – for he rocked from side to side with a gentle, yet constant and uniform, sway. Having rapidly taken notice of all this, I resumed the narrative of Sir Launcelot, which thus proceeded:

"And now, the champion, having escaped from the terrible fury of the dragon, bethinking himself of the brazen shield and of the breaking up of the enchantment which was upon it, removed the carcass from out of the way before him, and

approached valorously over the silver pavement of the castle to where the shield was upon the wall; which in sooth tarried not for his full coming, but fell down at his feet upon the silver floor, with a mighty great and terrible ringing sound."

No sooner had these syllables passed my lips, than — as if a shield of brass had indeed, at the moment, fallen heavily upon a floor of silver — I became aware of a distinct, hollow, metallic, and clangorous, yet apparently muffled reverberation. Completely unnerved, I leapt to my feet; but the measured rocking movement of Usher was undisturbed. I rushed to the chair in which he sat. His eyes were bent fixedly before him, and throughout his whole countenance there reigned a stony rigidity. But, as I placed my hand upon his shoulder, there came a strong shudder over his whole person; a sickly smile quivered on his lips; and I saw that he spoke in a low, hurried, and gibbering murmur, as if unconscious of my presence. Bending closely over him, I at length drank in the hideous import of his words.

"Not hear it? Yes, I hear it, and have heard it. Long — long — long — many minutes, many hours, many days, have I heard it yet I dared not — oh, pity me, miserable wretch that I am ! — I dared not speak! *We have put her living in the tomb!* Said I not that my senses were acute? I now tell you that I heard her first feeble movements in the hollow coffin. I heard them — many, many days ago — yet I dared not — *I dared not speak!* And now tonight Ethelred — the breaking of the hermit's door, and the death-cry of the dragon, and the clangour of the shield! Say, rather, the rending of her coffin, and the grating of the iron hinges of her prison, and her struggles within the coppered archway of the vault! Oh whither shall I fly? Will she not be here anon? Have I not heard her footstep on the stair? Do I not distinguish that heavy and horrible beating of her heart? Madman!" Here he sprang furiously to his feet, and shrieked out his syllables, as if in the effort he were giving up his soul: *"Madman! I tell you that she now stands outside the door!"*

As if in the superhuman energy of his utterance there had been found the potency of a spell – the huge antique panels to which the speaker pointed threw slowly back, upon the

instant, their ponderous jaws. It was the work of the rushing gust – but then outside those doors there *did* stand the lofty and enshrouded figure of the Lady Madeline of Usher. There was blood upon her white robes, and the evidence of some bitter struggle upon every portion of her emaciated frame. For a moment she remained trembling and reeling to and fro upon the threshold – then, with a low moaning cry, fell heavily inward upon the person of her brother, and in her violent and now final death-agonies, bore him to the floor a corpse, and a victim to the terrors he had anticipated.

From that chamber, and from that mansion, I fled aghast. Suddenly there shot along the path a wild light, and I turned to see whence a gleam so unusual could have issued; for the vast house and its shadows were alone behind me. The radiance was that of the full, blood-red moon, which now shone vividly through that once barely-discernible fissure, of which I have before spoken as extending from the roof of the building, in a zigzag direction, to the base. While I gazed, this fissure rapidly widened – there came a fierce breath of the whirlwind – the entire orb of the satellite burst at once upon my sight – my brain reeled as I saw the mighty walls rushing asunder – there was a long tumultuous shouting sound like the voice of a thousand waters – and the deep and dank tarn at my feet closed sullenly and silently over the fragments of the 'House of Usher'.

There was a Man Dwelt by a Churchyard

1924

M R James

This, you know, is the beginning of the story about sprites and goblins which Mamilius, the child in Shakespeare's *The Winter's Tale*, was telling to his mother the queen, and the court ladies, when the king came in with his guards and hurried her off to prison. There is no more of the story; Mamilius died soon after without having a chance of finishing it. Now what was it going to have been? Shakespeare knew, no doubt, and I will be bold to say that I do. It was not going to be a new story: it was to be one which you have most likely heard, and even told. Everybody may set it in what frame he likes best. This is mine: There was a man dwelt by a churchyard. His house had a lower storey of stone and an upper one of timber. The front windows looked out on the street and the back ones on the churchyard. It had once

belonged to the parish priest, but (this was in the days of Queen Elizabeth I) the priest was a married man and wanted more room; besides, his wife disliked seeing the churchyard at night out of her bedroom window. She said she saw — but never mind what she said; anyhow, she gave her husband no peace till he agreed to move into a larger house in the village street, and the old one was taken by John Poole, who was a widower, and lived there alone. He was an elderly man who kept very much to himself, and people said he was something of a miser.

It was very likely true: he was morbid in other ways, certainly. In those days it was common to bury people at night and by torchlight: and it was noticed that whenever a funeral was toward, John Poole was always at his window, either on the ground floor or upstairs, according as he could get the better view from one or the other.

There came a night when an old woman was to be buried. She was fairly well to do, but she was not liked in the place. The usual thing was said of her, that she was no Christian, and that on such nights as Midsummer Eve and All Hallows, she was not to be found in her house. She was red-eyed and dreadful to look at, and no beggar ever knocked at her door. Yet when she died she left a purse of money to the Church.

There was no storm on the night of her burial; it was fair and calm. But there was some difficulty about getting bearers, and men to carry the

torches, in spite of the fact that she had left larger fees than common for such as did that work. She was buried in woollen, without a coffin. No one was there but those who were actually needed – and John Poole, watching from his window. Just before the grave was filled in, the parson stooped down and cast something upon the body – something that clinked – and in a low voice he said words that sounded like "Thy money perish with thee." Then he walked quickly away, and so did the other men, leaving only one torch–bearer to light the sexton and his boy while they shovelled the earth in. They made no very neat job of it, and next day, which was a Sunday, the churchgoers were rather sharp with the sexton, saying it was the untidiest grave in the yard. And indeed, when he came to look at it himself, he thought it was worse than he had left it.

Meanwhile John Poole went about with a curious air, half exulting, as it were, and half nervous. More than once he spent an evening at the inn, which was clean contrary to his usual habit, and to those who fell into talk with him there he hinted that he had come into a little bit of money and was looking out for a somewhat better house. "Well, I don't wonder," said the smith one night, "I shouldn't care for that place of yours. I should be fancying things all night." The landlord asked him what sort of things.

"Well, maybe somebody climbing up to the chamber window, or the like of that," said the smith. "I don't know –

old mother Wilkins that was buried a week ago today, eh?"

"Come, I think you might consider of a person's feelings," said the landlord. "It ain't so pleasant for Master Poole, is it now?"

"Master Poole don't mind," said the smith. "He's been there long enough to know. I only says it wouldn't be my choice. What with the passing bell, and the torches when there's a burial, and all them graves laying so quiet when there's no one about: only they say there's lights – don't you never see no lights, Master Poole?"

"No, I don't never see no lights," said Master Poole sulkily, and called for another drink, and went home late.

That night, as he lay in his bed upstairs, a moaning wind began to play about the house, and he could not go to sleep. He got up and crossed the room to a little cupboard in the wall: he took out of it something that clinked, and put it in the breast of his bedgown. Then he went to the window and looked out into the churchyard.

Have you ever seen an old brass in a church with a figure of a person in a shroud? It is bunched together at the top of the head in a curious way. Something like that was sticking up out of the earth in a spot of the churchyard which John Poole knew very well. He

darted into his bed and lay there very still indeed.

Presently something made a very faint rattling at the casement. With a dreadful reluctance John Poole turned his eyes that way. Alas! Between him and the moonlight was the black outline of the curious bunched head… Then there was a figure in the room. Dry earth rattled on the floor. A low cracked voice said "Where is it?" and steps went hither and thither — faltering steps as of one walking with difficulty. It could be seen now and again, peering into corners, stooping to look under chairs; finally it could be heard fumbling at the doors of the cupboard in the wall, throwing them open. There was a scratching of long nails on the empty shelves. The figure whipped round, stood for an instant at the side of the bed, raised its arms, and with a horse scream of *"You've got it!"*

At this point HRH Prince Mamilius (who would, I think, have made the story a good deal shorter than this) flung himself with a loud yell upon the youngest of the court ladies present, who responded with an equally piercing cry. He was instantly seized upon by HM Queen Hermione, who, repressing an inclination to laugh, shook and slapped him very severely. Much flushed, and rather inclined to cry, he was about to be sent to bed: but, on the intercession of his victim, who had now recovered from the shock, he was eventually permitted to remain until his usual hour for retiring; by which time he too had so far recovered as to assert, in bidding goodnight to the company, that he knew another story quite three times as dreadful as that one, and would tell it on the first opportunity that offered.

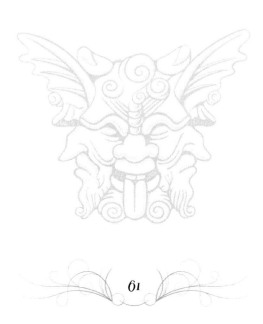

The Dead and the Countess

1905

Gertrude Atherton

It was an old cemetery, and they had been long dead. Those who died nowadays were put in the new burying place on the hill, close to the Bois d'Amour and within sound of the bells that called the living to Mass. But the little church where the Mass was celebrated stood faithfully beside the older dead; a new church, indeed, had not been built in that forgotten corner of Finisterre for centuries, not since the calvary on its pile of stones had been raised in the tiny square, surrounded then, as now, perhaps, by grey naked cottages; not since the castle with its round tower, down on the river, had been erected for the Counts of Croisac. But the stone walls enclosing that ancient cemetery had been kept in good repair, and there were no weeds within, nor toppling headstones. It looked cold and grey and desolate, like all the cemeteries of

Brittany, but it was made hideous neither by tawdry gew-gaws nor the licence of time.

And sometimes it was close to a picture of early beauty. When the village celebrated its yearly pardon, a great procession came out of the church – priests in glittering robes, young men in their gala costume of black and silver holding flashing standards aloft, and many maidens in flapping white head-dress and collar, black frocks and aprons flaunting with ribbons and lace. They marched, chanting, down the road beside the wall of the cemetery, where lay the generations that in their day had held the banners and chanted the service of the pardon. For the dead were peasants and priests – the Croisacs had their burying place in a hollow of the hills behind the castle – old men and women who had wept and died for the fishermen that had gone to the *grande pêche* and returned no more, and now and again a child, slept there. Those who walked past the dead at the pardon, or after the marriage ceremony, or took part in any one of the minor religious festivals with which the Catholic village enlivens its existence – all, young and old, looked grave and sad. For the women from childhood know that their lot is to wait and dread and weep, and the men that the ocean is treacherous and

cruel, but that bread can be wrung from no other master.

Therefore the living have little sympathy for the dead who have laid down their crushing burden; and the dead under their stones slumber contentedly enough. There is no envy among them for the young who wander at evening and pledge their troth in the Bois d'Amour, only pity for the groups of women who wash their linen in the creek that flows to the river. They look like pictures in the green quiet book of nature, these women, in their glistening white head-gear and deep collars; but the dead know better than to envy them, and the women – and the lovers – know better than to pity the dead.

The dead lay at rest in their boxes and thanked God they were quiet and had found everlasting peace.

And one day even this, for which they had patiently endured life, was taken from them.

The village was picturesque and there was none quite like it, even in Finisterre. Artists discovered it and made it famous. After the artists followed the tourists, and the old creaking diligence became an absurdity. Brittany was the fashion for three months of the year, and wherever there is fashion there is at least one railway. The one built to satisfy the thousands who wished to visit the wild, sad beauties of the west of France was laid along the road beside the little cemetery of this tale.

It takes a long while to awaken the dead. These heard neither the voluble working-men nor even the first snort of the engine. And, of course, they neither heard nor knew of the pleadings of the old priest that the line should be laid

elsewhere. One night he came out into the old cemetery and sat on a grave and wept. For he loved his dead and felt it to be a tragic pity that the greed of money, and the fever of travel, and the petty ambitions of men whose place was in the great cities where such ambitions were born, should shatter forever the holy calm of those who had suffered so much on earth. He had known many of them in life, for he was very old; and although he believed, like all good Catholics, in heaven and purgatory and hell, yet he always saw his friends as he had buried them, peacefully asleep in their coffins, the souls lying with folded hands like the bodies that held them, patiently awaiting the final call. He would never have told you, this good old priest, that he believed heaven to be a great echoing palace in which God and the archangels dwelt alone waiting for that great day when the elected dead should rise and enter the

Presence together, for he was a simple old man who had read and thought little. But he had a zigzag of fancy in his humble mind, and he saw his friends and his ancestors' friends as I have related to you: soul and body in the deep undreaming sleep of death – but *sleep*, not a rotted body deserted by its affrighted mate and to all who sleep there comes, sooner or later, the time of awakening.

He knew that they had slept through the wild storms that rage on the coast of Finisterre, when ships are flung on the rocks and trees crash down in the Bois d'Amour. He knew that the soft, slow chantings of the pardon never struck a chord in those frozen memories, meagre and monotonous as their store had been; nor the bagpipes down in the open village hall – a mere roof on poles – when the bride and her friends danced for three days without a smile on their sad brown faces.

All this the dead had known in life and it could not disturb nor interest them now. But that hideous intruder from modern civilization, a train of cars with a screeching engine, that would shake the earth which held them and rend the peaceful air with such discordant sounds that neither dead nor living could sleep! His life had been one long unbroken sacrifice, and he sought in vain to imagine one greater, which he would cheerfully assume could this disaster be spared his dead.

But the railway was built, and the first night the train went screaming by, shaking the earth and rattling the windows of the church, he went out and out and sprinkled every grave with holy water.

And thereafter twice a day, at dawn and at night, as the train tore a tunnel in the quiet air like the plebian upstart it was, he sprinkled every grave – rising sometimes from a bed of pain, at other times defying wind and rain and hail. And for a while he believed that his holy device had deepened the sleep of his dead, locked them beyond the power of man to awake. But one night he heard them muttering.

It was late. There were but a few stars on a black sky. Not a breath of wind came over the lonely plains beyond, or from the sea. There would be no wrecks tonight, and all the world seemed at peace. The lights were out in the village. One burned in the tower of Croisac, where the young wife of the count lay ill. The priest had been with her when the train

thundered by, and she had whispered to him:

"Would that I were on it! Oh, this lonely lonely land! This cold echoing chateau, with no one to speak to day after day! If it kills me, *mon père*, make him lay me in the cemetery by the road, that twice a day I may hear the train go by – the train that goes to Paris! If they put me down there over the hill, I will shriek in my coffin every night."

The priest had ministered as best he could to the ailing soul of the young noblewoman, with whose like he seldom dealt, and hastened back to his dead. He mused, as he toiled along the dark road with rheumatic legs, on the fact that the woman should have the same fancy as himself.

"If she is really sincere, poor young thing," he thought aloud, "I will forbear to sprinkle holy water on her grave. For those who suffer while alive should have all they desire after death, and I am afraid the count neglects her. But I pray God that my dead have not heard that monster tonight." And he tucked his gown under his arm and hurriedly told his rosary.

But when he went about among the graves with the holy water he heard the dead muttering.

"Jean-Marie," said a voice, fumbling among its unused tones for forgotten notes, "art thou ready? Surely that is the last call."

"Nay, nay," rumbled another voice, "that is not the sound of a trumpet, Francois. That will be sudden, loud and sharp, like the great blasts of the north when they come plunging over the sea from out the awful gorges of Iceland. Dost thou remember them, Francois? Thank the good God they spared us to die in

our beds with our grandchildren about us and only the little wind sighing in the Bois d'Amour. Ah, the poor comrades that died in their manhood, that went to the *grande pêche* once too often! Dost thou remember when the great wave curled round Ignace like his poor wife's arms, and we saw him no more? We clasped each other's hands, for we believed that we should follow, but we lived and went again and again to the *grande pêche*, and died in our beds. *Grace à Dieu!*"

"Why dost thou think of that now – here in the grave where it matters not, even to the living?"

"I know not; but it was of that night when Ignace went down that I thought as the living breath went out of me. Of what didst thou think as thou layest dying?"

"Of the money I owed to Dominique and could not pay. I sought to ask my son to pay it, but death had come suddenly and I could not speak. God knows how they treat my name today in the village of St. Hilaire."

"Thou art forgotten," murmured another voice. I died forty years after thee and men remember not so long in Finisterre. But thy son was my friend and I remember that he paid the money."

"And my son, what of him? Is he, too, here?"

"Nay; he lies deep in the northern sea. It was his second voyage, and he had returned with a purse for the young wife, the first time. But he returned no more, and she washed in the river for the dames of Croisac, and by-and-by she died. I would have married her but she said it was enough to lose one

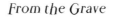

husband. I married another, and she grew ten years in every three that I went to the grande pêche. Alas for Brittany, she has no youth!"

"And thou? Wert thou an old man when thou camest here?"

"Sixty. My wife came first, like many wives. She lies here. Jeanne!"

"Is't thy voice, my husband? Not the Lord Jesus Christ's? What miracle is this? I thought that terrible sound was the trumpet of doom."

"It could not be, old Jeanne, for we are still in our graves. When the trump sounds we shall have wings and robes of light, and fly straight up to heaven. Hast thou slept well?"

"Ay! But why are we awakened? Is it time for purgatory?

Or have we been there?"

"The good God knows. I remember nothing. Art frightened? Would that I could hold thy hand, as when thou didst slip from life into that long sleep thou didst fear, yet welcome."

"I am frightened, my husband. But it is sweet to hear thy voice, hoarse and hollow as it is from the mould of the grave. Thank the good God thou didst bury me with the rosary in my hands," and she began telling the beads rapidly.

"If God is good," cried Francois, harshly, and his voice came plainly to the priest's ears, as if the lid of the coffin had rotted, "why are we awakened before our time? What foul fiend was it that thundered and screamed through the frozen avenues of my brain? Has God, perchance, been vanquished and does the Evil One reign in His stead?"

"Thou blasphemest! God reigns, now and always. It is but a punishment He has laid upon us for the sins of earth."

"Truly, we were punished enough before we descended to the peace of this narrow house. Ah, but it is dark and cold! Shall we lie like this for an eternity, perhaps? On earth we longed for death, but feared the grave. I would that I were alive again, poor and old and alone and in pain. It were better than this. Curse the foul fiend that woke us!"

"Curse not, my son," said a soft voice – and the priest stood up and uncovered and crossed himself, for it was the voice of his aged predecessor." I cannot tell thee what this is that has rudely shaken us in our graves and freed our spirits of their

blessed thraldom, and I like not the consciousness of this narrow house, this load of earth on my tired heart. But it is right, it must be right, or it would not be at all – ah, me!"

For a baby cried softly, hopelessly, and from a grave beyond came a mother's anguished attempt to still it.

"Ah, the good God!" she cried. "I, too, thought it was the great call, and that in a moment I should rise and find my child and go to my Ignace, my Ignace whose bones lie white on the floor of the sea. Will he find them, my father, when the dead shall rise again? To lie here and doubt! That were worse than life."

"Yes, yes," said the priest, "all will be well, my daughter."

"But all is not well, my father, for my baby cries and is alone in a little box in the ground. If I could claw my way to her with my hands – but my old mother lies between us."

"Tell your beads!" commanded the priest, sternly. "Tell your beads, all of you. All ye that have not your beads, say the 'Hail Mary!' one hundred times."

Immediately a rapid, monotonous muttering arose from every lonely chamber of that desecrated ground. All obeyed but the baby, who still moaned with the hopeless grief of deserted children. The living priest knew that they would talk no more that night, and went into the church to pray till dawn. He was sick with horror and terror, but not for himself. When the sky was pink and the air full of the sweet scents of morning, and a piercing scream tore a rent in the early silences, he hastened out and sprinkled his graves with a

double allowance of holy water. The train rattled by with two short derisive shrieks, and before the earth had ceased to tremble the priest laid his ear to the ground. Alas, they were still awake!

"The fiend is on the wing again, said Jean-Marie. "But as he passed I felt as if the finger of God touched my brow. It can do us no harm."

"I, too, felt that heavenly caress!" exclaimed the old priest. "And I!" "And I!" "And I!" came from every grave but the baby's.

The priest of earth, deeply thankful that his simple device had comforted them, went rapidly down the road to the castle. He forgot that he had not broken his fast nor slept. The count was one of the directors of the railroad, and to him he would make a final appeal.

It was early, but no one slept at Croisac. The young countess was dead. A great bishop had arrived in the night and administered the last rites. The priest hopefully asked if he might venture into the presence of the bishop. After a long wait in the kitchen, he was told that he could speak with Monsieur l' Eveque. He followed the servant up the wide spiral stair of the tower, and from its twenty-eighth step entered a room hung with purple cloth stamped with golden fleurs-de-lys. The bishop lay six feet above the floor on one of the splendid carved cabinet beds that are built against the walls in Brittany. Heavy curtains shaded his cold white face. The priest, who was small and bowed, felt immeasurably below

that august presence, and sought for words.

"What is it, my son?" asked the bishop, in his cold weary voice. "Is the matter so pressing? I am very tired."

Brokenly, nervously, the priest told his story, and as he strove to convey the tragedy of the tormented dead he not only felt the poverty of his expression – for was little used to narrative – but the torturing thought assailed him that what he said sounded wild and unnatural, real as it was to him. But he was not prepared for its effect on the bishop. He was standing in the middle of the room, whose gloom was softened and gilded by the waxen lights of a huge candelabra; his eyes, which had wandered unseeingly from one massive piece of carved furniture to another, suddenly lit on the bed, and he stopped abruptly, his tongue rolling out. The bishop was sitting up, livid with wrath.

"And this was thy matter of life and death, thou prating madman!" he thundered. "For this string of foolish lies I am kept from my rest, as if I were another old lunatic like thyself! Thou art not fit to be a priest and have the care of souls. Tomorrow——"

But the priest had fled, wringing his hands.

As he stumbled down the winding stair he ran straight into the arms of the count. Monsieur de Croisac had just closed a door behind him. He opened it, and, leading the priest into the room, pointed to his dead countess, who lay high up against the wall. On high pedestals at head and foot of her magnificent couch the pale flames rose from tarnished golden candlesticks.

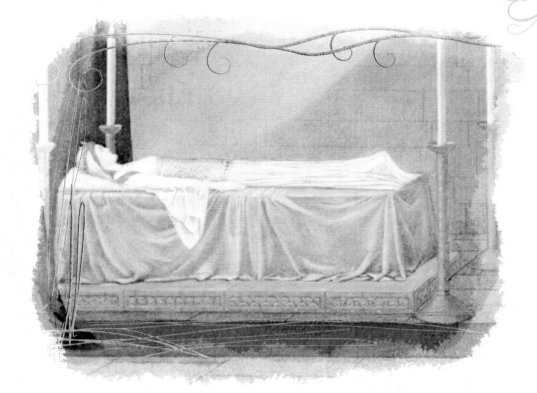

The blue hangings of the room were faded, like the rugs on the old dim floor; for the splendor of the Croisacs had departed with the Bourbons. The count lived in the old chateau because he must; but he reflected bitterly tonight that if he had made the mistake of bringing a young girl to it, there were several things he might have done to save her from despair and death.

"Pray for her," he said to the priest. "And you will bury her in the old cemetery. It was her last request."

He went out, and the priest sank on his knees and

mumbled his prayers for the dead. But his eyes wandered to the high narrow windows through which the countess had stared for hours and days, stared at the fishermen sailing north for the *grande pêche*, followed along the shore of the river by wives and mothers, until their boats were caught in the great waves of the ocean beyond; often at naught more animate than the dark flood, the wooded banks, the ruins, the rain driving like needles through the water. The priest had eaten nothing since his meagre breakfast at twelve the day before, and his imagination was active. He wondered if the soul up there rejoiced in the death of the beautiful restless body, the passionate brooding mind. He could not see her face from where he knelt, only the waxen hands. He wondered if the face were peaceful in death, or peevish and angry as when he had seen it last. If the great change had smoothed and sealed it, then perhaps the soul would sink deep under the dark waters, grateful for oblivion, and that cursed train could not awaken it for years to come. Curiosity succeeded wonder. He cut his prayers short, got to his weary swollen feet and pushed a chair to the bed. He mounted it and his face was close to the dead woman's. Alas! it was not peaceful. It was stamped with the tragedy of a bitter renunciation. After all, she had been young, and at the last had died unwillingly. There was still a fierce tenseness about the nostrils, and her upper lip was curled as if her last word had been a curse. But she was very beautiful, despite the emaciation of her features. Her lashes looked too heavy for the sunken cheeks.

"*Pauvre petite!*" thought the priest. " No, she will not rest, nor would she wish to. I will not sprinkle holy water on her grave. It is wondrous that monster can give comfort to any one, but if he can, so be it."

He went into the little oratory adjoining the bedroom and prayed more fervently. But when the watchers came an hour later they found him in a stupor, huddled at the foot of the altar.

When he awoke he was in his own house beside the church. It was four days before they would let him rise to go about his duties, and by that time the countess was in her grave.

The old housekeeper left him to take care of himself. It was raining thinly, a grey quiet rain that blurred the landscape and soaked the ground in the Bois d'Amour.

It was wet about the graves, too; but the priest had given little heed to the elements in his long life of crucified self, and as he heard the remote echo of the evening train he hastened out with his holy water, and had sprinkled every grave but one when the train sped by.

Then he knelt and listened eagerly. It was five days since he had knelt there last. Perhaps they had sunk again to rest. In a moment he wrung his hands and raised them to heaven. All the earth beneath him was filled with lamentation. They wailed for mercy, for peace, for rest; they cursed the foul fiend who had shattered the locks of death; and among the voices of men and children the priest distinguished the quavering notes of his

aged predecessor – not cursing, but praying with bitter entreaty. The baby was screaming with the accents of mortal terror and its mother was too frantic to care.

"Alas," cried the voice of Jean-Marie, "that they never told us what purgatory was like! What do the priests know? When we were threatened with punishment of our sins not a hint did we have of this. To sleep for a few hours, haunted with the moment of awakening! Then a cruel insult from the earth that is tired of us, and the orchestra of hell. Again! And again! And again! Oh God! How long? How long?"

The priest stumbled to his feet and ran over graves and paths to the mound above the countess. There he would hear a voice praising the monster of night and dawn, a note of content in this terrible chorus of despair which he believed would drive him mad. He vowed that on the morrow he would move his dead, if he had to unbury them with his own hands and carry them up the hill to graves of his own making.

For a moment he heard no sound. He knelt and laid his ear to the grave, then pressed it more closely and held his breath. A long rumbling moan reached it, then another and another. But there were no words.

"Is she moaning in sympathy with my poor friends?" he thought, "Or have they terrified her? Why does she not speak to them? Perhaps they would forget their plight were she to tell them of the world they have left so long. But it was not their world. Perhaps that it is which distresses her, for she will be lonelier here than on earth. Ah!"

A sharp horrified cry pierced to his ears, then a gasping shriek, and another; all dying away in a dreadful smothered rumble.

The priest rose and wrung his hands, looking to the wet skies for inspiration.

"Alas!" he sobbed, "She is not content. She has made a terrible mistake. She would rest in the deep sweet peace of death, and that monster of iron and fire and the frantic dead about her are tormenting a soul so tormented in life. There may be rest for her in the vault behind the castle, but not here. I know, and I shall do my duty – now, at once."

He gathered his robes about him and ran as fast as his old legs and rheumatic feet would take him towards the château, whose lights gleamed through the rain. On the bank of the river he met a fisherman and begged to be taken by boat. The fisherman wondered, but picked the priest up in his strong arms, lowered him into the boat, and rowed swiftly towards the château. When they landed, he made fast.

"I will wait for you in the kitchen, my father," he said; and the priest blessed him and hurried up to the castle.

Once more he entered through the door of the great kitchen, with its blue tiles, its glittering brass and bronze warming-pans which had comforted nobles and monarchs in the days of Croisac splendour. He sank into a chair beside the stove while a maid hastened to the count. She returned while the priest was still shivering, and announced that her master would see his holy visitor in the library.

It was a dreary room where the count sat waiting for the priest, and it smelled of musty calf, for the books on the shelves were old. A few novels and newspapers lay on the heavy table, a fire burned in the grate, but the paper on the wall was very dark and the fleurs-de-lys were tarnished and dull. The count, when at home, divided his time between this library and the water, when he could not chase the boar or the stag in the forests. But he often went to Paris, where he could afford the life of a bachelor in a wing of his great hotel; he had known too much of the extravagance of women to give his wife the key of the faded salons. He had loved the beautiful girl when he married her, but her repinings and bitter discontent had alienated him, and during the past year he had held himself aloof from her in sullen resentment. Too late he understood, and dreamed passionately of atonement. She had been a high-spirited brilliant eager creature, and her unsatisfied mind had dwelt constantly on the world she had vividly enjoyed for one year. And he had given her so little in return!

He rose as the priest entered, and bowed low. The visit bored him, but the good old priest commanded his respect; moreover, he had performed many offices and rites in his family. He moved a chair towards his guest, but the old man shook his head and nervously twisted his hands together.

"Alas, *monsieur le comte*," he said, "it may be that you, too, will tell me that I am an old lunatic, as did *Monsieur l' Eveque*. Yet I must speak, even if you tell your servants to fling me out of the château."

The count had started slightly. He recalled certain acid comments of the bishop, followed by a statement that a young curé should be sent, gently to supersede the old priest, who was in his dotage. But he replied suavely:

"You know, my father, that no one in this castle will ever show you disrespect. Say what you wish; have no fear. But will you not sit down? I am very tired."

The priest took the chair and fixed his eyes appealingly on the count.

"It is this, monsieur." He spoke rapidly, lest his courage should go. "That terrible train, with its brute of iron and live coals and foul smoke and screeching throat, has awakened my dead. I guarded them with holy water and they heard it not, until one night when I missed — I was with madame as the train shrieked by shaking the nail out of the coffins. I hurried back, but the mischief was done, the dead were awake, the dear sleep of eternity was shattered. They thought it was the last trump and wondered why they still were in their graves. But they talked together and it was not so bad at the first. But now they are frantic. They are in hell, and I have come to beseech you to see that they are moved far up on the hill. Ah, think, think, monsieur,

what it is to have the last long sleep of the grave so rudely disturbed – the sleep for which we live and endure so patiently!"

He stopped abruptly and caught his breath. The count had listened without change of countenance, convinced that he was facing a madman. But the farce wearied him, and involuntarily his hand had moved towards a bell on the table.

"Ah, monsieur, not yet! Not yet!" panted the priest. "It is of the countess I came to speak. I had forgotten. She told me she wished to lie there and listen to the train go by to Paris, so I sprinkled no holy water on her grave. But she, too, is wretched and horror-stricken, monsieur. Her coffin is new and strong, and I cannot hear her words, but I have heard those frightful sounds from her grave tonight, monsieur; I swear it on the cross. Ah, monsieur, thou dost believe me at last!"

For the count, as white as the woman had been in her coffin, and shaking from head to foot, had staggered from his chair and was staring at the priest as if he saw the ghost of his countess. "You heard—?" he gasped.

"She is not at peace, *monsieur*. She moans and shrieks in a terrible, smothered way, as if a hand were on her mouth—"

But he had uttered the last of his words. The count had suddenly recovered himself and dashed from the room. The

priest passed his hand across his forehead and sank slowly to the floor.

"He will see that I spoke the truth," he thought, as he fell asleep, "and tomorrow he will intercede for my poor friends."

The priest lies high on the hill where no train will ever disturb him, and his old comrades of the violated cemetery are close about him. For the Count and Countess of Croisac, who adore his memory, hastened to give him in death what he most had desired in the last of his life. And with them all things are well, for a man, too, may be born again, and without descending into the grave.

The Tell-Tale Heart

1843

EXTRACT

Edgar Allan Poe

TRUE! Nervous, very, very dreadfully nervous I had been and am; but why will you say that I am mad? The disease had sharpened my senses, not destroyed, not dulled them. Above all was the sense of hearing acute. I heard all things in the heaven and in the earth. I heard many things in hell. How then am I mad? Hearken! And observe how healthily, how calmly, I can tell you the whole story.

It is impossible to say how first the idea entered my brain, but, once conceived, it haunted me day and night. Object there was none. Passion there was none. I loved the old man. He had never wronged me. He had never given me insult. For his gold I had no desire. I think it was his eye! Yes, it was this! One of his eyes resembled that of a vulture – a pale blue eye with a film over it. Whenever it fell upon me my blood ran

cold, and so by degrees, very gradually, I made up my mind to take the life of the old man, and thus rid myself of the eye forever.

Now this is the point. You fancy me mad. Madmen know nothing. But you should have seen me. You should have seen how wisely I proceeded – with what caution, with what foresight, with what dissimulation, I went to work! I was never kinder to the old man than during the whole week before I killed him. And every night, about midnight, I turned the latch of his door and opened it oh – so gently! And then, when I had made an opening sufficient for my head, I put in a dark lantern all closed, closed so that no light shone out, and then I thrust in my head. Oh, you would have laughed to see how cunningly I thrust it in! I moved it slowly – very, very slowly, so that I might not disturb the old man's sleep. It took me an hour to place my whole head within the opening so far that I could see him as he lay upon his bed. Ha! Would a madman have been so wise as this? And then when my head was well in the room I undid the lantern cautiously – oh, so cautiously – cautiously (for the hinges creaked), I undid it just so much that a single thin ray fell upon the vulture eye. And this I did for seven long nights – every night just at midnight – but I found the eye always closed. And so it was impossible to do the work, for it was not the old man who vexed me but his Evil Eye. And every morning, when the day broke, I went boldly into the chamber and spoke courageously to him, calling him by name in a hearty tone, and inquiring how he had passed the night. So

you see he would have been a very profound old man indeed, to suspect that every night, just at twelve, I looked in upon him while he slept.

Upon the eighth night I was more than usually cautious in opening the door. A watch's minute hand moves more quickly than did mine! Never before that night had I *felt* the extent of my own powers, of my sagacity. I could scarcely contain my feelings of triumph. To think that there I was opening the door little by little, and he not even to dream of my secret deeds or thoughts. I fairly chuckled at the idea — and perhaps he heard me, for he moved on the bed suddenly, as if startled. Now you may think that I drew back — but no. His room was as black as pitch with the thick darkness (for the shutters were closed — fastened through fear of robbers), and so I knew that he could not see the opening of the door, and I kept pushing it on steadily, steadily.

I had my head in, and was about to open the lantern, when my thumb slipped upon the tin fastening, and the old man sprang up in the bed, crying out, "Who's there?"

I kept quite still and said nothing. For a whole hour I did not move a muscle, and in the meantime I did not hear him lie down. He was still sitting up in the bed, listening — just as I have done, night after night, hearkening to the deathwatch beetles in the wall.

Presently I heard a groan, and I knew it was the groan of mortal terror. It was not a groan of pain or of grief — oh, no! It was the low stifled sound that arises from the bottom of the

soul when overcharged with awe. I knew the sound well. Many a night, just at midnight, when all the world slept, it has welled up from my own bosom, deepening, with its dreadful echo, the terrors that distracted me. I say I knew it well. I knew what the old man felt, and pitied him — although I chuckled at heart. I knew that he had been lying awake ever since the first slight noise, when he had turned in the bed. His fears had been ever since growing upon him. He had been trying to fancy them causeless, but could not. He had been saying to himself, "It is nothing but the wind in the chimney, it is only a mouse crossing the floor," or, "It is merely a cricket which has made a single chirp." Yes, he has been trying to comfort himself with these suppositions; but he had found all in vain. *all in vain*, because Death, in approaching him, had stalked with his black shadow before him and enveloped the victim. And it was the mournful influence of the unperceived shadow that caused him to feel — although he neither saw nor heard — to *feel* the presence of my head within the room.

When I had waited a long time, very patiently, without hearing him lie down, I resolved to open a little — a very, very little — crevice in the lantern. So I opened it — you cannot imagine how stealthily, stealthily — until at length a single dim ray, like the thread of the spider, shot out from the crevice and fell upon the vulture eye.

It was open — wide, wide open — and I grew furious as I gazed upon it. I saw it with perfect distinctness — all a dull blue, with a hideous veil over it that chilled the very marrow

in my bones. But I could see nothing else of the old man's face or person, for I had directed the ray, as if by instinct, precisely upon the damned spot.

And now have I not told you that what you mistake for madness is but over-acuteness of the senses? Now, I say, there came to my ears a low, dull, quick sound, such as a watch makes when enveloped in cotton. I knew *that* sound well too. It was the beating of the old man's heart. It increased my fury as the beating of a drum stimulates the soldier into courage.

But even yet I refrained and kept still. I scarcely breathed. I held the lantern motionless. I tried how steadily I could maintain the ray upon the eye. Meantime the hellish tattoo of

the heart increased. It grew quicker and quicker, and louder and louder, every instant. The old man's terror *must* have been extreme! It grew louder, I say, louder every moment! Do you mark me well? I have told you that I am nervous: so I am. And now at the dead hour of the night, amid the dreadful silence of that old house, so strange a noise as this excited me to uncontrollable terror. Yet, for some minutes longer I refrained and stood still. But the beating grew louder, louder! I thought the heart must burst. And

now a new anxiety seized me — the sound would be heard by a neighbour! The old man's hour had come! With a loud yell, I threw open the lantern and leapt into the room. He shrieked once — once only. In an instant I dragged him to the floor, and pulled the heavy bed over him. I then smiled gaily, to find the deed so far done. But for many minutes the heart beat on with a muffled sound. This, however, did not vex me; it would not be heard through the wall. At length it ceased. The old man was dead. I removed the bed and examined the corpse. Yes, he was stone, stone dead. I placed my hand upon the heart and held it there many minutes. There was no pulsation. He was stone dead. His eye would trouble me no more.

If still you think me mad, you will think so no longer when I describe the wise precautions I took for the concealment of the body. The night waned, and I worked hastily, but in silence.

I took up three planks from the flooring of the chamber, and deposited all between the scantlings. I then replaced the boards so cleverly so cunningly, that no human eye — not even his — could have detected anything wrong. There was nothing to wash out — no stain of any kind — no blood-spot whatever. I had been too wary for that.

When I had made an end of these labours, it was four o'clock — still dark as midnight. As the bell sounded the hour, there came a knocking at the street door. I went down to open it with a light heart — for what had I *now* to fear? There entered three men, who introduced themselves, with perfect suavity, as officers of the police. A shriek had been heard by a neighbour

during the night; suspicion of foul play had been aroused; information had been lodged at the police office, and they (the officers) had been deputed to search the premises.

I smiled – for *what* had I to fear? I bade the gentlemen welcome. The shriek, I said, was my own in a dream. The old man, I mentioned, was absent in the country. I took my visitors all over the house. I bade them search – search *well*. I led them, at length, to his chamber. I showed them his treasures, secure, undisturbed. In the enthusiasm of my confidence, I brought chairs into the room, and desired them *here* to rest from their fatigues, while I myself, in the wild audacity of my perfect triumph, placed my own seat upon the very spot beneath which reposed the corpse of the victim.

The officers were satisfied. My manner had convinced them. I was singularly at ease. They sat, and while I answered cheerily, they chatted of familiar things. But, ere long, I felt myself getting pale and wished them gone. My head ached, and I fancied a ringing in my ears; but still they sat and still chatted. The ringing became more distinct: I talked more freely to get rid of the feeling: but it continued and gained definitiveness – until, at length, I found that the noise was *not* within my ears.

No doubt I now grew very pale; but I talked more fluently, and with a heightened voice. Yet the sound increased – and what could I do? It was *a low, dull, quick sound – much such a sound as a watch makes when enveloped in cotton*. I gasped for breath – and yet the officers heard it not. I talked more

quickly more vehemently, but the noise steadily increased. I arose and argued about trifles, in a high key and with violent gesticulations; but the noise steadily increased. Why *would* they not be gone? I paced the floor to and fro with heavy strides, as if excited to fury by the observations of the men, but the noise steadily increased. Oh God! What *could* I do? I foamed – I raved – I swore! I swung the chair upon which I had been sitting, and grated it upon the boards, but the noise arose over all and continually increased. It grew louder – louder – louder! And still the men chatted pleasantly, and smiled. Was it possible they heard not? Almighty God! – No, no! They heard! – They suspected! – They *knew!* – They were making a mockery of my horror! – This I thought, and this I think. But anything was better than this agony! Anything was more tolerable than this derision! I could bear those hypocritical smiles no longer! I felt that I must scream or die! – And now again – Hark! Louder! Louder! Louder! *Louder!*

"Villains!" I shrieked, "Dissemble no more! I admit the deed! – Tear up the planks! – Here, here! – It is the beating of his hideous heart!"

A Bottomless Grave

1888

Ambrose Bierce

My name is John Brenwalter. My father, a drunkard, had a patent for an invention for making coffee-berries out of clay; but he was an honest man and would not himself engage in the manufacture. He was, therefore, only moderately wealthy, his royalties from his really valuable invention bringing him hardly enough to pay his expenses of litigation with rogues guilty of infringement. So I lacked many advantages enjoyed by the children of unscrupulous and dishonourable parents, and had it not been for a noble and devoted mother, who neglected all my brothers and sisters and personally supervised my education, should have grown up in ignorance and been compelled to teach school. To be the favourite child of a good woman is better than gold.

When I was nineteen years of age my father had the

misfortune to die. He had always had perfect health, and his death, which occurred at the dinner table without a moment's warning, surprised no one more than himself. He had that very morning been notified that a patent had been granted him for a device to burst open safes by hydraulic pressure, without noise. The Commissioner of Patents had pronounced it the most ingenious, effective and generally meritorious invention that had ever been submitted to him, and my father had naturally looked forward to an old age of prosperity and honour. His sudden death was, therefore, a deep disappointment to him; but my mother, whose piety and resignation to the will of heaven were conspicuous virtues of her character, was apparently less affected. At the close of the meal, when my poor father's body had been removed from the floor, she called us all into an adjoining room and addressed us as follows:

"My children, the uncommon occurrence that you have just witnessed is one of the most disagreeable incidents in a good man's life, and one in which I take little pleasure, I assure you. I beg you to believe that I had no hand in bringing it about. Of course," she added, after a pause, during which her eyes were cast down in deep thought, "of course it is better that he is dead."

She uttered this with so evident a sense of its obviousness as a self-evident truth that none of us had the courage to brave her surprise by asking an explanation. My mother's air of surprise when any of us went wrong in any way was very

terrible to us. One day, when in a fit of peevish temper, I had taken the liberty to cut off the baby's ear, her simple words, "John, you surprise me!" appeared to me so sharp a reproof that after a sleepless night I went to her in tears, and throwing myself at her feet, exclaimed: "Mother, forgive me for surprising you." So now we all – including the one-eared baby – felt that it would keep matters smoother to accept without question the statement that it was better, somehow, for our dear father to be dead. My mother continued:

"I must tell you, my children, that in a case of sudden and mysterious death the law requires the coroner to come and cut the body into pieces and submit them to a number of men who, having inspected them, pronounce the person dead. For this the coroner gets a large sum of money. I wish to avoid that painful formality in this instance; it is one which never had the approval of – of the remains. John" – here my mother turned her angel face to me – "you are an educated lad, and very discreet. You have now an opportunity to show your gratitude for all the sacrifices that your education has entailed upon the rest of us. John, go and get rid of the coroner."

Inexpressibly delighted by this proof of my mother's confidence, and by the chance to distinguish myself by an act that squared with my natural disposition, I knelt before her, carried her hand to my lips and bathed it with tears of sensibility. Before five o'clock that afternoon I had got rid of the coroner.

I was immediately arrested and thrown into jail, where I

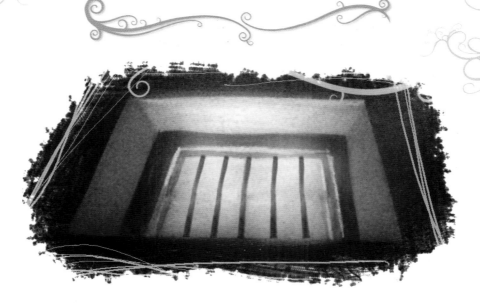

passed a most uncomfortable night, being unable to sleep because of the profanity of my fellow-prisoners: two clergymen, whose theological training had given them a fertility of impious ideas and a command of blasphemous language altogether unparalleled. But along towards morning the jailer – who, sleeping in an adjoining room, had been equally disturbed – entered the cell and with a fearful oath warned the reverend gentlemen that if he heard any more swearing their sacred calling would not prevent him from turning them into the street. After that they moderated their objectionable conversation, substituting an accordion, and I slept the peaceful and refreshing sleep of youth and innocence.

The next morning I was taken before the superior Judge, sitting as a committing magistrate, and put upon my preliminary examination. I pleaded not guilty, adding that the man whom I had murdered was a notorious Democrat (my

good mother was a Republican, and from early childhood I had been carefully instructed by her in the principles of honest government and the necessity of suppressing factional opposition). The judge, elected by a Republican ballot-box with a sliding bottom, was visibly impressed by the cogency of my plea and offered me a cigarette.

"May it please your honour," began the district attorney, "I do not deem it necessary to submit any evidence in this case. Under the law of the land you sit here as a committing magistrate. It is therefore your duty to commit. Testimony and argument alike would imply a doubt that your Honour means to perform your sworn duty. That is my case."

My counsel, a brother of the deceased coroner, rose and said: "May it please the court, my learned friend on the other side has so well and eloquently stated the law governing in this case that it only remains for me to inquire to what extent it has been already complied with. It is true, your honour is a committing magistrate, and as such it is your duty to commit — what? That is a matter which the law has wisely and justly left to your own discretion, and wisely you have discharged already every obligation that the law imposes. Since I have known your Honour you have done nothing but commit. You have committed embracery, theft, arson, perjury, adultery, murder — every crime in the calendar and every excess known to the sensual and depraved, including my learned friend, the district attorney. You have done your whole duty as a committing magistrate, and as there is no evidence against this worthy

young man, my client, I move that he be discharged."

An impressive silence ensued. The judge arose, and in a voice trembling with emotion sentenced me to life and liberty. Then turning to my counsel he said, coldly but significantly:

"I will see you later."

The next morning the lawyer who had defended me against a charge of murdering his own brother – with whom he had a quarrel about some land – had disappeared and his fate is to this day unknown.

In the meantime my poor father's body had been secretly buried at midnight in the back yard of his late residence, with his late boots on and the contents of his late stomach unanalysed. "He was opposed to display," said my dear mother, as she finished tamping down the earth above him and assisted the children to litter the place with straw; "his instincts were all domestic and he loved a quiet life."

My mother's application for letters of administration stated that she had good reason to believe that the deceased was dead, for he had not come home to his meals for several days; but the judge of the crow-bait court – as he ever afterwards contemptuously called it – decided that the proof of death was insufficient, and put the estate into the hands of the public administrator, who was his son-in-law. It was found that the liabilities were exactly balanced by the assets; there was left only the patent for the device for bursting open safes without noise by hydraulic pressure, and this had passed into the ownership of the probate judge and the public administrator –

as my dear mother preferred to spell it. Thus, within a few brief months a worthy and respectable family was reduced from prosperity to crime; necessity compelled us to go to work.

In the selection of occupations we were governed by a variety of considerations, such as personal fitness, inclination, and so forth. My mother opened a select private school for instruction in the art of changing the spots upon leopard-skin rugs; my eldest brother, George Henry, who had a turn for music, became a bugler in a neighbouring asylum for deaf mutes; my sister, Mary Maria, took orders for Professor Pumpernickel's Essence of Latchkeys for flavouring mineral springs; and I set up as an adjuster and gilder of crossbeams for gibbets. The other children, too young for labour, continued to steal small articles in front of shops, as they had been taught.

In our intervals of leisure we decoyed travellers into our house and buried the bodies in a cellar.

In one part of this cellar we kept wines, liquors and provisions. From the rapidity of their disappearance we acquired the superstitious belief that the spirits of the persons

buried there came at dead of night and held a festival. It was at least certain that frequently of a morning we would discover fragments of pickled meats, canned goods and such debris, littering the place, although it had been securely locked and barred against human intrusion. It was proposed to remove the provisions and store them elsewhere, but our dear mother, always generous and hospitable, said it was better to endure the loss than risk exposure: if the ghosts were denied this trifling gratification they might set on foot an investigation, which would overthrow our scheme of the division of labour, by diverting the energies of the whole family into the single industry pursued by me – we might all decorate the crossbeams of gibbets. We accepted her decision with filial submission, due to our reverence for her worldly wisdom and the purity of her character.

One night while we were all in the cellar – none dared to enter it alone – engaged in bestowing upon the Mayor of an adjoining town the solemn offices of Christian burial, my mother and the younger children, holding a candle each, while George Henry and I laboured with a spade and pick, my sister Mary Maria uttered a shriek and covered her eyes with her hands. We were all dreadfully startled and the Mayor's funeral rites were instantly suspended, while with pale faces and in trembling tones we begged her to say what had alarmed her. The younger children were so agitated that they held their candles unsteadily, and the waving shadows of our figures danced with uncouth and grotesque movements on the walls and flung themselves into the most uncanny attitudes. The face of the dead man, now gleaming ghastly in the light, and now extinguished by some floating shadow, appeared at each emergence to have taken on a new and more forbidding expression, a maligner menace. Frightened even more than ourselves by the girl's scream, rats raced in multitudes about the place, squeaking shrilly, or starred the black opacity of some distant corner with steadfast eyes, mere points of green light, matching the faint phosphorescence of decay that filled the half-dug grave and seemed the visible manifestation of that faint odour of mortality which tainted the unwholesome air. The children now sobbed and clung about the limbs of their elders, dropping their candles, and we were near being left in total darkness, except for that sinister light, which slowly welled upwards from the disturbed earth and overflowed the edges of the grave like a fountain.

Meanwhile my sister, crouching in the earth that had been thrown out of the excavation, had removed her hands from her face and was staring with expanded eyes into an obscure space between two wine casks.

"There it is! There it is!" she shrieked, pointing. "God in heaven! Can't you see it?"

And there indeed it was! A human figure, dimly discernible in the gloom — a figure that wavered from side to side as if about to fall, clutching at the wine-casks for support, had stepped unsteadily forwards and for one moment stood revealed in the light of our remaining candles; then it surged

heavily and fell prone upon the earth. In that moment we had all recognized the figure, the face and bearing of our father – dead these ten months and buried by our own hands! Our father, indubitably risen and ghastly drunk!

On the incidents of our precipitate flight from that horrible place, on the extinction of all human sentiment in that tumultuous, mad scramble up the damp and mouldy stairs: slipping, falling, pulling one another down and clambering over one another's back – the lights extinguished, babes trampled beneath the feet of their strong brothers and hurled backwards to death by a mother's arm! On all this I do not dare to dwell. My mother, my eldest brother and sister and I escaped; the others remained below, to perish of their wounds or of their terror – some, perhaps, by flame. For within an hour we four, hastily gathering together what money and jewels we had and what clothing we could carry, fired the dwelling and fled by its light into the hills. We did not even pause to collect the insurance, and my dear mother said on her death-bed – years afterwards in a distant land – that this was the only sin of omission that lay upon her conscience. Her confessor, a holy man, assured her that under the circumstances heaven would pardon the neglect.

About ten years after our removal from the scenes of my childhood I returned in disguise to the spot with a view to obtaining some treasure belonging to us, which had been buried in the cellar. I may say that I was unsuccessful: the discovery of many human bones in the ruins had set the authorities digging for more. They had found the treasure and had kept it for their honesty. The house had not been rebuilt; the whole suburb was, in fact, a desolation. So many unearthly 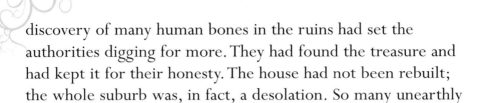 sights and sounds had been reported thereabout that nobody would live there. As there was none to question nor molest, I resolved to gratify my filial piety by gazing once more upon the face of my beloved father, if indeed our eyes had deceived us and he was still in his grave. I remembered that he had always worn an enormous diamond ring, and never having seen it nor heard of it since his death, I had reason to think he might have been buried in it. Procuring a spade, I soon located the grave in what had been the backyard and began digging. When I had got down about four feet the whole bottom fell out of the grave and I was precipitated into a large drain, falling through a long hole in its crumbling arch. There was no body, nor any vestige of one.

Unable to get out of the excavation, I crept through the drain, and having with some difficulty removed a mass of charred rubbish and blackened masonry that choked it, emerged into what had been that fateful cellar.

All was clear. My father, whatever had caused him to have been 'taken bad' at his meal (and I think it is possible that my sainted mother could have thrown some light upon that

matter) had indubitably been buried alive. The grave having been accidentally dug above the forgotten drain, and down almost to the crown of its arch, and no coffin having been used, his struggles on reviving had broken the long-rotted masonry and he had fallen through, eventually escaping into the cellar. Feeling that he was no longer welcome in his own house, yet having no other, he had lived in subterranean seclusion, a witness to our thrift and a pensioner on our providence. It was he who had eaten our food and it was he who had drunk our wine – he was no better than a common thief! In a moment of intoxication, and feeling – no doubt – that need of companionship which is the one sympathetic link between a drunken man and his race, he had left his place of concealment at a strangely inopportune time, entailing the most deplorable consequences upon those nearest and dearest to him – a blunder that had almost the dignity of crime.

Lost Hearts

1904

M R James

It was, as far as I can ascertain, in September of the year 1811 that a post-chaise drew up before the door of Aswarby Hall, in the heart of Lincolnshire. The little boy who was the only passenger in the chaise, and who jumped out as soon as it had stopped, looked about him with the keenest curiosity during the short interval that elapsed between the ringing of the bell and the opening of the hall door. He saw a tall, square, red-brick house, built in the reign of Anne; a stone-pillared porch had been added in the purer classical style of 1790; the windows of the house were many, tall and narrow, with small panes and thick white woodwork. A pediment, pierced with a round window, crowned the front. There were wings to right and left, connected by curious glazed galleries, supported by colonnades, with the central block. These wings

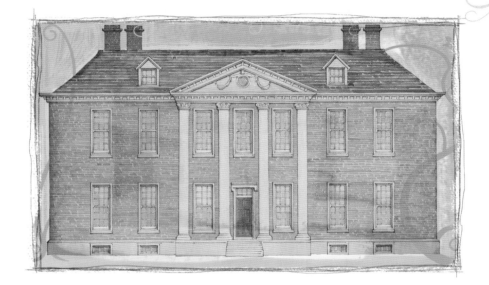

plainly contained the stables and offices of the house. Each was surmounted by an ornamental cupola with a gilded vane.

An evening light shone on the building, making the window-panes glow like so many fires. Away from the Hall in front stretched a flat park studded with oaks and fringed with firs, which stood out against the sky. The clock in the church-tower, buried in trees on the edge of the park, only its golden weather-cock catching the light, was striking six, and the sound came gently beating down the wind. It was altogether a pleasant impression, though tinged with the sort of melancholy appropriate to an evening in early autumn, that was conveyed to the mind of the boy who was standing in the porch waiting for the door to open to him.

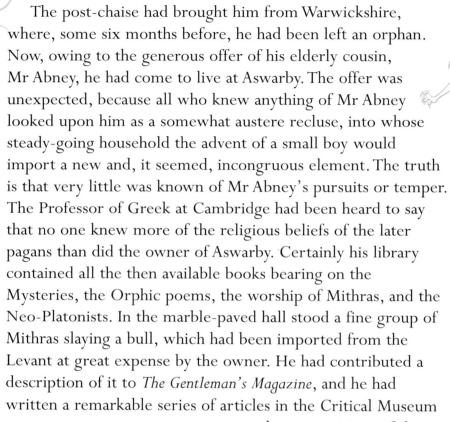

The post-chaise had brought him from Warwickshire, where, some six months before, he had been left an orphan. Now, owing to the generous offer of his elderly cousin, Mr Abney, he had come to live at Aswarby. The offer was unexpected, because all who knew anything of Mr Abney looked upon him as a somewhat austere recluse, into whose steady-going household the advent of a small boy would import a new and, it seemed, incongruous element. The truth is that very little was known of Mr Abney's pursuits or temper. The Professor of Greek at Cambridge had been heard to say that no one knew more of the religious beliefs of the later pagans than did the owner of Aswarby. Certainly his library contained all the then available books bearing on the Mysteries, the Orphic poems, the worship of Mithras, and the Neo-Platonists. In the marble-paved hall stood a fine group of Mithras slaying a bull, which had been imported from the Levant at great expense by the owner. He had contributed a description of it to *The Gentleman's Magazine*, and he had written a remarkable series of articles in the Critical Museum

on the superstitions of the Romans of the Lower Empire. He was looked upon, in fine, as a man wrapped up in his books, and it was a matter of great surprise among his neighbours that he should ever have heard of his

orphan cousin, Stephen Elliott, much more that he should have volunteered to make him an inmate of Aswarby Hall.

Whatever may have been expected by his neighbours, it is certain that Mr Abney – the tall, the thin, the austere – seemed inclined to give his young cousin a kindly reception. The moment the front-door was opened he darted out of his study, rubbing his hands with delight.

"How are you, my boy, how are you? How old are you?" said he. "That is, you are not too much tired, I hope, by your journey to eat your supper?"

"No, thank you, sir," said Master Elliott; "I am pretty well."

"That's a good lad," said Mr Abney. "And how old are you, my boy?"

It seemed a little odd that he should have asked the question twice in the first two minutes of their acquaintance.

"I'm twelve years old next birthday, sir," said Stephen.

"And when is your birthday, my dear boy? Eleventh of September, eh? That's well – that's very well. Nearly a year hence, isn't it? I like – ha, ha! – I like to get these things down in my book. Sure it's twelve? Certain?"

"Yes, quite sure, sir."

"Well, well! Take him to Mrs Bunch's room, Parkes, and let him have his tea – supper –whatever it is."

"Yes, sir," answered the staid Mr Parkes; and conducted Stephen to the lower regions.

Mrs Bunch was the most comfortable and human person whom Stephen had as yet met at Aswarby. She made him completely at home; they were great friends in a quarter of an hour: and great friends they remained. Mrs Bunch had been born in the neighbourhood some fifty-five years before the date of Stephen's arrival, and her residence at the Hall was of twenty years' standing. Consequently, if anyone knew the ins and outs of the house and the district, Mrs Bunch knew them; and she was by no means disinclined to communicate her information.

Certainly there were plenty of things about the Hall and the Hall gardens which Stephen, who was of an adventurous and inquiring turn, was anxious to have explained to him. 'Who built the temple at the end of the laurel walk? Who was the old man whose picture hung on the staircase, sitting at a

table, with a skull under his hand?' These and many similar points were cleared up by the resources of Mrs Bunch's powerful intellect. There were others, however, of which the explanations furnished were less satisfactory.

One November evening Stephen was sitting by the fire in the housekeeper's room reflecting on his surroundings.

"Is Mr Abney a good man, and will he go to heaven?" he suddenly asked, with the peculiar confidence which children possess in the ability of their elders to settle these questions, the decision of which is believed to be reserved for other tribunals.

"Good? – Bless the child!" said Mrs Bunch. "Master's as kind a soul as ever I see! Didn't I never tell you of the little boy as he took in out of the street, as you may say, this seven years back? And the little girl, two years after I first come here?"

"No. Do tell me all about them, Mrs Bunch – now, this minute!"

"Well," said Mrs Bunch, "the little girl I don't seem to recollect so much about. I know master brought her back with him from his walk one day, and give orders to Mrs Ellis, as was housekeeper then, as she should be took every care with. And the pore child hadn't no one belonging to her – she told me so her own self – and here she lived with us a matter of three weeks it might be; and then, whether she were somethink of a gipsy in her blood or what not, but one morning she out of her bed afore any of us had opened an eye, and neither track

nor yet trace of her have I set eyes on since. Master was wonderful put about, and had all the ponds dragged; but it's my belief she was had away by them gipsies, for there was singing round the house for as much as an hour the night she went, and Parkes, he declare as he heard them a-calling in the woods all that afternoon. Dear, dear! a hodd child she was, so silent in her ways and all, but I was wonderful taken up with her, so domesticated she was – surprising."

"And what about the little boy?" said Stephen.

"Ah, that pore boy!" sighed Mrs Bunch. "He were a foreigner – Jevanny he called hisself – and he come a-tweaking his 'urdy-gurdy round and about the drive one winter day, and master 'ad him in that minute, and ast all about where he came from, and how old he was, and how he made his way, and where was his relatives, and all as kind as heart could wish. But it went the same way with him. They're a hunruly lot, them foreign nations, I do suppose, and he was off one fine morning just the same as the girl. Why he went and what he done was our question for as much as a year after; for he never took his 'urdy-gurdy, and there it lays on the shelf."

The remainder of the evening was spent by Stephen in miscellaneous

cross-examination of Mrs Bunch and in efforts to extract a tune from the hurdy-gurdy.

That night he had a curious dream. At the end of the passage at the top of the house, in which his bedroom was situated, there was an old disused bathroom. It was kept locked, but the upper half of the door was glazed, and, since the muslin curtains which used to hang there had long been gone, you could look in and see the lead-lined bath affixed to the wall on the right hand, with its head towards the window.

On the night of which I am speaking, Stephen Elliott found himself, or so he thought, looking through the glazed door. The pale moon was shining through the window, and he was gazing down upon at a figure which lay in the bath.

His description of what he saw reminds me of what I once beheld myself in the famous vaults of St Michan's Church in Dublin, which possesses the horrid property of preserving corpses from decay for centuries. A figure inexpressibly thin and pathetic, of a dusty leaden colour, enveloped in a shroud-like garment, the thin lips crooked into a faint and dreadful smile, the hands pressed tightly over the region of the heart.

As he looked upon it, a distant, almost inaudible moan seemed to issue from its lips, and the arms began to stir. The terror of the sight forced Stephen backwards and he awoke to the fact that he was indeed standing on the cold boarded floor of the passage in the full light of the moon. With a courage which I do not think can be common among boys of his age, he went to the door of the bathroom to ascertain if the figure

of his dreams were really there. It was not, and he went back to bed.

Mrs Bunch was much impressed next morning by his story, and went so far as to replace the muslin curtain over the glazed door of the bathroom. Mr Abney, moreover, to whom he confided his experiences at breakfast, was greatly interested and made notes of the matter in what he called 'his book'.

The spring equinox was approaching, as Mr Abney frequently reminded his cousin, adding that this had been always considered by the ancients to be a critical time for the young: that Stephen would do well to take care of himself, and to shut his bedroom window at night; and that Censorinus had some valuable remarks on the subject. Two incidents that occurred about this time made an impression upon Stephen's mind.

The first was after an unusually uneasy and oppressed night that he had passed – though he could not recall any particular dream that he had had.

The following evening Mrs Bunch was occupying herself in mending his nightgown.

"Gracious me, Master Stephen!" she broke forth rather irritably, "How do you manage to tear your nightdress all to flinders this way? Look here, sir, what trouble you do give to poor servants that have to darn and mend after you!"

There was indeed a most destructive and apparently wanton series of slits or scorings in the garment, which would undoubtedly require a skilful needle to make good. They were

confined to the left side of the chest – long, parallel slits about six inches in length, some of them not quite piercing the texture of the linen. Stephen could only express his entire ignorance of their origin: he was sure they were not there the night before.

"But," he said, "Mrs Bunch, they are just the same as the scratches on the outside of my bedroom door: and I'm sure I never had anything to do with making them."

Mrs Bunch gazed at him open-mouthed, then snatched up a candle, departed hastily from the room, and was heard making her way upstairs. In a few minutes she came down.

"Well," she said, "Master Stephen, it's a funny thing to me how them marks and scratches can 'a' come there – too high up for any cat or dog to 'ave made 'em, much less a rat. They look for all the world like the marks of finger-nails. I wouldn't say nothing to master, not if I was you, Master Stephen, my dear; and just turn the key of the door when you go to your bed."

"I always do, Mrs Bunch, as soon as I've said my prayers."

"Ah, that's a good child: always say your prayers, and then no one can't hurt you."

Herewith Mrs Bunch addressed herself to mending the injured nightgown, with intervals of meditation, until bedtime. This was on a Friday night in March, 1812.

On the following evening the usual duet of Stephen and Mrs Bunch was augmented by the sudden arrival of Mr Parkes, the butler, who as a rule kept himself rather to himself in his own pantry. He did not see that Stephen was there: he was, moreover, flustered and less slow of speech than was his wont.

"Master may get up his own wine, if he likes, of an evening," was his first remark. "Either I do it in the daytime or not at all, Mrs Bunch. I don't know what it may be: very like it's the rats, or the wind got into the cellars; but I'm not so young as I was, and I can't go through with it as I have done."

"Well, Mr Parkes, you know it is a surprising place for the rats, is the Hall."

"I'm not denying that, Mrs Bunch; and, to be sure, many a time I've heard the tale from the men in the shipyards about the rat that could speak. I never laid no confidence in that before; but tonight, if I'd demeaned myself to lay my ear to the door of the further bin, I could pretty much have heard what they was saying."

"Oh, there, Mr Parkes, I've no patience with your fancies! Rats talking in the wine-cellar indeed!"

"Well, Mrs Bunch, I've no wish to argue with you: all I say is, if you choose to go to the far bin, and lay your ear to the door, you may prove my words this minute."

"What nonsense you do talk, Mr Parkes – not fit for children to listen to! Why, you'll be frightening Master Stephen there out of his wits."

"What! Master Stephen?" said Parkes, awaking to the consciousness of the boy's presence. "Master Stephen knows well enough when I'm a-playing a joke with you, Mrs Bunch."

In fact, Master Stephen knew much too well to suppose that Mr Parkes had in the first instance intended a joke. He was interested, not altogether pleasantly, in the situation; but

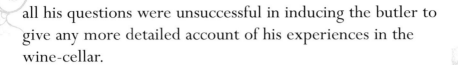

all his questions were unsuccessful in inducing the butler to give any more detailed account of his experiences in the wine-cellar.

We have now arrived at March 24, 1812. It was a day of curious experiences for Stephen: a windy, noisy day, which filled the house and the gardens with a restless impression. As Stephen stood by the fence of the grounds, and looked out into the park, he felt as if an endless procession of unseen people were sweeping past him on the wind, borne on resistlessly and aimlessly, vainly striving to stop themselves, to catch at something that might arrest their flight and bring them once again into contact with the living world of which they had formed a part. After luncheon that day Mr Abney said:

"Stephen, my boy, do you think you could manage to come to me tonight as late as eleven o'clock in my study? I shall be busy until that time, and I wish to show you something connected with your future life which it is most important that you should know. You are not to mention this matter to Mrs Bunch nor to anyone else in the house; and you had better go to your room at the usual time."

Here was a new excitement added to life: Stephen eagerly grasped at the opportunity of sitting up till eleven o'clock. He looked in at the library door on his way upstairs that evening, and saw a brazier, which he had often noticed in the corner of the room, moved out before the fire; an old silver-gilt cup

stood on the table, filled with red wine, and some written sheets of paper lay near it. Mr Abney was sprinkling some incense on the brazier from a round silver box as Stephen passed, but did not seem to notice his step.

The wind had fallen, and there was a still night and a full moon. At about ten o'clock Stephen was standing at the open window of his bedroom, looking out over the country. Still as the night was, the mysterious population of the distant moonlit woods was not yet lulled to rest. From time to time strange cries as of lost and despairing wanderers sounded from across the mere. They might be the notes of owls or water-birds, yet they did not quite resemble either sound. Were not they coming nearer? Now they sounded from the nearer side of the water, and in a few moments they seemed to be floating about among the shrubberies. Then they ceased; but just as Stephen was thinking of shutting the window and resuming his reading of Robinson Crusoe, he caught sight of two figures standing on the gravelled terrace that ran along the garden side of the Hall – the figures of a boy and girl, as it seemed; they stood side by side, looking up at the windows. Something in the form of the girl recalled irresistibly his dream of the figure in the bath. The boy inspired him with more acute fear.

Whilst the girl stood still, half smiling, with her hands clasped over her heart, the boy, a thin shape, with black hair and ragged clothing, raised his arms in the air with an appearance of menace and of unappeasable hunger and longing. The moon shone upon his almost transparent hands, and

Stephen saw that the nails were fearfully long and that the light shone through them. As he stood with his arms thus raised, he disclosed a terrifying spectacle. On the left side of his chest there opened a black and gaping rent; and there fell upon Stephen's brain, rather than upon his ear, the impression of one of those hungry and desolate cries that he had heard resounding over the woods of Aswarby all that evening. In another moment this dreadful pair had moved swiftly and noiselessly over the dry gravel, and he saw them no more.

Inexpressibly frightened as he was, he determined to take his candle and go down to Mr Abney's study, for the hour appointed for their meeting was near at hand. The study or library opened out of the front-hall on one side, and Stephen, urged on by his terrors, did not take long in getting there. To effect an entrance was not so easy. It was not locked, he felt sure, for the key was on the outside of the door as usual. His repeated knocks produced no answer. Mr Abney was engaged: he was speaking. What! Why did he try to cry out? and why was the cry choked in his throat? Had he, too, seen the mysterious children? But now everything was quiet, and the door yielded to Stephen's terrified and frantic pushing.

On the table in Mr Abney's study certain papers were found which explained the situation to Stephen Elliott when he was of an age to understand them. The most important sentences were as follows:

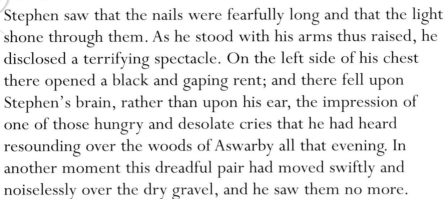

It was a belief very strongly and generally held by the ancients – of whose wisdom in these matters I have had such experience as induces me to place confidence in their assertions – that by enacting certain processes, which to us moderns have something of a barbaric complexion, a very remarkable enlightenment of the spiritual faculties in man may be attained: that, for example, by absorbing the personalities of a certain number of his fellow-creatures, an individual may gain a complete ascendancy over those orders of spiritual beings which control the elemental forces of our universe.

It is recorded of Simon Magus that he was able to fly in the air, to become invisible, or to assume any form he pleased, by the agency of the soul of a boy whom, to use the libellous phrase employed by the author of the Clementine Recognitions, he had 'murdered'. I find it set down, moreover, with considerable detail in the writings of Hermes Trismegistus, that similar happy results may be produced by the absorption of the hearts of not less than three human beings below the age of twenty-one years. To the testing of the truth of this receipt I have devoted the greater part of the last twenty years, selecting as the corpora vilia of my experiment such persons as could conveniently be removed without occasioning a sensible gap in society. The first step I effected by the removal of one Phoebe Stanley, a girl of gipsy extraction, on March 24, 1792. The second, by the removal of a wandering Italian

lad, named Giovanni Paoli, on the night of March 23, 1805. The final 'victim' – to employ a word repugnant in the highest degree to my feelings – must be my cousin, Stephen Elliott. His day must be this March 24, 1812.

The best means of effecting the required absorption is to remove the heart from the living subject, to reduce it to ashes, and to mingle them with about a pint of some red wine, preferably port. The remains of the first two subjects, at least, it will be well to conceal: a disused bathroom or wine-cellar will be found convenient for such a purpose. Some annoyance may be experienced from the psychic portion of the subjects, which popular language dignifies with the name of ghosts. But the man of philosophic temperament – to whom alone the experiment is appropriate – will be little prone to attach importance to the feeble efforts of these beings to wreak their vengeance on him. I contemplate with the liveliest satisfaction the enlarged and emancipated existence which the experiment, if successful, will confer on me; not only placing me beyond the reach of human justice (so-called), but eliminating to a great extent the prospect of death itself.

Mr Abney was found in his chair, his head thrown back, his face stamped with an expression of rage, fright, and mortal pain. In his left side was a terrible lacerated wound, exposing the heart. There was no blood on his hands, and a long knife that lay on the table was perfectly clean. A savage wild-cat

might have inflicted the injuries. The window of the study was open, and it was the opinion of the coroner that Mr Abney had met his death by the agency of some wild creature. But Stephen Elliott's study of the papers I have quoted led him to a very different conclusion.

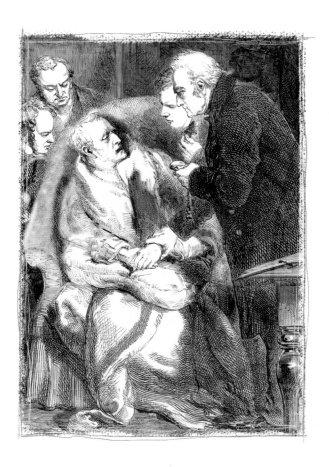

Silence

1837

Edgar Allan Poe

Ἐυδουσιν δ'ορεων κορυφαι τε και φαραγγες
Πρωνες τε και χαραδραι
ALCMAN.

(The mountain pinnacles slumber; valleys, crags and caves are silent.)

"Listen to me," said the Demon as he placed his hand upon my head. "The region of which I speak is a dreary region in Libya, by the borders of the river Zaire. And there is no quiet there, nor silence.

"The waters of the river have a saffron and sickly hue; and they flow not onwards to the sea, but palpitate forever and forever beneath the red eye of the sun with a tumultuous and convulsive motion. For many miles on either side of the river's

oozy bed is a pale desert of gigantic water-lilies. They sigh one unto the other in that solitude, and stretch towards the heaven their long and ghastly necks, and nod to and fro their everlasting heads. And there is an indistinct murmur which cometh out from among them like the rushing of subterrene water. And they sigh one unto the other.

"But there is a boundary to their realm — the boundary of
the dark, horrible, lofty forest. There, like the waves about the
Hebrides, the low underwood is agitated continually. But there
is no wind throughout the heaven. And the tall primeval trees
rock eternally hither and thither with a crashing and mighty
sound. And from their high summits, one by one, drop
everlasting dews. And at the roots strange poisonous flowers
lie writhing in perturbed slumber. And overhead, with a
rustling and loud noise, the grey clouds rush westwardly

forever, until they roll, a cataract, over the fiery wall of the horizon. But there is no wind throughout the heaven. And by the shores of the river Zaire there is neither quiet nor silence.

"It was night, and the rain fell; and, falling, it was rain, but, having fallen, it was blood. And I stood in the morass among the tall lilies, and the rain fell upon my head – and the lilies sighed one unto the other in the solemnity of their desolation.

"And, all at once, the moon arose through the thin ghastly mist, and was crimson in colour. And mine eyes fell upon a huge grey rock which stood by the shore of the river, and was lighted by the light of the moon. And the rock was grey, and ghastly, and tall – and the rock was grey. Upon its front were characters engraven in the stone; and I walked through the morass of water-lilies, until I came close unto the shore, that I might read the characters upon the stone. But I could not decipher them. And I was going back into the morass, when the moon shone with a fuller red, and I turned and looked again upon the rock, and upon the characters – and the characters were 'Desolation'.

"And I looked upwards, and there stood a man upon the summit of the rock; and I hid myself among the water-lilies that I might discover the actions of the man. And the man was tall and stately in form, and was wrapped up from his shoulders to his feet in the toga of old Rome. And the outlines of his figure were indistinct – but his features were the features of a deity; for the mantle of the night, and of the mist, and of the moon, and of the dew, had left uncovered the features of

his face. And his brow was lofty with thought, and his eye wild with care; and, in the few furrows upon his cheek I read the fables of sorrow, and weariness, and disgust with mankind, and a longing after solitude.

"And the man sat upon the rock, and leaned his head upon his hand, and looked out upon the desolation. He looked down into the low unquiet shrubbery, and up into the tall primeval trees, and up higher at the rustling heaven, and into the crimson moon. And I lay close within shelter of the lilies, and observed the actions of the man. And the man trembled in the solitude; but the night waned, and he sat upon the rock.

"And the man turned his attention from the heaven, and looked out upon the dreary river Zaire, and upon the yellow ghastly waters, and upon the pale legions of the water-lilies. And the man listened to the sighs of the water-lilies, and to the murmur that came up from among them. And I lay close within my covert and observed the actions of the man. And the man trembled in the solitude; – but the night waned and he sat upon the rock.

"Then I went down into the recesses of the morass, and waded far in among the wilderness of the lilies, and called unto the hippopotami which dwelt among the fens in the recesses of the morass. And the hippopotami heard my call, and came, with the behemoth, unto the foot of the rock, and

roared loudly and fearfully beneath the moon. And I lay close within my covert and observed the actions of the man. And the man trembled in the solitude; — but the night waned and he sat upon the rock.

"Then I cursed the elements with the curse of tumult; and a frightful tempest gathered in the heaven where, before, there had been no wind. And the heaven became livid with the violence of the tempest — and the rain beat upon the head of the man — and the floods of the river came down — and the river was tormented into foam — and the water-lilies shrieked within their beds — and the forest crumbled before the wind — and the thunder rolled — and the lightning fell — and the rock rocked to its foundation. And I lay close within my covert and observed the actions of the man. And the man trembled in the solitude; but the night waned and he sat upon the rock.

"Then I grew angry and cursed, with the curse of *silence*, the river, and the lilies, and the wind, and the forest, and the heaven, and the thunder, and the sighs of the water-lilies. And they became accursed, and *were still*. And the moon ceased to totter up its pathway to heaven — and the thunder died away — and the lightning did not flash — and the clouds hung motionless — and the waters sunk to their level and remained — and the trees ceased to rock — and the water-lilies sighed no more — and the murmur was heard no longer from among them, nor any shadow of sound throughout the vast illimitable desert. And I looked upon the characters of the rock, and they were changed; — and the characters were 'Silence'.

"And mine eyes fell upon the countenance of the man, and his countenance was wan with terror. And, hurriedly, he raised his head from his hand, and stood forth upon the rock and listened. But there was no voice throughout the vast illimitable desert, and the characters upon the rock were 'Silence'. And the man shuddered, and turned away, and fled afar off, in haste, so that I beheld him no more."

Now there are fine tales in the volumes of the Magi – in the iron-bound, melancholy volumes of the Magi. Therein, I say, are glorious histories of the heaven, and of the earth, and of the mighty sea – and of the Genii that over-ruled the sea, and the earth, and the lofty heaven. There was much lore too in the sayings which were said by the Sybils; and holy, holy things were heard of old by the dim leaves that trembled around Dodona – but, as Allah liveth, that fable which the Demon told me as he sat by my side in the shadow of the tomb, I hold to be the most wonderful of all! And as the Demon made an end of his story, he fell back within the cavity of the tomb and laughed. And I could not laugh with the Demon, and he cursed me because I could not laugh. And the lynx which dwelleth forever in the tomb, came out therefrom, and lay down at the feet of the Demon, and looked at him steadily in the face.

Haunted

Whether far or near, on land or at sea, long ago or right now, ghosts and ghouls haunt only an unfortunate few. This, of course, is lucky for most, but extremely unlucky for some...

132
The Legend of
Sleepy Hollow

144
The Canterville Ghost

168
Narrative of the
Ghost of a Hand

Wuthering Heights

182

The Legend of Sleepy Hollow

1820

EXTRACT

Washington Irving

Several of the Sleepy Hollow people were present at Van Tassel's and, as usual, were doling out their wild and wonderful legends. Many dismal tales were told about funeral trains, and mourning cries and wailings heard and seen about the great tree where the unfortunate Major André was taken, and which stood in the neighbourhood. Some mention was made also of the woman in white, that haunted the dark glen at Raven Rock, and was often heard to shriek on winter nights before a storm, having perished there in the snow. The chief part of the stories, turned upon the favourite spectre of Sleepy Hollow, the Headless Horseman, who had been heard several times of late, patrolling the country; and, it was said, tethered his horse nightly among the graves in the churchyard.

The sequestered situation of this church seems always to

have made it a favourite haunt of troubled spirits. It stands on a knoll, surrounded by locust, trees and lofty elms, from among which its decent, whitewashed walls shine modestly forth, like Christian purity beaming through the shades of retirement. A gentle slope descends from it to a silver sheet of water, bordered by high trees, between which, peeps may be caught at the blue hills of the Hudson. To look upon its grass-grown yard, where the sunbeams seem to sleep so quietly, one would think that there at least the dead might rest in peace. On one side of the church extends a wide woody dell, along which raves a large brook among broken rocks and trunks of fallen trees. Over a deep black part of the stream, not far from the church, was formerly thrown a wooden bridge; the road that led to it, and the bridge itself, were thickly shaded by overhanging trees, which cast a gloom about it, even in the daytime; but occasioned a fearful darkness at night. Such was one of the favourite haunts of the Headless Horseman, and the place where he was most frequently encountered. The tale was told of old Brouwer, a most heretical disbeliever in ghosts, how he met the Horseman returning from his foray into Sleepy Hollow, and was obliged to get up behind him; how they galloped over bush and brake, over hill and swamp, until they reached the bridge; when the Horseman suddenly turned into a skeleton, threw old Brouwer into the brook, and sprang away over the treetops with a clap of thunder.

This story was immediately matched by a thrice marvellous adventure of Brom Bones, who made light of the Headless

Horseman as an arrant jockey. He affirmed that on returning one night from the neighbouring village of Sing Sing, he had been overtaken by this midnight trooper; that he had offered to race with him for a bowl of punch, and should have won it too, for Daredevil beat the goblin horse all hollow, but just as they came to the church bridge, the Horseman bolted, and vanished in a flash of fire.

All these tales, told in that drowsy undertone with which men talk in the dark, the countenances of the listeners only now and then receiving a casual gleam from the glare of a pipe, sank deep in the mind of Ichabod. He repaid them in kind with large extracts from his invaluable author, Cotton Mather, and added many marvellous events that had taken place in his native state of Connecticut, and fearful sights which he had seen in his nightly walks about Sleepy Hollow.

The revel now gradually broke up. The old farmers gathered together their families in their wagons, and were heard for some time rattling along the hollow roads, and over the distant hills. Some of the damsels mounted on pillions behind their favourite swains, and their lighthearted laughter, mingling with the clatter of hoofs, echoed along the silent woodlands, sounding fainter and fainter, until they gradually died away – and the late scene of noise and frolic was all silent and deserted. Ichabod only lingered behind, according to the custom of country lovers, to have a tête-à-tête with the heiress; fully convinced that he was now on the high road to success. What passed at this interview I will not pretend to say,

for in fact I do not know. Something, however, I fear me, must have gone wrong, for he certainly sallied forth, after no very great interval, with an air quite desolate and chopfallen. Oh, these women! These women! Could that girl have been playing off any of her coquettish tricks? Was her encouragement of the poor Ichabod all a mere sham to secure her conquest of his rival? Heaven only knows, not I! Let it suffice to say, Ichabod stole forth with the air of one who had been sacking a hen roost, rather than a fair lady's heart. Without looking to the right or left to notice the scene of rural wealth on which he had so often gloated, he went straight to the stable, and with several hearty cuffs and kicks roused his steed most uncourteously from the comfortable quarters in which he was soundly sleeping, dreaming of mountains of corn and oats, and whole valleys of timothy and clover.

It was the very witching time of night that Ichabod, heavy-hearted and crest fallen, pursued his travels homewards, along the sides of the lofty hills which rise above Tarry Town, and which he had traversed so cheerily in the afternoon. The hour was as dismal as himself. Far below him, the Tappan Zee spread its dusky and indistinct waste of waters, with here and there the tall mast of a sloop, riding quietly at anchor under the land. In the dead hush of midnight, he could even hear the barking of the watchdog from the opposite shore of the Hudson; but it was so vague and faint as only to give an idea of his distance from this faithful companion of man. Now and then, too, the long-drawn crowing of a cock, accidentally

awakened, would sound far, far off, from some
farmhouse away among the hills – but it
was like a dreaming sound in his ear.
No signs of life occurred near him, but
occasionally the melancholy chirp of a
cricket, or perhaps the guttural twang of
a bullfrog from a neighbouring marsh, as
if sleeping uncomfortably and turning in
his bed.

All the stories of ghosts and goblins that
he had heard in the afternoon now came
crowding upon his recollection. The night
grew darker and darker; the stars seemed
to sink deeper in the sky, and driving
clouds occasionally hid them from his
sight. He had never felt so lonely and dismal.
He was, moreover, approaching the very
place where many of the scenes of the
ghost stories had been laid. In the centre
of the road stood an enormous tulip tree,
which towered like a giant above all the other
trees of the neighbourhood, and formed a
kind of landmark. Its limbs were gnarled and
fantastic, large enough to form trunks for
ordinary trees, twisting down almost to
the earth and rising again into the air. It
was connected with the tragical story of

the unfortunate André, who had been taken prisoner hard by; and was universally known by the name of Major André's tree. The common people regarded it with a mixture of respect and superstition, partly out of sympathy for the fate of its ill-starred namesake, and partly from the tales of strange sights, and doleful lamentations told concerning it.

As Ichabod approached this fearful tree, he began to whistle; he thought his whistle was answered — it was but a blast sweeping sharply through the dry branches. As he approached a little nearer, he thought he saw something white hanging in the midst of the tree. He paused, and ceased whistling; but on looking more narrowly, perceived that it was a place where the tree had been scathed by lightning, and the white wood laid bare. Suddenly he heard a groan — his teeth chattered, and his knees smote against the saddle: it was but the rubbing of one huge bough upon another, as they were swayed about by the breeze. He passed the tree in safety, but new perils lay before him.

About two hundred yards from the tree, a small brook crossed the road, and ran into a marshy and thickly wooded glen, known by the name of Wiley's Swamp. A few rough logs, laid side by side, served for a bridge over this stream. On that side of the road where the brook entered the wood, a group of oaks and chestnuts, matted thick with wild grape vines, threw a cavernous gloom over it. To pass this bridge was the severest trial. It was at this identical spot that the unfortunate André was captured, and under the covert of those chestnuts and

vines were the sturdy yeomen concealed who surprised him. This has ever since been considered a haunted stream, and fearful are the feelings of the school boy who has to pass it alone after dark.

As he approached the stream his heart began to thump; he summoned up, however, all his resolution, gave his horse half a score of kicks in the ribs, and attempted to dash briskly across the bridge. But instead of starting forward, the perverse old animal made a lateral movement, and ran broadside against the fence. Ichabod, whose fears increased with the delay, jerked the reins on the other side, and kicked lustily with the contrary foot. It was all in vain; his steed started, it is true, but it was only to plunge to the opposite side of the road into a thicket of brambles and alder bushes. The schoolmaster now bestowed both whip and heel upon the starveling ribs of old Gunpowder, who dashed forward, snuffling and snorting, but came to a stand just by the bridge, with a suddenness that had nearly sent his rider sprawling over his head. Just at this moment something by the side of the bridge caught the sensitive ear of Ichabod. In the dark shadow of the grove, on the margin of the brook, he beheld something huge, misshapen and towering. It stirred not, but seemed gathered up in the gloom, like some gigantic monster ready to spring upon the traveller.

The hair of the affrighted schoolmaster rose upon his head with terror. What was to be done? To turn and fly was now too late; and besides, what chance was there of escaping ghost or goblin, if such it was, which could ride upon the wings of the

wind? Summoning up, therefore, a show of courage, he demanded in stammering accents, "Who are you?" He received no reply. He repeated his demand in a still more agitated voice. Still there was no answer. Once more he cudgelled the sides of the inflexible Gunpowder, and, shutting his eyes, broke forth with involuntary fervour into a psalm tune. Just then the shadowy object of alarm put itself in motion, and with a scramble and a bound stood at once in the middle of the road. Though the night was dark and dismal, yet the form of the unknown might now in some degree be ascertained. He appeared to be a horseman of large dimensions, and mounted on a black horse of powerful frame. He made no offer of molestation or sociability, but kept aloof on one side of the road, jogging along on the blind side of old Gunpowder, who had now got over his fright and waywardness.

Ichabod, who had no relish for this strange midnight companion, and bethought himself of the adventure of Brom Bones with the Headless Horseman, now quickened his steed in hopes of leaving him behind. The stranger, however, quickened his horse to an equal pace. Ichabod pulled up, and fell into a walk, thinking to lag behind – the other did the same. His heart began to sink within him; he endeavoured to resume his psalm tune, but his parched tongue clove to the roof of his mouth, and he could not utter a stave. There was something in the moody and dogged silence of this pertinacious companion that was mysterious and appalling. It was soon fearfully accounted for. On mounting a rising

ground, which brought the figure of his fellow-traveller in relief against the sky, gigantic in height, and muffled in a cloak, Ichabod was horror-struck on perceiving that he was headless! But his horror was still more increased on observing that the head, which should have rested on his shoulders, was carried before him on the pommel of the saddle! His terror rose to desperation; he rained a shower of kicks and blows upon Gunpowder, hoping by a sudden movement to give his companion the slip – but the spectre started full jump with him. Away then they dashed, through thick and thin, stones flying and sparks flashing at every bound. Ichabod's flimsy

garments fluttered in the air, as he stretched his long lank body away over his horse's head, in the eagerness of his flight.

They had now reached the road which turns off to Sleepy Hollow; but Gunpowder, who seemed possessed with a demon, instead of keeping up it, made an opposite turn, and plunged headlong downhill to the left. This road leads through a sandy hollow shaded by trees for about a quarter of a mile, where it crosses the bridge famous in goblin story, and just beyond swells the green knoll on which stands the whitewashed church.

As yet the panic of the steed had given his unskilful rider an apparent advantage in the chase, but just as he had got halfway through the hollow, the girths of the saddle gave way, and he felt it slipping from under him. He seized it by the pommel, and endeavoured to hold it firm, but in vain; and had just time to save himself by clasping old Gunpowder round the neck, when the saddle fell to the earth, and he heard it trampled underfoot by his pursuer. For a moment the terror of Hans Van Ripper's wrath passed across his mind – for it was his Sunday saddle; but this was no time for petty fears; the goblin was hard on his haunches, and (unskilful rider that he was!) he had much ado to maintain his seat: sometimes slipping on one side, sometimes another, and sometimes jolted the ridge of his horse's backbone, with a violence that he feared would cleave him asunder.

An opening in the trees now cheered him with the hopes that the church bridge was at hand. The wavering reflection of

a silver star in the bosom of the brook told him that he was not mistaken. He saw the walls of the church dimly glaring under the trees beyond. He recollected the place where Brom Bones' ghostly competitor had disappeard. "If I can but reach that bridge," thought Ichabod, " I am safe." Just then he heard the black steed panting and blowing close behind him; he even fancied that he felt his hot breath. Another convulsive kick in the ribs, and old Gunpowder sprang upon the bridge; he thundered over the resounding planks; he gained the opposite side; and now Ichabod cast a look behind to see if his pursuer should vanish, according to rule, in a flash of fire and brimstone. Just then he saw the goblin rising in his stirrups, and in the very act of hurling his head at him. Ichabod endeavoured to dodge the horrible missile, but too late. It encountered his cranium with a tremendous crash – he was tumbled headlong into the dust, and Gunpowder, the black steed, and the goblin rider, passed by like a whirlwind.

The next morning the old horse was found without his saddle, soberly cropping the grass at his master's gate. Ichabod did not make his appearance at breakfast. Dinner-hour came, but no Ichabod. The boys assembled at the schoolhouse, but no schoolmaster. Hans Van Ripper now began to feel some uneasiness about the fate of poor Ichabod, and his saddle. An inquiry was set on foot, and after diligent investigation they came upon his traces. In one part of the road leading to the church was found the saddle trampled in the dirt; the tracks of horses' hoofs deeply dented in the road, and evidently at

furious speed, were traced to the bridge, beyond which, on the bank of a broad part of the brook, where the water ran deep and black, was found the hat of the unfortunate Ichabod, and close beside it a shattered pumpkin.

The brook was searched, but the body of the schoolmaster was not to be discovered.

The Canterville Ghost

1887

EXTRACT

Oscar Wilde

As Canterville Chase is seven miles from Ascot, the nearest railway station, Mr Otis had telegraphed for a waggonette to meet them, and they started on their drive in high spirits. It was a lovely July evening, and the air was delicate with the scent of the pine woods. Now and then they heard a wood pigeon brooding over its own sweet voice, or saw, deep in the rustling fern, the burnished breast of the pheasant. Little squirrels peered at them from the beech trees as they went by, and the rabbits scudded away through the brushwood and over the mossy knolls, with their white tails in the air. As they entered the avenue of Canterville Chase, however, the sky became suddenly overcast with clouds, a curious stillness seemed to hold the atmosphere, a great flight of rooks passed silently over their heads, and, before they

reached the house, some big drops of rain had fallen.

Standing on the steps to receive them was an old woman, neatly dressed in black silk, with a white cap and apron. This was Mrs Umney, the housekeeper, whom Mrs Otis, at Lady Canterville's earnest request, had consented to keep on in her former position. She made them each a low curtsey as they alighted, and said in a quaint, old-fashioned manner, "I bid you welcome to Canterville Chase." Following her, they passed through the fine Tudor hall into the library, a long, low room, panelled in black oak, at the end of which was a large stained-glass window. Here they found tea laid out for them, and, after taking off their wraps, they sat down and began to look round,

while Mrs Umney waited on them.

Suddenly Mrs Otis caught sight of a dull red stain on the floor just by the fireplace and, quite unconscious of what it really signified, said to Mrs Umney, "I am afraid something has been spilled there."

"Yes, madam," replied the old housekeeper in a low voice, "blood has been spilt on that spot."

"How horrid," cried Mrs Otis. "I don't at all care for bloodstains in a sitting room. It must be removed at once."

The old woman smiled, and answered in the same low, mysterious voice, "It is the blood of Lady Eleanore de Canterville, who was murdered on that very spot by her own husband, Sir Simon de Canterville, in 1575. Sir Simon survived her nine years, and disappeared suddenly under very mysterious circumstances. His body has never been discovered, but his guilty spirit still haunts the Chase. The bloodstain has been much admired by tourists and others, and cannot be removed."

"That is all nonsense," cried Washington Otis. "*Pinkerton's Champion Stain Remover* and *Paragon Detergent* will clean it up in no time," and before the terrified housekeeper could interfere he had fallen upon his knees, and was scouring the floor with a small stick of what looked like a black cosmetic. In a few moments no trace of the bloodstain could be seen.

"I knew Pinkerton would do it," he exclaimed triumphantly, as he looked round at his admiring family; but no sooner had he said these words than a terrible flash of lightning lit up the

sombre room, a fearful peal of thunder made them all start to their feet, and Mrs Umney fainted.

"What a monstrous climate!" said the American Minister calmly, as he lit a long cheroot. "I guess the old country is so overpopulated that they have not enough decent weather for everybody. I have always been of opinion that emigration is the only thing for England."

"My dear Hiram," cried Mrs Otis, "what can we do with a woman who faints?"

"Charge it to her like breakages," answered the Minister, "she won't faint after that." And in a few moments Mrs Umney certainly came to. There was no doubt, however, that she was extremely upset, and she sternly warned Mr Otis to beware of some trouble coming to the house.

"I have seen things with my own eyes, sir," she said, "that would make any Christian's hair stand on end, and many and many a night I have not closed my eyes in sleep for the awful

things that are done here." Mr Otis, however, and his wife warmly assured the honest soul that they were not afraid of ghosts, and, after invoking the blessings of Providence on her new master and mistress, and making arrangements for an increase of salary, the old housekeeper tottered off to her room.

The storm raged fiercely all that night, but nothing of particular note occurred. The next morning, however, when they came down to breakfast, they found the terrible stain of blood once again on the floor. "I don't think it can be the fault of the *Paragon Detergent*," said Washington, "for I have tried it with everything. It must be the ghost." He accordingly rubbed out the stain a second time, but the second morning it appeared again. The third morning also it was there, though the library had been locked up at night by Mr Otis himself, and the key carried upstairs. The whole family were now quite interested; Mr Otis began to suspect that he had been too dogmatic in his denial of the existence of ghosts, Mrs Otis expressed her intention of joining the Psychical Society, and Washington prepared a long letter to Messrs Myers and Podmore on the subject of the permanence of sanguineous stains when connected with crime. That night all doubts about the objective existence of phantasmata were removed forever.

The day had been warm and sunny; and, in the cool of the evening, the whole family went out for a drive. They did not return home till nine o'clock, when they had a light supper. The conversation in no way turned upon ghosts, so there were

not even those primary conditions of receptive expectation which so often precede the presentation of psychical phenomena. The subjects discussed, as I have since learned from Mr Otis, were merely such as form the ordinary conversation of cultured Americans of the better class, such as the immense superiority of Miss Fanny Davenport over Sarah Bernhardt as an actress; the difficulty of obtaining green corn, buckwheat cakes, and hominy, even in the best English houses; the importance of Boston in the development of the world-soul; the advantages of the baggage check system in railway travelling; and the sweetness of the New York accent as compared to the London drawl. No mention at all was made of the supernatural, nor was Sir Simon de Canterville alluded to in any way. At eleven o'clock the family retired and by half-past all the lights were out. Some time after, Mr Otis was awakened by a curious noise in the corridor, outside his room. It sounded like the clank of metal, and seemed to be coming nearer every moment. He got up at once, struck a match, and looked at the time. It was exactly one o'clock. He was quite calm, and felt his pulse, which

was not at all feverish. The strange noise still continued, and
with it he heard distinctly the sound of footsteps. He put on
his slippers, took a small oblong phial out of his dressing-case,
and opened the door. Right in front of him he saw, in the wan
moonlight, an old man of terrible aspect. His eyes were as red
as burning coals; long grey hair fell over his shoulders in
matted coils; his garments, which were of antique cut, were
soiled and ragged, and from his wrists and ankles hung heavy
manacles and rusty shackles.

"My dear sir," said Mr Otis, "I really must insist on your
oiling those chains, and have brought you for that purpose a
small bottle of the *Tammany Rising Sun Lubricator*. It is said to be
completely efficacious upon one application, and there are
several testimonials to that effect on the wrapper from some of
our most eminent native divines. I shall leave it here for you by
the bedroom candles, and will be happy to supply you with
more should you require it." With these words the United
States Minister laid the bottle down on a marble table, and,
closing his door, retired to rest.

For a moment the Canterville ghost stood quite motionless
in natural indignation; then, dashing the bottle violently upon
the polished floor, he fled down the corridor, uttering hollow
groans, and emitting a ghastly green light. Just, however, as he
reached the top of the great oak staircase, a door was flung
open, two little white-robed figures appeared, and a large
pillow whizzed past his head! There was evidently no time to
be lost, so, hastily adopting the Fourth Dimension of Space as a

means of escape, he vanished through the wainscoting, and the house became quite quiet.

On reaching a small secret chamber in the left wing, he leaned up against a moonbeam to recover his breath, and began to try and realize his position. Never, in a brilliant and uninterrupted career of three hundred years, had he been so grossly insulted. He thought of the Dowager Duchess, whom he had frightened into a fit as she stood before the glass in her lace and diamonds; of the four housemaids, who had gone off into hysterics when he merely grinned at them through the curtains of one of the spare bedrooms; of the rector of the parish, whose candle he had blown out as he was coming late one night from the library, and who had been under the care of Sir William Gull ever since, a perfect martyr to nervous disorders; and of old Madame de Tremouillac, who, having wakened up one morning early and seen a skeleton seated in an armchair by the fire reading her diary, had been confined to her bed for six weeks with an attack of brain fever, and, on her recovery, had become reconciled to the Church, and had broken off her connection with that notorious sceptic Monsieur de Voltaire. He remembered the terrible night when the wicked Lord Canterville was found choking in his dressing room, with the knave of diamonds half way down his throat, and confessed, just before he died, that he had cheated Charles James Fox out of £50,000 at Crockford's by means of that very card, and swore that the ghost had made him swallow it. All his great achievements came back to him again, from the

butler who had shot himself in the pantry because he had seen a green hand tapping at the window pane, to the beautiful Lady Stutfield, who was always obliged to wear a black velvet band round her throat to hide the mark of five fingers burnt upon her white skin, and who drowned herself at last in the carp-pond at the end of the King's Walk. With the enthusiastic egotism of the true artist he went over his most celebrated performances, and smiled bitterly to himself as he recalled to mind his last appearance as 'Red Ruben, or the Strangled Babe,' his debut as 'Gaunt Gibeon, the Blood-sucker of Bexley Moor,' and the furore he had excited one lovely June evening by merely playing ninepins with his own bones upon the lawn-tennis ground. And after all this, some wretched modern Americans were to come and offer him the *Rising Sun Lubricator*, and throw pillows at his head! It was unbearable. Besides, no ghosts in history had ever been treated in this manner. Accordingly, he determined to have vengeance, and remained till daylight in deep thought.

The next morning when the Otis family met at breakfast, they discussed the ghost at some length. The United States Minister was naturally a little annoyed to find that his present had not been accepted. "I have no wish," he said, "to do the ghost any personal injury, and I must say that, considering the length of time he has been in the house, I don't think it is at all polite to throw pillows at him" – a very just remark, at which, I am sorry to say, the twins burst into shouts of laughter.

"Upon the other hand," he continued, "if he really declines to use the *Rising Sun Lubricator*, we shall have to take his chains from him. It would be quite impossible to sleep, with such a noise going on outside the bedrooms."

For the rest of the week, however, they were undisturbed, the only thing that excited any attention being the continual renewal of the bloodstain on the library floor. This certainly was very strange, as the door was always locked at night by Mr Otis, and the windows kept closely barred. The chameleon-like colour, also, of the stain excited a good deal of comment. Some mornings it was a dull red, then it would be vermilion, then a rich purple, and once when they came down for family prayers, according to the simple rites of the Free American Reformed Episcopalian Church, they found it a bright emerald-green. These kaleidoscopic changes naturally amused the party very much, and bets on the subject were freely made every evening. The only person who did not enter into the joke was little Virginia, who, for some unexplained reason, was always a good deal distressed at the sight of the bloodstain, and very nearly cried the morning it was emerald-green. The second appearance of the ghost was on Sunday night. Shortly after they had gone to bed they were suddenly alarmed by a fearful crash in the hall. Rushing downstairs, they found that a large suit of old armour had become detached from its stand, and had fallen on the stone floor, while, seated in a high-backed chair, was the Canterville ghost, rubbing his knees with an expression of acute agony on his face. The twins,

having brought their peashooters with them, at once discharged two pellets on him, with that accuracy of aim which can only be attained by long and careful practice on a writing-master, while the United States Minister covered him with his revolver, and called upon him, in accordance with Californian etiquette, to hold up his hands! The ghost started up with a wild shriek of rage, and swept through them like a mist, extinguishing Washington Otis's candle as he passed, and so leaving them all in total darkness. On reaching the top of the staircase he recovered himself and determined to give his celebrated peal of demoniac laughter. This he had on more than one occasion found extremely useful. It was said to have turned Lord Raker's wig grey in a single night, and had certainly made three of Lady Canterville's French governesses give warning before their month was up. He accordingly laughed his most horrible laugh, till the old vaulted roof rang and rang again, but hardly had the fearful echo died away when a door opened, and Mrs Otis came out in a light blue dressing gown.

"I am afraid you are far from well," she said, "and have brought you a bottle of *Dr Dobell's Tincture*. If it is indigestion,

you will find it a most excellent remedy." The ghost glared at her in fury, and began at once to make preparations for turning himself into a large black dog, an accomplishment for which he was justly renowned, and to which the family doctor always attributed the permanent idiocy of Lord Canterville's uncle, the Hon. Thomas Horton. The sound of approaching footsteps, however, made him hesitate in his fell purpose, so he contented himself with becoming faintly phosphorescent, and vanished with a deep churchyard groan, just as the twins had come up to him.

On reaching his room he entirely broke down, and became a prey to the most violent agitation. The vulgarity of the twins, and the gross materialism of Mrs Otis, were naturally extremely annoying, but what really distressed him most was that he had been unable to wear the suit of mail. He had hoped that even modern Americans would be thrilled by the sight of a Spectre In Armour, if for no more sensible reason, at least out of respect for their national poet Longfellow, over whose graceful and attractive poetry he himself had whiled away many a weary hour when the Cantervilles were up in town. Besides, it was his own suit. He had worn it with success at the Kenilworth tournament, and had been highly complimented on it by no less a person than the Virgin Queen herself. Yet when he had put it on, he had been completely overpowered by the weight of the huge breastplate and steel casque, and had fallen heavily on the stone pavement, barking both his knees severely and bruising the knuckles of his right hand.

For some days after this he was extremely ill, and hardly stirred out of his room at all, except to keep the blood-stain in proper repair. However, by taking great care of himself he recovered, and resolved to make a third attempt to frighten the United States Minister and his family. He selected Friday the 17th of August for his appearance, and spent most of that day in looking over his wardrobe, ultimately deciding in favour of a large slouched hat with a red feather, a winding-sheet frilled at the wrists and neck, and a rusty sword. Towards evening a violent storm of rain came on, and the wind was so high that all the windows and doors in the old house shook and rattled. In fact, it was just such weather as he loved. His plan of action was this. He was to make his way quietly to Washington Otis's room, gibber at him from the foot of the bed, and stab himself three times in the throat to the sound of slow music. He bore Washington a special grudge, being quite aware that it was he who was in the habit of removing the famous Canterville blood-stain, by means of *Pinkerton's Paragon Detergent*. Having reduced the reckless and foolhardy youth to a condition of abject terror, he was then to proceed to the room occupied by the United States Minister and his wife, and there to place a clammy hand on Mrs Otis's forehead, while he hissed

into her trembling husband's ear the awful secrets of the charnel-house. With regard to little Virginia, he had not quite made up his mind. She had never insulted him in any way, and was pretty and gentle. A few hollow groans from the wardrobe, he thought, would be more than sufficient, or, if that failed to wake her, he might grabble at the counterpane with palsy-twitching fingers. As for the twins, he was quite determined to teach them a lesson. The first thing to be done was, of course, to sit upon their chests, so as to produce the stifling sensation of nightmare. Then, as their beds were quite close to each other, to stand between them in the form of a green, icy-cold corpse, till they became paralyzed with fear. And finally, to throw off the winding-sheet and crawl round the room, with white bleached bones and one rolling eyeball, in the character of 'Dumb Daniel, or the Suicide's Skeleton,' a role in which he had on more than one occasion produced a great effect, and which he considered quite equal to his famous part of 'Martin the Maniac, or the Masked Mystery.'

At half past ten he heard the family going to bed. For some time he was disturbed by wild shrieks of laughter from the twins, who, with the lighthearted gaiety of schoolboys, were evidently amusing themselves before they retired to rest, but at a quarter past eleven all was still, and, as midnight sounded, he sallied forth. The owl beat against the window panes, the raven croaked from the old yew tree, and the wind wandered moaning round the house like a lost soul; but the Otis family slept unconscious of their doom, and high above the rain and

storm he could hear the steady snoring of the Minister for the United States. He stepped stealthily out of the wainscoting, with an evil smile on his cruel, wrinkled mouth, and the moon hid her face in a cloud as he stole past the great oriel window, where his own arms and those of his murdered wife were blazoned in azure and gold. On and on he glided, like an evil shadow, the very darkness seeming to loathe him as he passed. Once he thought he heard something call, and stopped; but it was only the baying of a dog from the Red Farm, and he went on, muttering strange sixteenth-century curses, and ever and anon brandishing the rusty sword in the midnight air. Finally he reached the corner of the passage that led to luckless Washington's room. For a moment he paused there, the wind blowing his long grey locks about his head, and twisting into grotesque and fantastic folds the nameless horror of the dead man's shroud. Then the clock struck the quarter, and he felt the time was come. He chuckled to himself and turned the corner; but no sooner had he done so, than, with a piteous wail of terror, he fell back, and hid his blanched face in his long, bony hands. Right in front of him was standing a horrible spectre, motionless as a carven image, and monstrous as a madman's dream! Its head was bald and burnished; its face round, and fat, and white; and hideous laughter seemed to have writhed its features into an eternal grin. From the eyes streamed rays of scarlet light, the mouth was a wide well of fire, and a hideous garment, like to his own, swathed with its silent snows the Titan form. On its breast was a placard with

strange writing in antique characters – some scroll of shame it seemed, some record of wild sins, some awful calendar of crime – and, with its right hand, it bore aloft a fashion of gleaming steel.

Never having seen a ghost before, he naturally was terribly frightened and, after a second hasty glance at the awful phantom, he fled back to his room, tripping up in his long winding-sheet as he sped down the corridor, and finally dropping the rusty sword into the Minister's jack boots, where it was found in the morning by the butler. Once in the privacy of his own apartment, he flung himself down on a small pallet-bed and hid his face under the clothes. After a time, however, the brave old Canterville spirit asserted itself and he determined to go and speak to the other ghost as soon as it was daylight. Accordingly, just as the dawn was touching the hills with silver, he returned towards the spot where he had first laid eyes on the grisly phantom, feeling that, after all, two ghosts were better than one, and that, by the aid of his new friend, he might safely grapple with the twins. On reaching the spot, however, a terrible sight met his gaze. Something had evidently happened to the spectre, for the light had entirely faded from its hollow eyes, the gleaming sword had fallen from its hand, and it was leaning up against the wall in a strained and uncomfortable attitude. He rushed forward and seized it in his arms, when, to his horror, the head slipped off and rolled on the floor, the body assumed a recumbent posture, and he found himself clasping a white dimity bed-curtain, with

a sweeping-brush, a kitchen cleaver, and a hollow turnip lying at his feet! Unable to understand this curious transformation, he clutched the placard with feverish haste, and there, in the grey morning light, he read these fearful words:

YE OTIS GHOSTE

YE ONLIE TRUE AND ORIGINALE SPOOK
BEWARE OF YE IMITATIONES
ALL OTHERS ARE COUNTERFEITE

The whole thing flashed across him. He had been tricked, foiled, and outwitted! The old Canterville look came into his eyes; he ground his toothless gums together; and, raising his withered hands high above his head, swore, according to the picturesque phraseology of the antique school, that when Chanticleer had sounded twice his merry horn, deeds of blood would be wrought, and Murder walk abroad with silent feet.

Hardly had he finished this awful oath when, from the red-tiled roof of a distant homestead, a cock crew. He laughed a long, low, bitter laugh, and waited. Hour after hour he waited, but the cock, for some strange reason, did not crow again. Finally, at half past seven, the arrival of the housemaids made him give up his fearful vigil, and he stalked back to his room, thinking of his vain hope and baffled purpose. There he consulted several books of ancient chivalry, of which he was exceedingly fond, and found that, on every occasion on which his oath had been used,

Chanticleer had always crowed a second time. "Perdition seize the naughty fowl," he muttered, "I have seen the day when, with my stout spear, I would have run him through the gorge, and made him crow for me as 'twere in death!" He then retired to a comfortable lead coffin, and stayed there till evening.

The next day the ghost was very weak and tired. The terrible excitement of the last four weeks was beginning to have its effect. His nerves were completely shattered, and he started at the slightest noise. For five days he kept to his room, and at last made up his mind to give up the point of the bloodstain on the library floor. If the Otis family did not want it, they clearly did not deserve it. They were evidently people on a low, material plane of existence, and quite incapable of appreciating the symbolic value of sensuous phenomena. The question of phantasmic apparitions and the development of astral bodies, was of course quite a different matter, and really not under his control. It was his solemn duty to appear in the corridor once a week, and to gibber from the large oriel window on the first and third Wednesday in every month, and he did not see how he could honourably escape from his obligations. It is quite true that his life had been very evil, but, upon the other hand, he was most conscientious in all things connected with the supernatural. For the next three Saturdays, accordingly, he traversed the corridor as usual between midnight and three o'clock, taking every possible precaution against being either heard or seen. He removed his boots, trod

as lightly as possible on the old worm-eaten boards, wore a large black velvet cloak, and was careful to use the *Rising Sun Lubricator* for oiling his chains. I am bound to acknowledge that it was with a good deal of difficulty that he brought himself to adopt this last mode of protection. However, one night, while the family were at dinner, he slipped into Mr Otis's bedroom and carried off the bottle. He felt a little humiliated at first, but afterwards was sensible enough to see that there was a great deal to be said for the invention, and, to a certain degree, it served his purpose. Still, in spite of everything, he was not left unmolested. Strings were continually being stretched across the corridor, over which he tripped in the dark, and on one occasion, while dressed for the part of 'Black Isaac, or the Huntsman of Hogley Woods,' he met with a severe fall, through treading on a butter-slide, which the twins had constructed from the entrance of the Tapestry Chamber to the top of the oak staircase. This last insult so enraged him, that he resolved to make one final effort to assert his dignity and social position, and determined to visit the insolent young Etonians the next night in his celebrated character of "Reckless Rupert, or the Headless Earl.'

He had not appeared in this disguise for more than seventy years; in fact, not since he had so frightened pretty Lady Barbara Modish by means of it, that she suddenly broke off her engagement with the present Lord Canterville's grandfather, and ran away to Gretna Green with handsome Jack Castleton, declaring that nothing in the world would induce her to marry into a family that allowed such a horrible phantom to walk up and down the terrace at twilight. Poor Jack was afterwards shot in a duel by Lord Canterville on Wandsworth Common, and Lady Barbara died of a broken heart at Tunbridge Wells before the year was out, so, in every way, it had been a great success. It was, however, an extremely difficult 'make-up,' if I may use such a theatrical expression in connection with one of the greatest mysteries of the supernatural or – to employ a more scientific term – the higher-natural world, and it took him fully three hours to make his preparations. At last everything was ready, and he was very pleased with his appearance. The big leather riding boots that went with the dress were just a little too large for him, and he could only find one of the two horse-pistols, but, on the whole, he was quite satisfied, and at a quarter-past one he glided out of the wainscoting and crept down the corridor. On reaching the room occupied by the twins, which I should mention was called the Blue Bed Chamber, on account of the colour of its hangings, he found the door just ajar. Wishing to make an effective entrance, he flung it wide open, when a heavy jug of water fell right down on him, wetting him to the skin, and just

missing his left shoulder by a couple of inches. At the same moment he heard stifled shrieks of laughter proceeding from the four-poster bed. The shock to his nervous system was so great that he fled back to his room as hard as he could go, and the next day he was laid up with a severe cold. The only thing that at all consoled him in the whole affair was the fact that he had not brought his head with him, for, had he done so, the consequences might have been very serious.

He now gave up all hope of ever frightening this rude, noisy American family, and contented himself as a general rule, with creeping about the passages in list slippers, with a thick red muffler round his throat for fear of draughts, and a small gun, in case he should be attacked by the dreaded twins. The final blow he received occurred on the 19th of September. He had gone downstairs to the great entrance-hall, feeling sure that there, at any rate, he would be quite unmolested, and was amusing himself by making satirical remarks on the large Saroni photographs of the United States Minister and his wife, which had now taken the place of the Canterville family pictures. He was simply but neatly clad in a long

shroud, spotted with churchyard mould, and had tied up his jaw with a strip of yellow linen. He carried a small lantern and a sexton's spade. In fact, he was dressed for the character of "Jonas the Graveless, or the Corpse-Snatcher of Chertsey Barn," one of his most remarkable impersonations, and one which the Cantervilles had every reason to remember, as it was the real origin of their quarrel with their neighbour, Lord Rufford. It was about a quarter-past two o'clock in the morning, and, as far as he could ascertain, no one was stirring. As he was strolling towards the library, however, to see if there were any traces left of the blood-stain, suddenly there leaped out on him from a dark corner two figures, who waved their arms wildly above their heads, and shrieked "BOO!" in his ear.

Seized with a panic, which, under the circumstances, was only natural, he rushed for the staircase, but found Washington Otis waiting for him there with the big garden-syringe; and being thus hemmed in by his enemies on every side, and driven almost to bay, he vanished into the great iron stove, which, fortunately for him, was not lit, and had to make his way home through the flues and chimneys, arriving at his own room in a terrible state of dirt, disorder, and despair.

After this he was not seen again on any nocturnal expedition. The twins lay in wait for him on several occasions, and strewed the passages with nutshells every night to the great annoyance of their parents and the servants, but it was of no avail. It was quite evident that his feelings were so wounded that he would not appear. Mr Otis consequently resumed his

great work on the history of the Democratic Party, on which he had been engaged for some years; Mrs Otis organized a wonderful clambake, which amazed the whole county; the boys took to lacrosse, euchre, poker, and other American national games; and Virginia rode about the lanes on her pony, accompanied by the young Duke of Cheshire, who had come to spend the last week of his holidays at Canterville Chase. It was generally assumed that the ghost had gone away, and, in fact, Mr Otis wrote a letter to that effect to Lord Canterville, who, in reply, expressed his great pleasure at the news, and sent his best congratulations to the Minister's wife.

The Otises, however, were deceived, for the ghost was still in the house, and though now almost an invalid, was by no means ready to let matters rest, particularly as he heard that among the guests was the young Duke of Cheshire, whose grand-uncle, Lord Francis Stilton, had once bet a hundred guineas with Colonel Carbury that he would play dice with the Canterville ghost, and was found the next morning lying on the floor of the card room in such a helpless paralytic state, that though he lived on to a great age, he was never able to say anything again but 'Double Sixes.' The story was well known at the time, though, of course, out of respect to the feelings of the two noble families, every attempt was made to hush it up; and a full account of all the circumstances connected with it will be found in the third volume of

Lord Tattle's *Recollections of the Prince Regent and his Friends*. The ghost, then, was naturally very anxious to show that he had not lost his influence over the Stiltons, with whom indeed, he was distantly connected, his own first cousin having been married *en secondes noces* to the Sieur de Bulkeley, from whom, as everyone knows, the Dukes of Cheshire are lineally descended. Accordingly, he made arrangements for appearing to Virginia's little lover in his celebrated impersonation of 'The Vampire Monk, or, the Bloodless Benedictine,' a performance so horrible that when old Lady Startup saw it, which she did on one fatal New Year's Eve, in the year 1764, she went off into the most piercing shrieks, which culminated in violent apoplexy, and died in three days, after disinheriting the Cantervilles, who were her nearest relations, and leaving all her money to her London apothecary. At the last moment, however, his terror of the twins prevented his leaving his room, and the little Duke slept in peace under the great feathered canopy in the Royal Bedchamber, and dreamed of Virginia.

Narrative of the Ghost of a Hand

1863

J Sheridan Le Fanu

I'm sure she believed every word she related, for old Sally was veracious. But all this was worth just so much as such talk commonly is — marvels, fabulae, what our ancestors called winter's tales — which gathered details from every narrator and dilated in the act of narration. Still it was not quite for nothing that the house was held to be haunted. Under all this smoke there smouldered just a little spark of truth — an authenticated mystery, for the solution of which some of my readers may possibly suggest a theory, though I confess I can't.

Miss Rebecca Chattesworth, in a letter dated late in the autumn of 1753, gives a minute and curious relation of occurrences in the Tiled House, which, it is plain — although at starting she protests against all such fooleries — she has heard with a peculiar sort of interest and relates it certainly with an

awful sort of particularity.

I was for printing the entire letter, which is really very singular as well as characteristic. But my publisher meets me with his veto; and I believe he is right. The worthy old lady's letter is, perhaps, too long; and I must rest content with a few hungry notes of its tenor.

That year, and somewhere about the 24th October, there broke out a strange dispute between Mr Alderman Harper, of High Street, Dublin, and my Lord Castlemallard, who, in virtue of his cousinship to the young heir's mother, had undertaken for him the management of the tiny estate on which the Tiled or Tyled House – for I find it spelt both ways – stood.

This Alderman Harper had agreed for a lease of the house for his daughter, who was married to a gentleman named Prosser. He furnished it and put up hangings and otherwise went to considerable expense. Mr and Mrs Prosser came there sometime in June, and after having parted with a good many servants in the interval, she made up her mind that she could not live in the house; and her father waited on Lord Castlemallard and told him plainly that he would not take out the lease because the house was subjected to annoyances which he could not explain. In plain terms, he said it was haunted and that no servants would live there more than a few weeks and that after what his son-in-law's family had suffered there, not only should he be excused from taking a lease of it, but that the house itself ought to be pulled down as a nuisance and the habitual haunt of something worse than human malefactors.

Lord Castlemallard filed a bill in the Equity side of the Exchequer to compel Mr Alderman Harper to perform his contract, by taking out the lease. But the Alderman drew an answer, supported by no less than seven long affidavits, copies of all which were furnished to his lordship, and with the desired effect; for rather than compel him to place them upon the file of the court, his lordship struck, and consented to release him. I am sorry the cause did not proceed at least far enough to place upon the files of the court the very authentic and unaccountable story which Miss Rebecca relates.

The annoyances described did not begin till the end of August. One evening, Mrs Prosser, quite alone, was sitting in the twilight at the back parlour window. It was open, and looking out into the orchard she plainly saw a hand stealthily placed upon the stone window sill outside, as if by someone

beneath the window at her right side, intending to climb up. There was nothing but the hand, which was rather short but handsomely formed and white and plump, laid on the edge of the window sill; and it was not a very young hand, but one aged somewhere about forty, as she conjectured. It was only a few weeks before that the horrible robbery at Clondalkin had taken place and the lady fancied that the hand was that of one of the miscreants who was now about to scale the windows of the Tiled House. She uttered a loud scream and an exclamation of terror and at the same moment the hand was quietly withdrawn.

Search was made in the orchard, but no indications of any person's having been under the window, beneath which, ranged along the wall, stood a great column of flower pots, which it seemed must have prevented anyone's coming within reach of it.

The same night there came a hasty tapping every now and then at the window of the kitchen. The women grew frightened and the servant-man, taking firearms with him, opened the back door, but discovered nothing. As he shut it, however, he said, 'a thump came on it', and a pressure as of somebody striving to force his way in, which frightened him; and though the tapping went on upon the kitchen window panes, he made no further explorations.

About six o'clock on the Saturday evening following, the cook, 'an honest sober woman, now aged nigh sixty years', being alone in the kitchen, saw on looking up, it is supposed, the same fat but aristocratic-looking hand, laid with its palm against the glass, near the side of the window and this time moving slowly up and down, pressed all the while against the glass as if feeling carefully for some inequality in its surface. She cried out and said something like a prayer on seeing it. But it was not withdrawn for several seconds after.

After this, for a great many nights, there came at first a low and afterwards an angry rapping, as it seemed with a set of clenched knuckles, at the back door. And the servant-man would not open it, but called to know who was there; and there came no answer, only a sound as if the palm of the hand

was placed against it, and drawn slowly from side to side with a sort of soft, groping motion.

All this time, sitting in the back parlour, which for the time they used as a drawing room, Mr and Mrs Prosser were disturbed by rappings at the window, sometimes very low and furtive, like a clandestine signal, and at others sudden and so loud as to threaten the breaking of the pane.

This was all at the back of the house, which looked upon the orchard as you know. But on a Tuesday night, at about half past nine, there came precisely the same rapping at the hall door; and it went on, to the great annoyance of the master and terror of his wife, at intervals, for nearly two hours.

After this, for several days and nights, they had no annoyance whatsoever and began to think that the nuisance had expended itself. But on the night of the 13th September, Jane Easterbrook, an English maid, having gone into the pantry for the small silver bowl in which her mistress's bedtime drink was served, happening to look up at the little window of only four panes, observed through an augur-hole which was drilled through the window frame for the admission of a bolt to secure the shutter, a white pudgy finger – first the tip and then the two first joints introduced and turned about thus way and that, crooked against the inside, as if in search of a fastening which its owner destined to push aside. When the maid got back into the kitchen, we are told 'she fell into a swounde, and was all the next day very weak.'

Mr Prosser being, I've heard, a hard-headed and conceited

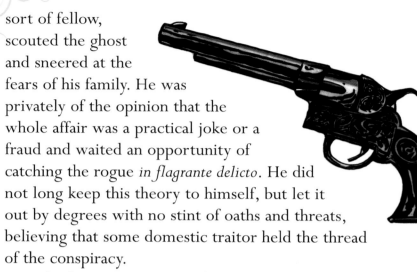

sort of fellow,
scouted the ghost
and sneered at the
fears of his family. He was
privately of the opinion that the
whole affair was a practical joke or a
fraud and waited an opportunity of
catching the rogue *in flagrante delicto*. He did
not long keep this theory to himself, but let it
out by degrees with no stint of oaths and threats,
believing that some domestic traitor held the thread
of the conspiracy.

Indeed it was time something were done; for not only his
servants, but good Mrs Prosser herself, had grown to look
unhappy and anxious. They kept at home from the hour of
sunset and would not venture about the house after nightfall,
except in couples.

The knocking had ceased for about a week; when one
night, Mrs Prosser being in the nursery, her husband, who was
in the parlour, heard it begin very softly at the hall door. The
air was quite still, which favoured his hearing distinctly. This
was the first time there had been any disturbance at that side
of the house and the character of the summons was changed.

Mr Prosser, leaving the parlour door open it seems, went
quietly into the hall. The sound was that of beating on
the outside of the stout door, softly and regularly,
'with the flat of the hand'. He was going to open it

suddenly, but changed his mind; and went back very quietly and on to the head of the kitchen stair, where was a 'strong closet' over the pantry, in which he kept his firearms, swords and canes.

Here he called his manservant, whom he believed to be honest, and with a pair of loaded pistols in his own coat pockets and giving another pair to him, he went as lightly as he could, followed by the man and with a stout walking-cane in his hand, forward to the door.

Everything went as Mr Prosser wished. The besieger of his house, so far from taking fright at their approach, grew more impatient; and the sort of patting which had aroused his attention at first assumed the rhythm and emphasis of a series of double knocks.

Mr Prosser, angry, opened the door with his right arm across, cane in hand. Looking, he saw nothing; but his arm was jerked up oddly, as it might be with the hollow of a hand and something passed under it, with a kind of gentle squeeze. The servant neither saw nor felt anything, and did not know why his master looked back so hastily, cutting with his cane and shutting the door with so sudden a slam.

From that time Mr Prosser discontinued his angry talk and swearing about it and seemed nearly as averse from the subject as the rest of his family. He grew, in fact, very uncomfortable, feeling an inward persuasion that when, in answer to the summons, he had opened the hall door, he had actually given admission to the besieger.

He said nothing to Mrs Prosser, but went up earlier to his bedroom, 'where he read a while in his Bible, and said his prayers'. I hope the particular relation of this circumstance does not indicate its singularity. He lay awake a good while, it appears; and, as he supposed, about a quarter past twelve he heard the soft palm of a hand patting on the outside of the bedroom door and then brushed slowly along it.

Up bounced Mr Prosser, very much frightened, and locked the door, crying, "Who's there?" but receiving no answer, but the same brushing sound of a soft hand drawn over the panels, which he knew only too well.

In the morning the housemaid was terrified by the impression of a hand in the dust of the little parlour table, where they had been unpacking delft and other things the day before. The print of the naked foot in the sea-sand did not frighten Robinson Crusoe half so much. They were by this time all nervous, and some of them half-crazed, about the hand.

Mr Prosser went to examine the mark and made light of it, but, as he swore afterwards,

rather to quiet his servants than from any comfortable feeling
about it in his own mind. However, he had them all one by one
into the room and made each place his or her hand, palm
downward, on the same table, thus taking a similar impression
from every person in the house, including himself and his wife.
And his 'affidavit' deposed that the formation of the hand so
impressed differed altogether from those of the living
inhabitants of the house and corresponded with that of the
hand seen by Mrs Prosser and by the cook.

Whoever or whatever the owner of that hand might be,
they all felt his subtle demonstration to mean that it was
declared he was no longer out of doors, but had established
himself in the house.

And now Mrs Prosser began to be troubled with strange
and horrible dreams, some of which as set out in detail, in
Aunt Rebecca's long letter, are really very appalling
nightmares. But one night, as Mr Prosser closed his
bedchamber door, he was struck somewhat by the utter silence
of the room, there being no sound of breathing, which seemed
strange to him, as he knew his wife was in bed and his ears
were particularly sharp.

There was a candle burning on a small table at the foot of
the bed, besides the one he held in one hand, a heavy ledger,
connected with his father-in-law's business being under his
arm. He drew the curtain at the side of the bed and saw
Mrs Prosser lying — as for a few seconds he mortally feared —
dead, her face being motionless, white, and covered with a

cold dew; and on the pillow, close beside her head and just within the curtains, was as he first thought a toad – but really the same fattish hand, the wrist resting on the pillow and the fingers extended towards her temple.

Mr Prosser, with a horrified jerk, pitched the ledger directly at the curtains, behind which the owner of the hand might be supposed to stand. The hand was instantaneously and smoothly snatched away, the curtains made a great wave and Mr Prosser got round the bed in time to see the closet door, which was at the other side, pulled to by the same white, puffy hand, as he believed.

He drew the door open with a fling and stared in: but the closet was empty, except for the clothes hanging from the pegs on the wall and the dressing table and looking-glass facing the windows. He shut it sharply and locked it and felt for a minute, he says, 'as if he were like to lose his wits'. Then, ringing at the bell, he brought the servants and with much ado they recovered Mrs Prosser from a sort of 'trance', in which, he says, from her looks, she seemed to have suffered 'the pains of death': and Aunt Rebecca adds, 'from what she told me of her visions, with her own lips, he might have added, "and of hell also".'

But the occurrence which seems to have determined the crisis was the strange sickness of their eldest child, a little boy aged between two and three years. He lay awake, seemingly in paroxysms of terror, and the doctors who were called in set down the symptoms to incipient water on the brain. Mrs

Prosser used to sit up with the nurse by the nursery fire, much troubled in mind about the condition of her child.

His bed was placed sideways along the wall, with its head against the door of a press or cupboard which, however, did not shut quite close. There was a little valance about a foot deep, round the top of the child's bed and this descended within some ten or twelve inches of the pillow on which it lay.

They observed that the little creature was quieter whenever they took it up and held it on their laps. They had just replaced him, as he seemed to have grown quite sleepy and tranquil, but he was not five minutes in his bed when he began to scream in one of his frenzies of terror; at the same moment the nurse for the first time detected, and Mrs Prosser equally plainly saw, following the direction of her eyes, the real cause of the child's sufferings. Protruding through the aperture of the press and shrouded in the shade of the valance, they plainly saw the white fat hand, palm downwards, presented

towards the head of the child. The mother uttered a scream and snatched the child from its little bed, and she and the nurse ran down to the lady's sleeping room, where Mr Prosser was in bed, shutting the door as they entered. They had hardly done so, when a gentle tap came to it from the outside.

There is a great deal more, but this will suffice. The singularity of the narrative seems to me to be this, that it describes the ghost of a hand and no more. The person to whom that hand belonged never once appeared; nor was it a hand separated from a body, but only a hand so manifested and introduced that its owner was always, by some crafty accident, hidden from view.

In the year 1819, at a college breakfast, I met a Mr Prosser – a thin, grave, but rather chatty old gentleman, with very white hair drawn back into a pigtail – and he told us all, with a concise particularity, a story of his cousin, James Prosser, who, when an infant, had slept for some time in what his mother said was a haunted nursery in an old house near Chapelizod and who, whenever he was ill, over-fatigued, or in anywise feverish, suffered all through his life as he had done from a time he could scarce remember, from a vision of a certain gentleman, fat and pale, every curl of whose wig, every button and fold of whose laced clothes and every feature and line of whose sensual, benignant and unwholesome face, was as minutely engraven upon his memory as the dress and lineaments of his own grandfather's portrait, which hung

before him every day at breakfast, dinner and supper.

Mr Prosser mentioned this as an instance of a curiously monotonous, individualized and persistent nightmare and hinted the extreme horror and anxiety with which his cousin, of whom he spoke in the past tense as 'poor Jemmie', was at any time induced to mention it.

I hope the reader will pardon me for loitering so long in the Tiled House, but this sort of lore has always had a charm for me; and people, you know – especially old people – will talk of what most interests themselves, too often forgetting that others may have had more than enough of it.

Wuthering Heights

1847

EXTRACT

Emily Brontë

The business of eating being concluded, I approached a window to examine the weather. A sorrowful sight I saw: dark night coming down prematurely, and sky and hills mingled in one bitter whirl of wind and suffocating snow.

"I don't think it possible for me to get home now without a guide," I could not help exclaiming. "The roads will be buried already. Mrs Heathcliff," I said earnestly, "you must excuse me for troubling you. I presume because, with that face, I'm sure you cannot help being good-hearted. Do point out some landmarks by which I may know my way home"

"Take the road you came," she answered, ensconcing herself in a chair, with a candle and the long book open before her. "It is brief advice, but as sound as I can give."

"Then, if you hear of me being discovered dead in a bog or

a pit full of snow, your conscience won't whisper that it is partly your fault?'"

"How so? I cannot escort you. They wouldn't let me go to the end of the garden wall."

"You! I should be sorry to ask you to cross the threshold, for my convenience, on such a night," I cried. "I want you to tell me my way, not to show it: or else to persuade Mr Heathcliff to give me a guide."

"Who? There is himself, Earnshaw, Zillah, Joseph and I."

"Are there no boys at the farm?"

"No; those are all."

"Then, it follows that I am compelled to stay."

"That you may settle with your host. I have nothing to do with it."

"I hope it will be a lesson to you to make no more rash journeys on these hills," cried Heathcliff's stern voice from the kitchen entrance. "As to staying here, I don't keep accommodations for visitors"

"I can sleep on a chair in this room," I replied.

"No, no! A stranger is a stranger, be he rich or poor: it will not suit me to permit anyone the range of the place while I am off guard!" said the unmannerly wretch.

With this insult, my patience was at an end. I uttered an expression of disgust and pushed past him into the yard, running against Earnshaw in my haste. It was so dark that I could not see the means of exit; and, as I wandered round, I heard another specimen of their civil behaviour amongst each

other. At first, the young man appeared about to befriend me.

"I'll go with him as far as the park," he said.

"You'll go with him to hell!" exclaimed his master, or whatever relation he bore. "And who is to look after the horses, eh?"

"A man's life is of more consequence than one evening's neglect of the horses; somebody must go," murmured Mrs Heathcliff, more kindly than I expected.

"Not at your command!" retorted Hareton. "If you set store on him, you'd better be quiet."

"Then I hope his ghost will haunt you; and I hope Mr Heathcliff will never get another tenant till the Grange is a ruin," she answered, sharply.

"Hearken, hearken, shoo's cursing on 'em!" muttered Joseph, towards whom I had been steering.

He sat within earshot, milking the cows by the light of a lantern, which I seized unceremoniously and, calling out that I would send it back on the morrow, rushed to the nearest postern.

"Maister, maister, he's staling t' lantern!" shouted the ancient, pursuing my retreat. "Hey, Gnasher! Hey, dog! Hey Wolf, holld him, holld him!"

On opening the little door, two hairy monsters flew at my throat, bearing me down, and extinguishing the light; while a mingled guffaw from Heathcliff and Hareton put the copestone on my rage and humiliation.

Fortunately, the beasts seemed more bent on stretching their paws, and yawning, and flourishing their tails, than devouring me alive; but they would suffer no resurrection, and I was forced to lie till their malignant masters pleased to deliver me. Then, hatless and trembling with wrath, I ordered the miscreants to let me out – on their peril to keep me one minute longer – with several incoherent threats of retaliation that, in their indefinite depth of virulency, smacked of King Lear.

The vehemence of my agitation brought on a copious bleeding at the nose. Still Heathcliff laughed, and still I scolded. I don't know what would have concluded the scene, had there not been one person at hand rather more rational than myself, and more benevolent than my entertainer. This was Zillah, the stout housewife; who at length issued forth to inquire into the nature of the uproar. She thought that some of them had been laying violent hands on me; and, not daring to attack her master, she turned her vocal artillery against the younger scoundrel.

"Well, Mr Earnshaw," she cried, "I wonder what you'll

have agait next? Are we going to murder folk on our very
door-stones? I see this house will never do for me – look at t'
poor lad, he's fair choking! Wisht, wisht; you mun'n't go on
so. Come in, and I'll cure that: there now, hold ye still."

With these words she suddenly splashed a pint of icy water
down my neck, and pulled me into the kitchen. Mr Heathcliff
followed, his accidental merriment expiring quickly.

I was sick exceedingly, and dizzy, and faint; and thus
compelled perforce to accept lodgings under his roof. He told
Zillah to give me a glass of brandy, and then passed on to the
inner room; while she condoled with me on my sorry
predicament, and having obeyed his orders, whereby I was
somewhat revived, ushered me to bed.

While leading the way upstairs, she recommended that I
should hide the candle, and not make a noise; for her master
had an odd notion about the chamber she would put me in,
and never let anybody lodge there willingly. I asked the reason.
She did not know, she answered: she had only lived there a
year or two; and they had so many queer goings on, she could
not begin to be curious.

Too stupefied to be curious myself, I fastened my door and
glanced round for the bed. The whole furniture consisted of a
chair, a clothes press, and a large oak case with squares cut out
near the top resembling coach windows. Having approached
this structure, I looked inside and perceived it to be a singular
sort of old-fashioned couch, very conveniently designed to
obviate the necessity for every member of the family having a

room to himself. In fact, it formed a little closet, and the ledge of a window, which it enclosed, served as a table. I slid back the panelled sides, pulled them together again, and felt secure against the vigilance of Heathcliff, and everyone else.

The ledge, where I placed my candle, had a few mildewed books piled up in one corner; and it was covered with writing scratched on the wood. This writing, however, was nothing but a name repeated in all kinds of characters, large and small – 'Catherine Earnshaw', here and there varied to 'Catherine Heathcliff', and then again to 'Catherine Linton'.

In vapid listlessness I leant my head against the window, and continued spelling over Catherine Earnshaw – Heathcliff – Linton, till my eyes closed; but they had not rested five minutes when a glare of white letters started from the dark – the air swarmed with Catherines; and rousing myself to dispel the obtrusive name, I discovered my candle-wick reclining on

one of the antique volumes, and perfuming the place with an odour of roasted calf-skin. I snuffed it off, and, very ill at ease under the influence of cold and nausea, sat up and spread open the injured tome on my knee. It was a Testament, in lean type, and smelling dreadfully musty: a fly-leaf bore the inscription – 'Catherine Earnshaw, her book,' and a date some quarter of a century back. I shut it, and took up another and another, till I had examined all. Catherine's library was select, and its state of dilapidation proved it to have been well used, though not altogether for a legitimate purpose: scarcely one chapter had

escaped a pen-and-ink commentary – at least the appearance of one – covering every morsel of blank that the printer had left. Some were detached sentences; other parts took the form of a regular diary, scrawled in an unformed, childish hand. At the top of an extra page (quite a treasure, probably, when first lighted on) I was greatly amused to behold an excellent

caricature of my friend Joseph, – rudely, yet powerfully sketched. An immediate interest kindled within me for the unknown Catherine, and I began forthwith to decipher her faded hieroglyphics.

'An awful Sunday,' commenced the paragraph beneath. 'I wish my father were back again. Hindley is a detestable substitute – his conduct to Heathcliff is atrocious. H and I are going to rebel – we took our initiatory step this evening.

'All day had been flooding with rain; we could not go to church, so Joseph must needs get up a congregation in the garret; and, while Hindley and his wife basked downstairs before a comfortable fire – doing anything but reading their Bibles, I'll answer for it – Heathcliff, myself, and the unhappy ploughboy were commanded to take our prayer books, and mount. We were ranged in a row on a sack of corn, groaning and shivering, and hoping that Joseph would shiver too, so that he might give us a short homily for his own sake. A vain idea! The service lasted precisely three hours; and yet my brother had the face to exclaim, when he saw us descending, "What, done already?" On Sunday evenings we used to be permitted to play, if we did not make much noise; now a mere titter is sufficient to send us into corners.

'"You forget you have a master here," says the tyrant. "I'll demolish the first who puts me out of temper! I insist on perfect sobriety and silence. Oh, boy! was that you? Frances darling, pull his hair as you go by: I heard him snap his fingers." Frances pulled his hair heartily and then went and

seated herself on her husband's knee, and there they were, like
two babies, kissing and talking nonsense by the hour – foolish
palaver that we should be ashamed of. We made ourselves as
snug as our means allowed in the arch of the dresser. I had just
fastened our pinafores together and hung them up for a
curtain, when in comes Joseph, on an errand from the stables.
He tears down my handiwork, boxes my ears, and croaks:

"'T' maister nobbut just buried, and Sabbath not o'ered,
und t' sound o' t' gospel still i' yer lugs, and ye darr be laiking!
Shame on ye! sit ye down, ill childer! There's good books
eneugh if ye'll read 'em: sit ye down, and think o' yer sowls!"

'Saying this, he compelled us so to square our positions that
we might receive from the far-off fire a dull ray to show us the
text of the lumber he thrust upon us. I could not bear the
employment. I took my dingy volume by the scroop, and
hurled it into the dog kennel, vowing I hated a good book.
Heathcliff kicked his to the same place. Then there was a
hubbub!

"'Maister Hindley!" shouted our chaplain. " Maister, coom
hither! Miss Cathy's riven th' back off 'Th' Helmet o'
Salvation,' un' Heathcliff's pawsed his fit into t' first part o'
'T' Brooad Way to Destruction!' It's fair flaysome that ye let
'em go on this gait. Ech! Th' owd man wad ha' laced 'em
properly – but he's goan!"

'Hindley hurried up from his paradise on the hearth, and
seizing one of us by the collar and the other by the arm, hurled
both into the back-kitchen; where, Joseph asseverated, 'owd

Nick' would fetch us as sure as we were living: and, so comforted, we each sought a separate nook to await his advent.

'I reached this book, and a pot of ink from a shelf, and pushed the house door ajar to give me light, and I have got the time on with writing for twenty minutes. But my companion is impatient, and proposes that we should appropriate the dairywoman's cloak, and have a scamper on the moors, under its shelter. A pleasant suggestion – and then, if the surly old man come in, he may believe his prophecy verified: we cannot be damper, or colder, in the rain than we are here.'

I suppose Catherine fulfilled her project, for the next sentence took up another subject: she waxed lachrymose.

'How little did I dream that Hindley would ever make me cry so!' she wrote. 'My head aches, till I cannot keep it on the pillow; and still I can't give over. Poor Heathcliff! Hindley calls him a vagabond, and won't let him sit with us, nor eat with us any more; and, he says, he and I must not play together, and threatens to turn him out of the house if we break his orders. He has been blaming our father (how dared he?) for treating H too liberally; and swears he will reduce him to his right place—'

I began to nod drowsily over the dim page: my eye wandered from manuscript to print. I saw a red ornamented title: *Seventy Times Seven, and the First of the Seventy-First. A Pious Discourse delivered by the Reverend Jabez Branderham, in the Chapel of Gimmerden Sough.* And while I was, half consciously, worrying my brain to guess what Jabez Branderham would make of his

subject, I sank back in bed, and fell asleep. Alas, for the effects of bad tea and bad temper! What else could it be that made me pass such a terrible night?

I began to dream, almost before I ceased to be sensible of my locality. I thought it was morning; and I had set out on my way home, with Joseph for a guide. The snow lay yards deep in our road; and, as we floundered on, my companion wearied me with constant reproaches that I had not brought a pilgrim's staff: telling me that I could never get into the house without one, and boastfully flourishing a heavy-headed cudgel, which I understood to be so denominated. For a moment I considered it absurd that I should need such a weapon to gain admittance into my own residence. Then a new idea flashed across me. I was not going there: we were journeying to hear the famous *Jabez Branderham preach, from the text — Seventy Times Seven; and* either Joseph, the preacher, or I had committed the 'First of the Seventy-First,' and were to be publicly exposed and excommunicated.

We came to the chapel. I have passed it really in my walks, twice or thrice; it lies in a hollow, between two hills: an elevated hollow, near a swamp, whose peaty moisture is said to answer all the purposes of embalming on the few corpses deposited there. The roof has been kept whole hitherto; but as the clergyman's stipend is only twenty pounds per annum, and a house with two rooms, threatening speedily to determine into one, no clergyman will undertake the duties of pastor: especially as it is currently reported that his flock would rather

let him starve than increase the living by one penny from their own pockets. However, in my dream, Jabez had a full and attentive congregation; and he preached – good God! What a sermon! Divided into *four hundred and ninety* parts, each fully equal to an ordinary address from the pulpit, and each discussing a separate sin! Where he searched for them, I cannot tell. He had his private manner of interpreting the phrase, and it seemed necessary the brother should sin different sins on every occasion.

Oh, how weary I grew. How I writhed, and yawned, and nodded, and revived! How I pinched and pricked myself, and rubbed my eyes, and stood up, and sat down again, and nudged Joseph to inform me if he would ever have done. I was condemned to hear all out: finally, he reached the 'First of the Seventy-First.' At that crisis, a sudden inspiration descended on me; I was moved to rise and denounce Jabez Branderham as the sinner of the sin that no Christian need pardon.

"Sir" I exclaimed, "sitting here within these four walls, at one stretch, I have endured and forgiven the four hundred and ninety heads of your discourse. Seventy times seven times have I plucked up my hat and been about to depart – seventy times seven times have you preposterously forced me to resume my seat. The four hundred and ninety-first is too much. Fellow-martyrs, have at him! Drag him down, and crush him to atoms, that the place which knows him may know him no more!"

'Thou art the man!' cried Jabez, after a solemn pause,

leaning over his cushion. "Seventy times seven times didst thou gapingly contort thy visage — seventy times seven did I take counsel with my soul. Lo, this is human weakness: this also may be absolved! The First of the Seventy-First is come. Brethren, execute upon him the judgment written. Such honour have all His saints!"

With that concluding word, the whole assembly, exalting their pilgrim's staves, rushed round me in a body; and I, having no weapon to raise in self-defence, commenced grappling with Joseph, my nearest and most ferocious assailant, for his. In the confluence of the multitude, several clubs crossed; blows, aimed at me, fell on other skulls. Presently the whole chapel resounded with rappings and counter rappings: every man's hand was against his neighbour; and Branderham, unwilling to remain idle, poured forth his zeal in a shower of loud taps on the boards of the pulpit, which responded so smartly that, at last, to my unspeakable relief, they woke me.

And what was it that had suggested the tremendous tumult? What had played Jabez's part in the row? Merely the branch of a fir tree that touched my lattice as the blast wailed by, and rattled its dry cones against the panes! I listened doubtingly an instant; detected the disturber, then turned and dozed, and dreamt again: if possible, still more disagreeably than before.

This time, I remembered I was lying in the oak closet, and I heard distinctly the gusty wind, and the driving of the snow. I heard, also, the fir bough repeat its teasing sound, and ascribed it to the right cause: but it annoyed me so much that I resolved

to silence it, if possible; and I thought I rose and endeavoured to unhasp the casement. The hook was soldered into the staple: a circumstance observed by me when awake, but forgotten. "I must stop it, nevertheless!" I muttered, knocking my knuckles through the glass, and stretching an arm out to seize the importunate branch; instead of which, my fingers closed on the fingers of a little, ice-cold hand!

The intense horror of nightmare came over me: I tried to draw back my arm, but the hand clung to it, and a most melancholy voice sobbed, "Let me in – let me in!"

"Who are you?" I asked, struggling, meanwhile, to disengage myself.

"Catherine Linton," it replied, shiveringly (why did I think of Linton? I had read 'Earnshaw' twenty times for Linton).

"I'm come home – I'd lost my way on the moor!"

As it spoke, I discerned, obscurely, a child's face looking through the window. Terror made me cruel; and, finding it useless to attempt shaking the creature off, I pulled its wrist onto the broken pane, and rubbed it to and fro till the blood ran down and soaked the bedclothes. Still it wailed, "Let me in!" and maintained its tenacious gripe, almost maddening me with fear.

"How can I!" I said at length. "Let *me* go, if you want me to let you in!"

The fingers relaxed, I snatched mine through the hole, hurriedly piled the books up in a pyramid against it, and stopped my ears to exclude the lamentable prayer.

I seemed to keep them closed above a quarter of an hour; yet, the instant I listened again, there was the doleful cry moaning on!

"Begone!" I shouted. "I'll never let you in, not if you beg for twenty years."

"It is twenty years," mourned the voice: "twenty years. I've been a waif for twenty years!"

Thereat began a feeble scratching outside, and the pile of books moved as if thrust forward.

I tried to jump up; but could not stir a limb; and so yelled aloud, in a frenzy of fright.

To my confusion, I discovered the yell was not ideal: hasty

footsteps approached my chamber door; somebody pushed it open with a vigorous hand, and a light glimmered through the squares at the top of the bed. I sat shuddering yet, and wiping the perspiration from my forehead. The intruder appeared to hesitate, and muttered to himself. At last, he said, in a half-whisper, plainly not expecting an answer, "Is anyone here?"

I considered it best to confess my presence; for I knew Heathcliff's accents, and feared he might search further, if I kept quiet. With this intention, I turned and opened the panels. I shall not soon forget the effect my action produced.

Heathcliff stood near the entrance, in his shirt and trousers; with a candle dripping over his fingers, and his face as white as the wall behind him. The first creak of the oak startled him like an electric shock: the light leapt from his hold to a distance of some feet, and his agitation was so extreme, that he could hardly pick it up.

"It is only your guest, sir," I called out, desirous to spare him the humiliation of exposing his cowardice further. "I had the misfortune to scream in my sleep, owing to a frightful nightmare. I'm sorry I disturbed you."

"Oh, God confound you, Mr Lockwood! I wish you were at the—" commenced my host, setting the candle on a chair, because he found it impossible to hold it steady. "And who showed you up into this room?" he continued, crushing his nails into his palms, and grinding his teeth to subdue the maxillary convulsions. "Who was it? I've a good mind to turn them out of the house this moment!"

"It was your servant, Zillah," I replied, flinging myself onto the floor, and rapidly resuming my garments. "I should not care if you did, Mr Heathcliff; she richly deserves it. I suppose that she wanted to get another proof that the place was haunted, at my expense. Well, it is — swarming with ghosts and goblins! You have reason in shutting it up, I assure you. No one will thank you for a doze in such a den!"

"What do you mean?" asked Heathcliff. "And what are you doing? Lie down and finish out the night, since you *are* here. But, for heaven's sake, don't repeat that horrid noise! Nothing could excuse it, unless you were having your throat cut!"

"If the little fiend had got in at the window, she probably would have strangled me!" I returned. "I'm not going to endure the persecutions of your hospitable ancestors again. Was not the Reverend Jabez Branderham akin to you on the mother's side? And that minx, Catherine Linton, or Earnshaw, or however she was called — she must have been a changeling — wicked little soul! She told me she had been walking the earth these twenty years: a just punishment for her mortal transgressions, I've no doubt!"

Scarcely were these words uttered when I recollected the association of Heathcliff's with Catherine's name in the book, which had completely slipped from my memory, till thus awakened. I blushed at my inconsideration: but, without showing further consciousness of the offence, I hastened to add:

"The truth is, sir, I passed the first part of the night in—"

Here I stopped afresh – I was about to say 'perusing those old volumes,' then it would have revealed my knowledge of their written, as well as their printed, contents; so, correcting myself, I went on, "in spelling over the name scratched on that window ledge. A monotonous occupation, calculated to set me asleep, like counting, or—"

"What *can* you mean by talking in this way to *me*!" thundered Heathcliff with savage vehemence. "How – how *dare* you, under my roof? God! He's mad to speak so!" And he struck his forehead with rage.

I did not know whether to resent this language or pursue my explanation; but he seemed so powerfully affected that I took pity and proceeded with my dreams; affirming I had never heard the appellation of 'Catherine Linton' before, but reading it often over produced an impression which personified itself when I had no longer my imagination under control. Heathcliff gradually fell back into the shelter of the bed, as I spoke; finally sitting down almost concealed behind it. I guessed, however, by his irregular and intercepted breathing, that he struggled to vanquish an excess of violent emotion. Not liking to show him that I had heard the conflict, I continued my toilette rather noisily, looked at my watch, and soliloquised on the length of the night: "Not three o'clock yet! I could have taken oath it had been six. Time stagnates here – we must surely have retired to rest at eight!"

"Always at nine in winter, and rise at four," said my host, suppressing a groan and, as I fancied, by the motion of his

arm's shadow, dashing a tear from his eyes. "Mr Lockwood," he added, "you may go into my room: you'll only be in the way, coming downstairs so early; and your childish outcry has sent sleep to the devil for me."

"And for me, too," I replied. "I'll walk in the yard till daylight, and then I'll be off; and you need not dread a repetition of my intrusion. I'm now quite cured of seeking pleasure in society, be it country or town. A sensible man ought to find sufficient company in himself."

"Delightful company!" muttered Heathcliff. "Take the candle, and go where you please. I shall join you directly. Keep out of the yard, though, the dogs are unchained; and the house – Juno mounts sentinel there, and – nay, you can only ramble about the steps and passages. But, away with you! I'll come in two minutes!"

I obeyed, so far as to quit the chamber; when, ignorant where the narrow lobbies led, I stood still, and was witness, involuntarily, to a piece of superstition on the part of my landlord which belied, oddly, his apparent sense. He got onto the bed and wrenched open the lattice, bursting, as he pulled at it, into an uncontrollable passion of tears. "Come in! Come in!" he sobbed. "Cathy, do come. Oh, do – once more! Oh! My heart's darling! Hear me *this* time, Catherine, at last!'

The spectre showed a spectre's ordinary caprice: it gave no sign of being; but the snow and wind whirled wildly through, even reaching my station, and blowing out the light.

There was such anguish in the gush of grief that accompanied

this raving, that my compassion made me overlook its folly, and I drew off, half angry to have listened at all, and vexed at having related my ridiculous nightmare, since it produced that agony – though *why* was beyond my comprehension.

I descended cautiously to the lower regions, and landed in the back-kitchen, where a gleam of fire, raked compactly together, enabled me to rekindle my candle. Nothing was stirring except a brindled, grey cat, which crept from the ashes, and saluted me with a querulous mew.

Two benches, shaped in sections of a circle, nearly enclosed the hearth; on one of these I stretched myself, and Grimalkin mounted the other. We were both of us nodding ere anyone invaded our retreat, and then it was Joseph, shuffling down a wooden ladder that vanished in the roof through a trap: the ascent to his garret, I suppose. He cast a sinister look at the little flame which I had enticed to play between the ribs, swept the cat from its elevation, and bestowing himself in the vacancy, commenced the operation of stuffing a three-inch pipe with tobacco. My presence in his sanctum was evidently esteemed a piece of impudence too shameful for remark: he silently applied the tube to his lips, folded his arms, and puffed away. I let him enjoy the luxury unannoyed; and after sucking out his last wreath and heaving a profound sigh, he got up, and departed as solemnly as he came.

A more elastic footstep entered next; and now I opened my mouth for a 'good morning,' but closed it again, the salutation unachieved; for Hareton Earnshaw was chanting *sotto voce*, in a series of curses directed against every object

he touched, while he rummaged a corner for a spade or shovel to dig through the drifts. He glanced over the back of the bench, dilating his nostrils, and thought as little of exchanging civilities with me as with my companion the cat. I guessed, by his preparations, that going out was allowed and, leaving my hard couch, made a movement to follow him. He noticed this, and thrust at an inner door with the end of his spade, intimating by an inarticulate sound that there was the place where I must go, if I changed my locality.

It opened into the house, where the females were already astir – Zillah urging flakes of flame up the chimney with a colossal bellows, and Mrs Heathcliff, kneeling on the hearth, reading a book by the aid of the blaze. She held her hand interposed between the furnace heat and her eyes, and seemed absorbed in her occupation; desisting from it only to chide the servant for covering her with sparks, or to push away a dog, now and then, that snoozled its nose overforwardly into her face. I was surprised to see Heathcliff there also. He stood by

the fire, his back towards me, just finishing a stormy scene with poor Zillah; who ever and anon interrupted her labour to pluck up the corner of her apron and heave an indignant groan.

"And you, you worthless—" he broke out as I entered, turning to his daughter-in-law, and employing an epithet as harmless as duck, or sheep, but generally represented by a dash. "There you are, at your idle tricks again! The rest of them do earn their bread – you live on my charity! Put your trash away, and find something to do. You shall pay me for the plague of having you eternally in my sight – do you hear, damnable jade?"

"I'll put my trash away, because you can make me if I refuse," answered the young lady, closing her book and throwing it on a chair. "But I'll not do anything, though you should swear your tongue out, except what I please!"

Heathcliff lifted his hand, and the speaker sprang to a safer distance, obviously acquainted with its weight.

Having no desire to be entertained by a cat-and-dog combat, I stepped forward briskly, as if eager to partake the warmth of the hearth, and innocent of any knowledge of the interrupted dispute. Each had enough decorum to suspend further hostilities. Heathcliff placed his fists, out of temptation, in his pockets; Mrs Heathcliff curled her lip and walked to a seat far off, where she kept her word by playing the part of a statue during the remainder of my stay.

The Haunted Dolls' House

1925

M R James

r Dillet pointed with his stick to an object which shall be described when the time comes and said: "I suppose you get stuff of that kind through your hands pretty often?" And when he said it, he lied in his throat and knew that he lied. Not once in twenty years – perhaps not once in a lifetime – could Mr Chittenden, skilled as he was in ferreting out the forgotten treasures of half a dozen counties, expect to handle such a specimen. It was a collector's palaver, and Mr Chittenden recognised it as such.

"Stuff of that kind, Mr Dillet! It's a museum piece, that is."

"Well, I suppose there are museums that'll take anything."

"I've seen one, not as good as that, years back," said Mr Chittenden, thoughtfully. "But that's not likely to come into the market: and I'm told they 'ave some fine ones of the

period over the water. No: I'm only telling you the truth, Mr Dillet, when I say that if you was to place an unlimited order with me for the very best that could be got – and you know I 'ave facilities for getting to know of such things and a reputation to maintain – well, all I can say is, I should lead you straight up to that one and say, 'I can't do no better for you than that, sir.'

"Hear, hear!" said Mr Dillet, applauding ironically with the end of his stick on the floor of the shop. "How much are you sticking the innocent American buyer for it, eh?"

"Oh, I shan't be over hard on the buyer, American or otherwise. You see, it stands this way, Mr Dillet – if I knew just a bit more about the pedigree—"

"Or just a bit less," Mr Dillet put in.

"Ha, ha! you will have your joke, sir. No, but as I was saying, if I knew just a little more than what I do about the piece – though anyone can see for themselves it's a genuine thing, every last corner of it, and there's not been one of my men allowed to so much as touch it since it came into the shop – there'd be another figure in the price I'm asking."

"And what's that: five and twenty?"

"Multiply that by three and you've got it, sir. Seventy-five's my price."

"And fifty's mine," said Mr Dillet.

The point of agreement was, of course, somewhere between the two, it does not matter exactly where – I think sixty guineas. But half an hour later the object was being

packed, and within an hour Mr Dillet had called for it in his car and driven away. Mr Chittenden, holding the cheque in his hand, saw him off from the door with smiles and returned, still smiling, into the parlour where his wife was making the tea. He stopped at the door.

"It's gone," he said.

"Thank God for that!" said Mrs Chittenden, putting down the teapot. "Mr Dillet, was it?"

"Yes, it was."

"Well, I'd sooner it was him than another."

"Oh, I don't know, he ain't a bad fellow, my dear."

"Maybe not, but in my opinion he'd be none the worse for a bit of a shake up."

"Well, if that's your opinion, it's my opinion he's put himself into the way of getting one. Anyhow, we shan't have no more of it and that's something to be thankful for."

And so Mr and Mrs Chittenden sat down to tea.

And what of Mr Dillet and of his new acquisition? What it was, the title of this story will have told you. What it was like, I shall have to indicate as well as I can.

There was only just room enough for it in the car and Mr Dillet had to sit with the driver: he had also to go slow, for though the rooms of the Dolls' House had all been stuffed carefully with soft cotton wool, jolting was to be avoided, in view of the immense number of small objects which thronged them; and the ten-mile drive was an anxious time for him, in

spite of all the precautions he insisted upon. At last his front door was reached and Collins, the butler, came out.

"Look here, Collins, you must help me with this thing – it's a delicate job. We must get it out upright, see? It's full of little things that mustn't be displaced more than we can help. Let's see, where shall we have it?" He paused, considering. "Really, I think I shall have to put it in my own room, to begin with at any rate. On the big table – that's it."

It was conveyed – with much talking – to Mr Dillet's spacious room on the first floor, looking out on the drive. The sheeting was unwound from it and the front thrown open, and for the next hour or two Mr Dillet was fully occupied in extracting the padding and setting in order the contents of the rooms.

When this thoroughly congenial task was finished, I must say that it would have been difficult to find a more perfect and attractive specimen of a Dolls' House in Strawberry Hill Gothic than that which now stood on Mr Dillet's large kneehole table, lighted up by the evening sun which came slanting through three tall sash-windows.

It was quite six feet long, including the chapel or oratory which flanked the front on the left as you faced it, and the stable on the right. The main block of the house was, as I have said, in the Gothic manner; that is to say, the windows had pointed arches and were surmounted by what are called ogival hoods, with crockets and finials such as we see on the canopies of tombs built into church walls. At the angles were absurd

turrets covered with arched panels. The chapel had pinnacles and buttresses and a bell in the turret and coloured glass in the windows. When the front of the house was open you saw four large rooms, bedroom, dining room, drawing room and kitchen, each with its appropriate furniture in a very complete state.

The stable on the right was in two storeys, with its proper complement of horses, coaches and grooms, and with its clock and Gothic cupola for the clock bell.

Pages, of course, might be written on the outfit of the mansion – how many frying pans, how many gilt chairs, what pictures, carpets, chandeliers, four-posters, table linen, glass, crockery and plate it possessed; but all this must be left to the imagination. I will only say that the base or plinth on which the house stood (for it was fitted with one of some depth which allowed of a flight of steps to the front door and a terrace, partly balustraded) contained a shallow drawer or drawers in which were neatly stored sets of embroidered curtains, changes of raiment for the inmates and, in short, all the materials for an infinite series of variations and refittings of the most absorbing and delightful kind.

"Quintessence of Horace Walpole, that's what it is: he must have had something to do with the making of it." Such was Mr Dillet's murmured reflection as he knelt before it in a reverent ecstasy. "Simply wonderful; this is my day and no mistake. Five hundred pound coming in this morning for that cabinet which I never cared about, and now this tumbling into my hands for a tenth, at the very most, of what it would fetch in town. Well, well! It almost makes one afraid something'll happen to counter it. Let's have a look at the population, anyhow."

Accordingly he set them before him in a row. Again, here is an opportunity, which some would snatch at, of making an

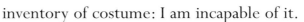

inventory of costume: I am incapable of it.

There were a gentleman and lady, in blue satin and brocade respectively. There were two children, a boy and a girl. There was a cook, a nurse, a footman and there were the stable servants, two postillions, a coachman, two grooms.

"Anyone else? Yes, possibly."

The curtains of the four-poster in the bedroom were closely drawn round four sides of it and he put his finger in between them and felt in the bed. He drew the finger back hastily, for it almost seemed to him as if something had – not stirred, perhaps, but yielded – in an odd, live way as he pressed it. Then he put back the curtains, which ran on rods in the proper manner, and extracted from the bed a white-haired old gentleman in a long linen nightdress and cap, and laid him down by the rest. The tale was complete.

Dinner time was now near, so Mr Dillet spent but five minutes in putting the lady and children into the drawing room, the gentleman into the dining room, the servants into the kitchen and stables and the old man back into his bed. He retired into his dressing room next door and we see or hear no more of him until something like one o'clock at night.

His whim was to sleep surrounded by some of the gems of his collection. The big room in which we have seen him contained his bed: bath, wardrobe, and all the appliances of

dressing were in a commodious room adjoining: but his four-poster, which itself was a valued treasure, stood in the large room where he sometimes wrote and often sat and received visitors. Tonight he repaired to it in a highly complacent frame of mind.

There was no striking clock within earshot – none on the staircase, none in the stable, none in the distant church tower. Yet it is indubitable that Mr Dillet was startled out of a very pleasant slumber by a bell tolling one.

He was so much startled that he did not merely lie breathlessly with wide-open eyes, but actually sat up in his bed.

He never asked himself, till the morning hours, how it was that, though there was no light at all in the room, the Dolls' House on the kneehole table, stood out with complete clearness. But it was so. The effect was that of a bright harvest moon shining full on the front of a big white stone mansion – a quarter of a mile away it might be and yet every detail was photographically sharp. There were trees about it too – trees rising behind the chapel and the house. He seemed to be conscious of the scent of a cool still September night. He

thought he could hear an occasional stamp and clink from the stables, as of horses stirring. And with another shock he realized that, above the house, he was looking – not at the wall of his room – but into the profound blue of a night sky.

There were lights, more than one, in the windows, and he quickly saw that this was no four-roomed house with a movable front, but one of many rooms, and staircases – a real house, but seen as if through the wrong end of a telescope. "You mean to show me something," he muttered to himself, and he gazed earnestly on the lighted windows. They would in real life have been shuttered or curtained, no doubt, he thought; but as it was there was nothing to intercept his view of what was being transacted inside the rooms.

Two rooms were lighted – one on the ground floor to the right of the door, one upstairs, on the left – the first brightly enough, the other rather dimly. The lower room was the dining room: a table was laid, but the meal was over and only wine and glasses were left on the table. The man of the blue satin and the woman of the brocade were alone in the room and they were talking very earnestly, seated close together at the table, their elbows on it: every now and again stopping to listen, as it seemed. Once *he* rose, came to the window and opened it and put his head out and his hand to his ear. There was a lighted taper in a silver candlestick on a sideboard. When the man left the window he seemed to leave the room also; and the lady, taper in hand, remained standing and listening. The expression on her face was that of one striving her utmost

to keep down a fear that threatened to master her – and succeeding. It was a hateful face, too; broad, flat and sly. Now the man came back and she took some small thing from him and hurried out of the room. He too, disappeared, but only for a moment or two. The front door slowly opened and he stepped out and stood on the top of the *perron*, looking this way and that; then turned towards the upper window that was lighted and shook his fist.

It was time to look at that upper window. Through it was seen a four-poster bed: a nurse or other servant in an armchair, evidently sound asleep; in the bed an old man lying: awake and, one would say, anxious, from the way in which he shifted about and moved his fingers, beating tunes on the coverlet. Beyond the bed a door opened. Light was seen on the ceiling and the lady came in: she set down her candle on a table, came to the fireside and roused the nurse. In her hand she had an old-fashioned wine bottle, ready uncorked. The nurse took it, poured some of the contents into a little silver saucepan, added some spice and sugar from casters on the table and set it to warm on the fire. Meanwhile the old man in the bed beckoned feebly to the lady, who came to him, smiling, took his wrist as if to feel his pulse and bit her lip as if in consternation. He looked at her anxiously and then pointed to the window and spoke. She nodded and did as the man below had done; opened the casement and listened – perhaps rather ostentatiously; then drew her head in and shook it, looking at the old man, who seemed to sigh.

By this time the posset on the fire was steaming and the nurse poured it into a small two-handled silver bowl and brought it to the bedside. The old man seemed disinclined for it and was waving it away, but the lady and the nurse together bent over him and evidently pressed it upon him. He must have yielded, for they supported him into a sitting position and put it to his lips. He drank most of it, in several draughts, and they laid him down. The lady left the room, smiling goodnight to him, and took the bowl, the bottle and the silver saucepan with her. The nurse returned to the chair and there was an interval of complete quiet.

Suddenly the old man started up in his bed – and he must have uttered some cry, for the nurse started out of her chair and made but one step of it to the bedside. He was a sad and terrible sight -– flushed in the face, almost to blackness, the eyes glaring whitely, both hands clutching at his heart, foam at his lips.

For a moment the nurse left him, ran to the door, flung it wide open, and one supposes, screamed aloud for help, then darted back to the bed and seemed to try feverishly to soothe him – to lay him down – anything. But as the lady, her husband and several servants, rushed into the room with horrified faces, the old man collapsed under the nurse's hands and lay back and the features, contorted with agony and rage, relaxed slowly into calm.

A few moments later, lights showed out to the left of the house and a coach with flambeaux drove up to the door. A

white-wigged man in black got nimbly out and ran up the
steps, carrying a small leather trunk-shaped box. He was met in
the doorway by the man and his wife, she with her
handkerchief clutched between her hands, he with a tragic face,
but retaining his self-control. They led the newcomer into the
dining room, where he set his box of papers on the table and,
turning to them, listened with a face of consternation at what
they had to tell. He nodded his head again and again, threw out
his hands slightly, declined, it seemed, offers of refreshment
and lodging for the night and within a few minutes came slowly
down the steps, entering the coach and driving off the way he
had come. As the man in blue watched him from the top of the
steps, a smile not pleasant to see stole slowly over his fat white
face. Darkness fell over the whole scene as the lights of the
coach disappeared.

But Mr Dillet remained sitting up in the bed: he had rightly
guessed that there would be a sequel. The house front
glimmered out again before long. But now there was a
difference. The lights were in other windows, one at the top of
the house, the other illuminating the range of coloured windows
of the chapel. How he saw through these is not quite obvious,
but he did. The interior was as carefully furnished as the rest of
the establishment, with its minute red cushions on the desks, its
Gothic stall-canopies and its western gallery and pinnacled
organ with gold pipes. On the centre of the black and white
pavement was a bier: four tall candles burned at the corners.
On the bier was a coffin covered with a pall of black velvet.

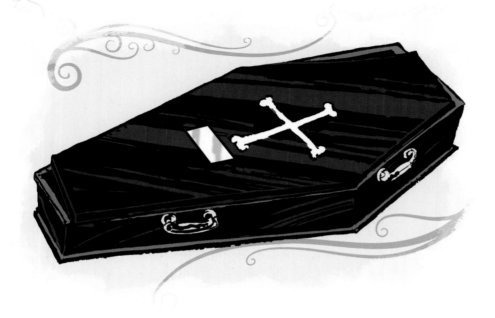

As he looked the folds of the pall stirred. It seemed to rise at one end: it slid downwards: it fell away, exposing the black coffin with its silver handles and nameplate. One of the tall candlesticks swayed and toppled over. Ask no more, but turn, as Mr Dillet hastily did, and look in at the lighted window at the top of the house, where a boy and girl lay in two truckle-beds, and a four-poster for the nurse rose above them. The nurse was not visible for the moment; but the father and mother were there, now in mourning, but with very little sign of mourning in their demeanour. Indeed, they were laughing and talking with a good deal of animation, sometimes to each

other and sometimes throwing a remark to one or other of the children and again laughing at the answers. Then the father was seen to go on tiptoe out of the room, taking with him as he went a white garment that hung on a peg near the door. He shut the door after him. A minute or two later it was slowly opened again and a muffled head poked round it. A bent form of sinister shape stepped across to the truckle-beds and suddenly stopped, threw up its arms and revealed, of course, the father, laughing. The children were in agonies of terror, the boy with the bedclothes over his head, the girl throwing herself out of bed into her mother's arms. Attempts at consolation followed – the parents took the children on their laps, patted them, picked up the white gown and showed there was no harm in it and so forth; and at last putting the children back into bed, left the room with encouraging waves of the hand. As they left it, the nurse came in and soon the light died down.

Still Mr Dillet watched immovable.

A new sort of light – not of lamp or candle – a pale ugly light, began to dawn around the door-case at the back of the room. The door was opening again. The seer does not like to dwell upon what he saw entering the room: he says it might be described as a frog – the size of a man – but it had scanty white hair about its head. It was busy about the truckle-beds, but not for long. The sound of cries – faint, as if coming out of a vast distance – but even so, infinitely appalling, reached the ear.

There were signs of a hideous commotion all over the house: lights passed along and up, and doors opened and shut, and running figures passed within the windows. The clock in the stable turret tolled one and darkness fell again.

It was only dispelled once more, to show the house front. At the bottom of the steps dark figures were drawn up in two lines, holding flaming torches. More dark figures came down the steps, bearing, first one, then another small coffin. And the lines of torch-bearers with the coffins between them moved silently onward to the left.

The hours of night passed on – never so slowly, Mr Dillet thought. Gradually he sank down from sitting to lying in his bed – but he did not close an eye: and early next morning he sent for the doctor.

The doctor found him in a disquieting state of nerves and recommended sea air. To a quiet place on the east coast he accordingly repaired by easy stages in his car.

One of the first people he met on the sea front was Mr Chittenden, who, it appeared, had likewise been advised to take his wife away for a bit of a change.

Mr Chittenden looked somewhat askance upon him when they met: and not without cause.

"Well, I don't wonder at you being a bit upset, Mr Dillet. What? Yes, well, I might say 'orrible upset, to be sure, seeing what me and my poor wife went through ourselves. But I put it to you, Mr Dillet, one of two things: was I going to scrap a

lovely piece like that on the one 'and, or was I going to tell customers: 'I'm selling you a regular picture-palace-drama in real life of the olden time, billed to perform regular at one o'clock a.m.'? Why, what would you 'ave said yourself? And next thing you know, two Justices of the Peace in the back parlour and pore Mr and Mrs Chittenden off in a spring cart to the County Asylum and everyone in the street saying, 'Ah, I thought it 'ud come to that. Look at the way the man drank!' – and me next door, or next door but one, to a total abstainer, as you know. Well, there was my position. What? Me 'ave it back in the shop? Well, what do you think? No, but I'll tell you what I will do. You shall have your money back, bar the ten pound I paid for it, and you make what you can."

Later in the day, in what is offensively called the 'smoke room' of the hotel, a murmured conversation between the two went on for some time.

"How much do you really know about that thing and where it came from?"

"Honest, Mr Dillet, I don't know the 'ouse. Of course, it came out of the lumber room of a country 'ouse – that anyone could guess. But I'll go as far as say this, that I believe it's not a hundred miles from this place. Which direction and how far I've no notion. I'm only judging by guesswork. The man as I actually paid the cheque to ain't one of my regular men and I've lost sight of him; but I 'ave the idea that this part of the country was his beat and that's every word I can tell you. But now, Mr Dillet, there's one thing that rather physicks me. That

old chap – I suppose you saw him drive up to the door – I thought so: now, would he have been the medical man, do you take it? My wife would have it so, but I stuck to it that was the lawyer, because he had papers with him and one he took out was folded up."

"I agree," said Mr Dillet. "Thinking it over, I came to the conclusion that was the old man's will, ready to be signed."

"Just what I thought," said Mr Chittenden, "and I took it that will would have cut out the young people, eh? Well, well! It's been a lesson to me, I know that. I shan't buy no more dolls' houses, nor waste no more money on the pictures – and as to this business of poisonin' grandpa, well, if I know myself, I never 'ad much of a turn for that. Live and let live: that's bin my motto throughout life and I ain't found it a bad one, that's for sure."

Filled with these elevated sentiments, Mr Chittenden retired to his lodgings. Mr Dillet next day repaired to the local Institute, where he hoped to find some clue to the riddle that absorbed him. He gazed in despair at a long file of the Canterbury and York Society's publications of the Parish Registers of the district. No print resembling the house of his nightmare was among those that hung on the staircase and in the passages. Disconsolate, he found himself in a derelict room, staring at a dusty model of a church in a dark and dusty glass case:

"Model of St Stephen's Church, Coxham. Presented by J. Merewether, Esq., of Ilbridge House, 1877. The work of his

ancestor James Merewether, d. 1786."

There was something in the fashion of it that reminded him dimly of his horror. He retraced his steps to a wall map he had noticed, and made out that Ilbridge House was in Coxham Parish. Coxham was, as it happened, one of the parishes of which he had retained the name when he glanced over the file of printed registers and it was not long before he found in them the record of the burial of Roger Milford, aged 76, on the 11th September 1757, and of Roger and Elizabeth Merewether, aged nine and seven, on the 19th of the same month. It seemed worthwhile to follow up this clue, frail as it was; and in the afternoon he drove out to Coxham. The east end of the north aisle of the church is a Milford chapel and on its north wall are tablets to the same persons; Roger, the elder, it seems, was distinguished by all the qualities which adorn 'the Father, the Magistrate, and the Man': the memorial was erected by his attached daughter Elizabeth, 'who did not long survive the loss of a parent ever solicitous for her welfare, and of two amiable children'. The last sentence was plainly an addition to the original inscription.

A yet later slab told of James Merewether, husband of Elizabeth, 'who in the dawn of life practised, not without success, those arts which, had he continued their exercise, might in the

opinion of the most competent judges have earned for him the name of the British Vitruvius: but who, overwhelmed by the visitation which deprived him of an affectionate partner and a blooming offspring, passed his Prime and Age in a secluded yet elegant Retirement: his grateful Nephew and Heir indulges a pious sorrow by this too brief recital of his excellences'.

The children were more simply commemorated. Both died on the night of the 12th of September.

Mr Dillet felt sure that in Ilbridge House he had found the scene of his drama. In some old sketch book, possibly even in some old print, he may yet find some convincing evidence that

he is right. But the Ilbridge House of today is not that which he sought; it is an Elizabethan erection of the forties, in mellow red brick, with stone quoins and dressings. A quarter of a mile from it, in a low part of the park, backed by ancient, stag-horned, ivy-strangled trees and thick undergrowth, are marks of a terraced platform overgrown with rough, dry grass. A few stone balusters lie here and there, and a heap or two, covered with nettles, brambles and ivy, of wrought stones with badly carved crockets. This, someone told Mr Dillet, was the site of a much older house. As he drove out of the village, the hall clock suddenly struck four and Mr Dillet started up and clapped his hands over his ears as if he had been struck. It was not the first time he had heard that bell.

Awaiting an offer from the other side of the Atlantic, the dolls' house still reposes, carefully sheeted, in a loft over Mr Dillet's stables, whither Collins conveyed it on the day when Mr Dillet started for the sea coast.

A Christmas Carol

1843

EXTRACT

Charles Dickens

Scrooge took his melancholy dinner in his usual melancholy tavern; and having read all the newspapers, and beguiled the rest of the evening with his banker's-book, went home to bed. He lived in chambers which had once belonged to his deceased partner. They were a gloomy suite of rooms, in a lowering pile of building up a yard, where it had so little business to be, that one could scarcely help fancying it must have run there when it was a young house, playing at hide-and-seek with other houses, and have forgotten the way out again. It was old enough now, and dreary enough, for nobody lived in it but Scrooge, the other rooms being all let out as offices. The yard was so dark that even Scrooge, who knew its every stone, was fain to grope with his hands. The fog and frost so hung about the black old gateway of the house,

that it seemed as if the Genius of the Weather sat in mournful meditation on the threshold.

Now, it is a fact, that there was nothing at all particular about the knocker on the door, except that it was very large. It is also a fact, that Scrooge had seen it, night and morning, during his whole residence in that place; also that Scrooge had as little of what is called fancy about him as any man in the City of London, even including – which is a bold word – the corporation, aldermen, and livery. Let it also be borne in mind that Scrooge had not bestowed one thought on Marley, since his last mention of his seven-years dead partner that afternoon. And then let any man explain to me, if he can, how it happened that Scrooge, having his key in the lock of the door, saw in the knocker, without its undergoing any intermediate process of change: not a knocker, but Marley's face.

Marley's face. It was not in impenetrable shadow as the other objects in the yard were, but had a dismal light about it, like a bad lobster in a dark cellar. It was not angry or ferocious, but looked at Scrooge as Marley used to look: with ghostly spectacles turned up upon its ghostly forehead. The hair was curiously

stirred, as if by breath or hot air; and, though the eyes were wide open, they were perfectly motionless. That, and its livid colour, made it horrible; but its horror seemed to be in spite of the face and beyond its control, rather than a part of its own expression.

As Scrooge looked fixedly at this phenomenon, it was a knocker again.

To say that he was not startled, or that his blood was not conscious of a terrible sensation to which it had been a stranger from infancy, would be untrue. But he put his hand upon the key he had relinquished, turned it sturdily, walked in, and lighted his candle.

He *did* pause, with a moment's irresolution, before he shut the door; and he *did* look cautiously behind it first, as if he half expected to be terrified with the sight of Marley's pigtail sticking out into the hall. But there was nothing on the back of the door, except the screws and nuts that held the knocker on, so he said "Pooh, pooh!'' and closed it with a bang.

The sound resounded through the house like thunder. Every room above, and every cask in the wine-merchant's cellars below, appeared to have a separate peal of echoes of its own. Scrooge was not a man to be frightened by echoes. He fastened the door, and walked across the hall, and up the stairs, slowly too: trimming his candle as he went.

You may talk vaguely about driving a coach-and-six up a

good old flight of stairs, or through a bad young Act of Parliament; but I mean to say you might have got a hearse up that staircase, and taken it broadwise, with the splinter-bar towards the wall and the door towards the balustrades: and done it easy. There was plenty of width for that, and room to spare; which is perhaps the reason why Scrooge thought he saw a locomotive hearse going on before him in the gloom. Half-a-dozen gas lamps out of the street wouldn't have lighted the entry too well, so you may suppose that it was pretty dark with Scrooge's dip.

Up Scrooge went, not caring a button for that: darkness is cheap, and Scrooge liked it. But before he shut his heavy door, he walked through his rooms to see that all was right. He had just enough recollection of the face to desire to do that.

Sitting room, bedroom, lumber room. All as they should be. Nobody under the table, nobody under the sofa; a small fire in the grate; spoon and basin ready; and the little saucepan of gruel (Scrooge had a cold in his head) upon the hob. Nobody under the bed; nobody in the closet; nobody in his dressing gown, which was hanging up in a suspicious attitude against the wall. Lumber room as usual. Old fire guard, old shoes, two fish-baskets, wash-stand on three legs, and a poker.

Quite satisfied, he closed his door, and locked himself in; double locked himself in, which was not his custom. Thus secured against surprise, he took off his cravat; put on his dressing gown and slippers, and his night cap; and sat down before the fire to take his gruel.

It was a very low fire indeed; nothing on such a bitter night. He was obliged to sit close to it, and brood over it, before he could extract the least sensation of warmth from such a handful of fuel. The fireplace was an old one, built by some Dutch merchant long ago, and paved all round with quaint Dutch tiles, designed to illustrate the Scriptures. There were Cains and Abels, Pharaoh's daughters, Queens of Sheba, Angelic messengers descending through the air on clouds like feather-beds, Abrahams, Belshazzars, Apostles putting off to sea in butter-boats, hundreds of figures to attract his thoughts; and yet that face of Marley, seven years dead, came like the ancient Prophet's rod, and swallowed up the whole. If each smooth tile had been a blank at first, with power to shape some picture on its surface from the disjointed fragments of his thoughts, there would have been a copy of old Marley's head on every one.

"Humbug!" said Scrooge; and walked across the room.

After several turns, he sat down again. As he threw his head back in the chair, his glance happened to rest upon a bell, a disused bell, that hung in the room, and communicated for some purpose now forgotten with a chamber in the highest storey of the building. It was with great astonishment, and with a strange, inexplicable dread, that as he looked, he saw this bell begin to swing. It swung so softly in the outset that it scarcely made a sound; but soon it rang out loudly, and so did every bell in the house.

This might have lasted half a minute, or a minute, but it

seemed an hour. The bells ceased as they had begun, together. They were succeeded by a clanking noise, deep down below; as if some person were dragging a heavy chain over the casks in the wine-merchant's cellar. Scrooge then remembered to have heard that ghosts in haunted houses were described as dragging chains.

The cellar door flew open with a booming sound, and then he heard the noise much louder, on the floors below; then coming up the stairs; then coming straight towards his door.

"It's humbug still!" said Scrooge. "I won't believe it."

His colour changed though, when, without a pause, it came on through the heavy door, and passed into the room before his eyes. Upon its coming in, the dying flame leaped up, as though it cried, "I know him! Marley's Ghost!" and fell again.

The same face: the very same. Marley in his pigtail, usual waistcoat, tights and boots; the tassels on the latter bristling, like his

pigtail, and his coat-skirts, and the hair upon his head. The chain he drew was clasped about his middle. It was long, and wound about him like a tail; and it was made (for Scrooge observed it closely) of cash boxes, keys, padlocks, ledgers, deeds, and heavy purses wrought in steel. His body was

transparent; so that Scrooge, observing him, and looking through his waistcoat, could see the two buttons on his coat behind.

Scrooge had often heard it said that Marley had no bowels, but he had never believed it until now.

No, nor did he believe it even now. Though he looked the phantom through and through, and saw it standing before him; though he felt the chilling influence of its death-cold eyes; and marked the very texture of the folded kerchief

bound about its head and chin, which wrapper he had not observed before; he was still incredulous, and fought against his senses.

"How now." said Scrooge, caustic and cold as ever. "What do you want with me?"

"Much." It was Marley's voice, no doubt about it.

"Who are you?"

"Ask me who I was."

"Who were you then?" said Scrooge, raising his voice. "You're particular – for a shade." He was going to say 'to a shade,' but substituted this, as more appropriate.

"In life I was your business partner, Jacob Marley."

"Can you – can you sit down?" asked Scrooge, looking doubtfully at him.

"I can."

"Do it, then."

Scrooge asked the question, because he didn't know whether a ghost so transparent might find himself in a condition to take a chair; and felt that in the event of its being impossible, it might involve the necessity of an embarrassing explanation. But the ghost sat down on the opposite side of the fireplace, as if he were quite used to it.

"You don't believe in me," observed the Ghost.

"I don't," said Scrooge.

"What evidence would you have of my reality beyond that of your senses?"

"I don't know," said Scrooge.

"Why do you doubt your senses?"

"Because," said Scrooge, "a little thing affects them. A slight disorder of the stomach makes them cheats. You may be an undigested bit of beef, a blot of mustard, a crumb of cheese, a fragment of an underdone potato. There's more of gravy than of grave about you, whatever you are!"

Scrooge was not much in the habit of cracking jokes, nor did he feel, in his heart, by any means waggish then. The truth is, that he tried to be smart, as a means of distracting his own attention, and keeping down his terror; for the spectre's voice disturbed the very marrow in his bones.

To sit, staring at those fixed glazed eyes in silence for a moment, would play, Scrooge felt, the very deuce with him. There was something very awful, too, in the spectre's being provided with an infernal atmosphere of its own. Scrooge could not feel it himself, but this was clearly the case; for though the Ghost sat perfectly motionless, its hair, and skirts, and tassels, were still agitated as by the hot vapour from an oven.

"You see this toothpick?" said Scrooge, returning quickly to the charge, for the reason just assigned; and wishing, though it were only for a second, to divert the vision's stony gaze from himself.

"I do," replied the Ghost.

"You are not looking at it," said Scrooge.

"But I see it," said the Ghost, "notwithstanding."

"Well," returned Scrooge, "I have but to swallow this, and

be for the rest of my days persecuted by a legion of goblins, all of my own creation. Humbug, I tell you: humbug!"

At this the spirit raised a frightful cry, and shook its chain with such a dismal and appalling noise, that Scrooge held on tight to his chair, to save himself from falling in a swoon. But how much greater was his horror, when the phantom taking off the bandage round its head, as if it were too warm to wear in-doors, its lower jaw dropped down upon its breast!

Scrooge fell upon his knees, and clasped his hands before his face.

"Mercy!" he said. "Dreadful apparition, why do you trouble me?"

"Man of the worldly mind!" replied the Ghost. "Do you believe in me or not?"

"I do," said Scrooge. "I must. But why do spirits walk the earth, and why do they come to me?"

"It is required of every man," the Ghost returned, "that the spirit within him should walk abroad among his fellow-men, and travel far and wide; and if that spirit goes not forth in life, it is condemned to do so after death. It is doomed to wander through the world – oh, woe is me! – and witness what it cannot share, but might have shared on earth, and turned to happiness."

Again the spectre raised a cry, and shook its chain and wrung its shadowy hands.

"You are fettered," said Scrooge, trembling. "Tell me why?"

"I wear the chain I forged in life," replied the Ghost. "I

made it link by link, and yard by yard; I girded it on of my own free will, and of my own free will I wore it. Is its pattern strange to you?"

Scrooge trembled more and more.

"Or would you know," pursued the Ghost, "the weight and length of the strong coil you bear yourself? It was full as heavy and as long as this, seven Christmas Eves ago. You have laboured on it, since. It is a ponderous chain!"

Scrooge glanced about him on the floor, in the expectation of finding himself surrounded by some fifty or sixty fathoms of iron cable: but he could see nothing.

"Jacob," he said, imploringly. "Old Jacob Marley, tell me more. Speak comfort to me, Jacob."

"I have none to give," the Ghost replied. "It comes from other regions, Ebenezer Scrooge, and is conveyed by other ministers, to other kinds of men. Nor can I tell you what I would. A very little more is all permitted to me. I cannot rest, I cannot stay, I cannot linger anywhere. My spirit never walked beyond our counting-house – mark me! – in life my spirit never roved beyond the narrow limits of our

money-changing hole; and weary journeys lie before me!"

It was a habit with Scrooge, whenever he became thoughtful, to put his hands in his breeches pockets. Pondering on what the Ghost had said, he did so now, but without lifting up his eyes, or getting off his knees.

"You must have been very slow about it, Jacob," Scrooge observed, in a businesslike manner, though with humility and deference.

"Slow!" the Ghost repeated.

"Seven years dead," mused Scrooge. "And travelling all the time?"

"The whole time," said the Ghost. "No rest, no peace. Incessant torture of remorse."

"You travel fast?" said Scrooge.

"On the wings of the wind," replied the Ghost.

"You might have got over a great quantity of ground in seven years," said Scrooge.

The Ghost, on hearing this, set up another cry, and clanked its chain so hideously in the dead silence of the night, that the Ward would have been justified in indicting it for a nuisance.

"Oh! Captive, bound, and double-ironed,"

cried the phantom, "not to know, that ages of incessant labour by immortal creatures, for this earth must pass into eternity before the good of which it is susceptible is all developed! Not to know that any Christian spirit working kindly in its little sphere, whatever it may be, will find its mortal life too short for its vast means of usefulness! Not to know that no space of regret can make amends for one life's opportunity misused! Yet such was I! Oh! such was I!"

"But you were always a good man of business, Jacob," faltered Scrooge, who now began to apply this to himself.

"Business!" cried the Ghost, wringing its hands again. "Mankind was my business. The common welfare was my business; charity, mercy, forbearance, and benevolence were all my business. The dealings of my trade were but a drop of water in the comprehensive ocean of my business!"

It held up its chain at arm's length, as if that were the cause of all its unavailing grief, and flung it heavily upon the ground again.

"At this time of the rolling year," the spectre said, "I suffer most. Why did I walk through crowds of fellow-beings with my eyes turned down, and never raise them to that blessed Star which led the Wise Men to a poor abode? Were there no poor homes to which its light would have conducted me?"

Scrooge was very much dismayed to hear the spectre going on at this rate, and began to quake exceedingly.

"Hear me!" cried the Ghost. "My time is nearly gone."

"I will," said Scrooge. "But don't be hard upon me. Don't be flowery, Jacob! Pray!"

"How it is that I appear before you in a shape that you can see, I may not tell. I have sat invisible beside you many and many a day."

It was not an agreeable idea. Scrooge shivered, and wiped the perspiration from his brow.

"That is no light part of my penance," pursued the Ghost. "I am here tonight to warn you, that you have yet a chance and hope of escaping my fate. A chance and hope of my procuring, Ebenezer."

"You were always a good friend to me," said Scrooge. "Thank'ee."

"You will be haunted," resumed the Ghost, "by Three Spirits."

Scrooge's countenance fell almost as low as the Ghost's had done.

"Is that the chance and hope you mentioned, Jacob?" he demanded, in a faltering voice.

"It is."

"I-I think I'd rather not," said Scrooge.

"Without their visits," said the Ghost, "you cannot hope to shun the path I tread. Expect the first tomorrow, when the bell tolls one."

"Couldn't I take them all at once, and have it over, Jacob?" hinted Scrooge.

"Expect the second on the next night at the same hour. The third upon the next night when the last stroke of twelve has ceased to vibrate. Look to see me no more; and look that, for your own sake, you remember what has passed between us!"

When it had said these words, the spectre took its wrapper from the table, and bound it round its head, as before. Scrooge knew this, by the smart sound its teeth made, when the jaws were brought together by the bandage. He ventured to raise his eyes again, and found his supernatural visitor confronting him in an erect attitude, with its chain wound over and about its arm.

The apparition walked backward from him; and at every step it took, the window raised itself a little, so that when the spectre reached it, it was wide open.

It beckoned Scrooge to approach, which he did. When they were within two paces of each other, Marley's Ghost held up its hand, warning him to come no nearer. Scrooge stopped.

Not so much in obedience, as in surprise and fear: for on the raising of the hand, he became sensible of confused noises in the air; incoherent sounds of lamentation and regret; wailings inexpressibly sorrowful and self-accusatory. The spectre, after listening for a moment, joined in the mournful dirge; and floated out upon the bleak, dark night.

Scrooge followed to the window: desperate in his curiosity. He looked out.

The air was filled with phantoms, wandering hither and thither in restless haste, and moaning as they went. Everyone of them wore chains like Marley's Ghost; some few (they might be guilty governments) were linked together; none were free.

Many had been personally known to Scrooge in their lives.

He had been quite familiar with one old ghost, in a white waistcoat, with a monstrous iron safe attached to its ankle, who cried piteously at being unable to assist a wretched woman with an infant, whom it saw below, upon a doorstep. The misery with them all was, clearly, that they sought to interfere, for good, in human matters, and had lost the power forever.

Whether these creatures faded into mist, or mist enshrouded them, he could not tell. But they and their spirit voices faded together; and the night became as it had been when he walked home.

Scrooge closed the window, and examined the door by which the Ghost had entered. It was double locked, as he had locked it with his own hands, and the bolts were undisturbed. He tried to say "Humbug!" but stopped at the first syllable. And being, from the emotion he had undergone, or the fatigues of the day, or his glimpse of the 'invisible world', or the dull conversation of the Ghost, or the lateness of the hour, much in need of repose; went straight to bed, without undressing, and fell asleep upon the instant.

The Ship that saw a Ghost

1902

EXTRACT

Frank Norris

So the *Glarus* plodded and churned her way onwards. Every day and all day the same pale blue sky and unwinking sun bent over that moving speck. Every day and all day the same black-blue water-world, untouched by any known wind, smooth as a slab of syenite, colourful as an opal, stretched out and around and beyond and before and behind us, forever, illimitable, empty. Every day, the smoke of our fires veiled the streaked whiteness of our wake. Every day Hardenberg (our skipper) at noon pricked a pin hole in the chart that hung in the wheel house, and that showed we were so much farther into the wilderness. Every day the world of men, of civilization, of newspapers, policemen, and street railways, receded, and we steamed on alone, lost and forgotten in that silent sea.

"Jolly lot o' room to turn raound in," observed Ally Bazan, the colonial, "withaout steppin' on y'r neighbour's toes."

"We're clean, clean out o' the track of navigation," Hardenberg told him. "An' a blessed good thing for us, too. Nobody ever comes down into these waters. Ye couldn't pick no course here. Everything leads to nowhere."

"Might as well be in a bally balloon," said Strokher.

I shall not tell of the nature of the venture on which the *Glarus* was bound, further than to say it was not legitimate. It had to do with an ill thing done more than two centuries ago. There was money in the venture, but it was to be gained by a violation of metes and bounds which are better left intact.

The island towards which we were heading is associated in the minds of men with a horror. A ship had called there once, two hundred years in advance of the *Glarus* – a ship not much unlike the crank high-prowed caravel of Hudson, and her company had landed, and having accomplished the evil they had set out to do, made shift to sail away. And then, just after the palms of the island had sunk from sight below the water's edge, the unspeakable had happened. The death that was not death had arisen from out the sea and stood before the ship; and over it and the blight of the thing lay along the decks like mould, and the ship sweated in the terror of that which is yet without a name. Twenty men died in the first week, all but six in the second. These six, with the shadow of insanity upon them, made out to launch a boat, returned to the island and died there, after leaving a record of what had happened.

The six left the ship exactly as she was, sails all set, lanterns all lit – left her in the shadow of the death that was not death. The wind made at the time, they said, and as they bent to their bars, she sailed after them, for all the world like a thing refusing to abandon them or be herself abandoned, till the wind died down. Then they left her behind, and she stood there, becalmed, and watched them go. She was never heard of again.

Or was she – well, that's as may be.

But the main point of the whole affair to my notion, has always been this. The ship was the last friend of those six poor wretches who made back for the island with their poor chests

of plunder. She was their guardian, as it were, would have defended and befriended them to the last; and also we, the Three Black Crows and myself, had no right under heaven, nor before the law of men, to come prying and peeping into this business – into this affair of the dead and buried past. There was sacrilege in it. We were no better than body snatchers.

When I heard the others complaining of the loneliness of our surroundings, I said nothing at first. I was no sailor man and I was on board only by tolerance. But I looked again at the maddening sameness of the horizon – the same vacant, void horizon that we had seen now for sixteen days on end, and felt in my wits and in my nerves that same formless rebellion and protest such as comes when the same note is reiterated over and over again.

It may seem a little thing that the mere fact of meeting with no other ship should have ground down the edge of the spirit. But let the incredulous – bound upon such a hazard as ours – sail straight into nothingness for sixteen days on end, seeing nothing but the sun, hearing nothing but the thresh of his own screw, and then put the question.

And yet, of all things, we desired no company. Stealth was our one great aim. But I think there were moments – towards the last – when the Three Crows would have welcomed even a cruiser.

On the seventh day, Hardenberg and I were forward by the cat-head adjusting the grain with some half formed intent of spearing the porpoises that of late had begun to appear under

our bows, and Hardenberg had been computing the number of days we were yet to run.

"We are some five hundred odd miles off that island by now," he said, "and she's doing her thirteen knots handsome. All's well so far – but do you know, I'd just as soon raise that point o' land as soon as convenient."

"How so?" said I, bending on the line. "Expect some weather?"

"Mr Dixon," said he, giving me a curious glance, "the sea is a queer proposition, put it any ways. I've been a sea-farin' man since I was as big as a minute, and I know the sea, and what's more, the Feel o' the Sea. Now, look out yonder. Nothin', hey? Nothin' but the same ol' skyline we've watched all the way out. The glass is as steady as a steeple, and this ol' hooker, I

reckon, is as sound as the day she went off the ways. But just
the same, if I were to home now, a-foolin' about Gloucester
way in my little dough-dish – d'ye know what? I'd put into
port. I sure would. Because why? Because I got the Feel o' the
Sea, Mr Dixon. I got the Feel o' the Sea."

I had heard old skippers say something of this before, and I
cited to Hardenberg the experience of a skipper captain I once
knew who had turned turtle in a calm sea off Trincomalee. I
asked what this Feel of the Sea was warning him against just
now (for on the high sea any premonition is a premonition of
evil, not of good). But he was not explicit.

"I don't know," he answered moodily, and as if in great
perplexity, coiling the rope as he spoke. "I don't know. There's
some blame thing or other close to us, I'll bet a hat. I don't
know the name of it, Mr Dixon, and I don't know the game of
it, but there's a big bird in the air, just out of sight someres,
and," he suddenly exclaimed, smacking his knee and leaning
forward, "I – don't – like – it – one – dam' – bit."

The same thing came up in our talk in the cabin that night,
after the dinner was taken off, and we settled down to tobacco.
Only, at this time, Hardenberg was on duty on the bridge. It
was Ally Bazan who spoke instead.

"Seems to me," he hazarded, "as haow they's somethin' or
other a-goin' to bump up, pretty blyme soon. I shouldn't be
surprized, naow, y'know, if we piled her up on some bally
uncharted reef along o' tonight and went strite daown afore
we'd had a bloomin' charnce to s'y 'So long, gen'lemen all'."

He laughed as he spoke, but when, just at that moment, a pan clattered in the galley, he jumped suddenly with an oath, and looked hard about the cabin.

Then Strokher confessed to a sense of distress also. He'd been having it since day before yesterday, it seemed.

"And I put it to you the glass is lovely," he said, "so it's no blow. I guess," he continued, "we're all a bit seedy and ship sore."

And whether or not this talk worked upon my own nerves, or whether in very truth the feel of the sea had found me also, I do not know; but I do know that after dinner that night, just before going to bed, a queer sense of apprehension came upon me, and that when I had come to my stateroom, I became furiously angry with nobody in particular, because I could not at once find the matches. But here was a difference. The other men had been merely vaguely uncomfortable.

I could put a name to my uneasiness. I felt that we were being watched.

It was a strange ship's company we made after that. I speak only of the crows and myself. We carried a scant crew of stokers, and there was also a chief engineer. But we saw so little of him that he did not count. The crows and I gloomed on the quarter deck from dawn to dark: silent, irritable, working upon each other's nerves till the creak of a block would make a man jump like cold steel laid to his flesh. We quarrelled over nothing, glowered at each other for half a word, and each one of us, at different times, was at some pains

to declare that never in the course of his career had he been associated with such a disagreeable trio of brutes. Yet we were always together and sought each other's company.

Only once were we all agreed, and that was when the cook, a Chinaman, spoiled a certain batch of biscuits. Unanimously we fell foul of the creature with so much vociferation as fishwives till he fled the cabin in actual fear of mishandling, leaving us suddenly seized with noisy hilarity — for the first time in a week. Hardenberg proposed a round of drinks from our single remaining case of beer. We stood up and formed an Elk's chain and then drained our glasses to each other's health.

That same evening, I remember, we all sat on the quarterdeck till late and — oddly enough — related each one his life's history up to date; and then went down to the cabin for a game of euchre before turning in.

We had left Strokher on the bridge — it was his watch — and had forgotten all about him in the interest of the game, when — I suppose it was about one in the morning — I heard him whistle long and shrill. I laid down my cards and said: "Hark!"

In the silence that followed we heard at first only the muffled lope of our engines, the cadenced snorting of the exhaust, and the ticking of Hardenberg's big watch in his waistcoat. Then from the bridge, above our deck, prolonged, intoned — a wailing cry in the night — came Strokher's voice: "Sail oh-h-h."

And the cards fell from our hands, and, like men turned to stone, we sat looking at each other across the soiled red cloth

for what seemed an immeasurably long minute. Then stumbling and swearing, in a hysteria of hurry, we gained the deck.

There was a moon, very low and reddish, but no wind. The sea beyond the taffrail was as smooth as lava, and so still that the swells from the cutwater of the *Glarus* did not break as they rolled away from the bows.

I remember that I stood staring and blinking at the empty ocean – where the moonlight lay like a painted stripe reaching to the horizon – stupid and frowning, till Hardenberg, who had gone on ahead, cried: "Not here – on the bridge!"

We joined Strokher, and as I came up the others were asking: "Where? Where?"

And there, before he had pointed, I saw – we all of us saw. And I heard Hardenberg's teeth come together like a spring trap, while Ally Bazan ducked as though to a blow, muttering: "Gord'a mercy, what nyme do ye put to a ship like that?"

And after that no one spoke for a long minute, and we stood there, moveless black shadows, huddled together for the sake of the blessed elbow touch that means so incalculably much, looking off over our port quarter.

For the ship that we saw there – oh, she was not a half-mile distant – was unlike any ship known to present day construction.

She was short, and high-pooped, and her stern, which was turned a little towards us, we could see, was set with curious windows, not unlike a house. And on either side of this stern were two great iron cressets such as once were used to burn

signal fires in. She had three masts with mighty yards swung 'thwart ship, but bare of all sails save a few rotting streamers. Here and there about her a tangled mass of rigging drooped and sagged.

And there she lay, in the red eye of the setting moon, in that solitary ocean, shadowy, antique, forlorn, a thing the most abandoned, the most sinister I ever remember to have seen.

Then Strokher began to explain volubly and with many repetitions.

"A derelict, of course. I was asleep; yes I was asleep. Gross neglect of duty. And we worked up to her. When I woke, why – you see, when I woke, there she was," he gave a weak little laugh, "and – and now, why, there she is, you see. I turned around and saw her sudden like – when I woke up, that is."

He laughed again, and as he laughed, the engines far below our feet gave a sudden hiccough. Something crashed and struck the ship's sides till we lurched as we stood. There was a shriek of steam, a shout – and then silence.

The noise of the machinery ceased; the *Glarus* slid through the still water, moving only by her own decreasing momentum.

Hardenberg sang, "Stand by!" and called down the tube to the engine room.

"What's up?"

I was standing close enough to him to hear the answer in a small faint voice:

"Shaft gone, sir."

"Broke?"

"Yes, sir."

Hardenberg faced about. "Come below. We must talk."

I do not think any of us cast a glance at the other ship again.

Certainly I kept my eyes away from her. But as we started down the companionway, I laid my hand on Strokher's shoulder. I looked him straight between the eyes as I asked: "*Were* you asleep? *Is* that why you saw her so suddenly?"

It is now five years since I asked the question. I am still waiting for Strokher's answer.

Well, our shaft was broken. We went down into the engine room and saw the jagged fracture that was the symbol of our broken hopes. And in the course of the next five minutes conversation with the chief, we found that there was to be no mending of it. We said nothing about the mishap coinciding with the appearance of the ship. But I know we did not consider the break with any degree of surprise after a few moments.

We came slowly up from the engine room and sat down at the cabin table in a dispirited fashion.

"Now what?" said Hardenberg, by way of beginning.

Nobody answered at first.

It was by now three in the morning. I recall it all perfectly. The ports opposite where I sat were open and I could see. The moon was all but full set. The dawn was coming up with a copper murkiness over the edge of the world. All the stars were yet out. The sea, for all the red moon and copper dawn, was grey, and there, less than half a mile away, still lay our consort. I could see her through the portholes with each slow careening of the *Glarus*.

"I vote for the island," cried Ally Bazan, "shaft or no shaft. We rigs a bit o' syle, y'know," – and thereat the discussion began.

For upwards of two hours it raged, with loud words and shaken forefingers, and great noisy bangings of the table, and how it would have ended I do not know, but at last – it was then maybe five in the morning – the lookout passed word down to the cabin: "Will you come on deck, gentlemen?" It was the mate who spoke, and the man was shaken – I could see that – to the very vitals of him.

We stared at one another, and I watched little Ally Bazan go slowly white to the lips. And even then no word of the Ship, except as it might be this from Hardenberg: "What is it? Good God Almighty, I'm no coward, but this thing is getting one too many for me." Then without further speech he went on deck.

The air was cool. The sun was not yet up. It was that strange, queer mid-period between dark and dawn, when the night is over and the day not yet come, just the grey that is neither light nor dark, the dim dead blink as of the refracted light from extinct worlds.

We stood at the rail. We did not speak, we stood watching. It was so still that the drip of steam from some loosened pipe far below was plainly audible, and it sounded in that lifeless, silent greyness, like – God knows what – a death tick.

"You see," said the mate, speaking just above a whisper, "there's no mistake about it. She is moving – this way."

"Oh, a current, of course," Strokher tried to say cheerfully, "sets her towards us."

Would the morning never come?

Ally Bazan – his parents were Catholic – began to mutter

to himself.

Then Hardenberg spoke aloud.

"I particularly don't want – that – out – there – to cross our bows. I don't want it to come to that. We must get some sails on her."

"And I put it to you as man to man," said Strokher, "where might be your wind?"

He was right. The *Glarus* floated in absolute calm. On all that slab of ocean nothing moved but the dead ship.

She came on slowly; her bows, the high clumsy bows pointed towards us, the water turning from her forefoot. She came on; she was near at hand. We saw her plainly – saw the rotted planks, the crumbling rigging, the rust-corroded metalwork, the broken rail, the gaping deck – and I could imagine that the clean water broke away from her sides in refluent wavelets as though in recoil from a thing unclean. She made no sound. No single thing stirred aboard the hulk of her – but she moved.

We were helpless. The *Glarus* could stir no boat in any direction; we were chained to the spot. Nobody had thought to put out our lights, and they still burned on through the dawn, strangely out of place in their red and green garishness.

And in the silence of that empty ocean, in that queer half-light between dawn and day, at six o'clock, silent as the settling of the dead to the bottomless bottom of the ocean, grey as fog, lonely, blind, soulless, voiceless, the dead ship crossed our bows.

I do not know how long after this the ship disappeared, or what was the time of day when we at last pulled ourselves together. But we came to some sort of decision at last. This was to go on – under sail. We were too close to the island now to turn back for – for a broken shaft.

The afternoon was spent fitting on the sails to her, and when after nightfall the wind at length came up fresh and favourable, I believe we all felt heartened and a deal more hardy – until the last canvass went aloft, and Hardenberg took the wheel.

We had drifted a good deal since the morning, and the bows of the *Glarus* were pointed homewards, but as soon as the breeze blew strong enough to get steerage way, Hardenberg put the wheel over, and headed for the island again.

We had not gone on this course half an hour – no, not twenty minutes – before the wind shifted a whole quarter of the compass and took the *Glarus* square in the teeth, so that there was nothing for it but to tack. And then the strangest thing befell.

I will make allowance for the fact that there was no centre board nor keel to speak of to the Glarus. I will admit that the sails upon a 900-tonne freighter are not calculated to speed her, nor steady her. I will even admit the possibility of a current that set from the island towards us. All this may be true, yet the *Glarus* should have advanced. We should have made a wake.

Instead of this our trusty old boat was – what shall I say?

I will say that no man may thoroughly understand a ship — after all. I will say that new ships are cranky and unsteady, that old and seasoned ships have their little crotchets, their little fussinesses that their skippers must learn and humour if they are to get anything out of them; that even the best ships may sulk at times, shirk their work, grow unstable, perverse, and refuse to answer helm and handling. And I will say that some ships that for years have sailed blue water as soberly and as docilely as a street-car horse has plodded the treadmill of the 'tween-tracks, have been known to balk, as stubbornly and as conclusively as any old Bay Billy that ever wore a bell. I know this has happened, because I have seen it. I saw, for instance, the *Glarus* do it.

Quite literally and truly we could do nothing with her. We will say, if you like, that that great jar and wrench when the shaft gave way shook her and crippled her. It is true, however, that whatever the cause may have been, we could not force her towards the island. Of course, we all said 'current;' but why didn't the log-line trail?

For three days and three nights we tried it. And the *Glarus* heaved and plunged and shook herself just as you have seen a horse plunge and rear when his rider tries to force him at the steam-roller.

I tell you I could feel the fabric of her tremble and shudder from bow to stern post, as though she were in a storm; I tell you she fell off from the wind, and broad-on drifted back from her course till the sensation of her shrinking was as plain as her

own staring lights and a thing pitiful to see.

We rowelled her and we crowded sail upon her, and we coaxed and bullied and humoured her, till the Three Crows, their fortune only a plain sail two days ahead, raved and swore like insensate brutes, or shall we say like *mahouts*, trying to drive their stricken elephant upon the tiger – and all to no purpose. "Damn the damned current and the damned luck and the damned shaft and all," Hardenberg would exclaim, as from the wheel he would watch the *Glarus* falling off. "Go on, you old hooker – you tub of junk! My God, you'd think she was scared!"

Perhaps the *Glarus* was scared; that point is debatable. But it was beyond doubt or debate that Hardenberg was scared.

A ship that will not obey is only one degree less terrible than a mutinous crew. And we were in a fair way to have both. The stokers whom we had impressed into duty as A.B.'s, were of course superstitious. They had seen – what we had seen and they knew how the *Glarus* was acting and it was only a question of time before they got out of hand.

That was the end. We held a final conference in the cabin and

decided that there was no help for it – we must turn back.

And back we accordingly turned, and at once the wind followed us, and the 'current' helped us, and the water churned under the forefoot of the *Glarus*, and the wake whitened under her stern, and the log-line ran out from the rail and strained back as the ship worked homewards.

We had never a mishap from the time we finally swung her about; and, considering the circumstances, the voyage back to San Francisco was propitious.

But an incident happened just after we had started back. We were perhaps some five miles on the homeward track. It was early evening and Strokher had the watch. At about seven o'clock he called me up on the bridge. "See her?" he said.

And there, far behind us, in the shadow of the twilight, loomed the other ship again, desolate, lonely beyond words. We were leaving her rapidly astern. Strokher and I stood looking at her till she dwindled to a dot. Then Strokher said: "She's on post again."

And when months afterwards we limped into the Golden Gate and cast anchor off the front, our crew went ashore as soon as discharged, and in half a dozen hours the legend was in every sailors' boarding house and in every seaman's dive, from Barbary Coast to Black Tom's.

It is still there, and that is why no pilot will take the *Glarus* out, no captain will navigate her, no stoker feed her fires, no sailor walk her decks. The *Glarus* is suspect. She will never smell blue water again. She has seen a ghost.

The Picture of Dorian Gray

1890

EXTRACT

Oscar Wilde

For some reason or other, the house was crowded that night, and the fat manager who met them at the door was beaming from ear to ear with an oily tremulous smile. He escorted them to their box with a sort of pompous humility, waving his fat jewelled hands and talking at the top of his voice. Dorian Gray loathed him more than ever. He felt as if he had come to look for Miranda and had been met by Caliban. Lord Henry, upon the other hand, rather liked him. At least he declared he did, and insisted on shaking him by the hand and assuring him that he was proud to meet a man who had discovered a real genius and gone bankrupt over a poet. Hallward amused himself with watching the faces in the pit. The heat was terribly oppressive, and the huge sunlight flamed like a monstrous dahlia with petals of yellow fire. The youths in

the gallery had taken off their coats and waistcoats and hung them over the side. The sound of the popping of corks came from the bar.

"What a place to find one's divinity in!" said Lord Henry.

"Yes!" answered Dorian Gray. "It was here I found her, and she is divine beyond all living things. When she acts, you will forget everything. These common rough people, with their coarse faces and brutal gestures, become quite different when she is on the stage. They sit silently and watch her. They weep and laugh as she wills them to do. She makes them as responsive as a violin. She spiritualizes them, and one feels that they are of the same flesh and blood as one's self."

"The same flesh and blood as one's self! Oh, I hope not!" exclaimed Lord Henry, who was scanning the occupants of the gallery through his opera-glass.

"Don't pay any attention to him, Dorian," said the painter. "I understand what you mean, and I believe in this girl. Anyone you love must be marvellous. If this girl can give a soul to those who have lived without one, if she can create the sense of beauty in people whose lives have been sordid and ugly, if she can strip them of their selfishness and lend them tears for sorrows that are not their own, she is worthy of all your adoration. This marriage is quite right. I did not think so at first, but I admit it now. The gods made Sibyl Vane for you. Without her you would have been incomplete."

"Thanks, Basil," answered Dorian Gray, pressing his hand. "I knew that you would understand me. Harry is so cynical, he terrifies me. But here is the orchestra. It is quite dreadful, but it only lasts for about five minutes. Then the curtain rises, and you will see the girl to whom I am going to give all my life, to whom I have given everything that is good in me."

A quarter of an hour afterwards, amidst an extraordinary turmoil of applause, Sibyl Vane stepped onto the stage. Yes, she was certainly lovely to look at – one of the loveliest creatures, Lord Henry thought, that he had ever seen. There was something of the fawn in her shy grace and startled eyes. A faint blush, like the shadow of a rose in a mirror of silver, came to her cheeks as she glanced at the crowded, enthusiastic house. She stepped back a few paces and her lips seemed to tremble. Basil Hallward leapt to his feet and began to applaud. Lord Henry peered through his glasses, murmuring, "Charming! charming!"

The scene was the hall of Capulet's house, and Romeo in his pilgrim's dress had entered with Mercutio and his other friends. The band, such as it was, struck up a few bars of music, and the dance began. Through the crowd of ungainly, shabbily dressed actors, Sibyl Vane moved like a creature from a finer world. The curves of her throat were the curves of a white lily. Her hands seemed to be made of cool ivory.

Yet she was curiously listless. She showed no sign of joy when her eyes rested on Romeo. The few words she had to speak were spoken in a thoroughly artificial manner. The voice was exquisite, but from the point of view of tone it was absolutely false. It was wrong in colour. It took away all the life from the verse. It made the passion unreal.

Dorian Gray grew pale as he watched her. He was puzzled and anxious. Neither of his friends dared to say anything to him. She seemed to them to be absolutely incompetent. They were horribly disappointed.

Yet they felt that the true test of any Juliet is the balcony scene of the second act. If she failed there, there was nothing in her.

She looked charming as she came out in the moonlight. That could not be denied. But the

staginess of her acting was unbearable, and grew worse as she went on. Her gestures became absurdly artificial. She overemphasized everything that she had to say. The beautiful passage:

> Thou knowest the mask of night is on my face,
> Else would a maiden blush bepaint my cheek
> For that which thou hast heard me speak tonight

was declaimed with the painful precision of a schoolgirl who has been taught to recite by some second-rate professor of elocution. When she leaned over the balcony and came to those wonderful lines:

> Although I joy in thee,
> I have no joy of this contract to-night:
> It is too rash, too unadvised, too sudden;
> Too like the lightning, which doth cease to be
> Ere one can say, "It lightens." Sweet, goodnight!
> This bud of love by summer's ripening breath
> May prove a beauteous flower when next we meet

she spoke the words as though they conveyed no meaning to her. It was not nervousness. Indeed, so far from being nervous, she was absolutely self-contained. It was simply bad art. She was a complete failure.

Even the common uneducated audience of the pit and gallery lost their interest in the play. They got restless, and

began to talk loudly and to whistle. The manager, who was standing at the back of the dress circle, stamped and swore with rage. The only person unmoved was the girl herself.

When the second act was over, there came a storm of hisses, and Lord Henry got up from his chair and put on his coat. "She is quite beautiful, Dorian," he said, "but she can't act. Let us go."

"I am going to see the play through," answered the lad, in a hard bitter voice. "I am awfully sorry that I have made you waste an evening, Harry. I apologize to you both."

"My dear Dorian, I should think Miss Vane was ill," interrupted Hallward. "We will come some other night."

"I wish she were ill," he rejoined. "But she seems to me to be simply callous and cold. She has entirely altered. Last night she was a great artist. This evening she is merely a commonplace mediocre actress."

"Don't talk like that about anyone you love, Dorian. Love is a more wonderful thing than art."

"They are both simply forms of imitation," remarked Lord Henry. "But do let us go. Dorian, you must not stay here any longer. It is not good for one's morals to see bad acting. Besides, I don't suppose you will want your wife to act, so what does it matter if she plays Juliet like a wooden doll? She is very lovely, and if she knows as little about life as she does about acting, she will be a delightful experience. Good heavens, my dear boy, don't look so tragic! The secret of remaining young is never to have an emotion that is

unbecoming. Come to the club with Basil and myself. We will smoke cigarettes and drink to the beauty of Sibyl Vane"

"Go away, Harry," cried the lad. "I want to be alone. Basil, you must go. Ah! Can't you see that my heart is breaking?" The hot tears came to his eyes. His lips trembled, and rushing to the back of the box, he leant up against the wall, hiding his face in his hands.

"Let us go, Basil," said Lord Henry with a strange tenderness in his voice, and the two men passed out together.

A few moments afterwards the footlights flared up and the curtain rose on the third act. Dorian Gray went back to his seat. He looked pale, and proud, and indifferent. The play dragged on. Half of the audience went out, tramping in heavy boots and laughing. The whole thing was a fiasco. The last act was played to almost empty benches. The curtain went down on a titter and some groans.

As soon as it was over, Dorian Gray rushed behind the scenes into the greenroom. The girl was standing there alone, with a look of triumph on her face. There was a radiance about her. Her parted lips were smiling over some secret of their own.

When he entered, she looked at him, and an expression of joy came over her. "How badly I acted tonight," she cried.

"Horribly!" he answered, gazing at her in amazement. "Horribly! It was dreadful. Are you ill? You have no idea what it was. You have no idea what I suffered."

The girl smiled. "Dorian," she answered, lingering over his name with long-drawn music in her voice, as though it were

sweeter than honey to the red petals of her mouth. "Dorian, you should have understood. You understand now, don't you?"

"Understand what?" he asked, angrily.

"Why I was so bad tonight. Why I shall always be bad. Why I shall never act well again."

He shrugged his shoulders. "You are ill, I suppose. When you are ill you shouldn't act. You make yourself ridiculous. My friends were bored. I was bored."

She seemed not to listen to him. She was transfigured with joy. An ecstasy of happiness dominated her.

"Dorian, Dorian," she cried, "before I knew you, acting was the one reality of my life. It was only in the theatre that I lived. I thought that it was all true. I was Rosalind one night and Portia the other. The joy of Beatrice was my joy, and the sorrows of Cordelia were mine also.

I believed in everything. The common people who acted with me seemed to me to be godlike. The painted scenes were my world. I knew nothing but shadows, and I thought them real. You came – oh, my beautiful love! – and you freed my soul from prison. You taught me what reality really is. Tonight, for the first time in my life, I saw through the hollowness, the sham, the silliness of the empty pageant in which I had always played. Tonight, for the first time, I became conscious that the Romeo was hideous and old and painted, that the moonlight in the orchard was false, that the scenery was vulgar, and that the words I had to speak were unreal, were not my words, were not what I wanted to say. You had brought me something higher, something of which all art is but a reflection. You had made me understand what love really is. My love! My love! Prince Charming! Prince of life! I have grown sick of shadows. You are more to me than all art can ever be. What have I to do with the puppets of a play? When I came on to-night, I could not understand how it was that everything had gone from me. I thought that I was going to be wonderful. I found that I could do nothing. Suddenly it dawned on my soul what it all meant. The knowledge was exquisite to me. I heard them hissing, and I smiled. What could they know of love such as ours? Take me away, Dorian – take me away with you, where we can be quite alone. I hate the stage. I might mimic a passion that I do not feel, but I cannot mimic one that burns me like fire. Oh, Dorian, Dorian, you understand now what it signifies? Even if I could do it, it would be profanation for me to play at being in

love. You have made me see that."

He flung himself down on the sofa and turned away his face. "You have killed my love," he muttered.

She looked at him in wonder and laughed. He made no answer. She came across to him, and with her little fingers stroked his hair. She knelt down and pressed his hands to her lips. He drew them away, and a shudder ran through him.

Then he leapt up and went to the door. "Yes," he cried, "you have killed my love. You used to stir my imagination. Now you don't even stir my curiosity. You simply produce no effect. I loved you because you were marvellous, because you had genius and intellect, because you realized the dreams of great poets and gave shape and substance to the shadows of art. You have thrown it all away. You are shallow and stupid. My God! How mad I was to love you! What a fool I have been! You are nothing to me now. I will never see you again. I will never think of you. I will never mention your name. You don't know what you were to me, once. Why, once . . . Oh, I can't bear to think of it! I wish I had never laid eyes upon you! You have spoiled the romance of my life. How little you can know of love, if you say it mars your art! Without your art, you are nothing. I would have made you famous, splendid, magnificent. The world would have worshipped you, and you would have borne my name. What are you now? A third-rate actress with a pretty face."

The girl grew white, and trembled. She clenched her hands together, and her voice seemed to catch in her throat. "You are

not serious, Dorian?" she murmured. "You are acting."

"Acting! I leave that to you. You do it so well," he answered, and there was a heavy and now unmistakable bitterness in his voice.

She rose from her knees and, with a piteous expression of pain in her face, came across the room to him. She put her hand upon his arm and looked into his eyes. He thrust her back. "Don't touch me!" he cried.

A low moan broke from her, and she flung herself at his feet and lay there like a trampled flower. "Dorian, Dorian, don't leave me!" she whispered. "I am so sorry I didn't act well. I was thinking of you all the time. But I will try — indeed, I will try. It came so suddenly across me, my love for you. I think I should never have known it if you had not kissed me — if we had not kissed each other. Kiss me again, my love. Don't go away from me. I couldn't bear it. Oh! don't go away from me. My brother... No; never mind. He didn't mean it. He was in jest... But you, oh! Can't you forgive me for tonight? I will work so hard and try to improve. Don't be cruel to me, because I love you better than anything in the world. After all, it is only once that I have not pleased you. But you are quite right, Dorian. I should have shown myself more of an artist. It was foolish of me, and yet I couldn't help it. Oh, don't leave me, don't leave me." A fit of passionate sobbing choked her. She crouched on the floor like a wounded thing, and Dorian Gray, with his beautiful eyes, looked down at her, and his chiselled lips curled in exquisite disdain. There is always

something ridiculous about the emotions of people whom one has ceased to love. Sibyl Vane seemed to him to be absurdly melodramatic. Her tears and sobs annoyed him.

"I am going," he said at last, in his calm clear voice. "I don't wish to be unkind, but I can't see you again. You have disappointed me."

She wept silently, and made no answer, but crept nearer. Her little hands stretched blindly out, and appeared to be seeking for him. He turned on his heel and left the room. In a few moments he was out of the theatre.

Where he went to he hardly knew. He remembered wandering through dimly lit streets, past gaunt, black-shadowed archways and evil-looking houses. Women with hoarse voices and harsh laughter had called after him. Drunkards had reeled by, cursing and chattering to themselves like monstrous apes. He had seen grotesque children huddled upon door steps, and heard shrieks and oaths from gloomy courts.

As the dawn was just breaking, he found himself close to Covent Garden. The darkness lifted, and, flushed with faint fires, the sky hollowed itself into a perfect pearl. Huge carts filled with nodding lilies rumbled slowly down the polished empty street. The air was heavy with the perfume of the flowers, and their beauty seemed to soothe his pain. He followed into the market and watched the men unloading their waggons. A white-smocked carter offered him some cherries. He thanked him, wondered why he refused to accept any

money for them, and began to eat them listlessly. They had been plucked at midnight, and the coldness of the moon had entered into them. A long line of boys carrying crates of striped tulips, and of yellow and red roses, filed in front of

him, threading their way through the huge, jade-green piles of vegetables. Under the portico, with its grey, sun-bleached pillars, loitered a troop of draggled bare-headed girls, waiting for the auction to be over. Others crowded round the swinging doors of the coffee house in the piazza. The heavy cart-horses slipped and stamped upon the rough stones, shaking their bells and trappings. Some of the drivers were lying asleep on a pile of sacks. Iris-necked and pink-footed, the pigeons ran about picking up seeds.

After a little while, he hailed a hansom and drove home. For a few moments he loitered upon the doorstep, looking round at the silent square, with its blank, close-shuttered windows and its staring blinds. The sky was pure opal now, and the roofs of the houses glistened like silver against it. From some chimney opposite a thin wreath of smoke was rising. It curled, a violet riband, through the nacre-coloured air.

In the huge gilt Venetian lantern, spoil of some Doge's barge, that hung from the ceiling of the great, oak-panelled hall of entrance, lights were still burning from three flickering jets: thin blue petals of flame they seemed, rimmed with white fire. He turned them out and, having thrown his hat and cape on the table, passed through the library towards the door of his bedroom, a large octagonal chamber on the ground floor that, in his new-born feeling for luxury, he had just had decorated for himself and hung with some curious Renaissance tapestries that had been discovered stored in a disused attic at Selby Royal. As he was turning the handle of the door, his eye fell

upon the portrait Basil Hallward had painted of him. He started back as if in surprise. Then he went on into his own room, looking somewhat puzzled. After he had taken the button hole out of his coat, he seemed to hesitate. Finally, he came back, went over to the picture, and examined it. In the dim arrested light that struggled through the cream-coloured silk blinds, the face appeared to him to be a little changed. The expression looked different. One would have said that there was a touch of cruelty in the mouth. It was certainly strange.

He turned round and, walking to the window, drew up the blind. The bright dawn flooded the room and swept the fantastic shadows into dusky corners, where they lay shuddering. But the strange expression that he had noticed in the face of the portrait seemed to linger there, to be more intensified even. The quivering ardent sunlight showed him the lines of cruelty round the mouth as clearly as if he had been looking into a mirror after he had done some dreadful thing.

He winced and, taking up from the table an oval glass framed in ivory Cupids – one of Lord Henry's many presents to him – glanced hurriedly into its polished depths. No line like that warped his red lips. What did it mean?

He rubbed his eyes, and came close to the picture, and examined it again. There were no signs of any change when he looked into the actual painting, and yet there was no doubt that the whole expression had altered. It was not a mere fancy of his own. The thing was horribly apparent.

He threw himself into a chair and began to think. Suddenly

there flashed across his mind what he had said in Basil Hallward's studio the day the picture had been finished. Yes, he remembered it perfectly. He had uttered a mad wish that he himself might remain young, and the portrait grow old; that his own beauty might be untarnished, and the face on the canvas bear the burden of his passions and his sins; that the painted image might be seared with the lines of suffering and thought, and that he might keep all the delicate bloom and loveliness of his then just conscious boyhood. Surely his wish had not been fulfilled? Such things were impossible. It seemed monstrous even to think of them. And, yet, there was the picture before him, with the touch of cruelty in the mouth that had not been there before.

Cruelty! Had he been cruel? It was the girl's fault, not his. He had dreamed of her as a great artist, had given his love to her because he had thought her great. Then she had disappointed him. She had been shallow and unworthy. And, yet, a feeling of infinite regret came over him, as he thought of her lying at his feet sobbing like a little child. He remembered with what callousness he had watched her. Why had he been made like that? Why had such a soul been given to him? But he had suffered also. During the three terrible hours that the play had lasted, he had lived centuries of pain, aeon upon aeon of torture. His life was well worth hers. She had marred him for a moment, if he had wounded her for an age. Besides, women were better suited to bear sorrow than men. They lived on their emotions. They only thought of their emotions. When

they took lovers, it was merely to have someone with whom they could have scenes. Lord Henry had told him that, and Lord Henry knew what women were. Why should he trouble about Sibyl Vane? She was nothing to him now.

But the picture? What was he to say of that? It held the

secret of his life, and told his story. It had taught him to love his own beauty. Would it teach him to loathe his own soul? Would he ever look at it again?

No; it was merely an illusion wrought on the troubled senses. The horrible night that he had passed had left phantoms behind it. Yet it was watching him, with its beautiful marred face and its cruel smile. Its bright hair gleamed in the early sunlight. Its blue eyes met his own. A sense of infinite pity, not for himself, but for the painted image of himself, came over him. It had altered already, and would alter more. Its gold would wither into grey. Its red and white roses would die. For every sin that he committed, a stain would fleck and wreck its fairness. But he would not sin again. The picture, changed or unchanged, would be to him the visible emblem of conscience. He would resist temptation. He would not see Lord Henry any more – would not, at any rate, listen to those subtle poisonous theories that in Basil Hallward's garden had first stirred within him the passion for impossible things. He would go back to Sibyl Vane, try to make her amends, marry her if she would have him, and try to love her again. Yes, it was his duty to do so. She must have suffered far more than he had. The poor child! He had been selfish and cruel to her. The fascination that she had once exercised over him would return.

He got up from his chair and drew a large screen right in front of the portrait, shuddering as he glanced at it. "How horrible!" he murmured to himself, and he walked across to the window and opened it.

When he stepped out onto the grass, he drew a long, deep breath. He could think only of Sibyl. A faint echo of his love had begun to come back to him. He repeated her name over and over again. The birds that were singing in the dew-drenched garden seemed to be telling the flowers about her.

It was long past noon when he awoke. His valet had crept several times on tiptoe into the room to see if he was stirring, and had wondered what made his young master sleep so late. Finally his bell sounded, and Victor came in softly with a cup of tea, and a pile of letters, on a small tray, and drew back the olive-satin curtains, with their shimmering blue lining, that hung in front of the three tall windows.

"*Monsieur* has slept well this morning," he said, smiling.

"What o'clock is it, Victor?" asked Dorian Gray drowsily.

"One hour and a quarter, *monsieur*."

How late it was! He sat up, and having sipped some tea, turned over his letters. One of them was from Lord Henry, and had been brought by hand that morning. He hesitated for a moment, and then put it aside. The others he opened listlessly. They contained the usual collection of cards, invitations to dinner, tickets for private views, programmes of charity concerts, and the like that are showered on fashionable young men every morning during the season.

After about ten minutes he got up, and throwing on an elaborate dressing-gown of silk-embroidered cashmere wool, passed into the onyx-paved bathroom. The cool water

refreshed him after his long sleep. He seemed to have forgotten all that he had gone through. A dim sense of having taken part in some strange tragedy came to him once or twice, but there was the unreality of a dream about it.

As soon as he was dressed, he went into the library and sat down to a light French breakfast that had been laid out for him on a small round table close to the open window. It was an exquisite day. The warm air seemed laden with spices. A bee flew in and buzzed round the blue-dragon bowl that, filled with roses, stood before him.

Suddenly his eye fell on the screen that he had placed in front of the portrait, and he started.

"Too cold for *monsieur?*" asked his valet, putting an omelette on the table. "I shut the window?"

Dorian shook his head. "I am not cold," he murmured.

Was it all true? Had the portrait really changed? Or had it been simply his own imagination that had made him see a look of evil where there had been a look of joy? The thing was absurd. It would serve as a tale to tell Basil some day. It would make him smile.

And, yet, how vivid was his recollection of the whole thing! First in the dim twilight, and then in the bright dawn, he had seen the touch of cruelty round the warped lips. He almost dreaded his valet leaving the room. He knew that when he was alone he would have to examine the portrait. He was afraid of certainty. As the door was closing behind him, he called him back. The man stood waiting for his orders. Dorian looked at

him for a moment. "I am not at home to anyone, Victor," he said with a sigh. The man bowed and retired.

Then he rose from the table, lit a cigarette, and flung himself down on a luxuriously cushioned couch that stood facing the screen. The screen was an old one, of gilt Spanish leather, stamped and wrought with a rather florid Louis-Quatorze pattern. He scanned it curiously, wondering if ever before it had concealed the secret of a man's life.

Should he move it aside, after all? Why not let it stay there? What was the use of knowing? If the thing was true, it was terrible. If it was not true, why trouble about it? But what if, by some fate or deadlier chance, eyes other than his spied behind and saw the horrible change? What should he do if Basil Hallward came and asked to look at his own picture? Basil would be sure to do that. No; the thing had to be examined. Anything would be better than this dreadful state of doubt.

He got up and locked both doors. At least he would be alone when he looked upon the mask of his shame. Then he drew the screen aside and saw himself face to face. It was perfectly true, no one could deny the fact that the potrait had altered.

As he often remembered afterwards, and always with no small wonder, he found himself at first gazing at the portrait with a feeling of almost scientific interest. That such a change should have taken place was incredible to him. And yet it was a fact. Was there some subtle affinity between the chemical atoms that shaped themselves into form and colour on the canvas and the soul that was within him? Could it be that what

that soul thought, they realized? That what it dreamed, they made true? Or was there some other, more terrible reason? He shuddered, and felt afraid, and, going back to the couch, lay there, gazing at the picture in sickened horror.

One thing, however, he felt that it had done for him. It had made him conscious how unjust, how cruel, he had been to Sibyl Vane. It was not too late to make reparation for that. She could still be his wife. His unreal and selfish love would yield to some higher influence, would be transformed into some nobler passion, and the portrait that Basil Hallward had painted of him would be a guide to him through life, would be to him what holiness is to some, and conscience to others. There were opiates for remorse, drugs that could lull the moral sense to sleep. But here was a visible symbol of the degradation of sin.

Three o'clock struck, and four, and the half-hour rang its double chime, but still Dorian Gray did not stir. He did not know what to do, or what to think. Finally, he went over to the table and wrote a passionate letter to the girl he had loved, imploring her forgiveness and accusing himself of madness. He covered page after page with wild words of sorrow and wilder words of pain. There is a luxury in self-reproach. When we blame ourselves, we feel that no one else has a right to blame us. It is the confession, not the priest, that gives us absolution. When Dorian had finished the letter, he felt comforted and that he had been forgiven.

Suddenly there came a knock to the door, and he heard

Lord Henry's voice outside. "My dear boy, I must see you."

He made no answer at first. The knocking still continued. Yes, it was better to let Lord Henry in, and to explain to him the new life he was going to lead. He would be firm and not listen to his friend's talk, he would explain his new plan to him and make him understand. Dorian jumped up, drew the screen across the picture, and unlocked the door.

"I am so sorry for it all, Dorian," said Lord Henry as he entered. "But you must not think too much about it."

"Do you mean about Sibyl Vane?" asked the lad.

"Yes, of course," answered Lord Henry, sinking into a chair, "It is dreadful, from one point of view, but it was not your fault. Did you go behind and see her, after the play was over?"

"Yes."

"I felt sure you had. Did you make a scene with her?"

"I was brutal. But it is all right now. I am not sorry for anything that has happened. It has taught me to know better."

"Ah, Dorian, I am so glad you take it in that way!"

"I am perfectly happy now." Said Dorian, "I know what conscience is, to begin with. It is not what you told me it was. It is the divinest thing in us. Don't sneer Harry, I want to be good. I can't bear the idea of my soul being hideous."

"A very charming artistic basis for ethics, Dorian! I congratulate you on it. But how are you going to begin?"

"By marrying Sibyl Vane."

"Marrying Sibyl Vane!" cried Lord Henry, standing up and looking at him in perplexed amazement. "But, my dear

Dorian—"

"Yes, Henry, I know what you are going to say. Something dreadful about marriage. I am not going to break my word. She is to be my wife."

"Your wife! Dorian! Didn't you get my letter?"

"Your letter? Oh, yes, I have not read it yet, Henry. I was afraid there might be something in it that I wouldn't like. It is over there if you wish to read it to me now."

"You know nothing then?"

"What do you mean?"

Lord Henry walked across the room, and sitting down by Dorian Gray, took both his hands in his own and held them tightly. "Dorian," he said, "my letter – don't be frightened – was to tell you that Sibyl Vane is dead."

Ghosts that have Haunted Me

1898

EXTRACT

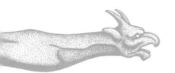

J K Bangs

It happened last Christmas, in my own home. I had provided as a little surprise for my wife a complete new solid silver service marked with her initials. The tree had been prepared for the children, and all had retired save myself. I had lingered later than the others to put the silver service under the tree, where its happy recipient would find it when she went

to the tree with the little ones the
next morning. It made a magnificent
display: the two dozen of each kind of
spoon, the forks, the knives, the coffee pot,
water urn, and all; the salvers, the vegetable dishes,
olive forks, cheese scoops, and other dazzling attributes
of a complete service, not to go into details, presented a
fairly scintillating picture which would have made me gasp if I
had not, at the moment when my own breath began to catch,
heard another gasp in the corner immediately behind me.
Turning about quickly to see whence it came, I observed a
dark figure in the pale light of the moon which streamed in
through the window.

"Who are you?" I cried, starting back, the
physical symptoms of a ghostly presence
manifesting themselves as usual.

"I am the ghost of one long gone before,"
was the reply, in sepulchral tones.

I breathed a sigh of relief,
for I had for a moment feared
it was a burglar.

"Oh!" I said. "You gave me
a start at first. I was afraid you
were a material thing come to
rob me." Then turning towards
the tree, I observed, with a wave
of the hand, "Fine layout, eh?"

"Beautiful," he said, hollowly. "Yet not so beautiful as things I've seen in realms beyond your ken."

And then he set about telling me of the beautiful gold and silverware they used in the Elysian Fields, and I must confess Monte Cristo would have had a hard time, with Sinbad the Sailor to help, to surpass the picture of royal magnificence the spectre drew. I stood enthralled until, even as he was talking, the clock struck three, when he rose up, and moving slowly across the floor, barely visible, murmured regretfully that he must be off, with which he faded away down the back stairs. I pulled my nerves, which were getting rather strained, together again, and went to bed.

Next morning, every bit of that silverware was gone; and, what is more, three weeks later I found the ghost's picture in the Rogue's Gallery in New York as that of the cleverest sneak-thief in the country.

All of which, let me say to you, dear reader, in conclusion, proves that when you are dealing with ghosts you mustn't give up all your physical resources until you have definitely ascertained that the thing by which you are confronted, horrid or otherwise, is a ghost, and not an all too material rogue with a light step, and a commodious jute bag for plunder concealed beneath his coat.

"How to tell a ghost?" you ask.

Well, as an eminent master of fiction frequently observes in his writings, that is another story, which I shall hope some day to tell for your instruction and my own aggrandisement.

Cursed Creatures

There are many things other than ghosts that go bump in the night. Here are tales of vampires and mummies, nameless monsters and phantom beasts, evil alter-egoes and scraps of corpses brought back to life. Welcome to the world of the undead...

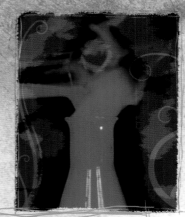

Dracula

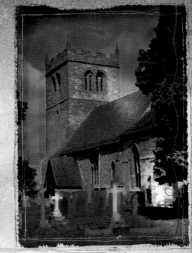

Man-Size in Marble

The Hound of the Baskervilles

Some Words with a Mummy

Carmilla

The Strange Case of Dr Jekyll and Mr Hyde

1886

EXTRACT

Robert Louis Stevenson

Twelve o'clock had scarce rung out over London, ere the knocker sounded very gently on the door. I went myself at the summons, and found a small man crouching against the pillars of the portico.

"Are you come from Dr Jekyll?" I asked.

He told me 'yes' by a constrained gesture, and when I had bidden him enter, he did not obey me without a searching backward glance into the darkness of the square. There was a policeman not far off, advancing with his bull's eye open; and at the sight, I thought my visitor started and made greater haste.

These particulars struck me, I confess, disagreeably; and as I followed him into the bright light of the consulting room, I kept my hand ready on my weapon. Here, at last, I had a

chance of clearly seeing him. I had never set eyes on him before, so much was certain. He was small, as I have said; I was struck besides with the shocking expression of his face, with his remarkable combination of great muscular activity and great apparent debility of constitution, and – last but not least – with the odd, subjective disturbance caused by his neighbourhood. This bore some resemblance to incipient rigour, and was accompanied by a marked sinking of the pulse. At the time, I set it down to some idiosyncratic, personal distaste, and merely wondered at the acuteness of the symptoms; but I have since had reason to believe the cause to lie much deeper in the nature of man, and to turn on some nobler hinge than the principle of hatred.

This person (who had thus, from the first moment of his entrance, struck in me what I can only describe as a disgustful curiosity) was dressed in a fashion that would have made an ordinary person laughable. His clothes, that is to say, although they were of rich and sober fabric, were enormously too large for him in every measurement – the trousers hanging on his legs and rolled up to keep them from the ground, the waist of the coat below his haunches and the collar sprawling wide upon his shoulders. Strange to relate, this ludicrous accoutrement was far from moving me to laughter. Rather, as there was something abnormal and misbegotten in the very essence of the creature that now faced me – something seizing, surprising and revolting – this fresh disparity seemed but to fit in with and to reinforce it, so that to my interest in the man's

nature and character there was added a curiosity as to his origin, his life, his fortune and status in the world.

These observations, though they have taken so great a space to be set down in, were yet the work of a few seconds. My visitor was, indeed, on fire with sombre excitement.

"Have you got it?" he cried. "Have you got it?" And so lively was his impatience that he even laid his hand upon my arm and sought to shake me.

I put him back, conscious at his touch of a certain icy pang along my blood. "Come, sir," said I. "You forget that I have not yet the pleasure of your acquaintance. Be seated, if you please." And I showed him an example, and sat down myself in my customary seat and with as fair an imitation of my ordinary manner to a patient, as the lateness of the hour, the nature of my preoccupations, and the horror I had of my visitor, would suffer me to muster.

"I beg your pardon, Dr Lanyon," he replied civilly enough. "What you say is very well founded and my impatience has shown its heels to my politeness. I come here at the instance of your colleague, Dr Henry Jekyll, on a piece of business of some moment, and I understood…" He paused and put his hand to his throat, and I could see, in spite of his collected manner, that he was wrestling against the approaches of the hysteria. " – I understood, a drawer…"

But here I took pity on my visitor's suspense, and some perhaps on my own growing curiosity.

"There it is, sir," said I, pointing to the drawer, where it lay

on the floor behind a table and still covered with the sheet.

He sprang to it, and then paused, and laid his hand upon his heart – I could hear his teeth grate with the convulsive action of his jaws – and his face was so ghastly to see that I grew alarmed both for his life and reason.

"Compose yourself," said I.

He turned a dreadful smile to me, and as if with the decision of despair, plucked away the sheet. At sight of the contents, he uttered one loud sob of such immense relief that I sat petrified. And the next moment, in a voice that was already fairly well under control, "Have you a graduated glass?" he asked.

I rose from my place with something of an effort and gave him what he asked.

He thanked me with a smiling nod, measured out a few minims of the red tincture and added one of the powders. The mixture, which was at first of a reddish hue, began, in proportion as the crystals melted, to brighten in colour, to effervesce audibly, and to throw off small fumes of vapour. Suddenly and at the same moment, the boiling ceased and the compound

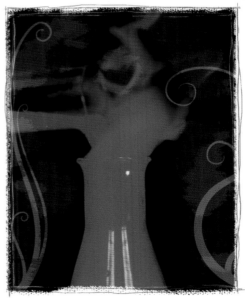

changed to a dark purple, which faded again more slowly to a watery green. My visitor, who had watched these metamorphoses with a keen eye, smiled, set down the glass upon the table, and then turned and looked upon me with an air of scrutiny.

"And now," said he, "to settle what remains. Will you be wise? Will you be guided? Will you suffer me to take this glass in my hand and to go forth from your house without further parley? Or has the greed of curiosity too much command of you? Think before you answer, for it shall be done as you decide. As you decide, you shall be left as you were before, and neither richer nor wiser, unless the sense of service rendered to a man in mortal distress may be counted as a kind of riches of the soul. Or, if you shall so prefer to choose, a new province of knowledge and new avenues to fame and power shall be laid open to you, here, in this room, upon the instant; and your sight shall be blasted by a prodigy to stagger the unbelief of Satan."

"Sir," said I, affecting a coolness that I was far from truly possessing, "you speak enigmas, and you will perhaps not wonder that I hear you with no very strong impression of belief. But I have gone too far in the way of inexplicable services to pause before I see the end."

"It is well," replied my visitor. "Lanyon, you remember your vows: what follows is under the seal of our profession. And now, you who have so long been bound to the most narrow and material views, you who have denied the virtue of

transcendental medicine, you who have derided your superiors – behold!"

He put the glass to his lips and drank at one gulp. A cry followed; he reeled, staggered, clutched at the table and held on, staring with injected eyes, gasping with open mouth; and as I looked there came, I thought, a change – he seemed to swell, his face became suddenly black and the features seemed to melt and alter – and the next moment, I had sprung to my feet and leapt back against the wall, my arm raised to shield me from that prodigy, my mind submerged in terror.

"O God!" I screamed, and "O God!" again and again; for there before my eyes – pale and shaken, and half-fainting, and groping before him with his hands, like a man restored from death – there stood Henry Jekyll!

What he told me in the next hour, I cannot bring my mind to set on paper. I saw what I saw, I heard what I heard, and my soul sickened at it – and yet now when that sight has faded from my eyes, I ask myself if I believe it and I cannot answer. My life is shaken to its roots. Sleep has left me; the deadliest terror sits by me at all hours; I feel that my days are numbered, and that I must die; and yet I shall die incredulous.

What was It?

1907

EXTRACT

Fitz-James O'Brien

It was the tenth of July. After dinner was over I repaired with my friend, Dr Hammond, to the garden to smoke my evening pipe. The Doctor and myself found ourselves in an unusually metaphysical mood. We lit our large meerschaums, filled with fine Turkish tobacco; we paced to and fro, conversing. A strange perversity dominated the currents of our thought. They would *not* flow through the sunlit channels into which we strove to divert them. For some unaccountable reason they constantly diverged into dark and lonesome beds, where a continual gloom brooded. It was in vain that, after our old fashion, we flung ourselves on the shores of the East, and talked of its gay bazaars, of the splendours of the time of Haroun, of harems and golden palaces. Black genies continually arose from the depths of our talk, and expanded, like the one the fisherman released from the copper vessel,

until they blotted everything bright from our vision. Insensibly, we yielded to the occult force that swayed us, and indulged in gloomy speculation. We had talked some time upon the proneness of the human mind to mysticism, and the almost universal love of the Terrible, when Hammond suddenly said to me, "What do you consider to be the greatest element of terror?"

The question, I own, puzzled me. That many things were terrible, I knew. Stumbling over a corpse in the dark; beholding, as I once did, a woman floating down a deep and rapid river, with wildly lifted arms and awful upturned face, uttering as she sank, shrieks that rent one's heart, while we, the spectators, stood frozen at a window which overhung the river at a height of sixty feet, unable to make the slightest effort to save her, but dumbly watching her last supreme agony and her disappearance. A shattered wreck, with no life visible, encountered floating listlessly on the ocean, is a terrible object, for it suggests a huge terror, the proportions of which are veiled. But it now struck me for the first time that there must be one great and ruling embodiment of fear – a 'king of terrors' to which all others must succumb. What might it be? To what train of circumstances would it owe its existence?

"I confess, Hammond," I replied to my friend, "I never considered the subject before. That there must be something more terrible than any other thing, I feel. I cannot attempt, however, even the most vague definition."

"I am somewhat like you, Harry," he answered. "I feel my

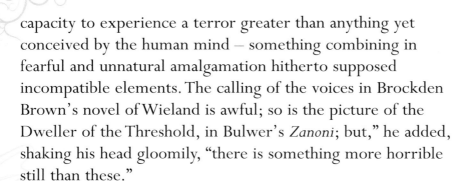

capacity to experience a terror greater than anything yet conceived by the human mind – something combining in fearful and unnatural amalgamation hitherto supposed incompatible elements. The calling of the voices in Brockden Brown's novel of Wieland is awful; so is the picture of the Dweller of the Threshold, in Bulwer's *Zanoni*; but," he added, shaking his head gloomily, "there is something more horrible still than these."

"Look here, Hammond," I rejoined, "let us drop this kind of talk, for heaven's sake!"

"I don't know what's the matter with me tonight," he replied, "but my brain is running upon all sorts of weird and awful thoughts. I feel as if I could write a story like Hoffman tonight, if I were only master of a literary style."

"Well, if we are going to be Hoffmanesque in our talk, I'm off to bed. How sultry it is! Goodnight, Hammond."

"Goodnight, Harry. Pleasant dreams to you."

"To you, gloomy wretch, genies, ghouls, and enchanters."

We parted, and each sought his respective chamber. I undressed quickly and got into bed, taking with me, according to my usual custom, a book, over which I generally read myself to sleep. I opened the volume as soon as I had laid my head upon the pillow, and instantly flung it to the other side of the room. It was Goudon's *History of Monsters* – a curious French work which I had lately imported from Paris, but which, in the state of mind I had then reached, was anything but an agreeable companion. I resolved to go to sleep at once so,

turning down my gas until nothing but a little blue point of light glimmered on the top of the tube, I composed myself to rest.

The room was in total darkness. The atom of gas that still remained lighted did not illuminate a distance of three inches round the burner. I desperately drew my arm across my eyes as if to shut out even the darkness, and tried to think of nothing. It was in vain. The confounded themes touched on by Hammond in the garden kept obtruding themselves on my brain. I battled against them. I erected ramparts of would-be blankness of intellect to keep them out. They still crowded upon me. While I was lying still as a corpse, hoping that by a perfect physical inaction I should hasten mental repose, an awful incident occurred. Something dropped, as it seemed, from the ceiling, plumb upon my chest, and I felt two bony hands encircling my throat, endeavouring to choke me.

I am no coward, and am possessed of considerable physical strength. The suddenness of the attack, instead of stunning me, strung every nerve to its highest tension. My body acted from instinct, before my brain had time to realize the terrors of my position. In an instant I wound two muscular arms around the creature and squeezed it, with all the strength of despair, against my chest. In a few seconds the bony hands that had fastened on my throat loosened their hold, and I was free to breathe once more. Then commenced a struggle of awful intensity. Immersed in the most profound darkness, totally ignorant of the nature of the thing by which I was so suddenly attacked, finding my grasp slipping every moment – by reason, it seemed to me, of the entire nakedness of my assailant – bitten with sharp teeth in the shoulder, neck and chest, having every moment to protect my throat against a pair of sinewy, agile hands, which my utmost efforts could not confine – these were a combination of circumstances to combat which required all the strength and skill and courage that I possessed.

At last, after a silent, deadly, exhausting struggle, I got my assailant under by a series of incredible efforts of strength. Once pinned, with my knee on what I made out to be its chest, I knew that I was victor. I rested for a moment to breathe. I heard the creature beneath me panting in the darkness, and felt the violent throbbing of a heart. It was apparently as exhausted as I was – that was one comfort. At this moment I remembered that I usually placed under my pillow, before going to bed, a large yellow silk pocket handkerchief, for use during the night. I felt for it instantly; it was there. In a few seconds more I had, after a fashion, pinioned the creature's arms.

I now felt tolerably secure. There was nothing more to be

done but to turn on the gas and, having first seen what my midnight assailant was like, arouse the household. I will confess to being actuated by a certain pride in not giving the alarm before; I wished to make the capture alone and unaided.

Never losing my hold for an instant, I slipped from the bed to the floor, dragging my captive with me. I had but a few steps to make to reach the gas-burner and these I made with the greatest caution, holding the creature in a grip like a vice. At last I got within arm's length of the tiny speck of blue light which told me where the gas-burner lay. Quick as lightning I released my grasp with one hand and let on the full flood of light. Then I turned to look at my captive.

I cannot even attempt to give any definition of my sensations the instant after I turned on the gas. I suppose I must have shrieked with terror, for in less than a minute afterward my room was crowded with the inmates of the house. I shudder now as I think of that awful moment. *I saw nothing!* I had one arm firmly clasped round a breathing, panting, corporeal shape, my other hand gripped with all its strength a throat as warm, and apparently fleshly, as my own; and yet, with this living substance in my grasp, with its body pressed against my own, and all in the bright glare of a large jet of gas, I absolutely beheld nothing! Not even an outline – a vapour!

I do not, even at this hour, realize the situation in which I found myself. I cannot recall the astounding incident thoroughly. Imagination in vain tries to compass the awful paradox.

It breathed. I felt its warm breath upon my cheek. It struggled fiercely. It had hands. They clutched me. Its skin was smooth, like my own. There it lay, pressed close up against me, solid as stone – and yet utterly invisible!

I wonder that I did not faint or go mad on the instant. Some wonderful instinct must have sustained me; for, absolutely, in place of loosening my hold on the terrible Enigma, I seemed to gain an additional strength in my moment of horror, and tightened my grasp with such wonderful force that I felt the creature shivering with agony.

Just then Hammond entered my room at the head of the household. As soon as he beheld my face – which, I suppose, must have been an awful sight to look at – he hastened forward, crying, "Great heaven, Harry! What has happened?"

"Hammond! Hammond!" I cried, "Come here. Oh! This is awful! I have been attacked in bed by something or other, which I have hold of; but I can't see it – I can't see it!"

Hammond, doubtless struck by the unfeigned horror expressed in my countenance, made one or two steps forward with an anxious yet puzzled expression. A very audible titter burst from the remainder of my visitors. This suppressed laughter made me furious. To laugh at a human being in my position! It was the worst species of cruelty. Now, I can understand why the appearance of a man struggling violently, as it would seem, with an airy nothing, and calling for assistance against a vision, should have appeared ludicrous. *Then*, so great was my rage against the mocking crowd that had

I the power I would have stricken them dead where they stood.

"Hammond! Hammond!" I cried again, despairingly. "For God's sake come to me. I can hold the – the Thing but a short while longer. It is overpowering me. Help me! Help me!"

"Harry," whispered Hammond, approaching me, "stop fooling about."

"I swear to you, Hammond, that this is no joke," I answered, in the same low tone. "Don't you see how it shakes my whole frame with its struggles? If you don't believe me, convince yourself. Feel it – touch it."

Hammond advanced and laid his hand on the spot I indicated. A wild cry of horror burst from him. He had felt it!

In a moment he had discovered somewhere in my room a long piece of cord, and was the next instant winding it and knotting it about the body of the unseen being that I clasped in my arms.

"Harry," he said, in a hoarse, agitated voice, for, though he preserved his presence of mind, he was deeply moved, "Harry, it's all safe now. You may let go, old fellow, if you're tired. The Thing can't move."

I was utterly exhausted, and I gladly loosed my hold.

Hammond stood holding the ends of the cord that bound the invisible thing, twisted round his hand, while before him, self-supporting as it were, he beheld a rope laced and interlaced, and stretching tightly round a vacant space. I never saw a man look so thoroughly

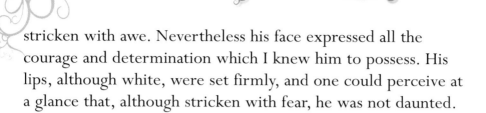

stricken with awe. Nevertheless his face expressed all the courage and determination which I knew him to possess. His lips, although white, were set firmly, and one could perceive at a glance that, although stricken with fear, he was not daunted.

The confusion that ensued among the guests of the house who were witnesses of this extraordinary scene between Hammond and myself – who beheld the pantomime of binding this struggling something – who beheld me almost sinking from physical exhaustion when my task of jailer was over – the confusion and terror that took possession of the bystanders, when they saw all this, was beyond description. The weaker ones fled from the apartment. The few who remained clustered near the door. Still incredulity broke out through their terror. They had not the courage to satisfy themselves, and yet they doubted. They were incredulous. How could a solid, breathing body be invisible, they asked. My reply was this. I gave a sign to Hammond, and both of us – conquering our fearful repugnance to touch the invisible creature – lifted it from the ground, manacled as it was, and took it to my bed.

"Now, my friends," I said, as Hammond and myself held the creature suspended over the bed, "I can give you self-evident proof that here is a solid, ponderable body which, nevertheless, you cannot see. Be good enough to watch the surface of the bed attentively."

I was astonished at my own courage in treating this strange event so calmly; but I had recovered from my first terror, and felt a sort of scientific pride in the affair which dominated

every other feeling.

The eyes of the bystanders were immediately fixed on my bed. At a given signal Hammond and I let the creature fall. There was the dull sound of a heavy body alighting on a soft mass. The timbers of the bed creaked. A deep impression marked itself distinctly on the pillow, and on the bed itself. The crowd who witnessed this gave a low, universal cry and rushed from the room. Hammond and I were left alone.

We remained silent for some time, listening to the low, irregular breathing of the creature on the bed, and watching the rustle of the bedclothes as it impotently struggled to free itself from confinement. Then Hammond spoke.

"Harry, this is awful."

"Aye, awful."

"But not unaccountable."

"Not unaccountable! What do you mean? Such a thing has never occurred since the birth of the world. God grant that I am not mad, and that this is not an insane fantasy!"

"Let us reason a little, Harry. Here is a solid body which we touch, but which we cannot see. The fact is so unusual that it strikes us with terror. Is there no parallel, though, for such a phenomenon? Take a piece of pure glass. It is tangible and transparent. A certain chemical coarseness is all that prevents its being so entirely transparent as to be totally invisible. It is not *theoretically impossible* to make a glass which shall not reflect a single ray of light — a glass so pure and homogeneous in its atoms that the rays from the sun shall pass through it. We do

not see the air, and yet we feel it."

"That's all very well Hammond, but these are inanimate substances. Glass does not breathe, air does not breathe. *This* thing has a heart that palpitates – a will that moves it."

"You forget the strange phenomena of which we have so often heard of late," answered the Doctor, gravely. "At the meetings called 'spirit circles,' invisible hands have been thrust into the hands of those persons round the table – warm, fleshly hands that seemed to pulsate with mortal life."

"What? Do you think, then, that this thing is——"

"I don't know what it is," was the solemn reply.

We watched together, smoking many pipes, all night long, by the bedside of the unearthly being that tossed and panted until it was apparently wearied out. Then we learned by the low, regular breathing that it slept.

The next morning the house was all astir. The boarders congregated on the landing outside my room, and Hammond and myself were lions. We had to answer many questions as to the state of our strange prisoner, for as yet not one person except ourselves could be induced to set foot in the apartment.

The creature was awake. This was evidenced by the convulsive manner in which the bedclothes were moved in its efforts to escape.

Hammond and myself had racked our brains during the long night to discover some means by which we might realize

the shape and general appearance of the Enigma. As well as we could make out by passing our hands over the creature's form, its outlines and lineaments were human. There was a mouth; a round, smooth head without hair; a nose, which, however, was little elevated above the cheeks; and its hands and feet felt like those of a boy. At first we thought of placing the being on a smooth surface and tracing its outline with chalk, as shoemakers trace the outline of the foot. This plan was given up as being of no value. Such an outline would give not the slightest idea of its conformation.

A happy thought struck me. We would take a cast of it in plaster of Paris. This would give us the solid figure, and satisfy all our wishes. But how to do it? The movements of the creature would disturb the setting of the plastic covering, and distort the mould. Another thought: why not give it chloroform? It had respiratory organs – that was evident by its breathing. Once reduced to a state of insensibility, we could do with it what we would. Dr X— was sent for; and after the worthy physician had recovered from the first shock of amazement, he proceeded to administer the chloroform. In three minutes afterward we were enabled to remove the fetters from the creature's body, and a well-known modeller of this city was busily engaged in covering the invisible form with the moist clay. In five minutes more we had a mould, and before evening a rough facsimile of the mystery. It was shaped like a man – distorted and horrible, but still a man. It was small, not over four feet in height, and its limbs revealed a

muscular development that was unparalleled. Its face surpassed in hideousness anything I had ever seen. Gustave Doré, or Callot, or Tony Johannot, never conceived anything so horrible. There is a face in one of the latter's illustrations to *Un Voyage où il vous plaira*, which somewhat approaches the countenance of this creature, but does not equal it. It was the physiognomy of what I should have fancied a ghoul to be. It looked as if it was capable of feeding on human flesh.

Having satisfied our curiosity, and bound everyone in the house to secrecy, it became a question what was to be done with our enigma. It was impossible that we should keep such a horror in our house. It was equally impossible that such an awful being should be let loose upon the world. I confess that I would have gladly voted for the creature's destruction. But who would shoulder the responsibility? Day after day this question was deliberated gravely.

The boarders all left the house. Mrs Moffat was in despair,

and threatened Hammond and myself with all sorts of legal penalties if we did not remove the horror. Our answer was, 'We will go if you like, but we decline taking this creature with us. It appeared in your house. On you the responsibility rests.' To this there was, of course, no answer.

The most singular part of the transaction was that we were entirely ignorant of what the creature habitually fed on. Everything in the way of nutriment that we could think of was placed before it, but was never touched. It was awful to stand by, day after day, and see the clothes toss, and hear the hard breathing, and know that it was starving.

Ten, twelve days, a fortnight passed, and it still lived. The pulsations of the heart, however, were daily growing fainter, and had now nearly ceased altogether. It was evident that the creature was dying for want of sustenance. I could not sleep of nights. Horrible as the creature was, it was pitiful to think of the pangs it was suffering.

At last it died. Hammond and I found it cold and stiff one morning in the bed. The heart had ceased to beat, the lungs to inspire. We hastened to bury it in the garden. It was a strange funeral, the dropping of that viewless corpse into the damp hole. The cast of its form I gave to Dr X——, who keeps it in his museum in Tenth Street.

As I am on the eve of a long journey from which I may not return, I have drawn up this narrative of an event the most singular that has ever come to my knowledge.

Frankenstein

1818

EXTRACT

Mary Shelley

Darkness had no effect upon my fancy, and a churchyard was to me merely the receptacle of bodies deprived of life, which, from being the seat of beauty and strength, had become food for the worm. Now I was led to examine the cause and progress of this decay and forced to spend days and nights in vaults and charnel-houses. My attention was fixed upon every object the most insupportable to the delicacy of the human feelings. I saw how the fine form of man was degraded and wasted; I beheld the corruption of death succeed to the blooming cheek of life; I saw how the worm inherited the wonders of the eye and brain. I paused, examining and analysing all the minutiae of causation, as exemplified in the change from life to death, and death to life, until from the midst of this darkness a sudden light broke in

upon me – a light so brilliant and wondrous, yet so simple, that while I became dizzy with the immensity of the prospect which it illustrated, I was surprised that among so many men of genius who had directed their inquiries towards the same science, that I alone should be reserved to discover so astonishing a secret.

It was on a dreary night of November that I beheld the accomplishment of my toils. With an anxiety that almost amounted to agony, I collected the instruments of life around me, that I might infuse a spark of being into the lifeless thing that lay at my feet. It was already one in the morning. The rain pattered dismally against the panes and my candle was nearly burnt out when, by the glimmer of the half-extinguished light, I saw the dull yellow eye of the creature open. It breathed hard, and a convulsive motion agitated its limbs.

How can I describe my emotions at this catastrophe, or how delineate the wretch whom with such infinite pains and care I had endeavoured to form? His limbs were in proportion, and I had selected his features as beautiful. Beautiful! Great God! His yellow skin scarcely covered the work of muscles and arteries beneath; his hair was of a lustrous black, and flowing; his teeth of a pearly whiteness; but these luxuriances only formed a more horrid contrast with his watery eyes, that seemed almost of the same colour as the dun white sockets in which they were set, his shrivelled complexion and straight black lips.

The different accidents of life are not so changeable as the feelings of human nature. I had worked hard for nearly two years, for the sole purpose of infusing life into an inanimate body. For this I had deprived myself of rest and health. I had desired it with an ardour that far exceeded moderation; but now that I had finished, the beauty of the dream vanished, and breathless horror and disgust filled my heart.

Unable to endure the aspect of the being I had created, I rushed out of the room, and continued a long time traversing my bedchamber, unable to compose my mind to sleep.

At length lassitude succeeded to the tumult I had before endured; and I threw myself on the bed in my clothes, endeavouring to seek a few moments of forgetfulness. But it was in vain. I slept, indeed, but I was disturbed by the wildest dreams. I thought I saw Elizabeth, in the bloom of health, walking in the streets of Ingolstadt. Delighted and surprised, I embraced her; but as I imprinted the first kiss on her lips, they became livid with the hue of death; her features appeared to change, and I thought that I held the corpse of my dead mother in my arms; a shroud enveloped her form, and I saw the grave-worms crawling in the folds of the flannel.

I started from my sleep with horror. A cold dew covered my forehead, my teeth chattered, and every limb became

convulsed: when, by the dim and yellow light of the moon, as it forced its way through the window shutters, I beheld the wretch – the miserable monster whom I had created. He held up the curtain of the bed; and his eyes, if eyes they may be called, were fixed on me. His jaws opened and he muttered some inarticulate sounds, while a grin wrinkled his cheeks. He might have spoken, but I did not hear. One hand was stretched out, seemingly to detain me – but I escaped and rushed downstairs. I took refuge in the courtyard belonging to the house which I inhabited; where I remained during the rest of the night, walking up and down in the greatest agitation, listening attentively, catching and fearing each sound as if it were to announce the approach of the demoniacal corpse to which I had so miserably given life. Oh! No mortal could support the horror of that countenance. A mummy again endued with animation could not be so hideous as that wretch. I had gazed on him while unfinished; he was ugly then, but when those muscles and joints were rendered capable of motion, it became a thing such as even Dante could not have conceived. I passed the night wretchedly. Sometimes my pulse beat so quickly and hardly that I felt the palpitation of every artery; at others, I nearly sank to the ground through languor and extreme weakness. Mingled with this horror, I felt the bitterness of disappointment; dreams that had been my food and pleasant rest for so long a space were now become a hell to me; and the change was so rapid, the overthrow so complete!

The Story of Baelbrow

1898

E and H Heron

It is a matter for regret that so many of Mr Flaxman Low's reminiscences should deal with the darker episodes of his experiences. Yet this is almost unavoidable, as the more purely scientific cases would not, perhaps, contain the same elements of interest for the general public, however valuable and instructive they might be to the expert student. It has also been considered better to choose the completer cases – those that ended in something like satisfactory proof – rather than the many instances where the thread broke off amongst surmisings, which it was never possible to subject to convincing tests.

North of a low-lying strip of country on the East Anglian coast, the promontory of Bael Ness thrusts out a blunt nose into the sea. On the Ness, backed by pinewoods, stands a

square, comfortable stone mansion, known to the countryside as Baelbrow. It has faced the east winds for close upon three hundred years, and during the whole period has been the home of the Swaffam family, who were never in anywise put out of conceit of their ancestral dwelling by the fact that it had always been haunted. Indeed, the Swaffams were proud of the Baelbrow Ghost, which enjoyed a wide notoriety, and no one dreamt of complaining of its behaviour until Professor Van der Voort of Louvain laid information against it, and sent an urgent appeal for help to Mr Flaxman Low.

The Professor, who was well acquainted with Mr Low, detailed the circumstances of his tenancy of Baelbrow, and the unpleasant events that had followed thereupon.

It appeared that Mr Swaffam, Senr., who spent a large portion of his time abroad, had offered to lend his house to the

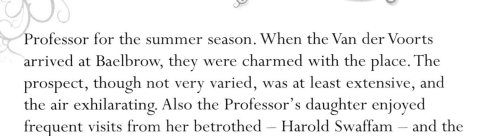

Professor for the summer season. When the Van der Voorts arrived at Baelbrow, they were charmed with the place. The prospect, though not very varied, was at least extensive, and the air exhilarating. Also the Professor's daughter enjoyed frequent visits from her betrothed – Harold Swaffam – and the Professor was delightfully employed in overhauling the Swaffam library.

The Van der Voorts had been duly told of the ghost, which lent distinction to the old house, but never in any way interfered with the comfort of the inmates. For some time they found this description to be strictly true, but with the beginning of October came a change. Up to this time and as far back as the Swaffam annals reached, the ghost had been a shadow, a rustle, a passing sigh – nothing definite or troublesome. But early in October strange things began to occur, and the terror culminated when a housemaid was found dead in a corridor three weeks later. Upon this the Professor felt that it was time to send for Flaxman Low.

Mr Low arrived upon a chilly evening when the house was already beginning to blur in the purple twilight, and the resinous scent of the pines came sweetly on the land breeze. Van der Voort welcomed him in the spacious, fire-lit hall. He was a stout man with a quantity of white hair, round eyes emphasized by spectacles, and a kindly, dreamy face. His life-study was philology, and his two relaxations: chess and the smoking of a big-bowled meerschaum.

"Now, Professor," said Mr Low when they had settled themselves in the smoking room. "How did it all begin?"

"I will tell you," replied Van der Voort, thrusting out his chin, and tapping his broad chest, and speaking as if an unwarrantable liberty had been taken with him. "First of all, it has shown itself to me!" Mr Flaxman Low smiled and assured him that nothing could be more satisfactory.

"But not at all satisfactory!" exclaimed the Professor. "I was sitting here alone, it might have been midnight, when I hear something come creeping like a little dog with its nails, *tick-tick*, upon the oak flooring of the hall. I whistle, for I think it is the little 'Rags' of my daughter, and afterwards opened the door, and I saw——' he hesitated and looked hard at Low through his spectacles, "something that was just disappearing into the passage which connects the two wings of the house. It was a figure, not unlike the human figure, but narrow and straight. I fancied I saw a bunch of black hair, and a flutter of something detached, which may have been a handkerchief. I was overcome by a feeling of repulsion. I heard a few clicking steps, then it stopped, as I thought, at the museum door. Come, I will show you the spot."

The Professor conducted Mr Low into the hall. The main staircase, dark and

massive, yawned above them, and directly behind it ran the passage referred to by the Professor. It was over twenty feet long, and about midway led past a deep arch containing a door reached by two steps.

Van der Voort explained that this door formed the entrance to a large room called the museum, in which Mr Swaffam, Senr., who was something of a collector, stored the various curios he picked up during his excursions abroad. The Professor went on to say that he immediately followed the figure, which he believed had gone into the museum, but he found nothing there except the cases containing Swaffam's treasures.

"I mentioned my experience to no one. I concluded that I had seen the ghost. But two days after, one of the female servants coming through the passage, in the dark, declared that a man leapt out at her from the embrasure of the museum door, but she released herself and ran screaming into the servants' hall. We at once made a search but found nothing to substantiate her story.

"I took no notice of this, though it coincided pretty well with my own experience. The week after, my daughter Lena came down late one night for a book. As she was about to cross the hall, something leapt upon her from behind. Women are of little use in serious investigations – she fainted! Since then she has been ill and the doctor says 'run down'." Here the Professor spread out his hands. "So she leaves for a change tomorrow. Since then other members of the household have

been attacked in much the same manner, with always the same result, they faint and are weak and useless when they recover.

"But, last Wednesday, the affair became a tragedy. By that time the servants had refused to come through the passage except in a crowd of three or four — most of them preferring to go round by the terrace to reach this part of the house. But one maid, named Eliza Freeman, said she was not afraid of the Baelbrow Ghost, and undertook to put out the lights in the hall one night. When she had done so, and was returning through the passage past the museum door, she appears to have been attacked, or at any rate frightened. In the grey of the morning they found her lying beside the steps, dead. There was a little blood upon her sleeve but no mark upon her body except a small raised pustule under the ear. The doctor said the girl was extraordinarily anaemic, and that she probably died from fright, her heart being weak. I was surprised at this, for she had always seemed to be a particularly strong and active young woman."

"Can I see Miss Van der Voort tomorrow before she goes?" asked Low, as the Professor signified he had nothing more to tell.

The Professor was rather unwilling that his daughter should be questioned, but he at last gave his permission, and next morning Low had a short talk with the girl before she left the house. He found her a very pretty girl, though listless and startlingly pale, and with a frightened stare in her light brown eyes. Mr Low asked if she could describe her assailant.

"No," she answered. "I could not see him for he was behind

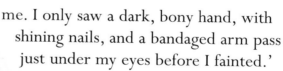

me. I only saw a dark, bony hand, with shining nails, and a bandaged arm pass just under my eyes before I fainted.'

"Bandaged arm? I have heard nothing of this."

"Tut-tut, mere fancy!" put in the Professor impatiently.

"I saw the bandages on the arm," repeated the girl, turning her head wearily away, "and I smelt the antiseptics it was dressed with."

"You have hurt your neck," remarked Mr Low, who noticed a small circular patch of pink under her ear.

She flushed and paled, raising her hand to her neck with a nervous jerk, as she said in a low voice: "It has almost killed me. Before he touched me, I knew he was there! I felt it!"

When they left her the Professor apologized for the unreliability of her evidence, and pointed out the discrepancy between her statement and his own.

"She says she sees nothing but an arm, yet I tell you it had no arms! Preposterous! Conceive a wounded man entering this house to frighten the young women! I do not know what to make of it! Is it a man, or is it the Baelbrow Ghost?" During the afternoon when Mr Low and the Professor returned from a stroll on the shore, they found a dark-browed young man with a bull neck and strongly marked features standing sullenly before the hall fire. The Professor presented him to Mr Low as Harold Swaffam.

Swaffam seemed to be about thirty, but was already known as a far-seeing and successful member of the Stock Exchange.

"I am pleased to meet you, Mr Low," he began, with a keen glance, "though you don't look sufficiently high-strung for one of your profession."

Mr Low merely bowed.

"Come, you don't defend your craft against my insinuations?" went on Swaffam. "And so you have come to rout out our poor old ghost from Baelbrow? You forget that he is an heirloom, a family possession! What's this about his having turned rabid, eh, Professor?" he ended, wheeling round upon Van der Voort in his brusque way.

The Professor told the story over again. It was plain that he stood rather in awe of his prospective son-in-law.

"I heard much the same from Lena, whom I met at the station," said Swaffam. "It is my opinion that the women in this house are suffering from an epidemic of hysteria. You agree with me, Mr Low?"

"Possibly. Though hysteria could hardly account for Freeman's death."

"I can't say as to that until I have looked further into the particulars. I have not been idle since I arrived. I have examined the museum. No one has entered it from the outside, and there is no other way of entrance except through the passage. The flooring is laid, I happen to know, on a thick layer of concrete. And there the case for the ghost stands at present." After a few moments of dogged reflection, he swung

round on Mr Low, in a manner that seemed peculiar to him when about to address any person. "What do you say to this plan, Mr Low? I propose to drive the Professor over to Ferryvale, to stop there for a day or two at the hotel, and I will also dispose of the servants who still remain in the house for, say, forty-eight hours. Meanwhile you and I can try to go further into the secret of the ghost's new pranks?"

Flaxman Low replied that this scheme exactly met his views, but the Professor protested against being sent away. Harold Swaffam, however, was a man who liked to arrange things in his own fashion, and within forty-five minutes he and Van der Voort departed in the dogcart.

The evening was lowering, and Baelbrow, like all houses built in exposed situations, was extremely susceptible to the changes of the weather. Therefore, before many hours were over, the place was full of creaking noises as the screaming gale battered at the shuttered windows, and the tree branches tapped and groaned against the walls.

Harold Swaffam on his way back was caught in the storm and drenched to the skin. It was therefore settled that after he had changed his clothes he should have a couple of hours' rest on the smoking-room sofa, while Mr Low kept watch in the hall.

The early part of the night passed over uneventfully. A light burned faintly in the great wainscotted hall, but the passage was dark. There was nothing to be heard but the wild moan and whistle of the wind coming in from the sea, and the squalls of rain dashing against the windows.

As the hours advanced, Mr Low lit a lantern that lay at hand and, carrying it along the passage, tried the museum door. It yielded, and the wind came muttering through to meet him. He looked round at the shutters and behind the big cases which held Mr Swaffam's treasures, to make sure that the room contained no living occupant but himself.

Suddenly he fancied he heard a scraping noise behind him, and turned round, but discovered nothing to account for it. Finally, he laid the lantern on a bench so that its light should fall through the door into the passage, and returned again to the hall, where he put out the lamp, and then once more took up his station by the closed door of the smoking room.

A long hour passed, during which the wind continued to roar down the wide hall chimney, and the old boards creaked as if furtive footsteps were gathering from every corner of the house. But Flaxman Low heeded none of these; he was awaiting for a certain sound.

After a while, he heard it – the cautious scraping of wood on wood. He leant forward to watch the museum door. *Click, click*, came the curious dog-like tread upon the tiled floor of the museum, till the thing, whatever it was, paused and listened behind the open door. The wind lulled at the moment, and Low listened also, but no further sound was to be heard, only slowly across the broad ray of light falling through the door grew a stealthy shadow.

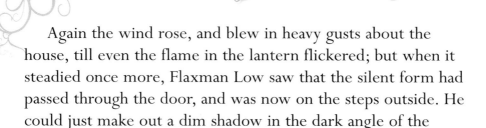

Again the wind rose, and blew in heavy gusts about the house, till even the flame in the lantern flickered; but when it steadied once more, Flaxman Low saw that the silent form had passed through the door, and was now on the steps outside. He could just make out a dim shadow in the dark angle of the embrasure.

Presently, from the shapeless shadow came a sound Mr Low was not prepared to hear. The thing sniffed the air with the strong, audible inspiration of a bear, or some large animal. At the same moment, carried on the draughts of the hall, a faint, unfamiliar odour reached his nostrils. Lena Van der Voort's words flashed back upon him – this, then, was the creature with the bandaged arm!

Again, as the storm shrieked and shook the windows, a darkness passed across the light. The thing had sprung out from the angle of the door, and Flaxman Low knew that it was making its way towards him through the illusive blackness of the hall. He hesitated for a second; then he opened the smoking-room door that creaked as he opened it.

Harold Swaffam sat up on the sofa, dazed with sleep. "What has happened? Has it come?"

Low told him what he had just seen. Swaffam listened half-smilingly.

"What do you make of it now?" he said.

"I must ask you to defer that question for a little," replied Low.

"Then you mean me to suppose that you have a theory to fit all these incongruous items?"

"I have a theory, which may be modified by further knowledge," said Low. "Meantime, am I right in concluding from the name of this house that it was built on a barrow or burying-place?'

"You are right, though that has nothing to do with the latest freaks of our ghost," returned Swaffam decidedly.

"I also gather that Mr Swaffam has lately sent home one of the many cases now lying in the museum?" went on Mr Low.

"He sent one, certainly, last September."

"And you have opened it," asserted Low.

"Yes – though I flattered myself I had left no trace of my handiwork."

"I have not examined the cases," said Low. "I inferred that you had done so from other facts."

"Now, one thing more," went on Swaffam, still smiling. "Do you imagine there is any danger – I mean to men like ourselves? Hysterical women cannot be taken into serious account."

"Certainly; the gravest danger to any person who moves about this part of the house alone after dark," replied Low.

Harold Swaffam leant back and crossed his legs.

"To go back to the beginning of our conversation, Mr Low, may I remind you of the various conflicting particulars you will have to reconcile before you can present any decent theory to the world?"

"I am quite aware of that."

"First of all, our original ghost was a mere misty presence, rather guessed at from vague sounds and shadows – now we

have a something that is tangible, and that can, as we have proof, kill with fright. Next Van der Voort declares the thing was a narrow, long and distinctly armless object, while Miss Van der Voort has not only seen the arm and hand of a human being, but saw them clearly enough to tell us that the nails were gleaming and the arm bandaged. She also felt its strength. Van der Voort, on the other hand, maintained that it clicked along like a dog — you bear out this description with the additional information that it sniffs like a wild beast. Now what can this thing be? It is capable of being seen, smelt and felt, yet it hides itself successfully in a room where there is no cavity or space sufficient to afford covert to a cat! You still tell me that you believe that you can explain this phenomenon?'

"Most certainly," replied Flaxman Low with conviction.

"I have not the slightest intention or desire to be rude, but as a mere matter of common sense, I must express my opinion plainly. I believe the whole thing to be the result of excited imaginations, and I am about to prove it. Do you think there is any further danger tonight?"

"Very great danger tonight," replied Low.

"Very well. As I said, I am going to prove it. I will ask you to allow me to lock you up in one of the distant rooms, where I can get no help from you, and I will pass the remainder of the night walking about the passage and hall in the dark."

"You can do so if you wish, but I must at least beg to be allowed to look on. I will leave the house and watch what goes on from the window in the passage, which I saw opposite the

museum door. You cannot, in any fairness, refuse to let me be a witness."

"I cannot, of course," returned Swaffam. "Still, the night is too bad to turn a dog out into, and I warn you that I shall lock you out."

"That will not matter. Lend me a macintosh, and leave the lantern lit in the museum, where I placed it."

Swaffam agreed to this.

Mr Low gives a graphic account of what followed. He left the house and was duly locked out, and, after groping his way round the house, found himself at length outside the window of the passage, which was almost opposite to the door of the museum. The door was still ajar and a thin band of light cut out into the gloom. Further down the hall gaped black and void. Low, sheltering himself as well as he could from the rain, waited for Swaffam 's appearance. Was the terrible yellow watcher balancing itself upon its lean legs in the dim corner opposite, ready to spring out with its deadly strength upon the passer-by?

Presently Low heard a door bang inside the house, and the next moment Swaffam appeared with a candle in his hand, an isolated spread of weak rays against the vast darkness behind. He advanced steadily down the passage, his dark face grim and set, and as he came Mr Low experienced that tingling sensation, which is so often the forerunner of some strange experience.

Swaffam passed on towards the other end of the passage.

There was a quick vibration of the museum door as a lean shape with a shrunken head leapt out into the passage after him. Then all together came a hoarse shout, the noise of a fall and utter darkness.

In an instant, Mr Low had broken the glass, opened the window, and swung himself into the passage. There he lit a match and as it flared he saw by its dim light a picture painted for a second upon the obscurity beyond.

Swaffam's big figure lay with outstretched arms, face downwards, and as Low looked a crouching shape extricated itself from the fallen man, raising a narrow vicious head from his shoulder.

The match spluttered feebly and went out, and Low heard a flying step click on the boards, before he could find the candle Swaffam had dropped. Lighting it, he stooped over Swaffam and turned him on his back. The man's strong colour had gone, and the wax-white face looked whiter still against the blackness of hair and brows. And upon his neck under the ear was a little raised pustule, from which a thin line of blood was streaked up to the angle of his cheekbone.

Some instinctive feeling prompted Low to glance up at this moment. Half extended from the museum doorway were a face and bony neck – a high-nosed, dull-eyed, malignant face, the eye sockets hollow, and the darkened teeth showing. Low plunged his hand into his pocket and a shot rang out in the echoing passageway and hall. The wind sighed through the broken panes, a ribbon of stuff fluttered along the polished

flooring, and that was all, as Flaxman Low half dragged, half carried Swaffam into the smoking room.

It was some time before Swaffam recovered consciousness. He listened to Low's story of how he had found him with a red angry gleam in his sombre eyes.

"The ghost has scored off me," he said, with an odd, sullen laugh, "but now I fancy it's my turn! But before we adjourn to the museum to examine the place, I will ask you to let me hear your notion of things. You have been right in saying there was real danger. For myself I can only tell you that I felt something spring upon me, and I knew no more. Had this not happened I am afraid I should never have asked you a second time what your idea of the matter might be," he added.

"There are two main indications," replied Low. "This strip of yellow bandage, which I have just now picked up from the passage floor, and the mark on your neck."

"What's that you say?" Swaffam rose quickly and examined his neck in a small glass beside the mantelshelf.

"Connect those two, and I think I can leave you to work it out for yourself," said Low.

"Pray let us have your theory in full," requested Swaffam shortly.

"Very well," answered Low good-humouredly – he thought Swaffam's annoyance natural in the circumstances. "The long, narrow figure that seemed to the Professor to be armless is developed on the next occasion. For Miss Van der Voort sees a

bandaged arm and a dark hand with gleaming – which means gilded – nails. The clicking sound of the footsteps coincides with these particulars, for we know that sandals made of strips of leather are not uncommon in company with gilt nails and bandages. Old and dry leather would naturally click upon your polished floor."

"Bravo, Mr Low! So you mean to say that this house is haunted by a mummy!"

"All that I have seen confirms this idea."

"To do you justice, you held this theory before to-night – before, in fact, you had seen anything for yourself. You gathered that my father had sent home a mummy, and you went on to conclude that I had opened the case?"

"Yes. I imagine you took off most of – or rather all – the outer bandages, thus leaving the limbs free, wrapped only in the inner bandages which were swathed round each separate limb. I fancy this mummy was preserved on the Theban method with aromatic spices, which left the skin olive-coloured, dry and flexible, like tanned leather, the features remaining distinct, and the hair, teeth and eyebrows perfect."

"So far, good," said Swaffam. "But now, how about the intermittent vitality? The pustule of blood on the neck of those whom it attacks? And where is our old friend the Baelbrow ghost to come in?"

Swaffam tried to speak in a rallying tone, but his excitement and lowering temper were visible enough, in spite of the attempts he made to suppress them.

"To begin at the beginning," said Flaxman Low, "everybody who, in a rational and honest manner, investigates the phenomena of spiritism will, sooner or later, meet in them some perplexing element, which is not to be explained by any of the ordinary theories. For reasons into which I need not now enter, this present case appears to me to be one of these. I am led to believe that the ghost which has for so many years given dim and vague manifestations of its existence in this house is, in fact, a vampire."

Swaffam threw back his head with an incredulous gesture.

"We no longer live in the middle ages, Mr Low! And besides, how could a vampire come here?" he said scoffingly.

"It is held by some authorities on these subjects that under certain conditions a vampire may be self-created. You tell me that this house is built upon an ancient barrow, in fact, on a spot where we might naturally expect to find such an elemental psychic germ. In those dead human systems were contained all the seeds for good and evil. The power which causes these psychic seeds or germs to grow is thought, and from being long dwelt on and indulged, a thought might finally gain a mysterious vitality, which could go on increasing more and more by attracting to itself suitable and appropriate elements from its environment. For a long period this germ remained a helpless intelligence, awaiting the opportunity to assume some material form, by means of which to carry out its desires. Now, we can only judge of the nature of the germ by its manifestation through matter. Here we have every

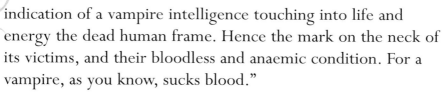

indication of a vampire intelligence touching into life and energy the dead human frame. Hence the mark on the neck of its victims, and their bloodless and anaemic condition. For a vampire, as you know, sucks blood."

"Now, for proof," said Swaffam. "Wait a second, Mr Low. You say you fired at this appearance?" And he took up the pistol which Low had laid down on the table.

"Yes, I aimed at a small portion of its foot which I saw on the step."

Without more words, and with the pistol still in his hand, Swaffam led the way to the Museum.

The wind howled round the house, and darkness lay upon the world, when the two men looked upon one of the strangest sights it has ever been given to men to shudder at.

Half in and half out of an oblong wooden box in a corner of the great room, lay a lean shape in its rotten yellow bandages, the scraggy neck surmounted by a mop of frizzled hair. The toe

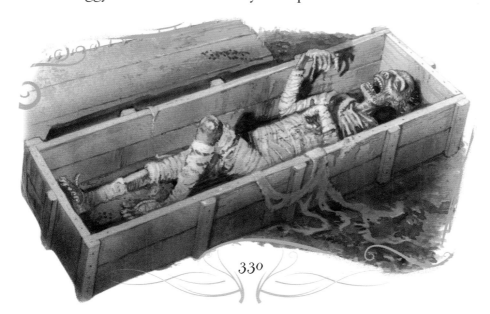

strap of a sandal and a portion of the left foot had been shot away.

Swaffam, with a working face, gazed down at it, then seizing it by its tearing bandages, he flung it into the box, where it fell into a lifelike posture, its wide, moist-lipped mouth gaping up at them.

For a moment Swaffam stood over the thing; then with a curse he raised the revolver and shot into the grinning face again and again with a deliberate vindictiveness. Finally he rammed the thing down into the box, and, clubbing the weapon, smashed the head into fragments with a vicious energy that coloured the whole horrible scene with a suggestion of murder done.

Then, turning to Low, he said "Help me to fasten the cover on it."

"Are you going to bury it?"

"No, we must rid the earth of it," he answered savagely. "I'll put it into the old canoe and burn it."

The rain had ceased when in the daybreak they carried the old canoe down to the shore. In it they placed the mummy case with its ghastly occupant. The sail was raised and the vessel set alight, and Low and Swaffam watched it drift away, at first a tiny spark, then a flare and waving fire – until far out to sea the history of that dead thing ended three thousand years after the priests of Armen had laid it to rest in its appointed pyramid.

Dracula

1897

EXTRACT

Bram Stoker

I was awakened by the Count, who looked at me as grimly as a man could look as he said, "Tomorrow, my friend, we must part. You return to your beautiful England, I to some work which may have such an end that we may never meet. Your letter home has been despatched. Tomorrow I shall not be here, but all shall be ready for your journey. In the morning come the Szgany, who have some labours of their own here, and also come some Slovaks. When they have gone, my carriage shall come for you, and shall bear you to the Borgo Pass to meet the diligence from Bukovina to Bistritz. But I am in hopes that I shall see more of you at Castle Dracula."

I suspected him, and determined to test his sincerity. Sincerity! It seems like a profanation of the word to write it in connection with such a monster, so I asked him point-blank,

"Why may I not go tonight?"

"Because, dear sir, my coachman and horses are away on a mission."

"But I would walk with pleasure. I want to get away at once."

He smiled, such a soft, smooth, diabolical smile that I knew there was some trick behind it. He said, "And your baggage?"

"I do not care about it. I can send for it some other time."

The Count stood up, and said, with a sweet courtesy which made me rub my eyes, it seemed so real, "You English have a saying which is close to my heart, for its spirit is that which rules our *boyars*, 'Welcome the coming, speed the parting guest.' Come with me, my dear young friend. Not an hour shall you wait in my house against your will, though sad am I at your going, and that you so suddenly desire it. Come!" With a stately gravity, he, with the lamp, preceded me down the stairs and along the hall. Suddenly he stopped. "Hark!"

Close at hand came the howling of many wolves. It was almost as if the sound sprang up at the rising of his hand, just as the music of a great orchestra seems to leap under the baton of the conductor. After a pause of a moment, he proceeded, in his stately way, to the door, drew back the ponderous bolts, unhooked the heavy chains, and began to draw it open.

To my astonishment I saw that it was unlocked. Suspiciously, I looked all round, but could see no key of any kind.

As the door began to open, the howling of the wolves outside grew louder and angrier. Their red jaws, with champing teeth, and their blunt-clawed feet as they leapt, came in through the opening door. I knew then that to struggle at the moment against the Count was useless. With such allies as these at his command, I could do nothing.

But still the door continued slowly to open, and only the Count's body stood in the gap. Suddenly it struck me that this might be the moment and means of my doom. I was to be given to the wolves, and at my own instigation. There was a diabolical wickedness in the idea great enough for the Count, and as the last chance I cried out, "Shut the door! I shall wait till morning." And I covered my face with my hands to hide my tears of disappointment.

With one sweep of his powerful arm the Count threw the door shut, and the great bolts clanged and echoed through the hall.

In silence we returned to the library, and after a minute or two I went to my own room. The last I saw of Count Dracula was his kissing his hand to me, with a red light of triumph in his eyes and a smile that Judas in hell might be proud of.

When I was in my room and about to lie down, I thought I heard a whispering at my door. I went to it softly and listened. Unless my ears deceived me, I heard the voice of the Count.

"Back to your own place! Your time is not yet come. Wait! Have patience! Tonight is mine. Tomorrow night is yours!"

There was a low, sweet ripple of laughter, and in a rage I threw open the door, and saw beyond the three terrible women licking their lips. As I appeared, they all joined in a horrible laugh, and ran away.

I came back to my room and threw myself on my knees. It is then so near the end? Tomorrow! Lord, help me!

I slept till just before the dawn, and when I woke threw myself on my knees, for I determined that if Death came he should find me ready.

At last I felt that subtle change in the air, and knew that the morning had come. Then came the welcome cock crow, and I felt that I was safe. With a glad heart, I opened the door and ran down the hall. I had seen that the door was unlocked, and now escape was before me. With hands that trembled with eagerness, I unhooked the chains and threw back the massive bolts.

But the door would not move. Despair seized me. I pulled and pulled at the door, and shook it till, massive as it was, it rattled in its casement. I could see the bolt shot. It had been locked after I left the Count.

Then a wild desire took me to obtain the key at any risk, and I determined then and there to scale the wall again, and gain the Count's room. He might kill me, but death now seemed the happier choice of evils. Without a pause I rushed

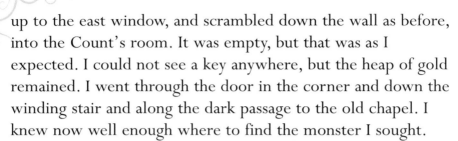

up to the east window, and scrambled down the wall as before, into the Count's room. It was empty, but that was as I expected. I could not see a key anywhere, but the heap of gold remained. I went through the door in the corner and down the winding stair and along the dark passage to the old chapel. I knew now well enough where to find the monster I sought.

The great box was in the same place, close against the wall, but the lid was laid on it, not fastened down, but with the nails ready in their places to be hammered home.

I knew I must search the body for the key, so I raised the lid, and laid it back against the wall. And then I saw something which filled my very soul with horror. There lay the Count, but looking as if his youth had been half restored. For the white hair and moustache were changed to dark iron-grey. The cheeks were fuller, and the white skin seemed ruby-red underneath. The mouth was redder than ever, for on the lips were gouts of fresh blood, which trickled from the corners of the mouth and ran down over the chin and neck. Even the deep, burning eyes seemed set amongst swollen flesh, for the lids and pouches underneath were bloated. It seemed as if the whole awful creature were simply gorged with blood. He lay like a filthy leech, exhausted with his repletion.

I shuddered as I bent over to touch him and every sense in me revolted at the contact – but I had to search, or I was lost. The coming night might see my own body a banquet in a similar way to those horrid three. I felt all over the body, but no sign could I find of the key. Then I stopped and looked at

the Count. There was a mocking smile on the bloated face which seemed to drive me mad. This was the being I was helping to transfer to London, where, perhaps, for centuries to come he might, amongst its teeming millions, satiate his lust for blood, and create a new and ever-widening circle of semi-demons to batten on the helpless.

The very thought drove me mad. A terrible desire came upon me to rid the world of such a monster. There was no lethal weapon at hand, but I seized a shovel that the workmen had been using to fill the cases, and lifting it high, struck, with the edge downward, at the hateful face. But as I did so the head turned, and the eyes fell upon me, with all their blaze of basilisk horror. The sight seemed to paralyze me, and the shovel turned in my hand and glanced from the face, merely making a deep gash above the forehead. The shovel fell from my hand across the box, and as I pulled it away the flange of the blade caught the edge of the lid, which fell over again, and hid the horrid thing from my sight. The last glimpse I had was of the bloated face, bloodstained and fixed with a grin of malice which would have held its own in the nethermost hell.

I thought and thought what should be my next move, but my brain seemed on fire, and I waited with a despairing feeling

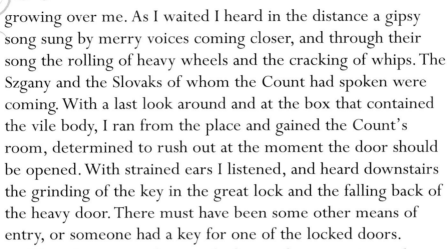

growing over me. As I waited I heard in the distance a gipsy
song sung by merry voices coming closer, and through their
song the rolling of heavy wheels and the cracking of whips. The
Szgany and the Slovaks of whom the Count had spoken were
coming. With a last look around and at the box that contained
the vile body, I ran from the place and gained the Count's
room, determined to rush out at the moment the door should
be opened. With strained ears I listened, and heard downstairs
the grinding of the key in the great lock and the falling back of
the heavy door. There must have been some other means of
entry, or someone had a key for one of the locked doors.

Then there came the sound of many feet tramping and
dying away in some passage which sent up a clanging echo. I
turned to run down again towards the vault, where I might
find the new entrance, but at the moment there seemed to come
a violent puff of wind, and the door to the winding stair blew
to with a shock that set the dust from the lintels flying. When I
ran to push it open, I found that it was hopelessly fast. I was
again a prisoner, and the net of doom was closing round me.

As I write there is in the passage below a sound of many
tramping feet and the crash of weights being set down heavily,
doubtless the boxes, with their freight of earth. There is a
sound of hammering. It is the box being nailed down. Now I
can hear the heavy feet tramping again along the hall, with
many other idle feet coming behind them.

The door is shut; the chains rattle. There is a grinding of
the key in the lock. I can hear the key withdrawn, then another

door opens and shuts. I hear the creaking of lock and bolt.

Hark! In the courtyard and down the rocky way the roll of heavy wheels, the crack of whips, and the chorus of the Szgany as they pass into the distance.

I am alone in the castle with those horrible women. Faugh! Mina is a woman, and there is nought in common. They are devils of the Pit!

I shall not remain alone with them. I shall try to scale the castle wall farther than I have yet attempted. I may find a way from this dreadful place.

And then away for home! Away to the quickest and nearest train! Away from the cursed spot, from this cursed land, where the devil and his children still walk with earthly feet!

At least God's mercy is better than that of those monsters, and the precipice is steep and high. At its foot a man may sleep – as a man. Goodbye, all Mina!

Man-size in Marble

1893

E Nesbit

Although every word of this story is as true as despair, I do not expect people to believe it. Nowadays a 'rational explanation' is required before belief is possible. Let me then, at once, offer the 'rational explanation' which finds most favour among those who have heard the tale of my life's tragedy. It is held that we were 'under a delusion,' Laura and I, on that 31st of October; and that this supposition places the whole matter on a satisfactory and believable basis. The reader can judge, when he, too, has heard my story, how far this is an 'explanation,' and in what sense it is 'rational.' There were three who took part in this; Laura and I and another man. The other man still lives, and can speak to the truth of the least credible part of my story.

I never knew in my life what it was to have as much money as I required to supply the most ordinary needs of life: good colours, canvases, brushes, books and cab-fares and when we were married, we knew quite well that we should only be able to live at all by 'strict punctuality and attention to business.' I used to paint in those days, and Laura used to write, and we felt sure we could keep the pot at least simmering. Living in town was out of the question, so we went to look for a cottage in the country, which should be at once sanitary and picturesque. So rarely do these two qualities meet in one cottage that our search was for some time quite fruitless. We tried advertisements, but most of the desirable rural residences which we did look at, proved to be lacking in both essentials; and when a cottage chanced to have drains, it always had stucco as well and was shaped like a tea-caddy. And if we found a vine or rose-covered porch, corruption invariably lurked within. Our minds got so befogged by the eloquence of estate agents, and the rival disadvantages of the fever-traps and outrages to beauty which we had seen and scorned, that I very much doubt whether either of us on our wedding morning, knew the difference between a house and a haystack. But when we got away from friends and estate agents, on our honeymoon, our wits grew clear again, and we knew a pretty cottage when at last we saw one.

It was at Brenzett a little village set on a hill over against the southern marshes. We had gone there, from the seaside village where we were staying, to see the church, and two

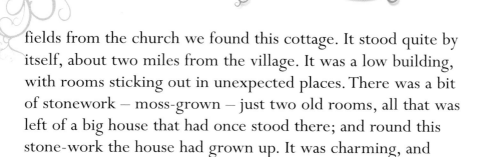

fields from the church we found this cottage. It stood quite by itself, about two miles from the village. It was a low building, with rooms sticking out in unexpected places. There was a bit of stonework — moss-grown — just two old rooms, all that was left of a big house that had once stood there; and round this stone-work the house had grown up. It was charming, and after a brief examination we took it. It was absurdly cheap.

The rest of our honeymoon we spent in grubbing about in second-hand shops in the county town, picking up bits of old oak and Chippendale chairs for our furnishing. We wound up with a run up to town and a visit to Liberty's, and soon the low oak-beamed lattice-windowed rooms began to be home. There was a jolly old-fashioned garden at the back, with grass paths, and no end of hollyhocks and sunflowers, and big lilies. From the window you could see the marsh pastures, and beyond them the beautiful blue, thin line of the sea.

We were as happy as the summer was glorious, and settled down into work sooner than we ourselves expected. I was never tired of sketching the view and the wonderful cloud effects from the open lattice, and Laura would sit at the table and write verses about them, in which I mostly played the part of foreground.

We got a tall old peasant woman to housekeep for us. Her face and figure were good, though her cooking was of the homeliest; but she understood all about gardening, and told us all the old names of the coppices and cornfields, and the stories of the smugglers and highwaymen, and, better still, of

the 'things that walked,' and of the 'sights' which met one in lonely glens of a starlight night. She was a great comfort to us, because Laura hated housekeeping as much as I loved folklore, and we soon came to leave all the domestic business to Mrs Dorman, and to use her legends in little magazine stories which brought in the jingling guinea.

We had three months of married happiness, and did not have a single quarrel. One October evening I had been down to smoke a pipe with the doctor – our only neighbour – a pleasant young Irishman. Laura had stayed at home to finish a comic sketch of a village episode for the *Monthly Marplot*. I left her laughing over her own jokes, and came in to find her a crumpled heap of pale muslin weeping on the window seat.

"Good heavens, my darling, what's the matter?" I cried, taking her in my arms. She leaned her little dark head against my shoulder and went on crying. I had never seen her cry before – we had always been so happy, you see – and I felt sure some frightful misfortune had happened.

"What *is* the matter? Do speak."

"It's Mrs Dorman," she sobbed.

"What has she done?" I inquired, immensely relieved that it was not a serious matter.

"She says she must go before the end of the month, that her niece is ill – she's gone down to see her now – tonight. But I don't believe that's the real, true reason, because her niece is always ill. I believe someone in the village may have been been setting her against us. Her manner was so very peculiar – she

was not at all like her usual self."

"Never mind darling," I said. "Whatever you do, don't cry, or I shall have to cry too, to keep you in countenance, and then you'll never respect your man again!"

She dried her eyes obediently on my handkerchief, and even tried to smile, though it was a faint version of her usual pretty one. "But you see," she went on, "it is really serious, because these village people are so sheepy, and if one won't do a thing you may be quite sure none of the others will. And I shall have to cook the dinners, and wash up the hateful greasy plates; and you'll have to carry cans of water about, and clean the boots and knives and we shall never have any time for work, or to earn any money, or anything. We shall have to work hard all day, and only be able to have a slight respite when we are waiting for the kettle to boil!"

I represented to her that even if we had to perform these duties, the day would still present some margin for other toils and recreations. But would not see the matter in any but the greyest light. She was very unreasonable but I could not have loved her more if she had been as reasonable as Whately.

"I'll speak to Mrs Dorman when she comes back, and see if I can't come to terms with her," I said. "Perhaps she only wants a rise in her pay. I am sure it will be all right. Let's walk up to the church together."

The church was a large and lonely one, and we loved to go there, especially upon bright nights. The path skirted a wood, cut through it once, and ran along the crest of the hill through two meadows, and round the churchyard wall, over which the old yews loomed in black masses of shadow. This path, which was partly paved, was called 'the bier-balk,' for it had long been the way by which the corpses had been carried to burial. The churchyard was richly treed, and was shaded by great elms which stood just outside and stretched their majestic arms in benediction over the happy dead. A large, low porch let one into the building by a Norman doorway and a heavy oak door studded with iron.

Inside, the arches rose into darkness, and between them the reticulated windows, which stood out white in the moonlight. In the chancel, the windows were of rich glass, which showed in faint light their noble colouring, and made the black oak of the choir pews hardly more solid than the shadows. But on each side of the altar lay a grey marble figure of a knight in full plate armour lying upon a low slab, with hands held up in everlasting prayer. And these figures, oddly enough, were

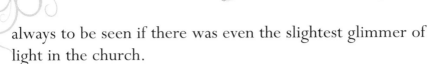

always to be seen if there was even the slightest glimmer of
light in the church.

Their names were lost, but the peasants told of them that
they had been fierce and wicked men, marauders by land and
sea, who had been the scourge of their time, and had been
guilty of deeds so foul that the house they had lived in – the
big house, by the way, that had stood on the site of our cottage
– had been stricken by lightning and the vengeance of heaven.
But for all that, the gold of their heirs had bought them a place
in the church. Looking at the bad, hard faces reproduced in the
marble, this story was easily believed.

The church looked at its best and weirdest on that night,
for the shadows of the yew trees fell through the windows
upon the floor of the nave and touched the pillars with
tattered shade. We sat down together without speaking, and

watched the solemn beauty of the old church, with some of that awe which inspired its early builders. We walked to the chancel and looked at the sleeping warriors. Then we rested some time on the stone seat in the porch, looking out over the stretch of quiet moonlit meadows, feeling in every fibre of our being the peace of the night and of our happy love; and came away at last with a sense that even scrubbing and blackleading were but small troubles at their worst.

Mrs Dorman had come back from the village, and I at once invited her to a *tête-à-tête*. "Now, Mrs Dorman," I said, when I had got her into my painting room, "what's all this about your not staying with us?"

"I should be glad to get away, sir, before the end of the month," she answered, with her usual placid dignity.

"Have you any fault to find, Mrs Dorman?"

"None at all, sir. You and your lady have always been most kind, I'm sure—"

"Well, what is it? Are your wages not high enough?"

"No, sir, I gets quite enough."

"Then why not stay?"

"I'd rather not," she said with some hesitation, "my niece is very ill."

"But your niece has been ill ever since we came."

No answer. There was a long and awkward silence. Eventually I broke it.

"Can't you stay for another month?" I asked.

"No, sir. I'm bound to go by Thursday."

And this was Monday!

"Well, I must say, I think you might have let us know before. There's no time now to get anyone else, and your mistress is not fit to do heavy housework. Can't you stay till next week?"

"I might be able to come back next week."

I was now convinced that all she wanted was a brief holiday, which we should have been willing enough to let her have, as soon as we could get a substitute.

"But why must you go this week?" I persisted. "Come, out with it."

Mrs Dorman drew the little shawl, which she always wore, tightly across her bosom, as though she were cold. Then she said, with a sort of effort: "They say, sir, as this was a big house in Catholic times, and there was a many deeds done here."

The nature of the 'deeds' might be vaguely inferred from the inflection of Mrs Dorman's voice which was enough to make one's blood run cold. I was glad that Laura was not in the room. She was always nervous, as highly-strung natures are, and I felt that these tales about our house, told by this old peasant woman, with her impressive manner and contagious credulity, might have made our home less dear to my wife.

"Tell me all about it, Mrs Dorman," I said "You needn't mind about telling me. I'm not like the young people who make fun of such things."

Which was partly true.

"Well, sir," she sank her voice, "you may have seen in the church, beside the altar, two shapes."

"You mean the effigies of the knights in armour," I said cheerfully.

"I mean them two bodies, drawed out man-size in marble," she returned, and I had to admit that her description was a thousand times more graphic than mine, to say nothing of a certain weird force and uncanniness about the phrase 'drawed out man-size in marble'.

"They do say, as on All Saints' Eve them two bodies sits up on their slabs, and gets off of them, and then walks down the aisle, *in their marble* and as the church clock strikes eleven they walks out of the church door, and along the bier-balk, and if it's wet there'll be footprints left in the morning."

"And where do they go?" I asked.

"They comes back here to their home, sir, and if anyone meets them—"

"Well, what then?" I asked.

But she only repeated that her niece was ill and she must go. I scorned to discuss the niece, and tried to get from Mrs Dorman more details of the legend. I could get nothing but warnings.

"Whatever you do, sir, lock the door early on All Saints' Eve, and make the cross sign over the doorstep and on the windows."

"But is their evidence that anyone has ever seen these dreadful things?" I persisted.

"That's not for me to say. I know what I know, sir."

"Well, who was here last year?"

"No one, sir. The lady as owned the house only stayed here in summer, and she always went to London a full month afore *the* night. And I'm sorry to inconvenience you and your lady, but my niece is ill and I must go on Thursday."

I could have shaken her for her absurd reiteration of that obvious fiction, after she had told me her real reasons. She was determined to go, nor could our united entreaties move her in the least.

I did not tell Laura the legend of the shapes that walked in their marble, partly because a legend concerning our house might perhaps trouble my wife, and partly, I think, from some more occult reason. This was not quite the same to me as any other story, and I did not want to talk about it till the day was over. I had very soon ceased to think of the legend, however.

I was painting a portrait of Laura, against the lattice window, and I could not think of much else. I had got a splendid background of yellow and grey sunset, and was working away with enthusiasm at her lace.

On Thursday Mrs Dorman went. She relented, at parting, so far as to say, "Don't you put yourself about too much, ma'am, and if there's any little thing I can do next week, I'm sure I shan't mind." From which I inferred that she wished to

come back to us after Halloween. Up to the last she adhered to the fiction of the niece with touching fidelity.

Thursday passed off pretty well. Laura showed marked ability in the matter of steak and potatoes, and I confess that my knives, and the plates, which I insisted upon washing, were better done than I had dared to expect.

Friday came. It is about what happened on that Friday that this is written. I wonder if I should have believed it, if anyone had told it to me. I will write the story of it as quickly and plainly as I can. Everything that happened on that day is burnt into my brain. I shall not forget anything, nor leave anything out.

I got up early, I remember, and lighted the kitchen fire, and had just achieved a smoky success, when my little wife came running down, as sunny and sweet as the clear October morning

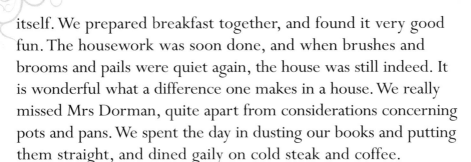

itself. We prepared breakfast together, and found it very good fun. The housework was soon done, and when brushes and brooms and pails were quiet again, the house was still indeed. It is wonderful what a difference one makes in a house. We really missed Mrs Dorman, quite apart from considerations concerning pots and pans. We spent the day in dusting our books and putting them straight, and dined gaily on cold steak and coffee.

Laura was, if possible, brighter and gayer and sweeter than usual, and I began to think that a little domestic toil was really good for her. We had never been so merry since we were married, and the walk we had that afternoon was, I think, the happiest time of all my life. When we had watched the deep scarlet clouds slowly pale into leaden grey against a pale-green sky, and saw the white mists curl up along the hedgerows in the distant marsh, we came back to the house, silently, hand in hand.

"You are sad, my darling," I said, half-jestingly, as we sat down together in our little parlour. I expected a disclaimer, for my own silence had been the silence of complete happiness.

To my surprise she said, "Yes. I think I am sad, or rather I am uneasy. I don't think I'm very well. I have shivered three or four times since we came in, and it is not cold, is it?"

"No," I said, and hoped it was not a chill caught from the treacherous mists that roll up from the marshes in the dying light. No she said, she did not think so. Then, after a silence, she spoke suddenly,

"Do you ever have presentiments of evil?"

"No," I said, smiling, "and I shouldn't believe in them even if I had."

"I do," she went on; "the night my father died I knew it, though he was right away in the north of Scotland." I did not answer in words.

She sat looking at the fire for some time in silence, gently stroking my hand. At last she sprang up, came behind me, and, drawing my head back, kissed me. "There, it's over now," she said. "What a baby I am! Come, light the candles, and we'll have some of these new Rubinstein duets."

And we spent a happy hour or two at the piano.

At about half past ten I began to long for the goodnight pipe, but Laura looked so white that I felt it would be brutal of me to fill our sitting-room with the fumes of strong cavendish. "I'll take my pipe outside," I said.

"Let me come, too."

"No, sweetheart, not tonight; you're much too tired. I shan't be long. Get to bed, or I shall have an invalid to nurse tomorrow as well as the boots to clean."

I kissed her and was turning to go, when she flung her arms round my neck, and held me as if she would never let me go again. I stroked her hair.

"Come darling, you're over-tired. The housework has been too much for you."

She loosened her clasp a little and drew a deep breath. "No. We've been very happy today, Jack, haven't we? Don't stay out too long."

"I won't, my dearie."

I strolled out of the front door, leaving it unlatched. What a night it was! The jagged masses of heavy dark cloud were rolling at intervals from horizon to horizon, and thin white wreaths covered the stars. Through all the rush of the cloud river, the moon swam, breasting the waves and disappearing again in the darkness. When now and again her light reached the woodlands they seemed to be slowly and noiselessly waving in time to the swing of the clouds above them. There was a strange grey light over all the earth; the fields had that shadowy bloom over them, which only comes from the marriage of dew and moonshine, or frost and starlight.

I walked up and down, drinking in the beauty of the quiet earth and the changing sky. The night was absolutely silent. Nothing seemed to be abroad. There was no skurrying of rabbits, or twitter of the half-asleep birds. And though the clouds went sailing across the sky, the wind that drove them never came low enough to rustle the dead leaves in the woodland paths. Across the meadows I could see the church tower standing out black and grey against the sky. I walked there thinking over our three months of happiness — and of my wife, her dear eyes, her loving ways. Oh, my little girl! My own little girl; what a vision came then of a long, glad life for you and me together!

I heard a bell-beat from the church. Eleven already! I turned to go in, but the night held me. I could not go back into our little warm rooms yet. I would go up to the church.

I felt vaguely that it would be good to carry my love and thankfulness to the sanctuary whither so many loads of sorrow and gladness had been borne by the men and women of the dead years.

I looked in at the low window as I went by. Laura was half lying on her chair in front of the fire. I could not see her face; only her little head showed dark against the pale blue wall. She was quite still. Asleep, no doubt. My heart reached out to her, as I went on. There must be a God, I thought, and a God who was good. How otherwise could anything so sweet and dear as she have ever been imagined?

I walked slowly along the edge of the wood. A sound broke the stillness of the night; it was a rustling in the wood. I stopped and listened. The sound stopped too. I went on, and now distinctly heard another step than mine answer mine like an echo. It was a poacher or a wood-stealer, most likely, for these were not unknown in our Arcadian neighbourhood. But whoever it was, he was a fool not to step more lightly. I turned into the wood, and now the footstep seemed to come from the path I had just left. It must be an echo, I thought. The wood looked perfect in the moonlight. The large dying ferns and the brushwood showed where through thinning foliage the pale light came down. The tree trunks stood up like Gothic columns all around me. They reminded me of the church, and I turned into the bier-balk, and passed through the corpse-gate between the graves to the low porch. I paused for a moment on the stone seat where Laura and I had watched the fading

landscape. Then I noticed that the door of the church was open, and I blamed myself for having left it unlatched the other night. We were the only people who ever cared to come to the church except on Sundays, and I was vexed to think that through our carelessness the damp autumn airs had had a chance of getting in and injuring the old fabric. I went in. It will seem strange, perhaps, that I should have gone halfway up the aisle before I remembered with a sudden chill, followed by as sudden a rush of self-contempt that this was the very day and hour when, according to tradition, the shapes drawed out man-size in marble began to walk.

Having thus remembered the legend, and remembered it with a shiver, of which I was ashamed, I could not do otherwise than walk up towards the altar, just to look at the figures as I said to myself; really what I wanted was to assure myself, first, that I did not believe the legend, and, secondly, that it was not true. I was rather glad that I had come. I thought now I could tell Mrs Dorman how vain her fancies were, and how peacefully the marble figures slept on through the ghastly hour. With my hands in my pockets I passed up the aisle. In the grey dim light the eastern end of the church looked larger than usual, and the arches above the two tombs looked larger too. The moon came out and showed me the reason. I stopped short, my heart gave a leap that nearly choked me, and then sank sickeningly.

The 'bodies drawed out man-size' *were gone*, and their marble slabs lay wide and bare in the vague moonlight that

slanted through the east window.

Were they really gone? Or was I mad? Clenching my nerves, I stooped and passed my hand over the smooth slabs, and felt their flat unbroken surface. Had someone taken the things away? Was it some vile practical joke? I would make sure, anyway. In an instant I had made a torch of a newspaper, which happened to be in my pocket, and lighting it held it high above my head. Its yellow glare illumined the dark arches and those slabs. The figures *were* gone. And I was alone in the church; or was I alone?

And then a horror seized me, a horror indefinable and indescribable – an overwhelming certainty of supreme and accomplished calamity. I flung down the torch and tore along the aisle and out through the porch, biting my lips as I ran to keep myself from shrieking aloud. Oh, was I mad – or what was this that possessed me? I leapt the churchyard wall and took the straight cut across the fields, led by the light from our windows. Just as I got over the first stile, a dark figure seemed to spring out of the ground. Mad still with that certainty of misfortune, I made for the thing that stood in my path, shouting, "Get out of the way, can't you!"

But my push met with a more vigorous resistance than I had expected. My arms were caught just above the elbow and held as in a vice, and the raw-boned Irish doctor actually shook me.

"Would ye?" he cried, in his own unmistakable accents – "would ye, then?"

"Let me go, you fool," I gasped. "The marble figures have gone from the church; I tell you they've gone."

He broke into a ringing laugh. "I'll have to give ye a draught tomorrow, I see. Ye've listening to old wives' tales."

"I tell you, I've seen the bare slabs."

"Well, come back with me. I'm going up to old Palmer's his daughter's ill. We'll look in at the church and let me see the bare slabs."

"You go, if you like," I said, a little less frantic for his laughter. "I'm going home to my wife."

"Rubbish, man," said he. "D'ye think I'll permit of that? Are ye to go saying all yer life that ye've seen solid marble endowed with vitality, and me to go all me life saying ye were a coward? No, sir ye shan't do ut."

The night air, a human voice, and I think also the physical contact with this six feet of solid common sense, brought me back a little to my ordinary self, and the word 'coward' was a mental shower-bath.

"Come on, then," I said sullenly, "perhaps you're right."

He still held my arm tightly. We got over the stile and back to the church. All was still as death. The place smelt very damp and earthy. We walked up the aisle. I am not ashamed to confess that I shut my eyes: I knew the figures would not be there. I heard Kelly strike a match.

"Here they are, ye see, right enough; ye've been dreaming or drinking, asking yer pardon for the imputation."

I opened my eyes. By Kelly's expiring vesta I saw two

shapes lying 'in their marble' on their slabs. I drew a deep breath, and caught his hand.

"I'm awfully indebted to you," I said. "It must have been some trick of light, or I have been working rather hard, perhaps that's it. Do you know, I was quite convinced they were gone."

"I'm aware of that," he answered, rather grimly, "ye'll have to be careful of that brain of yours, my friend, I assure ye."

He was leaning over and looking at the right-hand figure, whose stony face was the most villainous and deadly in expression.

"By Jove," he said, "something has been afoot here – this hand is broken."

And so it was. I was certain that it had been perfect the last time Laura and I had been there.

"Perhaps someone has tried to remove them," said the young doctor.

"That won't account for my impression," I objected.

"Too much painting and not enough rest will account for that, well enough."

"Come along," I said, "or my wife will be getting anxious. You'll come in and have a drop of whisky and drink confusion to ghosts and better sense to me."

"I ought to go up to Palmer's, but it's so late now I'd best leave it till the morning," he replied. "I was kept late at the Union, and I've had to see a lot of people since. All right, I'll come back with ye."

I think he fancied I needed him more than did Palmer's girl, so, discussing how such an illusion could have been possible, and deducing from this experience large generalities concerning ghostly apparitions, we walked up to our cottage. We saw, as we walked up the garden path, that bright light streamed out of the front door, and presently saw that the parlour door was open too. Had she gone out?

"Come in," I said, and Dr Kelly followed me into the parlour. It was ablaze with candles, not only the wax ones, but at least a dozen guttering, tallow dips, stuck in vases and ornaments in unlikely places. Light was Laura's remedy for nervousness. Poor child! Why had I left her? Brute that I was.

We glanced round the room, and at first we did not see her. The window was open, and the draught set all the candles flaring one way. Her chair was empty and her handkerchief and book lay on the floor. I turned to the window. There, in the recess of the window, I saw her. Oh, my child, my love, had she gone to that window to watch for me? And what had come into the room behind her? To what had she turned with that look of frantic fear and horror? Oh, my little one, had she thought that it was I whose step she heard, and turned to meet what?

She had fallen back across a table in the window, and her body lay half on it and half on the window-seat, and her head hung down over the table, the brown hair loosened and fallen to the carpet. Her lips were drawn back, and her eyes wide open. They saw nothing now. What had they seen last?

The doctor moved towards her, but I pushed him aside and sprang to her; caught her in my arms and cried: "It's all right, Laura! I've got you safe darling." She fell into my arms in a heap. I clasped her and kissed her, and called her name, but I think I knew all the time that she was dead. Her hands were tightly clenched. In one of them she held something fast. When I was quite sure that she was dead, and that nothing mattered at all any more, I let him open her hand to see what she held.

It was a grey marble finger.

The Hound of the Baskervilles

1901

EXTRACT

Sir Arthur Conan Doyle

I have said that over the great Grimpen Mire there hung a dense, white fog. It was drifting slowly in our direction and banked itself up like a wall on that side of us, low but thick and well defined. The moon shone on it, and it looked like a great shimmering ice-field. Holmes' face was turned towards it, and he muttered impatiently as he watched its sluggish drift.

"It's moving towards us, Watson."

"Is that serious?"

"Very serious, indeed – the one thing upon earth which could have disarranged my plans. He can't be very long, now. It is already ten o'clock. Our success and even his life may depend upon his coming out before the fog is over the path."

The night was clear and fine. The stars shone cold and

bright, while a half-moon bathed the whole scene in a soft, uncertain light. Before us lay the dark bulk of the house, its serrated roof and bristling chimneys hard outlined against the silver-spangled sky. Broad bars of golden light from the lower windows stretched across the orchard and the moor. One of them was suddenly shut off. There only remained the lamp in the dining room where the two men, the murderous host and the unconscious guest, still chatted over their cigars.

Every minute that white woolly plain that covered one-half of the moor was drifting closer and closer to the house. Already the first thin wisps of it were curling across the golden square of the lighted window. The farther wall of the orchard was already invisible, and the trees were standing out of a swirl of white vapour. As we watched it the fog-wreaths came crawling round both corners of the house and rolled slowly into one dense bank on which the upper floor and the roof floated like a strange ship upon a shadowy sea. Holmes struck his hand passionately upon the rock in front of us and stamped his feet in his impatience.

"If he isn't out in a quarter of an hour the path will be covered. In half an hour we won't be able to see our hands."

"Shall we move farther back upon higher ground?"

"Yes, I think it would be as well."

So as the fog-bank flowed onward we fell back before it until we were half a mile from the house, our footsteps crunching in the remains of the snow, and still that dense white sea, with the moon silvering its upper edge, swept on.

"We are going too far," said Holmes. "We dare not take the chance of his being overtaken before he can reach us. At all costs we must hold our ground where we are." He dropped on his knees and clapped his ear to the ground. "Thank God, I think that I hear him coming."

A sound of quick steps broke the silence of the moor. Crouching among the stones we stared intently at the silver-tipped bank in front of us. The steps grew louder, and through the fog, as through a curtain, there stepped the man whom we were awaiting. He looked round him in surprise as he emerged into the clear, starlit night. Then he came swiftly along the path, passed close to where we lay, and went on up the long slope behind us. As he walked he glanced continually over either shoulder, like a man who is ill at ease.

"Hist!" cried Holmes, and I heard the sharp click of a cocking pistol. "Look out! It's coming!"

There was a thin, crisp, continuous patter from somewhere in the heart of that crawling bank. The cloud was within fifty yards of where we lay, and we glared at it, all three, uncertain what horror was about to break from the heart of it. I was at holmes' elbow, and I glanced at his face. It was pale and

exultant, his eyes shining brightly in the moonlight. But suddenly they started forward in a rigid, fixed stare, and his lips parted in amazement. At the same instant Lestrade gave a yell of terror and threw himself face downward upon the ground. I sprang to my feet, my inert hand grasping my pistol, my mind paralyzed by the dreadful shape that had sprung out upon us from the shadows of the fog. A hound it was, an enormous coal-black hound, but not such a hound as mortal eyes have ever seen. Fire burst from its open mouth, its eyes glowed with a smouldering glare, its muzzle and hackles and dewlap were outlined in flickering flame. Never could anything more savage, more hellish be conceived than that dark form and savage face which broke upon us out of the wall of fog.

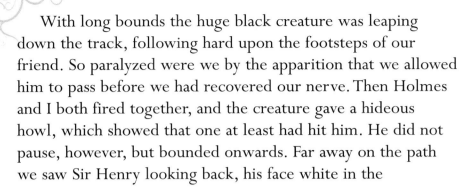

With long bounds the huge black creature was leaping down the track, following hard upon the footsteps of our friend. So paralyzed were we by the apparition that we allowed him to pass before we had recovered our nerve. Then Holmes and I both fired together, and the creature gave a hideous howl, which showed that one at least had hit him. He did not pause, however, but bounded onwards. Far away on the path we saw Sir Henry looking back, his face white in the

moonlight, his hands raised in horror, glaring helplessly at the frightful thing.

But that cry of pain from the hound had blown all our fears to the winds. If he was vulnerable he was mortal, and if we could wound him we could kill him. Never have I seen a man run as Holmes ran that night. I am reckoned fleet of foot, but he outpaced me as much as I outpaced the little professional. In front of us as we flew up the track we heard scream after scream from Sir Henry and the deep roar of the hound. I was in time to see the beast spring upon its victim, hurl him to the ground, and worry at his throat. But the next instant Holmes had emptied five barrels of his revolver into the creature's flank. With a last howl of agony and a vicious snap in the air, it rolled upon its back, four feet pawing furiously, and then fell limp upon its side. The giant hound was dead.

Sir Henry lay insensible where he had fallen. We tore away his collar, and Holmes breathed a prayer of gratitude when we saw that there was no sign of a wound and that the rescue had been in time. Already our friend's eyelids shivered. Lestrade thrust his brandy flask between the baronet's teeth, and two frightened eyes were looking up at us.

"My God!" he whispered. "Whatever, was it?"

"It's dead, whatever it is," said Holmes. "We've laid the family ghost once and forever."

Some Words with a Mummy

1845

EXTRACT

Edgar Allan Poe

I could not have completed my third snore when there came
a furious ringing at the doorbell, and then an impatient
thumping at the knocker, which awakened me at once. In a
minute afterward, and while I was still rubbing my eyes, my
wife thrust in my face a note, from my old friend,
Dr Ponnonner. It ran thus:

Come to me, by all means, my dear good friend, as soon as
you receive this. Come and help us to rejoice. At last, by
long persevering diplomacy, I have gained the assent of the
Directors of the City Museum, to my examination of the
mummy — you know the one I mean. I have permission to
unswathe it and open it, if desirable. A few friends only will
be present — you, of course. The mummy is now at my

house, and we shall begin to unroll it at eleven tonight. Yours, ever, Ponnonner.

By the time I had reached the Ponnonner, it struck me that I was as wide awake as a man need be. I leapt out of bed in an ecstacy, overthrowing all in my way; dressed myself with a rapidity truly marvellous; and set off, at the top of my speed, for the doctor's.

There I found a very eager company assembled. They had been awaiting me with much impatience; the mummy was extended upon the dining table; and the moment I entered its examination was commenced.

It was one of a pair brought, several years previously, by Captain Arthur Sabretash, a cousin of Ponnonner's from a tomb near Eleithias, in the Lybian mountains, a considerable distance above Thebes on the Nile. The grottoes at this point, although less magnificent than the Theban sepulchres, are of higher interest, on account of affording more numerous illustrations of the private life of the Egyptians. The chamber from which our specimen was taken, was said to be very rich in such illustrations; the walls being completely covered with fresco paintings and bas-reliefs, while statues, vases, and mosaic work of rich patterns, indicated the vast wealth of the deceased.

The treasure had been deposited in the Museum precisely in the same condition in which Captain Sabretash had found it – that is to say, the coffin had not been disturbed. For eight

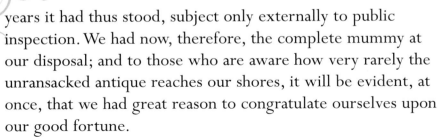

years it had thus stood, subject only externally to public inspection. We had now, therefore, the complete mummy at our disposal; and to those who are aware how very rarely the unransacked antique reaches our shores, it will be evident, at once, that we had great reason to congratulate ourselves upon our good fortune.

Approaching the table, I saw on it a large box, or case, nearly seven feet long, and perhaps three feet wide, by two feet and a half deep. It was oblong – not coffin-shaped. The material was at first supposed to be the wood of the sycamore (*platanus*), but, upon cutting into it, we found it to be pasteboard, or, more properly, pâpier-maché, composed of papyrus. It was thickly ornamented with paintings, representing funeral scenes, and other mournful subjects – interspersed among which, in every variety of position, were certain series of hieroglyphical characters, intended, no doubt, for the name of the departed. By good luck Mr Gliddon formed one of our party, and he had no difficulty in translating

the letters, which were simply phonetic, and represented the word, *Allamistakeo*.

We had some difficulty in getting this case open without injury; but having at length accomplished the task, we came to a second, coffin-shaped, and very considerably less in size than the exterior one, but resembling it precisely in every other respect. The interval between the two was filled with resin, which had, in some degree, defaced the colours of the interior box.

Upon opening this latter (which we did quite easily), we arrived at a third case, also coffin-shaped, and varying from the second one in no particular, except in that of its material, which was cedar, and still emitted the peculiar and highly aromatic odour of that wood. Between the second and the third case there was no interval – the one fitting accurately within the other.

Removing the third case, we discovered and took out the body itself. We had expected to find it, as usual, enveloped in frequent rolls or bandages, of linen; but, in place of these, we found a sort of sheath, made of papyrus, and coated with a layer of plaster, thickly gilt and painted. The paintings represented subjects connected with the various supposed duties of the soul, and its presentation to different divinities, with numerous identical human figures intended, very probably, as portraits of the persons embalmed. Extending from head to foot was a columnar, or perpendicular, inscription, in phonetic hieroglyphics, giving again his name

and titles, and the names and titles of his relations.

Around the neck thus ensheathed, was a collar of cylindrical glass beads, diverse in colour, and so arranged as to form images of deities, of the scarabaeus, etc. with the winged globe. Around the small of the waist was a similar collar or belt.

Stripping off the papyrus, we found the flesh in excellent preservation, with no perceptible odour. The colour was reddish. The skin was hard, smooth, and glossy. The teeth and hair were in good condition. The eyes (it seemed) had been removed, and glass ones substituted, which were very beautiful and wonderfully lifelike, with the exception of somewhat too determined a stare. The fingers and the nails were brilliantly gilded.

Mr Gliddon was of opinion, from the redness of the epidermis, that the embalmment had been effected altogether by asphaltum; but, on scraping the surface with a steel instrument, and throwing into the fire some of the powder thus obtained, the flavour of camphor and other sweet-scented gums became apparent.

We searched the corpse very carefully for the usual openings through which the entrails are extracted, but, to our surprise, we could discover none. No member of the party was at that period aware that entire or unopened mummies are not infrequently met. The brain it was customary to withdraw through the nose; the intestines through an incision in the side. The body was then shaved, washed, and salted; then laid aside for several weeks, when the operation of embalming, properly so called, began.

As no trace of an opening could be found, Dr Ponnonner was preparing his instruments for dissection, when I observed that it was then past two o'clock. Hereupon it was agreed to postpone the internal examination until the next evening; and we were about to separate for the present, when someone suggested an experiment or two with the Voltaic pile.

The application of electricity to a mummy that was at least three or four thousand years old, was an idea, if not particularly sage, still sufficiently original, and we all caught it at once. About one-tenth in earnest and nine-tenths in jest, we arranged a battery in the doctor's study, and conveyed thither the Egyptian.

It was only after much trouble that we succeeded in laying bare some portions of the temporal muscle which appeared of less stony rigidity than other parts of the frame, but which, as we had anticipated, of course, gave no indication of galvanic susceptibility when brought in contact with the wire. This, the first trial, indeed, seemed decisive, and, with a hearty laugh at our own absurdity, we were bidding each other goodnight, when my eyes, happening to fall upon those of the mummy, were there immediately riveted in amazement. My brief glance, in fact, had sufficed to assure me that the orbs which we had all supposed to be glass, and which were originally very noticeable for a certain wild stare, were now so far covered by the lids, that only a small portion of the *tunica albuginea* remained visible.

With a shout I called attention to the fact, and it became immediately obvious to all.

I cannot say that I was *alarmed* at the phenomenon, because alarmed is, in my case, not exactly the word. It is possible, however, that, but for the brown stout, I might have been a little nervous. As for the rest of the company, they really made no attempt at concealing the downright fright which possessed them. Dr Ponnonner was a man to be pitied. Mr Gliddon, by some peculiar process, managed to render himself invisible. Mr Silk Buckingham, I fancy, will scarcely be so bold as to deny the fact that he immediately made his way, upon all fours, under the table.

After the first shock of astonishment, however, we

resolved, as a matter of course, upon further experiment forthwith. Our operations were now directed against the great toe of the right foot. We made an incision over the outside of the exterior *os sesamoideum pollicis pedis*, and thus got at the root of the *abductor* muscle. Readjusting the battery, we now applied the fluid to the bisected nerves – when, with a movement of exceeding life-likeness, the mummy first drew up its right knee so as to bring it nearly in contact with the abdomen, and then, straightening the limb with inconceivable force, bestowed a kick upon Dr Ponnonner, which had the effect of discharging that gentleman, like an arrow from a catapult, through a window into the street below.

We rushed out *en masse* to bring in the mangled remains of the victim, but had the happiness to meet him upon the staircase, coming up in an unaccountable hurry, brimful of the most ardent philosophy, and impressed with the necessity of prosecuting our experiment with vigour and with zeal.

It was by his advice, accordingly, that we made, upon the spot, a profound incision into the tip of the subject's nose, while the doctor himself, laying violent hands upon it, pulled it into vehement contact with the wire.

Morally and physically – figuratively and literally – was the effect electric. In the first place, the corpse opened its eyes and winked very rapidly for several minutes, as does Mr Barnes in the pantomime, in the second place, it sneezed and in the third it sat up on end…

Carmilla

1872

EXTRACT

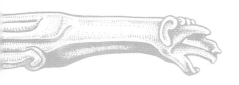

J Sheridan Le Fanu

The old general's eyes were fixed on the ground, as he leaned with his hand upon the basement of a shattered monument.

Under a narrow, arched doorway, surmounted by one of those demoniacal grotesques in which the cynical and ghastly fancy of old Gothic carving delights, I saw very gladly the beautiful face and figure of Carmilla enter the shadowy chapel.

I was just about to rise and speak, having nodded, smiling, in answer to her peculiarly engaging smile; when with a cry, the old man by my side caught up the woodman's hatchet, and

started forward. On seeing him, a brutalised change came over her features. It was an instantaneous and horrible transformation, as she made a crouching step backwards. Before I could utter a scream, he struck at her with all his force; but she dived under his blow, and unscathed, caught him in her tiny grasp by the wrist. He struggled for a moment to release his arm, but his hand opened, the axe fell to the ground, and the girl was gone.

He staggered against the wall. His grey hair stood upon his head, and a moisture shone over his face, as if he were at the point of death.

The frightful scene had passed in a moment. The first thing I recollect after, is *madame* standing before me, and impatiently repeating again and again, the question, "Where is Mademoiselle Carmilla?"

I answered at length, "I don't know – I can't tell – she went there," and I pointed to the door through which *madame* had just entered, "only a minute or two since."

"But I have been standing there, in the passage, ever since Mademoiselle Carmilla entered; and she did not return."

She then began to call Carmilla, through every door and passage and from the windows, but no answer came.

"She called herself Carmilla?" asked the general, still agitated.

"Carmilla, yes," I answered.

"Aye," he said; "that is Millarca. That is the same person who long ago was called many other names – Mircalla,

Countess Karnstein. Depart from this accursed ground, my poor child, as quickly as you can. Drive to the clergyman's house, and stay there till we come. Only there will you be safe. Begone! May you never behold Carmilla more; for you will not see her face here again."

As he spoke, one of the strangest-looking men I ever beheld entered the chapel at the door through which Carmilla had made her entrance and her exit. He was tall, narrow-chested, stooping, with high shoulders, and dressed in black. His face was brown and dried in with deep furrows and he wore an oddly-shaped hat with a broad leaf. His hair, long and grizzled, hung on his shoulders. He wore a pair of gold spectacles, and walked slowly with an odd shambling gait, with his face sometimes turned up to the sky and sometimes bowed down towards the ground, seemed to wear a perpetual smile. His long thin arms were swinging, and his lank hands, in old black gloves ever so much too wide for them, waving and gesticulating in utter abstraction.

"The very man!" exclaimed the general, advancing with manifest delight. "My dear baron, how happy I am to see you, I had no hope of meeting you so soon." He signed to my father, who had by this time returned, and leading the fantastic old gentleman, whom he called the baron, to meet him, he introduced him formally, and they at once entered into earnest conversation. The stranger took a roll of paper from his pocket, and spread it on the worn surface of a tomb that stood by. He had a pencilcase in his fingers, with which he traced

imaginary lines from point to point on the paper, which from their often glancing from it together at certain points of the building, I concluded to be a plan of the chapel. He accompanied what I may term his lecture, with occasional readings from a dirty little book, whose yellow leaves were closely written over.

They sauntered together down the side aisle, opposite to the spot where I was standing, conversing as they went. Then they began measuring distances by paces, and finally they all stood together, facing a piece of the sidewall, which they began to examine with great minuteness; pulling off the ivy that clung over it, and rapping the plaster with the ends of their sticks, scraping here, and knocking there. At length they ascertained the existence of a broad marble tablet, with letters carved in relief upon it.

With the assistance of the woodman, who soon returned, a monumental inscription, and carved coat-of-arms, were disclosed. They proved to be those of the long-lost monument of Mircalla, Countess Karnstein.

The old general, though not I fear given to the praying mood, raised his hands and eyes to heaven, in mute thanksgiving for some moments.

"Tomorrow," I heard him say; "the commissioner will be here, and the inquisition will be held according to law."

Then turning to the old man with the gold spectacles, whom I have described, he shook him warmly by both hands and said: "How can I thank you? How can we all thank you?

You will have delivered this region from a plague that has scourged its inhabitants for more than a century. The horrible enemy, thank God, is at last tracked."

My father led the stranger aside, and the general followed. I knew that he had led them out of hearing, that he might relate my case, and I saw them glance often quickly at me, as the discussion proceeded.

My father came to me, kissed me again and again, and leading me from the chapel, said: "It is time to return, but before we go home, we must add to our party the good priest, who lives but a little way from this; and persuade him to accompany us to the *schloss*."

In this quest we were successful: and I was glad, being unspeakably fatigued when we reached home. But my satisfaction was changed to dismay, on discovering that there were no tidings of Carmilla. Of the scene that had occurred in the ruined chapel, no explanation was offered to me, and it was clear that it was a secret which my father for the present determined to keep from me.

The sinister absence of Carmilla made the remembrance of the scene more horrible to me. The arrangements for the night were singular. Two servants, and *madame* were to sit up in my room that night; and the ecclesiastic with my father kept watch in the adjoining dressing room.

The priest had performed certain solemn rites that night, the purport of which I did not understand any more than I comprehended the reason of this extraordinary precaution

taken for my safety during sleep.

I saw all clearly a few days later.

The disappearance of Carmilla was followed by the discontinuance of my nightly sufferings.

You have heard, no doubt, of the appalling superstition that prevails in Upper and Lower Styria, in Moravia, Silesia, in Turkish Servia, in Poland, even in Russia; the superstition, so we must call it, of the vampire.

If human testimony – taken with every care and solemnity, judicially, before commissions innumerable, each consisting of many members all chosen for integrity and intelligence, and constituting reports more voluminous perhaps than exist upon any one other class of cases – is worth anything, it is difficult to deny, or even to doubt the existence of such a phenomenon as the vampire.

For my part I have heard no theory by which to explain what I myself have witnessed and experienced, other than that supplied by the ancient and well-attested belief of the country.

The next day the formal proceedings took place in the Chapel of Karnstein. The grave of the Countess Mircalla was opened; and the general and my father recognized each his perfidious and beautiful guest, in the face now disclosed to view. The features, though a hundred and fifty years had passed since her funeral, were tinted with the warmth of life. No cadaverous smell exhaled from the coffin. The two medical men, one officially present, the other there on the part of the promoter of the inquiry, attested the marvellous fact that there

was a faint but appreciable respiration, and a corresponding action of the heart. The limbs were perfectly flexible, the flesh elastic; and the leaden coffin floated with blood. Here then, were all the admitted signs and proofs of vampirism. The body therefore, in accordance with the ancient practice, was raised and a sharp stake driven through the heart of the vampire, who uttered a piercing shriek at the moment, in all respects such as might escape from a living person in the last agony. Then the head was struck off, and a torrent of blood flowed from the severed neck. The body and head was next placed on a pile of wood, and reduced to ashes, which were thrown upon the river and borne away, and that territory has never since been plagued by the visits of a vampire.

My father has a copy of the report of the Imperial Commission, with the signatures of all who were present at these proceedings, attached in verification of the statement. It is from this official paper that I have summarized my account of this last shocking scene.

The Doomed and the Dead

Why do the dead choose to intrude upon the living? To haunt us with things that have been. To plague us to change things that are now. To warn us about things that will be, and sometimes even play a part in our own demise...

386

The Turn of the Screw

392

The Trial for Murder

410

In Kropfsberg Keep

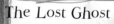

424

The Lost Ghost

The Turn of the Screw

1898

EXTRACT

Henry James

Round the corner of the house, she loomed again into view. "What in the name of goodness is the matter?" She was now flushed and out of breath.

I said nothing till she came quite near. "With me?" I must have made a wonderful face. "Do I show it?"

"You're as white as a sheet. You look awful."

I considered; I could meet on this without scruple, any innocence. My need to respect the bloom of Mrs Grose's had dropped, without a rustle, from my shoulders, and if I wavered for the instant it was not with what I kept back. I put out my hand to her and she took it; I held her hard a little, liking to feel her close to me. There was a kind of support in the shy heave of her surprise. "You came for me for church, but I can't go."

"Has anything happened?"

"Yes. You must know now. Did I look very queer?"

"Through this window? Dreadful!"

"Well," I said, "I've been frightened." Mrs Grose's eyes expressed plainly that *she* had no wish to be, yet also that she knew too well her place not to be ready to share with me any marked inconvenience. Oh, it was quite settled that she *must* share! "Just what you saw from the dining room a minute ago was the effect of that. What *I* saw — just before — was much worse."

Her hand tightened. "What was it?"

"An extraordinary man. Looking in."

"What extraordinary man?"

"I haven't the least idea."

Mrs Grose gazed round us in vain. "Then where is he gone?"

"I know still less."

"Have you seen him before?"

"Yes — once. On the old tower."

She could only look at me harder. "Do you mean he's a stranger?"

"Oh, very much!"

"Yet you didn't tell me?"

"No — for reasons. But now that you've guessed…"

Mrs Grose's round eyes encountered this charge. "Ah, I haven't guessed!" she said. "How can I if *you* don't imagine?"

"I don't in the very least."

"You've seen him nowhere but on the tower?"

"And on this spot just now."

Mrs Grose looked round again. "What was he doing on the tower?"

"Only standing there and looking down at me."

She thought a minute. "Was he a gentleman?"

I found I had no need to think. "No." She gazed in deeper wonder. "No."

"Then nobody about the place? Nobody from the village?"

"Nobody – nobody. I didn't tell you, but I made sure."

She breathed a vague relief: this was, oddly, so much to the good. It only went indeed a little way, "But if he isn't a gentleman—"

"What *is* he? He's a horror."

"A horror?"

"He's – God help me if I know what he is!"

Mrs. Grose looked round once more; she fixed her eyes on the duskier distance, then, pulling herself together, turned to me with abrupt inconsequence. "It's time we should be at church."

"Oh, I'm not fit for church!"

"Won't it do you good?"

"It won't do them—" I nodded at the house.

"The children?"

"I can't leave *them* now."

"You're afraid?"

I spoke boldly. "I'm afraid of *him*."

Mrs Grose's large face showed me, at this, for the first time, the faraway faint glimmer of a consciousness more acute. I somehow made out in it the delayed dawn of an idea I myself had not given her and that was as yet quite obscure to me. It comes back to me that I thought instantly of this as something I could get from her; and I felt it to be connected with the desire she presently showed to know more. "When was it – on the tower?"

"About the middle of the month. At this same hour."

"Almost at dark," said Mrs Grose.

"Oh, no, not nearly. I saw him as I see you."

"Then how did he get in?"

"And how did he get out?" I laughed. "I had no opportunity to ask him! This evening, you see," I pursued, "he has not been able to get in."

"He only peeps?"

"I hope it will be confined to that!"

She had now let go my hand. She turned away a little.

I waited an instant; then I brought out: "Go to church. Goodbye. I must watch."

Slowly she faced me again. "Do you fear for them?"

We met in another long look, "Don't *you*?" Instead of answering she came nearer to the window and, for a minute, applied her face to the glass. "You see how he could see," I meanwhile went on.

She didn't move. "How long was he here?"

"Till I came out. I came to meet him."

Mrs Grose at last turned round, and there was still more in her face. "*I* couldn't have come out."

"Neither could *I*!" I laughed again. "But I did come. I have my duty."

"So have I mine," she replied; after which she added: "What is he like?"

"I've been dying to tell you. But he's like nobody."

"Nobody?" she echoed.

"He has no hat." Then seeing in her face that she already, in this, with a deeper dismay found a touch of picture, I quickly added stroke to stroke. "He has red hair, very red, close-curling, and a pale face, long in shape, with straight, good features and little, rather queer whiskers that are as red as his hair. His eyebrows are, somehow, darker; they look particularly arched and as if they might move a good deal. His eyes are sharp and strange, they're rather small and very fixed. His mouth's wide, and his lips are thin, and except for his little whiskers he's quite clean-shaven. He gives me a sort of sense of looking like an actor."

"An actor!" It was impossible to resemble one less, at least, than Mrs Grose at that moment.

"I've never seen one, but so I suppose them. He's tall, active, erect," I continued, "but never – no, never! – a gentleman."

My companion's face had blanched as I went on; her round

eyes started and her mild mouth gaped. "A gentleman?" she gasped, confounded, stupefied: "A gentleman, *he*?"

"You know him then?"

She visibly tried to hold herself. "But he *is* handsome?"

I saw the way to help her. "Remarkably!"

"And dressed?"

"In somebody's clothes. They're smart, but they're not his."

She broke into a breathless affirmative groan: "They're the master's!"

I caught it up. "You *do* know him?"

She faltered but a second. "Quint!" she cried. "Peter Quint – his own man, his valet, when he was here!"

"When the master was?"

Gaping still, but meeting me, she pieced it all together. "He never wore his hat, but he did wear – well, there were waistcoats missed. They were both here – last year. Then the master went, and Quint was alone."

I followed, but halting a little. "Alone?"

"Alone with *us*." Then, as from a deeper depth, "In charge," she added.

"And what became of him?"

"He went, too," she brought out at last.

"Went where?"

Her expression became extraordinary. "God knows! He died."

"Died?" I almost shrieked.

She seemed fairly to square herself, plant herself more firmly to utter the wonder of it. "Yes. Mr Quint is dead."

The Trial for Murder

1865

Charles Dickens

with Charles Allston Collins

I have always noticed a prevalent want of courage, even among persons of superior intelligence and culture, as to imparting their own psychological experiences when those have been of a strange sort. Almost all men are afraid that what they could relate in such wise would find no parallel or response in a listener's internal life, and might be suspected or laughed at. A truthful traveller, having seen some extraordinary creature in the likeness of a sea-serpent, would have no fear of mentioning it; but the same traveller, having had some singular presentiment, impulse, vagary of thought, vision (so-called), dream, or other remarkable mental impression, would hesitate considerably before he would own to it. To this reticence I attribute much of the obscurity in which such subjects are involved. We do not habitually

communicate our experiences of these subjective things as we do our experiences of objective creation. The consequence is, that the general stock of experience in this regard appears exceptional, and really is so, in respect of being miserably imperfect.

In what I am going to relate, I have no intention of setting up, opposing, or supporting, any theory whatever. I know the history of the bookseller in Berlin, I have studied the case of the wife of a late Astronomer Royal as related by Sir David Brewster, and I have followed the minutest details of a much more remarkable case of spectral illusion occurring within my private circle of friends. It may be necessary to state as to this last, that the sufferer (a lady) was in no degree, however distant, related to me. A mistaken assumption on that head might suggest an explanation of a part of my own case — but only a part — which would be wholly without foundation. It cannot be referred to my inheritance of any developed peculiarity, nor had I ever before any at all similar experience, nor have I ever had any at all similar experience since.

It does not signify how many years ago, or how few, a certain murder was committed in England, which attracted great attention. We hear more than enough of murderers as they rise in succession to their atrocious eminence, and I would bury the memory of this particular brute, if I could, as his body was buried, in Newgate Jail. I purposely abstain from giving any direct clue to the criminal's individuality.

When the murder was first discovered, no suspicion fell —

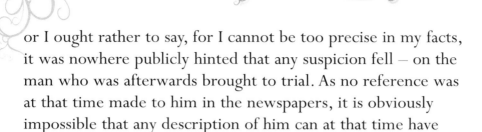

or I ought rather to say, for I cannot be too precise in my facts, it was nowhere publicly hinted that any suspicion fell – on the man who was afterwards brought to trial. As no reference was at that time made to him in the newspapers, it is obviously impossible that any description of him can at that time have been given in the newspapers. It is essential that this fact be remembered.

Unfolding at breakfast my morning paper, containing the account of that first discovery, I found it to be deeply interesting, and I read it with close attention. I read it twice, if not three times. The discovery had been made in a bedroom, and when I laid down the paper I was aware of a flash – rush – flow – I do not know what to call it, no word I can find is satisfactorily descriptive – in which I seemed to see that bedroom passing through my room, like a picture impossibly painted on a running river. Though almost instantaneous in its passing, it was perfectly clear; so clear that I distinctly, and with a sense of relief, observed the absence of the dead body from the bed.

It was in no romantic place that I had this curious sensation, but in chambers in Piccadilly, very near to the corner of St James's Street. It was entirely new to me. I was in my easy-chair at the moment, and the sensation was accompanied with a peculiar shiver which started the chair from its position. (But it is to be noted that the chair ran easily on castors.) I went to one of the windows (there are two in the room, and the room

is on the second floor) to refresh my eyes with the moving objects down in Piccadilly. It was a bright autumn morning, and the street was sparkling and cheerful. The wind was high. As I looked out, it brought down from the park a quantity of fallen leaves, which a gust took and whirled into a spiral pillar. As the pillar fell and the leaves dispersed, I saw two men on the opposite side of the way, going from west to east. They were one behind the other. The foremost man often looked back over his shoulder. The second man followed him, at a distance of some thirty paces, with his right hand menacingly raised. First, the singularity and steadiness of this threatening gesture in so public a thoroughfare attracted my attention; and next, the more remarkable circumstance that nobody heeded it. Both men threaded their way among the other passengers with a smoothness hardly consistent even with the action of walking on a pavement; and no single creature, that I could see, gave them place, touched them, or looked after them. In passing before my windows, they both stared up at me. I saw their two faces very distinctly, and I knew that I could recognize them anywhere. Not that I had consciously noticed anything very remarkable in either face, except that the man who went first had an unusually lowering appearance, and that the face of the man who followed him was of the colour of impure wax.

I am a bachelor, and my valet and his wife constitute my whole establishment. My occupation is in a certain branch

bank, and I wish that my duties as head of a department were as light as they are popularly supposed to be. They kept me in town that autumn, when I stood in need of change. I was not ill, but I was not well. My reader is to make the most that can be reasonably made of my feeling jaded, having a depressing sense upon me of a monotonous life, and being 'slightly dyspeptic'. I am assured by my renowned doctor that my real state of health at that time justifies no stronger description, and I quote his own from his written answer to my request for it.

As the circumstances of the murder, gradually unravelling, took stronger and stronger possession of the public mind, I kept them away from mine by knowing as little about them as was possible in the midst of the universal excitement. But I knew that a verdict of wilful murder had been found against the suspected murderer, and that he had been committed to Newgate for trial. I also knew that his trial had been postponed over one sessions of the Central Criminal Court, on the ground of general prejudice and want of time for the preparation of the defence. I may further have known, but I believe I did not, when, or about when, the sessions to which his trial stood postponed would come on.

My sitting room, bedroom, and dressing room, are all on one floor. With the last there is no communication but through the bedroom. True, there is a door in it, once communicating with the staircase; but a part of the fitting of

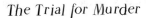
my bath has been – and had then been for some years – fixed across it. At the same period, and as a part of the same arrangement – the door had been nailed up and canvassed over.

I was standing in my bedroom late one night, giving some directions to my servant before he went to bed. My face was towards the only available door of communication with the dressing room, and it was closed. My servant's back was towards that door. While I was speaking to him, I saw it open and a man look in, who very earnestly and mysteriously beckoned to me. That man was the man who had gone second of the two along Piccadilly, and whose face was of the colour of impure wax.

The figure, having beckoned, drew back and closed the door. With no longer pause than was made by my crossing the bedroom, I opened the dressing room door and looked in. I had a lighted candle already in my hand. I felt no inward expectation of seeing the figure in the dressing room, and I did not see it there.

Conscious that my servant stood amazed, I turned round to him, and said: "Derrick, could you believe that in my cool senses I fancied I saw a…" As I there laid my hand upon his breast, with a sudden start he trembled violently, and said, "Oh Lord, yes, sir! A dead man beckoning!"

Now I do not believe that this John Derrick, who has been my trusty and attached servant for more than twenty years, had any impression whatever of having seen any such ghostly

figure, until I happened to touched him. The change in him was so startling, when I touched him, that I fully believe he derived his impression in some occult manner from me at that instant.

I bade John Derrick bring some brandy, and I gave him a dram, and was glad to take one myself. Of what had preceded that night's phenomenon, I told him not a single word. Reflecting on it, I was absolutely certain that I had never seen that face before, except on the one occasion in Piccadilly. Comparing its expression when beckoning at the door with its expression when it had stared up at me as I stood at my window, I came to the conclusion that on the first occasion it had sought to fasten itself upon my memory, and that on the second occasion it had made sure of being immediately remembered.

I was not very comfortable that night, though I felt a certainty, difficult to explain, that the figure would not return. At daylight I fell into a heavy sleep, and was awakened by John Derrick's coming to my bedside with a paper in his hand.

This paper, it appeared, had been the subject of an altercation at the door between its bearer and my servant. It was a summons to me to serve upon a jury at the forthcoming sessions of the Central Criminal Court at the Old Bailey. I had never before been summoned on such a jury, as John Derrick well knew. He believed that that class of jurors were customarily chosen on a lower qualification than mine, and he had at first refused to accept the summons. The man who

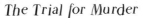

served it had taken the matter very coolly. He had said that my attendance or non-attendance was nothing to him. There the summons was; and I should deal with it at my own peril.

For a day or two I was undecided whether to respond to this call or take no notice of it. I was not conscious of the slightest mysterious bias, influence, or attraction, one way or other. Of that I am as strictly sure as of every other statement that I make here. Ultimately I decided, as a break in the monotony of my life, that I would go.

The appointed morning was a raw morning in the month of November. There was a dense brown fog in Piccadilly, and it became positively black and in the last degree oppressive east of Temple Bar. I found the passages and staircases of the courthouse flaringly lighted with gas, and the court itself similarly illuminated. I *think* that, until I was conducted by officers into the old court and saw its crowded state, I did not know that the murderer was to be tried that day. I think that, until I was so helped into the old court with considerable difficulty, I did not know into which of the two courts sitting my summons would take me. But this must not be received as a positive assertion, for I am not completely satisfied in my mind on either point.

I took my seat in the place appropriated to jurors in waiting, and I looked about the court as well as I could through the cloud of fog and breath that was heavy in it. I noticed the black vapour hanging like a murky curtain outside the great windows, and I noticed the stifled sound of wheels on the straw or tan that was littered in the street; also, the hum of the people gathered there, which a shrill whistle, or a louder song or hail than the rest, occasionally pierced. Soon afterwards the judges, two in number, entered, and took their seats. The buzz in the court was hushed. The direction was given to put the murderer to the bar. He appeared, and in that same instant I recognized in him the first of the two men who had gone down Piccadilly.

If my name had been called then, I doubt if I could have answered to it audibly. But it was called about sixth or eighth in the panel, and I was by that time able to say, "Here!" Now, observe. As I stepped into the box, the prisoner became violently agitated, and beckoned to his attorney. The prisoner's wish to challenge me was so manifest, that it occasioned a pause, during which the attorney, with his hand upon the dock, whispered with his client, and shook his head. I afterwards had it from that gentleman, that the prisoner's first affrighted words to him were, "At all hazards, challenge that man!" But that, as he would give no reason for it, and admitted that he had not even known my name until he heard it called, it was not done.

Both on the ground already explained, that I wish to avoid reviving the unwholesome, unwelcome memory of that murderer, and also because a detailed account of his trial is by

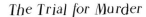

no means indispensable to my narrative, I shall confine myself to such incidents in the ten days and nights during which we, the members of the jury, were kept together, as directly bear on my own very curious personal experience. It is in that, and not in the murderer, that I seek to interest my reader.

I was chosen foreman of the jury. On the second morning of the trial, after evidence had been taken for two hours, happening to cast my eyes over my brother jurymen, I found an inexplicable difficulty in counting them. I counted them several times, yet always with the same difficulty. In short, I made them one too many.

I touched the brother juryman whose place was next me, and I whispered to him, "Oblige me by counting us." He looked surprised by the request, but turned his head and counted. "Why," says he, suddenly, "we are Thirt——; but no, it's not possible. No. We are twelve."

According to my counting that day, we were always right in detail, but in the gross we were always one too many. There was no appearance – no figure – to account for it; but I had now a foreshadowing of the figure that was surely coming.

The jury were housed at the London Tavern. We all slept in one large room on separate tables, and we were constantly in the charge and under the eye of the officer sworn to hold us in safe-keeping. I see no reason for suppressing the real name of that officer. He was intelligent, highly polite, and obliging, and much respected in the City. His name was Mr Harker.

When we turned into our twelve beds at night,
Mr Harker's bed was drawn across the door. On the night of
the second day, not being disposed to lie down, and seeing
Mr Harker sitting on his bed, I went and sat beside him, and
offered him a pinch of snuff. As Mr Harker's hand touched
mine in taking it from my box, a peculiar shiver crossed him,
and he said, "Who is this?"

Following Mr Harker's eyes, and looking along the room, I
saw again the figure I expected – the second of the two men
who had gone down Piccadilly. I rose, and advanced a few
steps; then stopped, and looked round at Mr Harker. He was
quite unconcerned, and said in a pleasant way, "I thought for a
moment we had a thirteenth man but I see it is the moonlight."

Making no revelation to Mr Harker, but inviting him to
take a walk with me to the end of the room, I watched what
the figure did. It stood for a few moments by the bedside of
each of my eleven brother jurymen, close to the pillow. It
always went to the right-hand side of the bed, and always
passed out crossing the foot of the next bed. It seemed, from
the action of the head, merely to look down pensively at each
recumbent figure. It took no notice of me, or of my bed,
which was that nearest to Mr Harker's. It seemed to go out
where the moonlight came in, through a high window, as by an
aerial flight of stairs.

Next morning at breakfast, it appeared that everybody
present had dreamed of the murdered man last night, except
myself and Mr Harker.

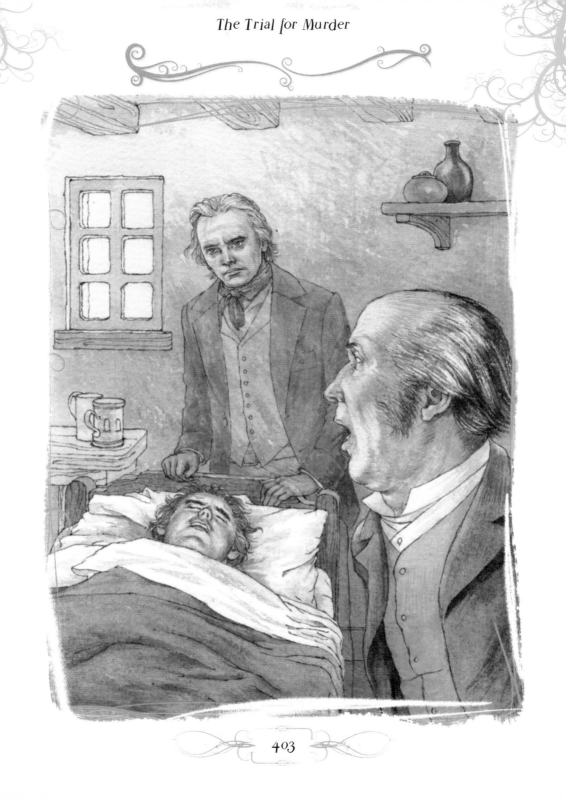

I now felt as convinced that the second man who had gone down Piccadilly was the murdered man (so to speak), as if it had been borne into my comprehension by his immediate testimony. On the fifth day of the trial, when the case for the prosecution was drawing to a close, a miniature of the murdered man, missing from his bedroom upon the discovery of the deed, and afterwards found in a hiding place where the murderer had been seen digging, was put in evidence. Having been identified by the witness under examination, it was handed up to the bench, and thence handed down to be inspected by the jury. As an officer in a black gown was making his way with it across to me, the figure of the second man who had gone down Piccadilly impetuously started from the crowd, caught the miniature from the officer, and gave it to me with his own hands, at the same time saying, in a low and hollow tone – before I saw the miniature, which was in a locket – "I was younger then, and my face was not then drained of blood." It also came between me and the brother juryman to whom I would have given the miniature, and between him and the brother juryman to whom he would have given it, and so passed it on through the whole of our number, and back into my possession. Not one of them, however, detected this.

At table, and generally when we were shut up together in Mr Harker's custody, we had from the first naturally discussed the day's proceedings a good deal. On that fifth day, the case

for the prosecution being closed, and we having that side of the question in a completed shape before us, our discussion was more animated and serious. Among our number was a vestryman – the densest idiot I have ever seen at large – who met the plainest evidence with the most preposterous objections, and who was sided with by two flabby parochial parasites; all the three impanelled from a district so delivered over to fever that they ought to have been upon their own trial for five hundred murders. When these mischievous blockheads were at their loudest, which was towards midnight, while some of us were already preparing for bed, I again saw the murdered man. He stood grimly behind them, beckoning to me. On my going towards them, and striking into the conversation, he immediately retired. This was the beginning of a separate series of appearances, confined to that long room in which we were confined. Whenever a knot of my brother jurymen laid their heads together, I saw the head of the murdered man among theirs. Whenever their comparison of notes was going against him, he would solemnly and irresistibly beckon to me.

It will be borne in mind that down to the production of the miniature, on the fifth day of the trial, I had never seen the appearance in court. Three changes occurred now that we entered on the case for the defence. Two of them I will mention together, first. The figure was now in court continually, and it never there addressed itself to me, but always to the person who was speaking at the time. For

instance: the throat of the murdered man had been cut straight across. In the opening speech for the defence, it was suggested that the deceased might have cut his own throat. At that very moment, the figure – with its throat in the dreadful condition referred to (this it had concealed before) – stood at the speaker's elbow, motioning across and across its windpipe, now with the right hand, now with the left, vigorously suggesting to the speaker himself the impossibility of such a wound having been self-inflicted by either hand. For another instance: a witness to character – a woman – deposed to the prisoner's being the most amiable of mankind. The figure at that instant stood on the floor before her, looking her full in the face, and pointing out the prisoner's evil countenance with an extended arm and an outstretched finger.

The third change now to be added impressed me strongly as the most marked and striking of all. I do not theorize upon it; I accurately state it, and there leave it. Although the appearance was not itself perceived by those whom it addressed, its coming close to such persons was invariably attended by some trepidation or disturbance on their part. It seemed to me as if it were prevented, by laws to which I was not amenable, from fully revealing itself to others, and yet as if it could invisibly, dumbly, and darkly overshadow their minds. When the leading counsel for the defence suggested that hypothesis of suicide, and the figure stood at the learned gentleman's elbow, frightfully sawing at its severed throat, it is undeniable that the counsel faltered in his speech, lost for a

few seconds the thread of his ingenious discourse, wiped his forehead with his handkerchief, and turned extremely pale. When the witness to character was confronted by the appearance, her eyes most certainly did follow the direction of its pointed finger, and rest in great hesitation and trouble upon the prisoner's face.

Two additional illustrations will suffice. On the eighth day of the trial I came back into court with the rest of the jury some little time before the return of the judges. Standing up in the box and looking about me, I thought the figure was not there, until, chancing to raise my eyes to the gallery, I saw it bending forward and leaning over a very decent woman, as if to assure itself whether the judges had resumed their seats or not. Immediately afterwards that woman screamed, fainted, and was carried out. So with the venerable, sagacious, and patient judge who conducted the trial. When the case was over, and he settled himself and his papers to sum up, the murdered man, entering by the judges' door, advanced to his lordship's desk, and looked eagerly over his shoulder at the pages of his notes which he was turning. A change came over his lordship's face; his hand stopped; the peculiar shiver, that I knew so well, passed over him; he faltered, "Excuse me, gentlemen. I am somewhat oppressed by the vitiated air;" and did not recover until he had drunk a glass of water.

Through all the monotony of six of those interminable ten days – the same judges and others on the bench, the same

murderer in the dock, the same lawyers at the table, the same tones of question and answer rising to the roof of the court, the same ushers going in and out, the same lights kindled at

the same hour when there had been any natural light of day, the same rain pattering and dripping when it was rainy, the same footmarks of turnkeys and prisoner day after day on the same sawdust – through all the wearisome monotony which made me feel as if I had been foreman of the jury for a vast period of time, and Piccadilly had flourished at the same time as Babylon, the murdered man never lost one trace of his distinctness in my eyes, nor was he at any moment less distinct than anybody else. I must not omit, as a matter of fact, that I never once saw the appearance which I call by the name of the murdered man look at the murderer. Again and again I wondered, "Why does he not?" But he never did.

Nor did he look at me, after the production of the miniature, until the last closing minutes of the trial arrived.

We retired to consider, at seven minutes before ten at night. The idiotic vestryman and his two parochial parasites gave us so much trouble that we twice returned into court to beg to have certain extracts from the judge's notes re-read. Nine of us had not the smallest doubt about those passages, neither, I believe, had any one in the court. At length we prevailed, and finally the jury returned into court.

The murdered man at that time stood directly opposite the jury box. As I took my place, his eyes rested on me with great attention; he seemed satisfied, and slowly shook a great grey veil, which he carried on his arm for the first time, over his head and whole form. As I gave in our verdict, "Guilty," the veil collapsed, all was gone, and his place was empty.

The murderer, being asked by the judge, according to usage, whether he had anything to say before sentence of death should be passed upon him, indistinctly muttered something which was described in the leading newspapers of the following day as a few rambling, incoherent, and half-audible words, in which he was understood to complain that he had not had a fair trial, because the foreman of the jury was prepossessed against him. The remarkable declaration that he really made was this: "My lord, I knew I was a doomed man when the foreman of the jury came into the box. My lord I knew he would never let me off, because, before I was taken, he somehow got to my bedside in the night, woke me, and put a rope round my neck."

In Kropfsberg Keep

1895

EXTRACT

Ralph A Cram

A great many years ago, soon after my grandfather died,
and Matzen came to us, when I was a little girl, and so
young that I remember nothing of the affair except as
something dreadful that frightened me very much, two young
men who had studied painting with my grandfather came
down to Brixleg from Munich, partly to paint, and partly to
amuse themselves, "ghost-hunting" as they said, for they were
very sensible young men and prided themselves on it, laughing
at all kinds of superstition, and particularly at that form which
believed in ghosts and feared them. They had never seen a real
ghost, you know, and they belonged to a certain set of people
who believed nothing they had not seen themselves – which
always seemed to me *very* conceited. Well, they knew that we
had lots of beautiful castles here in the lower valley, and they

assumed, and rightly, that every castle has at least *one* ghost story connected with it – so they chose this as their hunting ground, only the game they sought was ghosts, not chamois. Their plan was to visit every place that was supposed to be haunted, and to meet every reputed ghost, and prove that it really was no ghost at all.

There was a little inn down in the village then, kept by an old man named Peter Rosskopf, and the two young men made this their headquarters. The very first night they began to draw from the old innkeeper all that he knew of legends and ghost stories connected with Brixleg and its castles, and as he was a most garrulous old gentleman he filled them with the wildest delight by his stories of the ghosts of the castles about the mouth of the Zillerthal. Of course the old man believed every word he said, and you can imagine his horror and amazement when, after telling his

guests the particularly blood-curdling story of Kropfsberg and its haunted keep, the elder of the two boys, whose surname I have forgotten, but whose Christian name was Rupert, calmly said, "Your story is most satisfactory: we will sleep in Kropfsberg Keep tomorrow night, and you must provide us with all that we may need to make ourselves comfortable."

The old man nearly fell into the fire. "What for a blockhead are you?" he cried, with big eyes. "The keep is haunted by Count Albert's ghost, I tell you!"

"That is why we are going there tomorrow night; we wish to make the acquaintance of Count Albert."

"But there was a man stayed there once, and in the morning he was dead."

"Very silly of him. There are two of us, and we carry revolvers."

"But it's a *ghost*, I tell you," almost screamed the innkeeper. "Are ghosts afraid of firearms?"

"Whether they are or not, we are *not* afraid of *them*."

Here the younger boy broke in – he was named Otto von Kleist. I remember the name, for I had a music teacher once by that name. He abused the poor old man shamefully; told him that they were going to spend the night in Kropfsberg in spite of Count Albert and Peter Rosskopf, and that he might as well make the most of it and earn his money with cheerfulness.

In a word, they finally bullied the old fellow into submission, and when the morning came he set about

preparing for the suicide, as he considered it, with sighs and mutterings and ominous shakings of the head.

You know the condition of the castle now — nothing but scorched walls and crumbling piles of fallen masonry. Well, at the time I tell you of, the keep was still partially preserved. It was finally burned out only a few years ago by some wicked boys who came over from Jenbach to have a good time. But when the ghost hunters came, though the two lower floors had fallen into the crypt, the third floor remained. The peasants said it *could* not fall, but that it would stay until the Day of Judgment, because it was in the room above that the wicked Count Albert sat watching the flames destroy the great castle and his imprisoned guests, and where he finally hung himself in a suit of armour that had belonged to his mediaeval ancestor, the first Count Kropfsberg.

No one dared touch him, and so he hung there for twelve

years, and all the time venturesome boys and daring men used to creep up the turret steps and stare awfully through the chinks in the door at that ghostly mass of steel that held within itself the body of a murderer and suicide, slowly returning to the dust from which it was made. Finally it disappeared, none knew whither, and for another dozen years the room stood empty but for the old furniture and the rotting hangings.

So, when the two men climbed the stairway to the haunted room, they found a very different state of things from what exists now. The room was absolutely as it was left the night Count Albert burned the castle, except that all trace of the suspended suit of armour and its ghastly contents had vanished.

No one had dared to cross the threshold, and I suppose that for forty years no living thing had entered that dreadful room.

On one side stood a vast canopied bed of black wood, the damask hangings of which were covered with mould and mildew. All the clothing of the bed was in perfect order, and on it lay a book, open and face downward. The only other furniture in the room consisted of several old chairs, a carved oak chest; and a big inlaid table covered with books and papers, and on one corner two or three bottles with dark solid sediment at the bottom, and a glass, also dark with the dregs of wine that had been poured out almost half a century before. The tapestry on the walls was green with mould, but hardly torn or otherwise defaced, for although the heavy dust of forty years lay on everything, the room had been preserved from

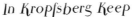

further harm. No spider web was to be seen, no trace of nibbling mice, not even a dead moth or fly on the sills of the diamond-paned windows; life seemed to have shunned the room utterly and finally.

The men looked at the room curiously, and, I am sure, not without some feelings of awe and unacknowledged fear; but, whatever they may have felt of instinctive shrinking, they said nothing, and quickly set to work to make the room passably inhabitable. They decided to touch nothing that had not absolutely to be changed, and therefore they made for themselves a bed in one corner with the mattress and linen from the inn. In the great fireplace they piled a lot of wood on the caked ashes of a fire dead for forty years, turned the old chest into a table, and laid out on it all their arrangements for the evening's amusement: food, two or three bottles of wine, pipes and tobacco, and the chessboard that was their inseparable travelling companion.

All this they did themselves: the innkeeper would not even come within the walls of the outer court; he insisted that he had washed his hands of the whole affair, the silly dunderheads might go to their death their own way. *He* would not aid and abet them. One of the stable boys brought the basket of food and the wood and the bed up the winding stone stairs, to be sure, but neither money nor prayers nor threats would bring him within the walls of the accursed place, and he stared fearfully at the hare-brained boys as they worked around the dead old room preparing for the night that was coming so fast.

At length everything was in readiness, and after a final visit
to the inn for dinner, Rupert and Otto started at sunset for the
Keep. Half the village went with them – for Peter Rosskopf
had babbled the whole story to an open-mouthed crowd of
wondering men and women – and as to an execution the awestruck crowd followed the two boys dumbly, curious to see if
they surely would put their plan into execution. But none
went farther than the outer doorway of the stairs, for it was
already growing twilight. In absolute silence they watched the
two foolhardy youths with their lives in their hands enter the

terrible keep, standing like a
tower in the midst of the piles
of stones that had once
formed walls joining it with
the mass of the castle beyond.
When a moment later a light
showed itself in the high
windows above, they sighed
resignedly and went their
ways, to wait stolidly until
morning should come and
prove the truth of their fears
and warnings.

In the meantime the ghost hunters built a huge fire, lighted
their many candles, and sat down to await developments.
Rupert afterwards told my uncle that they really felt no fear
whatever, only a contemptuous curiosity, and they ate their

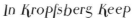

supper with good appetite and an unusual relish. It was a long
evening. They played many games of chess, waiting for
midnight. Hour passed after hour, and nothing occurred to
interrupt the monotony of the evening. Ten, eleven, came and
went – it was almost midnight. They piled more wood in the
fireplace, lighted new candles, looked to their pistols – and
waited. The clocks in the village struck twelve; the sound
coming muffled through the high, deep-embrasured windows.
Nothing happened, nothing to break the heavy silence; and
with a feeling of disappointed relief they looked at each other
and acknowledged that they had met another rebuff.

Finally they decided that there was no use in sitting up and
boring themselves any longer, they had much better rest; so
Otto threw himself down on the mattress, falling almost
immediately asleep. Rupert sat a little longer, smoking, and
watching the stars creep along behind the shattered glass and
the bent leads of the lofty windows; watching the fire fall
together, and the strange shadows move mysteriously on the
mouldering walls. The iron hook in the oak beam, that crossed
the ceiling midway fascinated him, not with fear, but morbidly.
So, it was from that hook that for twelve years, twelve long
years of changing summer and winter, the body of Count
Albert, murderer and suicide, hung in its strange casing of
mediaeval steel; moving a little at first, and turning gently
while the fire died out on the hearth, while the ruins of the
castle grew cold, and horrified peasants sought for the bodies
of the score of gay, reckless, wicked guests whom Count

Albert had gathered in Kropfsberg for a last debauch, gathered to their terrible and untimely death. What a strange and fiendish idea it was, the young, handsome noble who had ruined himself and his family in the society of the splendid debauchees, gathering them all together, men and women who had known only love and pleasure, for a glorious and awful riot of luxury. And then, when they were all dancing in the great ballroom, locking the doors and burning the whole castle about them, the while he sat in the great keep listening to their screams of agonized fear, watching the fire sweep from wing to wing until the whole mighty mass was one enormous and awful pyre, and then, clothing himself in his great-great-grandfather's armour, hanging himself in the midst of the ruins of what had been a proud and noble castle. So ended a great family, a great house. But that was forty years ago. He was growing drowsy; the light flickered and flared in the fireplace; one by one the candles went out; the shadows grew thick in the room. Why did that great iron hook stand out so plainly? Why did that dark shadow dance and quiver so mockingly behind it? Why? But he ceased to wonder at anything. He was asleep.

It seemed to him that he woke almost immediately; the fire still burned, though low and fitfully on the hearth. Otto was sleeping, breathing quietly and regularly. The shadows had

gathered close around him, thick and murky. With every passing moment the light died in the fireplace; he felt stiff with cold. In the utter silence he heard the clock in the village strike two. He shivered with a sudden and irresistible feeling of fear, and abruptly turned and looked towards the hook in the ceiling.

Yes, It was there, he knew that it would be. It seemed quite natural, he would have been disappointed had he seen nothing; but now he knew that the story was true, knew that he was wrong, and that the dead *do* sometimes return to earth. For there, in the fast-deepening shadow, hung the black mass of wrought steel, turning a little now and then, with the light flickering on the tarnished and rusty metal. He watched it quietly; he hardly felt afraid it was rather a sentiment of sadness and fatality that filled him, of gloomy forebodings of something unknown, unimaginable. He sat and watched the thing disappear in the gathering dark, his hand on his pistol as it lay by him on the great chest. There was no sound but the regular breathing of the sleeping boy on the mattress.

It had grown absolutely dark; a bat fluttered against the broken glass of the window. He wondered if he was growing mad, for – he hesitated to acknowledge it to himself – he heard music; far, curious music, a strange and luxurious dance, very faint, very vague, but unmistakable.

Like a flash of lightning came a jagged line of fire down the blank wall opposite him, a line that remained, that gradually grew wider, that let a pale cold light into the room, showing

him now all its details — the empty fireplace, where a thin smoke rose in a spiral from a bit of charred wood, the mass of the great bed, and, in the very middle, black against the curious brightness, the armoured man or ghost or devil, standing, not suspended, beneath the rusty hook. And with the rending of the wall the music grew more distinct, though sounding still very far away.

Count Albert raised his mailed hand and beckoned to him; then turned, and stood in the riven wall.

Without a word, Rupert rose and followed him, his pistol in hand. Count Albert passed through the mighty wall and disappeared in the unearthly light. Rupert followed mechanically. He felt the crushing of the mortar beneath his feet, the roughness of the jagged wall where he rested his hand.

The keep rose absolutely isolated among the ruins, yet on passing through the wall Rupert found himself in a long, uneven corridor, the floor of which was warped and sagging, while the walls were covered on one side with big faded portraits of an inferior quality, like those in the corridor that connects the Pitti and Uffizi in Florence. Before him moved the figure of Count Albert — a black silhouette in the ever-increasing light. And always the music grew stronger and stranger, a mad, evil, seductive dance that bewitched, even while it disgusted.

In a final blaze of vivid, intolerable light, in a burst of hellish music that might have come from Bedlam, Rupert

stepped from the corridor into a vast and curious room where
at first he saw nothing, distinguished nothing but a mad,
seething whirl of sweeping figures, white, in a white room,
under white light – Count Albert standing before him, the
only dark object to be seen. As his eyes grew accustomed to
the fearful brightness, he knew that he was looking on a dance
such as the damned might see in hell, but such
as no living man had ever seen before.

Around the long, narrow hall, under the
fearful light that came from nowhere but
was omni-present, swept a rushing stream
of unspeakable horrors, dancing insanely,
laughing, gibbering hideously; the dead of
forty years. White, polished skeletons, bare
of flesh and vesture, some still clothed in the
dreadful rags of dried and rattling sinews, the
tags of tattering grave-clothes flaunting behind
them. These were the dead of many years ago.
Then the dead of more recent times, with yellow
bones showing only here and there, the long and
insecure hair of their hideous heads writhing in the beating air.
Then green and grey horrors, bloated and shapeless, stained
with earth or dripping with spattering water; and here and
there white, beautiful things, like chiselled ivory, the dead of
yesterday, in the mummy arms of rattling skeletons.

Round and round the cursed room, a swaying, swirling
maelstrom of death, while the air grew thick with miasma, the

floor foul with shreds of shrouds, and yellow parchment, clattering bones, and wisps of tangled hair.

And in the very midst of this ring of death, a sight not for words nor for thought, a sight to blast forever the mind of the man who looked upon it: a leaping, writhing dance of Count Albert's victims, the score of beautiful women and reckless men who danced to their awful death while the castle burned around them, charred and shapeless now, a living charnel house of nameless horror.

Count Albert, who had stood silent, watching the dance of the damned, turned to Rupert, and for the first time spoke.

"We are ready for you now; dance!"

A prancing horror, dead some dozen years, leered at Rupert with eyeless skull.

"Dance!"

Rupert stood frozen, motionless.

"Dance!"

His hard lips moved. "Not if the devil came from hell to make me."

Count Albert swept his vast two-handed sword into the fœtid air while the tide of corruption paused in its swirling, and swept down on Rupert with gibbering grins.

The room, and the howling dead, and the black portent before him circled dizzily around, as with a last effort of departing consciousness he drew his pistol and fired full in the face of Count Albert.

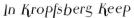

Perfect silence, perfect darkness; not a breath, not a sound: the dead stillness of a long-sealed tomb. Rupert lay on his back, stunned, helpless, his pistol clenched in his frozen hand, a smell of powder in the black air. Where was he? Dead? In hell? He reached his hand out cautiously; it fell on dusty boards. Outside, far away, a clock struck three. Had he dreamed? Of course; but how ghastly a dream! With chattering teeth he called softly, "Otto!"

There was no reply, and none when he called again and again. He staggered weakly to his feet, groping for matches and candles. A panic of abject terror came on him: the matches were gone!

He turned towards the fireplace: a single coal glowed in the white ashes. He swept a mass of papers and dusty books from the table, and with trembling hands cowered over the embers, until he succeeded in lighting the dry tinder. Then he piled the old books on the blaze, and looked fearfully around.

No: It was gone – thank God for that; the hook was empty.

But why did Otto sleep so soundly; why did he not awake?

He stepped unsteadily across the room in the flaring light of the burning books, and knelt by the mattress.

So they found him in the morning, when no one came to the inn from Kropfsberg Keep, and the quaking Peter Rosskopf arranged a relief party – found him kneeling beside the mattress where Otto lay, shot in the throat and quite dead.

The Lost Ghost

1903

Mary E Wilkins Freeman

Mrs John Emerson, sitting with her needlework beside the window, looked out and saw Mrs Rhoda Meserve coming down the street, and knew at once by a thrusting forward of the neck and a bustling hitch of the shoulders that she had important news. Rhoda Meserve always had the news as soon as the news was in being, and generally Mrs John Emerson was the first to whom she imparted it. The two women had been friends ever since Mrs Meserve had married Simon Meserve and come to the village to live.

Mrs Meserve was a pretty woman, moving with graceful flirts of ruffling skirts; her clear-cut, nervous face as delicately tinted as a shell looked brightly from the plumy brim of a black hat at Mrs Emerson in the window. Mrs Emerson was glad to see her coming. She returned the greeting with

enthusiasm, then rose hurriedly, ran into the cold parlour and brought out one of the best rocking-chairs. She was just in time, after drawing it up beside the opposite window, to greet her friend at the door.

"Good-afternoon," said she. "I declare, I'm real glad to see you. I thought of coming over to your house this afternoon, but I couldn't bring my sewing very well. I am putting the ruffles on my new black dress skirt."

"Well, I didn't have a thing on hand except my crochet work," responded Mrs Meserve, "and I thought I'd just run over a few minutes."

"I'm real glad you did," repeated Mrs Emerson. "Take your things right off and take the rocking-chair."

Mrs Meserve settled herself, while Mrs Emerson carried her shawl and hat into the adjoining bedroom. When she returned Mrs Meserve was rocking peacefully and was already at work hooking blue wool in and out.

"That's real pretty," said Mrs Emerson. "I suppose it's for the church fair?"

"Yes. I don't suppose it'll bring enough to pay for the worsted, let alone the work, but I suppose I've got to make something."

"How much did that one you made for the fair last year bring?"

"Only twenty-five cents. It takes me a week every minute I can get to make one. Well, I suppose I oughtn't to complain as long as it is for the Lord, but sometimes it does seem as if the Lord didn't get much out of it."

"Well, it's very pretty work," said Mrs Emerson, sitting down at the opposite window and taking up her dress skirt.

"Yes, it is real pretty work. I just *love* to crochet."

The two women rocked and sewed and crocheted in silence. They were both waiting. Mrs Meserve waited for the other's curiosity to develop in order that her news might have, as it were, a befitting stage entrance. Mrs Emerson waited for the news. Finally she could wait no longer.

"Well, what's the news?" said she.

"Well, I don't know as there's anything very particular."

"Yes, there is; you can't cheat me," replied Mrs Emerson. "Now, how do you know?"

"By the way you look."

Mrs Meserve laughed consciously and rather vainly.

"Well, there is some news. Simon came home with it today. He heard it in South Dayton. The old Sargent place is let."

Mrs Emerson dropped her sewing and stared.

"You don't say so!"

"Yes, it is."

"Who to?"

"Why, some folks from Boston that moved to South Dayton last year. They haven't been satisfied with the house they had there – it wasn't large enough. He's got a wife and his unmarried sister in the family. The sister's got money, too. You know the old Sargent house is a splendid place."

"Yes, it's the handsomest house in town, but—"

"Oh, Simon said they told him about that and he just laughed. Said he wasn't afraid and neither was his wife and sister. Said he'd risk ghosts rather than little tucked-up sleeping rooms without any sun, like they've had in the Dayton house. Said he'd risk *seeing* ghosts, than risk being ghosts themselves."

"Oh, well," said Mrs Emerson, "it is a beautiful house, and maybe there isn't anything in those stories."

"Nothing in creation would hire me to go into a house that I'd ever heard a word against of that kind," declared Mrs Meserve with emphasis. "I wouldn't go into that house if they would give me the rent. I've seen enough of haunted houses to last me as long as I live."

Mrs Emerson's face acquired the expression of a hunting hound.

"Have you?" she asked in an intense whisper.

"Yes, I have. I don't want any more of it."

"Before you came here?"

"Yes; before I was married – when I was quite a girl."

Mrs Meserve had not married young. Mrs Emerson had mental calculations when she heard that.

"Did you really live in a house that was——" she whispered fearfully.

Mrs Meserve nodded solemnly.

"Did you really ever——see——anything? Anything that did you any harm?"

"No, I didn't see anything that did me harm looking at it in one way, but it don't do anybody in this world any good to see things that haven't any business to be seen in it. You never get over it."

Mrs Emerson's features seemed to sharpen.

"Well, of course I don't want to urge you," said she, "if you don't feel like talking about it; but maybe it might do you good to tell it out, if it's on your mind, worrying you."

"I try to put it out of my mind," said Mrs Meserve.

"Well, it's just as you feel."

"I never told anybody but Simon," said Mrs Meserve. "I never felt as if it was wise perhaps. I didn't know what folks might think. So many don't believe in anything they can't understand. Simon advised me not to talk about it. He said he

didn't believe it was anything supernatural, but he had to own up that he couldn't give any explanation for it to save his life. He said lots of folks would sooner tell folks my head wasn't right than to own up they couldn't see through it."

"I'm sure I wouldn't say so," returned Mrs Emerson.

"You know better than that, I hope."

"Yes," replied Mrs Meserve. "I know you wouldn't say so."

"And I wouldn't tell it to a soul if you didn't want me to."

"Well, I'd rather you wouldn't."

"I won't speak of it even to Mr Emerson."

"I'd rather you wouldn't even to him."

"I won't."

Mrs Emerson took up her dress skirt again; Mrs Meserve hooked up another loop of blue wool. Then she began:

"Of course," said she, "I ain't going to say positively that I believe or disbelieve in ghosts, but all I tell you is what I saw. I can't explain it. If you can, well and good; I shall be glad, for it will stop tormenting me as it has done and always will. There hasn't been a day nor a night since it happened that I haven't thought of it."

"That's awful," Mrs Emerson said.

"Ain't it? Well, it happened before I was married, when I was a girl and lived in East Wilmington. It was the first year I lived there. You know my family all died five years before that."

Mrs Emerson nodded.

"Well, I went there to teach school, and I went to board with a Mrs Amelia Dennison and her sister, Abby, her name

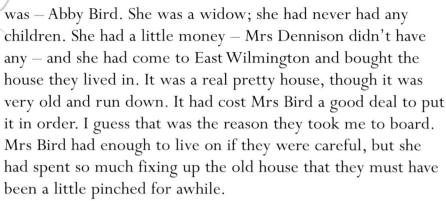

was – Abby Bird. She was a widow; she had never had any children. She had a little money – Mrs Dennison didn't have any – and she had come to East Wilmington and bought the house they lived in. It was a real pretty house, though it was very old and run down. It had cost Mrs Bird a good deal to put it in order. I guess that was the reason they took me to board. Mrs Bird had enough to live on if they were careful, but she had spent so much fixing up the old house that they must have been a little pinched for awhile.

"Anyhow, they took me to board, and I thought I was pretty lucky to get in there. I had a nice room, big and sunny and furnished pretty, the paper and paint all new, and everything as neat as wax. Mrs Dennison was one of the best cooks I ever saw, and I had a little stove in my room, and there was always a nice fire there when I got home from school. I thought I hadn't been in such a nice place since I lost my own home, until I had been there about three weeks.

"I had been there about three weeks before I found it out, though I guess it had been going on ever since they had been in the house, and that was most four months. They hadn't said anything about it, and I didn't wonder.

"Well, I went there in September. I begun my school the first Monday. I remember it was a real cold fall, there was a frost the middle of September, and I had to put on my winter coat. I remember when I came home that night (let me see, I began school on a Monday, and that was two weeks from the next Thursday), I took off my coat downstairs and laid it on the

table in the front entry. It was a real nice coat — heavy black broadcloth trimmed with fur; I had had it the winter before. Mrs Bird called after me as I went upstairs that I ought not to leave it in the front entry in case somebody might come in and take it, but I only laughed and called back to her that I wasn't afraid. I never was much afraid of burglars.

"Well, though it was hardly the middle of September, it was a real cold night. I remember my room faced west, and the sun was getting low, and the sky was a pale yellow and purple, just as you see it sometimes in the winter when there is going to be a cold snap. I rather think that was the night the frost came the first time. I know Mrs Dennison covered up some flowers she had in the front yard, anyhow. I remember looking out and seeing an old green plaid shawl of hers over the verbena bed. There was a fire in my little wood-stove. Mrs Bird made it, I know. She was a real motherly sort of woman; she always seemed to be the happiest when she was doing something to make other folks happy and comfortable. Mrs Dennison told me she had always been so. 'It's lucky Abby never had any children,' she said, 'for she would have spoilt them.'

"Well, that night I sat down beside my nice little fire and was having a beautiful time, and thinking how lucky I was to have got board in such a place with such nice folks, when I heard a queer little sound at my door. It was such a little hesitating sort of sound that it sounded more like a fumble than a knock, as if someone very timid, with little hands, was feeling along the door, not quite daring to knock. For a minute

I thought it was a mouse. But I waited and it came again, and then I made up my mind it was a knock, but a very little scared one, so I said, 'Come in.'

"But nobody came in, and then presently I heard the knock again. Then I got up and opened the door, thinking it was very queer, and I had a frightened feeling without knowing why.

"Well, I opened the door, and the first thing I noticed was a draught of cold air, as if the front door downstairs was open, but there was a strange close smell about the cold draught. It smelled more like a cellar that had been shut up for years, than out-of-doors. Then I saw something. I saw my coat first. The thing that held it

was so small that I couldn't see much of anything else. Then I saw a little white face with eyes so scared and wishful that they seemed as if they might eat a hole in anybody's heart. It was a dreadful little face, with something about it which made it different from any other face on earth, but it was so pitiful that somehow it did away a good deal with the dreadfulness. And there were two little hands spotted purple with the cold, holding up my winter coat, and a strange little far-away voice said: 'I can't find my mother.'

"'For heaven's sake,' I said, 'who are you?'

"Then the little voice said again: 'I can't find my mother.'

"All the time I could smell the cold and I saw that it was about the child; that cold was clinging to her as if she had come out of some deadly cold place. Well, I took my coat, I did not know what else to do, and the cold was clinging to that. It was as cold as if it had come off ice. When I had the coat I could see the child more plainly. She was dressed in one little white garment made very simply. It was a nightgown, and I could see dimly through it her thin body mottled purple with the cold. Her face was a clear waxen white. Her hair was dark, but it looked as if it might be dark only because it was so damp, almost wet, and might really be light hair. It clung very close to her forehead, which was round and white. She would have been very beautiful if she had not been so dreadful.

"'Who are you?' says I again, looking at her.

"She looked at me with her terrible pleading eyes and did not say anything.

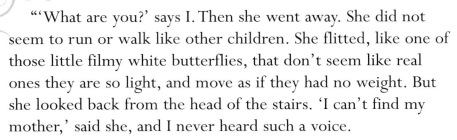

"'What are you?' says I. Then she went away. She did not seem to run or walk like other children. She flitted, like one of those little filmy white butterflies, that don't seem like real ones they are so light, and move as if they had no weight. But she looked back from the head of the stairs. 'I can't find my mother,' said she, and I never heard such a voice.

"'Who is your mother?' says I, but she was gone.

"Well, I thought for a moment I should faint away. The room got dark and I heard a singing in my ears. I stood in my door, and called first Mrs Bird and then Mrs Dennison. I didn't dare go down over the stairs where that had gone. It seemed to me I should go mad if I didn't see somebody or something like other folks on the face of the earth. I thought I should never make anybody hear, but I could hear them stepping about downstairs, and I could smell biscuits baking for supper. Somehow the smell of those biscuits seemed the only natural thing left to keep me in my right mind. I just stood there and called, and finally I heard the entry door open and Mrs Bird called back: "'What is it? Did you call, Miss Arms?'

"'Come up here; come up here as quick as you can, both of you,' I screamed out. 'Quick, quick, quick!'

"I heard Mrs Bird tell Mrs Dennison: 'Come quick, Amelia, something is the matter in Miss Arms' room.' It struck me even then that she expressed herself rather queerly, and it struck me as very queer, indeed, when they both got upstairs and I saw that they knew what had happened, or that they knew of what nature the happening was.

"'What is it, dear?' asked Mrs Bird, and her pretty, loving voice had a strained sound. I saw her look at Mrs Dennison and I saw Mrs Dennison look back at her.

"'For God's sake,' says I, and I never spoke so before – 'for God's sake, what was it brought my coat upstairs?'

"'What was it like?' asked Mrs Dennison in a sort of failing voice, and she looked at her sister and her sister looked at her.

"'It was a child I have never seen here before. It looked like a child,' says I, 'but I never saw a child so dreadful, and it had on a nightgown, and said she couldn't find her mother.'

"I thought for a minute Mrs Dennison was going to faint, but Mrs Bird hung onto her and rubbed her hands, and whispered in her ear (she had the cooingest kind of voice), and I ran and got her a glass of cold water. I tell you it took considerable courage to go downstairs alone, but they had set a lamp on the entry table so I could see. I don't believe I could have plucked up enough to have gone downstairs in the dark, thinking every second that child might be close to me. The lamp and the smell of the biscuits baking seemed to sort of keep my courage up, but I tell you I didn't waste much time going down those stairs and out into the kitchen for a glass

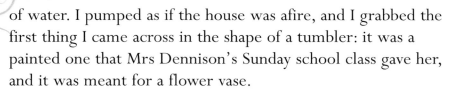

of water. I pumped as if the house was afire, and I grabbed the first thing I came across in the shape of a tumbler: it was a painted one that Mrs Dennison's Sunday school class gave her, and it was meant for a flower vase.

"Well, I filled it and then ran upstairs. I felt every minute as if something would catch my feet, and I held the glass to Mrs Dennison's lips, while Mrs Bird held her head up, and she took a good long swallow, then she looked hard at the tumbler.

"'Yes,' says I, 'I know I got this one, but I took the first I came across, and it isn't hurt a mite.'

"'Don't get the painted flowers wet,' says Mrs Dennison very feebly, 'they'll wash off if you do.'

"'I'll be real careful,' says I. I knew she set a sight by that painted tumbler.

"The water seemed to do Mrs Dennison good, for presently she pushed Mrs Bird away and sat up. She had been laying down on my bed.

"'I'm all over it now,' says she, but she was terribly white, and her eyes looked as if they saw something outside things. Mrs Bird wasn't much better, but she always had a sort of settled, good, sweet look that nothing could disturb. I knew I looked dreadful, for I saw myself in the glass, and I would hardly have known who it was.

"Mrs Dennison, she slid off the bed and walked sort of tottery to a chair. 'I was silly to give way so,' says she.

"'No, you wasn't silly, sister,' says Mrs Bird. 'I don't know what this means any more than you do, but whatever it is, no

one ought to be called silly for being overcome by anything so different from other things which we have known all our lives.'

"Mrs Dennison looked at her sister, then she looked at me, then back at her sister again, and Mrs Bird spoke as if she had been asked a question.

"'Yes,' says she, 'I do think Miss Arms ought to be told – that is, I think she ought to be told all we know ourselves.'

"'That isn't much,' said Mrs Dennison with a dying-away sort of sigh. She looked as if she might faint away again any minute. She was a real delicate-looking woman, but it turned out she was a good deal stronger than poor Mrs Bird.

"'No, there isn't much we do know,' says Mrs Bird, 'but what little there is she ought to know. I felt as if she ought to when she first came here.'

"'Well, I didn't feel quite right about it,' said Mrs Dennison, 'but I kept hoping it might stop, and any way, that it might never trouble her, and you had put so much in the house, and we needed the money, and I didn't know but she might be nervous and think she couldn't come, and I didn't want to take a man boarder.'

"'And aside from the money, we were very anxious to have you come, my dear,' says Mrs Bird.

"'Yes,' says Mrs Dennison, 'we wanted the young company in the house; we were lonesome, and we both of us took a great liking to you the minute we set eyes on you.'

"And I guess they meant what they said, both of them. They were beautiful women, and nobody could be any kinder to me

than they were, and I never blamed them for not telling me before, and, as they said, there wasn't really much to tell.

"They hadn't any sooner fairly bought the house, and moved into it, than they began to see and hear things. Mrs Bird said they were sitting together in the sitting-room one evening when they heard it the first time. She said her sister was knitting lace (Mrs Dennison made beautiful knitted lace) and she was reading the *Missionary Herald* (Mrs Bird was very much interested in mission work), when all of a sudden they heard something. She heard it first and she laid down her *Missionary Herald* and listened, and then Mrs Dennison she saw her listening and she drops her lace. 'What is it you are listening to, Abby?' says she. Then it came again and they both heard, and the cold shivers went down their backs to hear it, though they didn't know why. 'It's the cat, isn't it?' says Mrs Bird.

"'It isn't any cat,' says Mrs Dennison.

"'Oh, I guess it *must* be the cat; maybe she's got a mouse,' says Mrs Bird, real cheerful, to calm down Mrs Dennison, for she saw she was 'most scared to death, and she was always afraid of her fainting away. Then she opens the door and calls, 'Kitty, kitty, kitty!' They had brought their cat with them in a basket when they came to East Wilmington to live. It was a real handsome tiger cat, a tommy, and he knew a lot.

"Well, she called 'Kitty, kitty, kitty!' and sure enough the kitty came, and when he came in the door he gave a big yawl that didn't sound unlike what they had heard.

"'There, sister, here he is; you see it was the cat,' says Mrs Bird. 'Poor kitty!'

"But Mrs Dennison she eyed the cat, and she give a great screech.

"'What's that? What's that?' says she.

"'What's what?' says Mrs Bird, pretending to herself that she didn't see what her sister meant.

"'Somethin's got hold of that cat's tail,' says Mrs Dennison. 'Somethin's got hold of his tail. It's pulled straight out, an' he can't get away. Just hear him yawl!'

"'It isn't anything,' says Mrs Bird, but even as she said that she could see a little hand holding fast to that cat's tail, and then the child seemed to sort of clear out of the dimness behind the hand, and the child was sort of laughing then, instead of looking sad, and she said that was a great deal worse. She said that laugh was the most awful and the saddest thing she ever heard.

"Well, she was so dumbfounded that she didn't know what to do, and she couldn't sense at first that it was anything supernatural. She thought it must be one of the neighbour's children who had run away and was making free of their house, and was teasing their cat, and that they must be just nervous to feel so upset by it. So she speaks up sort of sharp.

"'Don't you know that you mustn't pull the kitty's tail?' says she. 'Don't you know you hurt the poor kitty, and she'll scratch you if you don't take care. Poor kitty, you mustn't hurt her.'

"And with that she said the child stopped pulling that cat's tail and went to stroking her just as soft and pitiful, and the cat put his back up and rubbed and purred as if he liked it. The cat never seemed a mite afraid, and that seemed queer, for I had always heard that animals were dreadfully afraid of ghosts; but then, that was a pretty harmless little sort of ghost.

"Well, Mrs Bird said the child stroked that cat, while she and Mrs Dennison stood watching it, and holding onto each other, for, no matter how hard they tried to think it was all right, it didn't look right. Finally Mrs Dennison she spoke.

"'What's your name, little girl?' says she.

"Then the child looks up and stops stroking the cat, and says she can't find her mother, just the way she said it to me. Then Mrs Dennison she gave such a gasp that Mrs Bird thought she was going to faint away, but she didn't. 'Well, who is your mother?' says she. But the child just says again, 'I can't find my mother – I can't find my mother.'

"'Where do you live, dear?' says Mrs Bird.

"'I can't find my mother,' says the child.

"Well, that was the way it was. Nothing happened. Those two women stood there hanging onto each other, and the child stood in front of them, and they asked her questions, and everything she would say was: 'I can't find my mother.'

"Then Mrs Bird tried to catch hold of the child, for she thought in spite of what she saw that perhaps she was nervous and it was a real child, only perhaps not quite right in its head, that had run away in her little nightgown after she had been put to bed.

"She tried to catch the child. She had an idea of putting a shawl around it and going out – she was such a little thing she could have carried her easy enough – and trying to find out to which of the neighbours she belonged. But the minute she moved toward the child there wasn't any child there; there was only that little voice seeming to come from nothing, saying 'I can't find my mother,' and presently that died away.

"Well, that same thing kept happening, or something very much the same. Once in awhile Mrs Bird would be washing dishes, and all at once the child would be standing beside her with the dish-towel, wiping them. Of course, that was terrible. Mrs Bird would wash the dishes all over. Sometimes she didn't tell Mrs Dennison, it made her so nervous. Sometimes when they were making cake they would find the raisins all picked over, and sometimes little sticks of kindling-wood would be found laying beside the kitchen stove. They never knew when they would come across that child, and always she kept saying over and over that she couldn't find her mother. They never tried talking to her, except once in awhile Mrs Bird would get desperate and ask her something, but the child never seemed to hear it; she always kept right on saying that she couldn't find her mother.

"After they had told me all they had to tell about their experience with the child, they told me about the house and the people that had lived there before they did. It seemed something dreadful had happened in that house. And the land agent had never let on to them. I don't think they would have

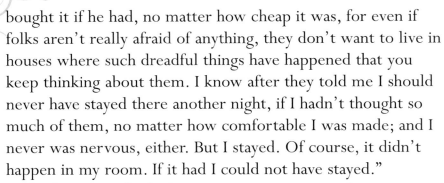

bought it if he had, no matter how cheap it was, for even if folks aren't really afraid of anything, they don't want to live in houses where such dreadful things have happened that you keep thinking about them. I know after they told me I should never have stayed there another night, if I hadn't thought so much of them, no matter how comfortable I was made; and I never was nervous, either. But I stayed. Of course, it didn't happen in my room. If it had I could not have stayed."

"What was it?" asked Mrs Emerson in an awed voice.

"It was an awful thing. That child had lived in the house with her father and mother two years before. They had come – or the father had – from a real good family. He had a good situation: he was a drummer for a big leather house in the city, and they lived real pretty, with plenty to do with. But the mother was a real wicked woman. She was as handsome as a picture, and they said she came from good sort of people enough in Boston, but she was bad clean through, though she was real pretty spoken and most everybody liked her. She used to dress out and make a great show, and she never seemed to take much interest in the child, and folks began to say she wasn't treated right.

"The woman had a hard time keeping a maid. For some reason one wouldn't stay. They would leave and then talk about her awfully, telling all kinds of things. People didn't believe it at first; then they began to. They said that the woman made that little thing, though she wasn't much over five years old, and small and babyish for her age, do most of the work, what

there was done; they said the house used to look like a pigsty when she didn't have help. They said the little thing used to stand on a chair and wash dishes, and they'd seen her carrying in sticks of wood most as big as she was many a time, and they'd heard her mother scolding her. The woman was a fine singer, and had a voice like a screech-owl when she scolded.

"The father was away most of the time, and when that happened he had been away out west for some weeks. There had been a married man hanging about the mother for some time, and folks had talked some; but they weren't sure there was anything wrong, and he was a man very high up, with money, so they kept pretty still for fear he would hear of it and make trouble for them, and of course nobody was sure, though folks did say afterward that the father of the child had ought to have been told.

"But that was very easy to say; it wouldn't have been so easy to find anybody who would have been willing to tell him such a thing as that, especially when they weren't any too sure. He set his eyes by his wife, too. They said all he seemed to think of was to earn money to buy things to deck her out in. And he about worshipped the child, too. They said he was a real nice man. The men that are treated so bad mostly are real nice men. I've always noticed that.

"Well, one morning that man that there had been whispers about was missing. He had been gone quite a while, though, before they really knew that he was missing, because he had gone away and told his wife that he had to go to New York on

business and might be gone a week, and not to worry if he didn't get home, and not to worry if he didn't write, because he should be thinking from day to day that he might take the next train home and there would be no use in writing. So the wife waited, and she tried not to worry until it was two days over the week, then she run into a neighbour's and fainted dead away on the floor. And then they made inquiries and found out that he had skipped – with some money that didn't belong to him, too.

"Then folks began to ask where was that woman, and they found out by comparing notes that nobody had seen her since the man went away. But three or four women remembered that she had told them that she thought of taking the child and going to Boston to visit her folks, so when they hadn't seen her around, and the house shut, they jumped to the conclusion that was where she was. They were the neighbours that lived right around her, but they didn't have much to do with her, and she'd gone out of her way to tell them about her Boston plan, and they didn't make much reply when she did.

"Well, there was this house shut up, and the man and woman missing and the child. Then all of a sudden one of the women that lived the nearest remembered something. She remembered that she had waked up three nights running, thinking she heard a child crying somewhere, and once she waked up her husband, but he said it must be the Bisbees' little girl, and she thought it must be. The child wasn't well and was always crying. It used to have colic spells, especially at night.

So she didn't think any more about it until this came up, then
all of a sudden she did think of it. She told what she had heard,
and finally folks began to think they had better enter that
house and see if there was anything wrong.

"Well, they did enter it, and they found that child dead,
locked in one of the rooms. (Mrs Dennison and Mrs Bird
never used that room; it was a back bedroom on the second
floor.)

"Yes, they found that poor child there, starved to death, and
frozen – though they weren't sure she had frozen to death, for
she was in bed with clothes enough to keep her pretty warm
when she was alive. But she had been there a week, and she
was nothing but skin and bone. It looked as if the mother had
locked her into the house when she went away, and told her
not to make any noise for fear the neighbours would hear her
and find out that she herself had gone.

"Mrs Dennison said she couldn't really believe that the
woman had meant to have her own child starved to death.
Probably she thought the little thing would raise somebody, or
folks would try to get in the house and find her. Well,
whatever she thought, there the child was, dead.

"But that wasn't all. The father came home, right in the
midst of it; the child was just buried, and he was beside
himself. And – he went on the track of his wife, and he found
her, and he shot her dead; it was in all the papers at the time;
then he disappeared. Nothing had been seen of him since.
Mrs Dennison said that she thought he had either made way

with himself or got out of the country, nobody knew, but they did know there was something wrong with the house.

"'I knew folks acted queer when they asked me how I liked it when we first came here,' says Mrs Dennison, 'but I never dreamed why till we saw the child that night.'"

"I never heard anything like it in my life," said Mrs Emerson, staring at the other woman with awestruck eyes.

"I thought you'd say so," said Mrs Meserve. "You don't wonder that I ain't disposed to speak light when I hear there is anything queer about a house, do you?"

"No, I don't, after that," Mrs Emerson said.

"But that ain't all," said Mrs Meserve.

"Did you see it again?" Mrs Emerson asked.

"Yes, I saw it a number of times before the last time. It was lucky I wasn't nervous, or I never could have stayed there, much as I liked the place and much as I thought of those two women; they were beautiful women, and no mistake. I loved those women. I hope Mrs Dennison will come and see me sometime.

"Well, I stayed, and I never knew when I'd see that child. I got so I was very careful to bring everything of mine upstairs, and not leave any little thing in my room that needed doing, for fear she would come lugging up my coat or hat or gloves or I'd find things done when there'd been no live being in the room to do them. I can't tell you how I dreaded seeing her; and worse than the seeing her was the hearing her say, 'I can't find my mother.' It was enough to make your blood run cold. I

never heard a living child cry for its mother that was anything so pitiful as that dead one. It was enough to break your heart.

"She used to come and say that to Mrs Bird oftener than to any one else. Once I heard Mrs Bird say she wondered if it was possible that the poor little thing couldn't really find her mother in the other world, she had been such a wicked woman.

"But Mrs Dennison told her she didn't think she ought to speak so nor even think so, and Mrs Bird said she shouldn't wonder if she was right. Mrs Bird was always very easy to put in the wrong. She was a good woman, and one that couldn't do things enough for other folks. It seemed as if that was what she lived on. I don't think she was ever so scared by that poor little ghost, as much as she pitied it, and she was 'most heartbroken because she couldn't do anything for it, as she could have done for a live child.

"'It seems to me sometimes as if I should die if I can't get that awful little white robe off that child and get her in some clothes and feed her and stop her looking for her mother,' I heard her say once, and she was in earnest. She cried when she said it. That wasn't long before she died.

"Now I am coming to the strangest part of it all. Mrs Bird died very sudden. One morning – it was Saturday, and there wasn't any school – I went downstairs to breakfast, and Mrs Bird wasn't there; there was nobody but Mrs Dennison. She was pouring out the coffee when I came in. 'Why, where's Mrs Bird?' says I.

"'Abby ain't feeling very well this morning,' says she; 'there isn't much the matter, I guess, but she didn't sleep very well, and her head aches, and she's sort of chilly, and I told her I thought she'd better stay in bed till the house gets warm.' It was a very cold morning.

"'Maybe she's got cold,' says I.

"'Yes, I guess she has,' says Mrs Dennison. 'I guess she's got cold. She'll be up before long. Abby ain't one to stay in bed a minute longer than she can help.'

"Well, we went on eating our breakfast, and all at once a shadow flickered across one wall of the room and over the ceiling the way a shadow will sometimes when somebody passes the window outside.

"Mrs Dennison and I both looked up, then out of the window; then Mrs Dennison she gives a scream.

"'Why, Abby's crazy!' says she. 'There she is out this bitter cold morning, and – and – ' She didn't finish, but she meant the child. For we were both looking out, and we saw, as plain as we ever saw anything in our lives, Mrs Abby Bird walking off over the white snow-path with that child holding fast to her hand, nestling close to her as if she had found her own mother.

"'She's dead,' says Mrs Dennison, clutching hold of me hard. 'She's dead; my sister is dead!'

"She was. We hurried upstairs as fast as we could go, and she was dead in her bed, and smiling as if she was dreaming, and one arm and hand was stretched out as if something had hold of it; and it couldn't be straightened even at the last – it lay out over her casket at the funeral."

"Was the child ever seen again?" asked Mrs Emerson in a shaking voice.

"No," replied Mrs Meserve; "that child was never seen again after she went out of the yard with Mrs Bird."

The Adventure of the German Student

1824

Washington Irving

On a stormy night, in the tempestuous times of the French Revolution, a young German was returning to his lodgings, at a late hour, across the old part of Paris. The lightning gleamed, and the loud claps of thunder rattled through the lofty narrow streets – but I should first tell you something about this young German.

Gottfried Wolfgang was a young man of good family. He had studied for some time at Göttingen, but being of a visionary and enthusiastic character, he had wandered into those wild and speculative doctrines which have so often bewildered German students. His secluded life, his intense application, and the singular nature of his studies, had an effect on both mind and body. His health was impaired; his imagination diseased. He had been indulging in fanciful

speculations on spiritual essences, until, like Swedenborg, he had an ideal world of his own around him. He took up a notion, I do not know from what cause, that there was an evil influence hanging over him; an evil genius or spirit seeking to ensnare him and ensure his perdition. Such an idea working on his melancholy temperament produced the most gloomy effects. He became haggard and desponding. His friends discovered the mental malady preying upon him, and determined that the best cure was a change of scene; he was sent, therefore, to finish his studies amidst the splendours and gaieties of Paris.

Wolfgang arrived at Paris at the breaking out of the

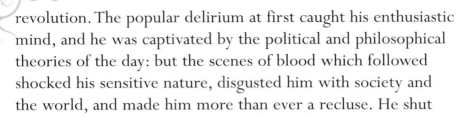

revolution. The popular delirium at first caught his enthusiastic mind, and he was captivated by the political and philosophical theories of the day: but the scenes of blood which followed shocked his sensitive nature, disgusted him with society and the world, and made him more than ever a recluse. He shut

himself up in a solitary apartment in the Pays Latin, the quarter of students. There, in a gloomy street not far from the monastic walls of the Sorbonne, he pursued his favorite speculations. Sometimes he would spend hours together in the great libraries of Paris, those catacombs of departed authors, rummaging among their hoards of dusty and obsolete works in quest of food for his unhealthy appetite. He was, in a manner, a literary ghoul, feeding in the

charnel house of decayed literature.

Wolfgang, though solitary and reclusive, was of an ardent temperament, but for a time it operated merely upon his imagination. He was too shy and ignorant of the world to make any advances to the fair, but he was an admirer of female beauty, and in his lonely chamber would often lose himself in reveries on forms and faces which he had seen, and his fancy would deck out images of loveliness far surpassing the reality.

While his mind was in this excited and sublimated state, a dream produced an extraordinary effect upon him. It was of a female face of transcendent beauty. So strong was the impression made, that he dreamt of it again and again. It haunted his thoughts by day, his slumbers by night; in fine, he became passionately enamoured of this shadow of a dream. This lasted so long that it became one of those fixed ideas which haunt the minds of melancholy men, and are at times mistaken for madness.

Such was Gottfried Wolfgang, and such his situation at the time I mentioned. He was returning home late on stormy night, through some of the old and gloomy streets of the Marais, the ancient part of Paris. The loud claps of thunder rattled among the high houses of the narrow streets. He came to the Place de Grève, the square where public executions are performed. The lightning quivered about the pinnacles of the ancient *hôtel de ville*, and shed flickering gleams over the open space in front. As Wolfgang was crossing the square, he shrank back with horror at finding himself close by the guillotine. It

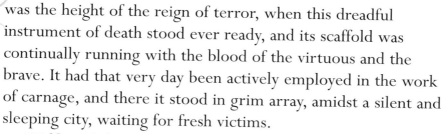

was the height of the reign of terror, when this dreadful instrument of death stood ever ready, and its scaffold was continually running with the blood of the virtuous and the brave. It had that very day been actively employed in the work of carnage, and there it stood in grim array, amidst a silent and sleeping city, waiting for fresh victims.

Wolfgang's heart sickened within him, and he was turning shuddering from the horrible engine, when he beheld a shadowy form, cowering as it were at the foot of the steps which led up to the scaffold. A succession of vivid flashes of lightning revealed it more distinctly. It was a female figure, dressed in black. She was seated on one of the lower steps of the scaffold, leaning forward, her face hidden in her lap; and her long dishevelled tresses hanging to the ground, streaming with the rain which fell in torrents. Wolfgang paused. There was something awful in this solitary monument of woe. The female had the appearance of being above the common order. He knew the times to be full of vicissitude, and that many a fair head, which had once been pillowed on down, now wandered houseless. Perhaps this was some poor mourner whom the dreadful axe had rendered desolate and alone, and who sat here heart-broken on the strand of existence, from which all that was dear to her had been launched into eternity.

He approached, and addressed her in the accents of sympathy. She raised her head and gazed wildly at him. What was his astonishment at beholding, by the bright glare of the lighting, the very face which had haunted him in his dreams. It

was pale and disconsolate, but ravishingly beautiful.

Trembling with violent and conflicting emotions, Wolfgang again accosted her. He spoke something of her being exposed at such an hour of the night, and to the fury of such a storm, and offered to conduct her to her friends. She pointed to the guillotine with a gesture of dreadful signification.

"I have no friend on earth!" said she.

"But you have a home," said Wolfgang.

"Yes – in the grave!"

The heart of the student melted at the words.

"If a stranger dare make an offer," said he, "without danger of being misunderstood, I would offer my humble dwelling as a shelter; myself as a devoted friend. I am friendless myself in Paris, and a stranger in the land; but if my life could be of service, it is at your disposal, and should be sacrificed before harm or indignity should come to you."

There was an honest earnestness in the young man's manner that had its effect. His foreign accent, too, was in his favour; it showed him not to be a hackneyed inhabitant of Paris. Indeed, there is an eloquence in true enthusiasm that is not to be doubted. The homeless stranger confided herself implicitly to the protection of the student.

He supported her faltering steps across the Pont Neuf, and by the place where the statue of Henry IV had been overthrown by the populace. The storm had abated, and the thunder rumbled at a distance. All Paris was quiet; that great volcano of human passion slumbered for a while, to gather

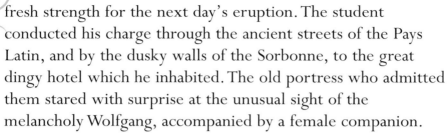

fresh strength for the next day's eruption. The student
conducted his charge through the ancient streets of the Pays
Latin, and by the dusky walls of the Sorbonne, to the great
dingy hotel which he inhabited. The old portress who admitted
them stared with surprise at the unusual sight of the
melancholy Wolfgang, accompanied by a female companion.

On entering his apartment, the student, for the first time,
blushed at the scantiness and indifference of his dwelling. He
had but one chamber – an old-fashioned saloon – heavily
carved, and fantastically furnished with the remains of former
magnificence, for it was one of those hotels in the quarter
of the Luxembourg palace, which had once belonged to
nobility. It was lumbered with books and papers, and all the
usual apparatus of a student, and his bed stood in a recess at
one end.

When lights were brought, and Wolfgang had a better
opportunity of contemplating the stranger, he was more than
ever intoxicated by her beauty. Her face was pale, but of a
dazzling fairness, set off by a profusion of raven hair that hung
clustering about it. Her eyes were large and brilliant, with a
singular expression approaching almost to wildness. As far as
her black dress permitted her shape to be seen, it was of
perfect symmetry. Her whole appearance was highly striking,
though she was dressed in the simplest style. The only thing
approaching to an ornament which she wore, was a broad
black band round her neck, clasped by diamonds.

The perplexity now commenced with the student how to

dispose of the helpless being thus thrown upon his protection. He thought of abandoning his chamber to her, and seeking shelter for himself elsewhere. Still, he was so fascinated by her charms, there seemed to be such a spell upon his thoughts and senses, that he could not tear himself from her presence. Her manner, too, was singular and unaccountable. She spoke no more of the guillotine. Her grief had abated. The attentions of the student had first won her confidence, and then, apparently, her heart. She was evidently an enthusiast like himself, and enthusiasts soon understand each other.

In the infatuation of the moment, Wolfgang avowed his passion for her. He told her the story of his mysterious dream, and how she had possessed his heart before he had even seen her. She was strangely affected by his recital, and acknowledged to have felt an impulse towards him equally unaccountable. It was the time for wild theory and wild actions. Old prejudices and superstitions were done away; everything was under the sway of the Goddess of Reason. Among other rubbish of the old times, the forms and ceremonies of marriage began to be considered superfluous bonds for honourable minds. Social compacts were the vogue. Wolfgang was far too much of theorist not to be tainted by the liberal doctrines of the day.

"Why should we separate?" said he. "Our hearts are united; in the eye of reason and honour we are as one. What need is there of sordid forms to bind high souls together?"

The stranger listened with emotion: she had evidently

received illumination at the same school.

"You have no home nor family," continued he. "Let me be everything to you, or rather let us be everything to one another. If form is necessary, form shall be observed – there is my hand. I pledge myself to you forever."

"Forever?" said the stranger, solemnly.

"Forever!" repeated Wolfgang.

The stranger clasped the hand extended to her: "Then I am yours," murmured she, and sank upon his bosom.

The next morning the student left his bride sleeping, and sallied forth at an early hour to seek more spacious apartments suitable to the change in his situation. When he returned, he found the stranger lying with her head hanging over the bed, and one arm thrown over it. He spoke to her, but received no reply. He advanced to awaken her from her uneasy posture. On taking her hand, it was cold – there was no pulsation – her face was pallid and ghastly. In a word, she was a corpse.

Horrified and frantic, he alarmed the house. A scene of confusion ensued. The police was summoned. As the officer entered the room, he started back on beholding the corpse.

"How did this woman come here?" he cried.

"Do you know anything about her?" said Wolfgang eagerly.

"Do I?" exclaimed the officer. "She was guillotined yesterday."

He stepped forward; undid the black collar round the neck

of the corpse, and the head rolled on the floor!

The student burst into a frenzy. "The fiend! The fiend has gained possession of me!" shrieked he; "I am lost forever."

They tried to soothe him, but all in vain. He was possessed with the belief that an evil spirit had reanimated the dead body to ensnare him. He went distracted, and died in a madhouse.

The Phantom Coach

1864

Amelia B Edwards

The circumstances I am about to relate to you have truth to recommend them. They happened to myself, and my recollection of them is vivid as if they had taken place only yesterday. Twenty years, however, have gone by since that night. During those twenty years I have told the story to but one other person. I tell it now with a reluctance which I find it difficult to overcome. All I entreat, meanwhile, is that you will abstain from forcing your own conclusions upon me. I want nothing explained away. I desire no arguments. My mind on this subject is quite made up, and having the testimony of my own senses to rely upon, I prefer to abide by it.

Well! It was just twenty years ago, and within a day or two of the end of the grouse season. I had been out all day with my gun, and had had no sport to speak of. The wind was due east;

the month, December; the place, a bleak wide moor in the far north of England. And I had lost my way. It was not a pleasant place in which to lose one's way, with the first feathery flakes of a coming snowstorm just fluttering down upon the heather, and the leaden evening closing in all around. I shaded my eyes with my hand, and stared anxiously into the gathering darkness, where the purple moorland melted into a range of low hills, some ten or twelve miles distant. Not the faintest smoke-wreath, not the tiniest cultivated patch, or fence, or sheep-track, met my eyes in any direction. There was nothing for it but to walk on, and take my chance of finding what shelter I could, by the way. So I shouldered my gun again and pushed wearily forward, for I had been on foot since an hour after daybreak and had eaten nothing since breakfast.

Meanwhile, the snow began to come down with ominous steadiness, and the wind fell. After this, the cold became more intense, and the night came rapidly up. As for me, my prospects darkened with the darkening sky, and my heart grew heavy as I thought how my young wife was already watching for me through the window of our little inn parlour, and thought of all the suffering in store for her throughout this weary night. We had been married four months, and, having spent our autumn in the Highlands, were now lodging in a remote little village situated just on the verge of the great English moorlands. We were very much in love, and, of course, very happy. This morning, when we parted, she had implored me to return before dusk, and I had promised her that I

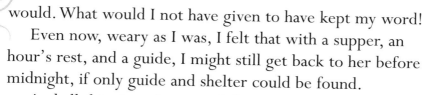

would. What would I not have given to have kept my word!

Even now, weary as I was, I felt that with a supper, an hour's rest, and a guide, I might still get back to her before midnight, if only guide and shelter could be found.

And all this time the snow fell and the night thickened. I stopped and shouted every now and then, but my shouts seemed only to make the silence deeper. Then a vague sense of uneasiness came upon me, and I began to remember stories of travellers who had walked on and on in the falling snow until, wearied out, they were fain to lie down and sleep their lives away. Would it be possible, I asked myself, to keep on thus through all the long dark night? Would there not come a time when my limbs must fail, and my resolution give way? When I, too, must sleep the sleep of death. Death! I shuddered. How hard to die just now, when life lay all so bright before me! How hard for my darling, whose whole loving heart – but that thought was not to be borne! To banish it, I shouted again, louder and longer, and then listened eagerly. Was my shout answered, or did I only fancy that I heard a far-off cry? I halloed again and again the echo followed. Then a wavering speck of light came suddenly out of the dark, shifting, disappearing, growing momentarily nearer and brighter. Running towards it at full speed, I found myself, to my great joy, face to face with an old man and a lantern.

"Thank God!" was the exclamation that burst involuntarily from my lips. Blinking and frowning, he lifted his lantern and peered into my face.

"What for?" growled he, sulkily.

"Well for you. I began to fear I should be lost in the snow."

"Eh, then, folks do get cast away hereabouts fra' time to time, an' what's to hinder you from bein' cast away likewise, if the Lord's so minded?"

"If the Lord is so minded that you and I shall be lost together my friend, we must submit," I replied; "but I don't mean to be lost without you. How far am I now from Dwolding?"

"A gude twenty mile, more or less."

"And the nearest village?"

"The nearest village is Wyke, an' that's twelve miles t'other side."

"Where do you live, then?"

"Out yonder," said he, with a vague jerk of the lantern.

"You're going home, I presume?"

"Maybe I am."

"Then I'm going with you."

The old man shook his head, and rubbed his nose reflectively with the handle of the lantern.

"It ain't no use," growled he. "He 'ont let you in – not he."

"We'll see about that," I replied, briskly. "Who is he?"

"The master."

"Who is the master?"

"That's nowt to you," was the unceremonious reply.

"Well, well; you lead the way, and I'll engage that the master shall give me shelter and a supper tonight."

"Eh, you can try him!" muttered my reluctant guide; and, still shaking his head, he hobbled, gnome-like, away through the falling snow.

A large mass loomed up presently out of the darkness, and a huge dog rushed out barking furiously.

"Is this the house?" I asked.

"Ay, it's the house. Down, Bey!" And he fumbled in his pocket for the key.

I drew up close behind him, prepared to lose no chance of entrance, and saw in the little circle of light shed by the lantern that the door was heavily studded with iron nails, like the door of a prison. In another minute he had turned the key and I had pushed past him into the house.

Once inside, I looked round with curiosity and found myself in a great raftered hall, which served, apparently, a variety of uses. One end was piled to the roof with corn, like a barn. The other was stored with flour-sacks, agricultural implements, casks, and all kinds of miscellaneous lumber; while from the beams overhead hung rows of hams, flitches,

and bunches of dried herbs for winter use. In the centre of the floor stood some huge object gauntly dressed in a dingy wrapping-cloth, and reaching halfway to the rafters. Lifting a corner of this cloth, I saw, to my surprise, a telescope of very considerable size, mounted on a rude movable platform, with four small wheels. The tube was made of painted wood bound round with bands of metal rudely fashioned; the speculum, so far as I could estimate its size in the dim light, measured at least fifteen inches in diameter. While I was yet examining the instrument, and asking myself whether it was not the work of some self-taught optician, a bell rang sharply.

"That's for you," said my guide, with a malicious grin. "Yonder's his room."

He pointed to a low black door at the opposite side of the hall. I crossed over, rapped somewhat loudly, and went in, without waiting for an invitation. A huge, white-haired old man rose from a table covered with books and papers, and confronted me sternly.

"Who are you?" said he. "How came you here? What do you want?"

"James Murray, barrister-at-law. On foot across the moor. Meat, drink, and sleep."

He bent his bushy brows into a portentous frown.

"Mine is not a house of entertainment," he said, haughtily. "Jacob, how dare you admit this stranger?"

"I didn't admit him," grumbled the old man. "He followed me over the muir, and shouldered his way in before me. I'm no

match for six foot two."

"And pray, sir, by what right have you forced an entrance into my house?"

"The same by which I should have clung to your boat, if I were drowning. The right of self-preservation."

"Self-preservation?"

"There's an inch of snow on the ground already," I replied, briefly, "and it would be deep enough to cover my body before daybreak."

He strode to the window, pulled aside a heavy black curtain, and looked out.

"It is true," he said. "You can stay, if you choose, till morning. Jacob, serve the supper."

With this he waved me to a seat, resumed his own, and became at once absorbed in the studies from which I had disturbed him.

I placed my gun in a corner, drew a chair to the hearth, and examined my quarters at leisure. Smaller and less incongruous in its arrangements than the hall, this room contained, nevertheless, much to awaken my curiosity. The floor was carpetless. The whitewashed walls were in parts scrawled over with strange diagrams, and in others covered with shelves crowded with philosophical instruments, the uses of many of which were unknown to me. On one side of the fireplace stood a bookcase filled with dingy folios; on the other, a small organ, fantastically decorated with painted carvings of medieval saints and devils. Through the half-opened door of a

cupboard at the further end of the room I saw a long array of
geological specimens, surgical preparations, crucibles, retorts,
and jars of chemicals; while on the mantelshelf beside me,
amid a number of small objects stood a model of the solar
system, a small galvanic battery, and a microscope. Every chair
had its burden. Every corner was heaped high with books. The

very floor was littered over with maps, casts, papers, tracings, and learned lumber of all conceivable kinds.

I stared about me with an amazement increased by every fresh object upon which my eyes chanced to rest. So strange a room I had never seen; yet seemed it stranger still, to find such a room in a lone farmhouse amid those wild and solitary moors! Over and over again I looked from my host to his surroundings, and from his surroundings back to my host, asking myself who and what he could be? His head was singularly fine; but it was more the head of a poet than of a philosopher. Broad in the temples, prominent over the eyes, and clothed with a rough profusion of perfectly white hair, it had all the ideality and much of the ruggedness that characterizes the head of Ludwig von Beethoven. There were the same deep lines about the mouth, and the same stern furrows in the brow. There was the same concentration of expression. While I was yet observing him, the door opened and Jacob brought in the supper. His master then closed his book, rose, and with more courtesy of manner than he had yet shown, invited me to the table.

A dish of ham and eggs, a loaf of brown bread, and a bottle of admirable sherry, were placed before me.

"I have but the homeliest farmhouse fare to offer you, sir," said my entertainer. "Your appetite, I trust, will make up for the deficiencies of our larder."

I had already fallen upon the viands, and now protested, with the enthusiasm of a starving sportsman, that I had never

eaten anything so delicious.

He bowed stiffly, and sat down to his own supper, which consisted, primitively, of a jug of milk and a basin of porridge. We ate in silence, and, when we had done, Jacob removed the tray. I then drew my chair back to the fireside. My host, somewhat to my surprise, did the same, and turning abruptly towards me, said: "Sir, I have lived here in strict retirement for three-and-twenty years. During that time I have not seen as many strange faces and I have not read a single newspaper. You are the first stranger who has crossed my threshold for more than four years. Will you favour me with a few words of information respecting that outer world from which I have parted company so long?"

"Pray interrogate me," I replied. "I am heartily at your service."

He bent his head in acknowledgment; leaned forward, with his elbows resting on his knees and his chin supported in the palms of his hands; stared fixedly into the fire; and proceeded to question me.

His inquiries related chiefly to scientific matters, with the later progress of which, as applied to the practical purposes of life, he was almost wholly unacquainted. No student of science myself, I replied as well as my slight information permitted; but the task was far from easy, and I was much relieved when, passing from interrogation to discussion, he began pouring forth his own conclusions upon the facts which I had been attempting to place before him. He talked, and I listened spellbound. He talked till I believe he almost forgot my presence, and only thought aloud. I had never heard anything like it then; I have never heard anything like it since. Familiar with all systems of all philosophies, subtle in analysis, bold in generalization, he poured forth his thoughts in an uninterrupted stream, and, still leaning forward in the same moody attitude with his eyes fixed upon the fire, wandered from topic to topic, from speculation to speculation, like an inspired dreamer. From practical science to mental philosophy; from electricity in the wire to electricity in the nerve; from Watts to Mesmer, from Mesmer to Reichenbach, from Reichenbach to Swedenborg, Spinoza, Condillac, Descartes, Berkeley, Aristotle, Plato, and the Magi and mystics of the East, were transitions which – however bewildering in their variety and scope – seemed easy and harmonious upon his lips as sequences in music. By and by – I forget now by what link of conjecture or illustration – he passed on to that field which lies beyond the boundary line or even conjectural philosophy, and reaches no man knows whither. He spoke of the soul and its aspirations; of the spirit and its powers; of second sight; of prophecy; of those phenomena which, under the names of ghosts, spectres and supernatural appearances, have been denied by the sceptics and attested by the credulous, of all ages.

"The world," he said, "grows hourly more and more sceptical of all that lies beyond its own narrow radius; and our men of science foster the fatal tendency. They condemn as

fable all that resists experiment. They reject as false all that cannot be brought to the test of the laboratory or the dissecting room. Against what superstition have they waged so long and obstinate a war, as against the belief in apparitions? And yet what superstition has maintained its hold upon the minds of men so long and so firmly. Show me any fact in physics, in history, in archaeology, which is supported by testimony so wide and so various. Attested by all races of men, in all ages, and in all climates, by the soberest sages of antiquity, by the rudest savage of today, by the Christian, the Pagan, the Pantheist, the Materialist, this phenomenon is treated as a nursery tale by the philosophers of our century. Circumstantial evidence weighs with them as a feather in the balance. The comparison of causes with effects, however valuable in physical science, is put aside as worthless and unreliable. The evidence of competent witnesses, however conclusive in a court of justice, counts for nothing. He who pauses before he pronounces, is condemned as a trifler. He who believes, is a dreamer or a fool."

He spoke with bitterness, and, having said thus, relapsed for some minutes into silence. Presently he raised his head from his hands, and added, with an altered voice and manner: "I, sir, paused, investigated, believed, and was not ashamed to state my convictions to the world. I, too, was branded as a visionary, held up to ridicule by my contemporaries, and hooted from that field of science in which I had laboured with honour during all the best years of my fife. These things

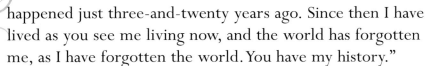

happened just three-and-twenty years ago. Since then I have lived as you see me living now, and the world has forgotten me, as I have forgotten the world. You have my history."

"It is a very sad one," I murmured, scarcely knowing what to answer.

"It is a very common one," he replied. "I have only suffered for the truth, as many a better and wiser man has suffered before me."

He rose, as if desirous of ending the conversation, and went over to the window.

"It has ceased snowing," he observed, as he dropped the curtain and came back to the fireside.

"Ceased!" I exclaimed, starting eagerly to my feet, "Oh, if it were only possible – but no! it is hopeless. Even if I could find my way across the moor, I could not walk twenty miles tonight."

"Walk twenty miles tonight!" repeated my host. "What are you thinking of?"

"Of my wife," I replied impatiently. "Of my young wife, who does not know that I have lost my way, and who is at this moment breaking her heart with suspense and terror."

"Where is she?"

"At Dwolding, twenty miles away."

"At Dwolding," he echoed, thoughtfully. "Yes, the distance, it is true, is twenty miles; but – are you so very anxious to save the next six or eight hours?"

"So very, very anxious, that I would give ten guineas at this moment for a guide and a horse."

"Your wish can be gratified at a less costly rate," said he, smiling. "The night mail from the north, which changes horses at Dwolding, passes within five miles of this spot, and will be due at a certain crossroad in about an hour and a quarter. If Jacob were to go with you across the moor and put you into the old coachroad, you could find your way, I suppose, to where it joins the new one?"

"Easily – gladly."

He smiled again, rang the bell, gave the old servant his directions, and, taking a bottle of whisky and wineglass from the cupboard in which he kept his chemicals said: "The snow lies deep and it will be difficult walking tonight on the moor. A glass of usquebaugh before you start?"

I would have declined the spirit, but he pressed it on me, and so I drank it. It was so strong that it went down my throat like liquid flame and almost took my breath away.

"It is strong," he said; "but it will help to keep out the cold. And now you have no moments to spare. Goodnight!"

I thanked him for his hospitality and would have shaken hands with him but that he had turned away almost before I could finish my sentence. In another minute I had traversed the hall, Jacob had locked the two locks on the outer door behind me, and we were out on the wide, white moor. Although the wind had fallen, it was still bitterly cold. Not a star glimmered in the black vault overhead. Not a sound, save the rapid crunching of the snow beneath our feet, disturbed the heavy stillness of the night. Jacob, not too well pleased with his mission, shambled on before in sullen silence, his lantern in his hand and his shadow at his feet. I followed, with my gun over my shoulder, as little inclined for conversation as himself. My thoughts were full of my late host. His voice yet rang in my ears. His eloquence yet held my imagination captive. I remember to this day, with surprise, how my over-excited brain retained whole sentences and parts of sentences, troops of brilliant images, and fragments of splendid reasoning, in the very words in which he had uttered them. Musing thus over what I had heard, and striving to recall a lost link here and there, I strode on at the heel of my guide, absorbed and unobservant. Presently – at the end, as it seemed to me, of only a few minutes – he came to a sudden halt, and said:

"Yon's your road. Keep the stone fence to your right hand and you can't fail of the way."

"This, then, is the old coach road?"

"Ay, 'tis the old coach road."

"And how far do I go before I reach the crossroads?"

"Nigh upon three mile."

I pulled out my purse, and he became more communicative.

"The road's a fair road enough," said he, "for foot passengers; but 'twas over-steep and narrow for the northern traffic. You'll mind where the parapet's broken away, close again' the signpost.

It's never been mended since the accident."

"What accident?"

"Eh, the night mail pitched right over into the valley below – a gude fifty feet an' more – just at the worst bit o'road in the whole county."

"Horrible! Were many lives lost?"

"All. Four were found dead, and t'other two died next morning."

"How long is it since this happened?"

"Just nine year."

"Near the signpost, you say? I will bear it in mind. Good night."

"Gude night, sit, and thankee." Jacob pocketed his half-crown, made a faint pretence of touching his hat, and trudged back by the way he had come.

I watched the fight of his lantern till it quite disappeared, and then turned to pursue my way alone. This was no longer matter of the slightest difficulty, for, despite the dead darkness overhead, the line of stone fence showed distinctly enough against the pale gleam of the snow. How silent it seemed now, with only my footsteps to listen to; how silent and how solitary! A strange disagreeable sense of loneliness stole over me. I walked faster. I hummed a fragment of a tune. I cast up enormous sums in my head, and accumulated them at compound interest. I did best, in short, to forget the startling speculations to which I had but just been listening, and, to some extent, I succeeded.

Meanwhile, the night air seemed to become colder and colder. My feet were like ice. I lost sensation in my hands, and grasped my gun mechanically. I even breathed with difficulty, as though, instead of traversing a quiet north-country highway, I were scaling the uppermost heights of some gigantic alp. This last symptom became so distressing that I was forced to stop and lean against the stone fence. As I did so I chanced to look back up the road, and there, to my infinite relief, I saw a distant point of light, like the gleam of an approaching lantern. I at first concluded that Jacob had retraced his steps and followed me; but then a second light flashed into sight – a light evidently parallel with the first, and approaching at the same rate of motion. It needed no second thought to show me that these must be the carriage-lamps of some private vehicle, though it seemed strange that any private vehicle should take a road professedly disused and dangerous.

There could be no doubt, however, of the fact, for the lamps grew larger and brighter every moment, and I even fancied I could already see the dark outline of the carriage between them. It was coming up very fast, and quite noiselessly, the snow being nearly a foot deep under the wheels.

And now the body of the vehicle became distinctly visible behind the lamps. It looked strangely lofty. A sudden suspicion flashed upon me. Was it possible that I had passed the crossroads in the dark without observing the signpost, and could this be the very coach which I had come to meet?

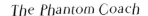

No need to ask myself that question a second time, for here it came round the bend of the road: guard and driver, one outside passenger, and four steaming greys, all wrapped in a soft haze of light, through which the lamps blazed out like a pair of fiery meteors.

I jumped forward, waved my hat. The mail came down at full speed and passed me. For a moment I feared that I had not been seen or heard, but it was only for a moment. The coachman pulled up; the guard, muffled to the eyes in capes and comforters, and apparently sound asleep in the rumble, neither answered my hail nor made the slightest effort to dismount; the outside passenger did not even turn his head. I opened the door for myself. There were but three travellers inside, so I stepped in, shut the door, slipped into the vacant corner, and congratulated myself of my good fortune.

The atmosphere of the coach seemed, if possible, colder than that of the outer air and was pervaded by a singularly damp and disagreeable smell. I looked round at my fellow-passengers. They were all three men, and all silent. They did not seem to be asleep, but each leaned back in his corner of the vehicle, as if absorbed in his own reflections.

"How intensely cold it is tonight," I said, addressing my opposite neighbour.

He lifted his head, looked at me, but made no reply.

"The winter," I added, "seems to have begun in earnest."

Although the corner in which he sat was so dim that I could distinguish none of his features very clearly, I saw that his eyes were still turned full upon me. And yet he answered never a word.

At any other time I should have felt, and perhaps expressed, some annoyance, but at the moment I felt too ill to do either. The icy coldness of the night air had struck a chill to my very marrow, and the strange smell inside the coach was affecting me with an intolerable nausea. I shivered from head to foot, and, turning to my left-hand neighbour, asked if he had any objection to an open window?

He neither spoke nor stirred.

I repeated the question somewhat more loudly, but with the same result. Then I lost my patience and let the sash down. As I did so, the leather strap broke in my hand, and I observed that the glass was covered with a thick coat of mildew, the accumulation, apparently, of years. My attention being thus drawn to the condition of the coach, I examined it more narrowly, and saw by the uncertain light of the outer lamps that it was in the last state of dilapidation. Every part of it was not only out of repair but in a condition of decay. The sashes splintered at a touch. The leather fittings were crusted over with mould, and literally rotting from the woodwork. The floor was almost breaking away beneath my feet. The whole machine, in short, was foul with damp, and had evidently been dragged from some outhouse in which it had been mouldering away for years, to do another day or two of duty on the road.

I turned to the third passenger, whom I had not yet addressed, and hazarded one more remark.

"This coach," I said, "is in deplorable condition. The regular mail, I suppose, is under repair."

He moved his head slowly, and looked me in the face, without speaking a word. I shall never forget that look while I live. I turned cold at heart under it. I turn cold at heart even now when I recall it. His eyes glowed with a fiery unnatural lustre. His face was livid as the face of a corpse. His bloodless lips were drawn back as if in the agony of death, and showed the gleaming teeth between.

The words that I was about to utter died upon my lips, and a strange horror – a dreadful horror – came upon me. My sight had by this time become used to the gloom of the coach and I could see with tolerable distinctness. I turned to my opposite neighbour. He, too, was looking at me with the same startling pallor in his face and the same stony glitter in his eyes. I passed my hand across my brow. I turned to the passenger on the seat beside my own, and saw – oh, heaven! how shall I describe what I saw? I saw that he was no living man – that none of them were living men, like myself A pale phosphorescent light – the fight of putrefaction – played upon their awful faces; upon their hair, dank with the dews of the grave; upon their clothes – earth stained and dropping to pieces; upon their hands, which were as the hands of corpses long buried. Only their eyes, their terrible eyes, were living; and those eyes were all turned menacingly upon me!

A shriek of terror, a wild, unintelligible cry for help and mercy, burst from my lips as I flung myself against the door and strove in vain to open it.

In that single instant, brief and vivid as a landscape beheld in the flash of summer lightning, I saw the moon shining down through a rift of stormy cloud – the ghastly signpost rearing its warning finger by the wayside – the broken parapet – the plunging horses – the black gulf below. Then the coach reeled like a ship at sea. Then came a mighty crash – a sense of crushing pain – and then darkness.

It seemed as if years had gone by when I awoke one morning from a deep sleep and found my wife watching by my bedside. I will pass over the scene that ensued and give you, in half a dozen words, the tale she told me with tears of thanksgiving. I had fallen over a precipice, close against the junction of the old coach-road and the new, and had only been saved from certain death by lighting upon a deep snowdrift that had accumulated at the foot of the rock beneath. In this snowdrift I was discovered at daybreak by a couple of shepherds, who carried me to the nearest shelter and brought a surgeon to my aid. The surgeon found me in a state of raving delirium, with a broken arm and a compound fracture of the skull. The letters in my pocket-book showed my name and address; my wife was summoned to nurse me; and, thanks to youth and a fine constitution, I came out of danger at last. The place of my fall, I need scarcely say, was precisely that at which a frightful accident had happened to the north mail nine years before.

I never told my wife the fearful events which I have just related to you. I told the surgeon who attended me; but he treated the whole adventure as a dream born of brain fever. We discussed the question over and over until we found that we could discuss it no longer, and then we dropped it. Others may form what conclusions they please – I *know* that twenty years ago I was the fourth inside passenger in that phantom coach.

The Signal-Man

1866

Charles Dickens

"Halloa! Below there!"

When he heard a voice calling to him, he was standing at the door of his box, with a flag in his hand, furled round its short pole. One would have thought, considering the nature of the ground, that he could not have doubted from what quarter the voice came; but instead of looking up to where I stood on the top of the steep cutting nearly over his head, he turned himself about, and looked down the line. There was something remarkable in his manner of doing so, though I could not have said for my life what. But I know it was remarkable enough to attract my notice, even though his figure was foreshortened and shadowed, down in the deep trench, and mine was high above him, so steeped in the glow

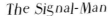

of an angry sunset, that I had shaded my eyes with my hand before I saw him at all.

"Halloa! Below!"

From looking down the line, he turned himself about again, and, raising his eyes, saw my figure high above him.

"Is there any path by which I can come down and speak to you?"

He looked up at me without replying, and I looked down at him without pressing him too soon with a repetition of my idle question. Just then there came a vague vibration in the earth and air, quickly changing into a violent pulsation, and an oncoming rush that caused me to start back, as though it had force to draw me down. When such vapour as rose to my height from this rapid train had passed me, and was skimming away over the landscape, I looked down again, and saw him refurling the flag he had shown while the train went by.

I repeated my inquiry. After a pause, during which he seemed to regard me with fixed attention, he motioned with his rolled-up flag towards a point on my level, some two or three hundred yards distant. I called down to him, "All right!" and made for that point. There, by dint of looking closely about me, I found a rough zigzag descending path notched out, which I followed.

The cutting was extremely deep and unusually precipitate. It was made through a clammy stone that became oozier and wetter as I went down. For these reasons, I found the way long enough to give me time to recall a singular air of reluctance or

compulsion with which he had pointed out the path.

When I came down low enough upon the zigzag descent to see him again, I saw that he was standing between the rails on the way by which the train had lately passed, in an attitude as if he were waiting for me to appear. He had his left hand at his chin, and that left elbow rested on his right hand, crossed over his breast. His attitude was one of such expectation and watchfulness that I stopped a moment, wondering at it.

I resumed my downward way, and stepping out upon the level of the railroad, and drawing nearer to him, saw that he was a dark sallow man, with a dark beard and rather heavy eyebrows. His post was in as solitary and dismal a place as ever I saw. On either side, a dripping-wet wall of jagged stone, excluding all view but a strip of sky; the perspective one way only a crooked prolongation of this great dungeon; the shorter perspective in the other direction terminating in a gloomy red light, and the gloomier entrance to a black tunnel, in whose massive architecture there was a barbarous, depressing, and forbidding air. So little sunlight ever found its way to this spot, that it had an earthy, deadly smell; and so much cold wind rushed through it, that it struck chill to me, as if I had left the natural world.

Before he stirred, I was near enough to him to have touched him. Not even then removing his eyes from mine, he stepped back one step, and lifted his hand.

This was a lonesome post to occupy (I said), and it had riveted my attention when I looked down from up yonder. A

visitor was a rarity, I should suppose; not an unwelcome rarity, I hoped? In me, he merely saw a man who had been shut up within narrow limits all his life, and who, being at last set free, had a newly-awakened interest in these great works. To such purpose I spoke to him; but I am far from sure of the terms I used; for, besides that I am not happy in opening any conversation, there was something in the man that daunted me.

He directed a most curious look towards the red light near the tunnel's mouth, and looked all about it, as if something were missing from it, and then looked it me.

That light was part of his charge? Was it not?

He answered in a low voice, "Don't you know it is?"

The monstrous thought came into my mind, as I perused the fixed eyes and the saturnine face, that this was a spirit, not a man. I have speculated since, whether there may have been infection in his mind.

In my turn, I stepped back. But in making the action, I detected in his eyes that he had some latent fear of me, and this succeeded in putting the monstrous thought to flight.

"You look at me," I said, forcing a smile, "as if you had a dread of me."

"I was doubtful," he returned, "whether I had seen you before."

"Where?"

He pointed to the red light he had looked at.

"There?" I said.

Intently watchful of me, he replied (but without sound), 'yes.'

"My good fellow, what should I do there? However, be that as it may, I never was there, you may swear."

"I think I may," he rejoined. "Yes; I am sure I may."

His manner cleared, like my own. He replied to my remarks with readiness, and in well-chosen words. Had he much to do there? Yes; that was to say, he had enough responsibility to bear; but exactness and watchfulness were what was required of him, and of actual work – manual labour – he had next to none. To change that signal, to trim those lights, and to turn this iron handle now and then, was all he had to do under that head. Regarding those many long and lonely hours of which I seemed to make so much, he could only say that the routine of his life had shaped itself into that form, and he had grown used to it. He had taught himself a language down here, if only to know it by sight, and to have formed his own crude ideas of its pronunciation, could be called learning it. He had also worked at fractions and decimals, and tried a little algebra; but he was, and had been as a boy, a poor hand at figures. Was it necessary for him when on duty always to remain in that channel of damp air, and could he never rise into the sunshine from between those high stone walls? Why, that depended upon times and circumstances. Under some conditions there would be less upon the line than under others, and the same held good as to certain hours of the day and night. In bright weather, he did choose occasions for getting a little above these lower shadows; but, being at all

times liable to be called by his electric bell, and at such times listening for it with redoubled anxiety, the relief was less than I would suppose.

He took me into his box, where there was a fire, a desk for an official book in which he had to make certain entries, a telegraphic instrument with its dial, face, and needles, and the little bell of which he had spoken. On my trusting that he would excuse the remark that he had been well educated, and (I hoped I might say without offence) perhaps educated above that station, he observed that instances of slight incongruity in such wise would rarely be found wanting among large bodies of men; that he had heard it was so in workhouses, in the police force, even in that last desperate resource, the army; and that he knew it was so, more or less, in any great railway staff. He had been, when young (if I could believe it, sitting in that hut, he scarcely could), a student of natural philosophy, and had attended lectures; but he had run wild, misused his opportunities, gone down, and never risen again. He had no complaint to offer

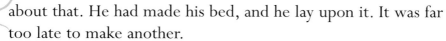

about that. He had made his bed, and he lay upon it. It was far too late to make another.

All that I have here condensed he said in a quiet manner, with his grave, dark regards divided between me and the fire. He threw in the word, 'Sir,' from time to time, and especially when he referred to his youth, as though to request me to understand that he claimed to be nothing but what I found him. He was several times interrupted by the little bell, and had to read off messages and send replies. Once he had to stand outside the door and display a flag as a train passed, and make some verbal communication to the driver. In the discharge of his duties, I observed him to be remarkably exact and vigilant, breaking off his discourse at a syllable, and remaining silent until what he had to do was done.

In a word, I should have set this man down as one of the safest of men to be employed in that capacity, but for the circumstance that while he was speaking to me he twice broke off with a fallen colour, turned his face towards the little bell when it did not ring, opened the door of the hut (which was kept shut to exclude the unhealthy damp), and looked out towards the red light near the mouth of the tunnel. On both of those occasions, he came back to the fire with the inexplicable air upon him which I had remarked, without being able to define, when we were so far asunder.

Said I, when I rose to leave him, "You almost make me think that I have met with a contented man."

(I am afraid I must acknowledge that I said it to lead him on.)

"I believe I used to be so," he rejoined, in the low voice in which he had first spoken, "but I am troubled, sir, I am troubled."

He would have recalled the words if he could. He had said them, however, and I took them up quickly.

"With what? What is your trouble?"

"It is very difficult to impart, sir. It is very, very difficult to speak of. If ever you make me another visit, I will try to tell you."

"But I expressly intend to make you another visit. Say, when shall it be?"

"I go off early in the morning, and I shall be on again at ten tomorrow night, sir."

"I will come at eleven."

He thanked me, and went out at the door with me. "I'll show my white light, sir," he said, in his peculiar low voice, "till you have found the way up. When you have found it, don't call out! And when you are at the top, don't call out!"

His manner seemed to make the place strike colder to me, but I said no more than, "Very well."

"And when you come down tomorrow night, don't call out! Let me ask you a parting question. What made you cry, 'Halloa! Below there!' tonight?"

"Heaven knows," said I. "I cried something to that effect."

"Not to that effect, sir. Those were the very words. I know them well."

"I admit those were the very words. I said them, no doubt,

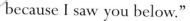

because I saw you below."

"For no other reason?"

"What other reason could I possibly have?"

"You had no feeling that they were conveyed to you in any supernatural way?"

"No."

He wished me goodnight, and held up his light. I walked by the side of the down line of rails (with a very disagreeable sensation of a train coming behind me) until I found the path. It was easier to mount than to descend, and I got back to my inn without any adventure.

Punctual to my appointment, I placed my foot on the first notch of the zigzag next evening, as the distant clocks were striking eleven. He was waiting for me at the bottom, with his white light on. "I have not called out," I said, when we came close together. "May I speak now?"

"By all means, sir."

"Goodnight, then, and here's my hand."

"Goodnight, sir, and here's mine." With that we walked side by side to his box, entered it, closed the door, and sat down by the fire.

"I have made up my mind, sir," he began,

bending forward as soon as we were seated, and speaking in a tone but a little above a whisper, "that you shall not have to ask me twice what troubles me. I took you for someone else yesterday evening. That troubles me."

"That mistake?"

"No. That someone else."

"Who is it?"

"I don't know."

"Like me?"

"I don't know. I never saw the face. The left arm is across the face, and the right arm is waved, violently waved. This way."

I followed his action with my eyes, and it was the action of an arm gesticulating, with the utmost passion and vehemence, 'For God's sake, clear the way!'

"One moonlight night," said the man, "I was sitting here, when I heard a voice cry, 'Halloa! Below there!' I started up, looked from that door, and saw this someone else standing by the red light near the tunnel, waving as I just now showed you. The voice seemed hoarse with shouting, and it cried, 'Look out! Look out!' And then again, 'Halloa! Below there! Look out!' I caught up my lamp, turned it on red, and ran towards the figure, calling, 'What's wrong? What has happened? Where?' It stood just outside the blackness of the tunnel. I advanced so close upon it that I wondered at its keeping the sleeve across its eyes. I ran right up at it, and had my hand stretched out to pull the sleeve away, when it was gone."

"Into the tunnel?" said I.

"No. I ran on into the tunnel, five hundred yards. I stopped, and held my lamp above my head, and saw the figures of the measured distance, and saw the wet stains stealing down the walls and trickling through the arch. I ran out again faster than I had run in (for I had a mortal abhorrence of the place upon me), and I looked all round the red light with my own red light, and I went up the iron ladder to the gallery atop of it, and I came down again, and ran back here. I telegraphed both ways, 'An alarm has been given. Is anything wrong?' The answer came back, both ways, 'All well.'"

Resisting the slow touch of a frozen finger tracing out my spine, I showed him how that this figure must be a deception of his sense of sight; and how that figures, originating in disease of the delicate nerves that minister to the functions of the eye, were known to have often troubled patients, some of whom had become conscious of the nature of their affliction, and had even proved it by experiments upon themselves. "As to an imaginary cry," said I, "do but listen for a moment to the wind in this unnatural valley while we speak so low, and to the wild harp it makes of the telegraph wires."

That was all very well, he returned, after we had sat listening for a while, and he ought to know something of the wind and the wires – he who so often passed long winter nights there, alone and watching. But he would beg to remark that he had not finished.

I asked his pardon, and he slowly added these words,

touching my arm,

"Within six hours after the Appearance, the memorable accident on this line happened, and within ten hours the dead and wounded were brought along through the tunnel over the spot where the figure had stood."

A disagreeable shudder crept over me, but I did my best against it. It was not to be denied, I rejoined, that this was a remarkable coincidence, calculated deeply to impress his mind. But it was unquestionable that remarkable coincidences did continually occur, and they must be taken into account in dealing with such a subject. Though to be sure I must admit, I added (for I thought I saw that he was going to bring the objection to bear upon me), men of common sense did not allow much for coincidences in making the ordinary calculations of life.

He again begged to remark that he had not finished.

I again begged his pardon for being betrayed into interruptions.

"This," he said, again laying his hand upon my arm, and glancing over his shoulder with hollow eyes, "was just a year ago. Six or seven months passed, and I had recovered from the surprise and shock, when one morning, as the day was breaking, I, standing at the door, looked towards the red light, and saw the spectre again." He stopped, with a fixed look at me.

"Did it cry out?"

"No. It was silent."

"Did it wave its arm?"

"No. It leaned against the shaft of the light, with both hands before the face. Like this."

Once more I followed his action with my eyes. It was an action of mourning. I have seen such an attitude in stone figures on tombs.

"Did you go up to it?"

"I came in and sat down, partly to collect my thoughts, partly because it had turned me faint. When I went to the door

again, daylight was above me, and the ghost was gone."

"But nothing followed? Nothing came of this?"

He touched me on the arm with his forefinger twice or thrice giving a ghastly nod each time:

"That very day, as a train came out of the tunnel, I noticed, at a carriage window on my side, what looked like a confusion of hands and heads, and something waved. I saw it just in time to signal the driver, Stop! He shut off, and put his brake on, but the train drifted past here a hundred and fifty yards or more. I ran after it, and, as I went along, heard terrible screams and cries. A young lady had died instantaneously in one of the compartments, and was brought in here, and laid down on this floor between us."

Involuntarily I pushed my chair back, as I looked from the boards at which he pointed to himself.

"True, sir. True. Precisely as it happened, so I tell it you."

I could think of nothing to say, to any purpose, and my mouth was very dry. The wind and the wires took up the story with a long lamenting wail.

He resumed. "Now, sir, mark this, and judge how my mind is troubled. The spectre came back a week ago. Ever since, it has been there, now and again, by fits and starts."

"At the light?"

"At the dangerlight."

"What does it seem to do?"

He repeated, if possible with increased passion and vehemence, that former gesticulation of, 'For God's sake, clear

the way!'

Then he went on. "I have no peace or rest for it. It calls to me, for many minutes together, in an agonized manner, 'Below there! Look out!' It stands waving to me. It rings my bell—"

I caught at that. "Did it ring your bell yesterday evening when I was here, and you went to the door?"

"Twice."

"Why, see," said I, "how your imagination misleads you. My eyes were on the bell, and my ears were open to the bell, and if I am a living man, it did *not* ring at those times. No, nor at any other time, except when it was rung in the natural course of physical things by the station communicating with you."

He shook his head. "I have never made a mistake as to that yet, sir. I have never confused the spectre's ring with the man's. The ghost's ring is a strange vibration in the bell that it derives from nothing else, and I have not asserted that the bell stirs to the eye. I don't wonder that you failed to hear it. But I heard it."

"And did the spectre seem to be there, when you looked out?"

"It *was* there."'

"Both times?"

He repeated firmly: "Both times."

"Will you come to the door with me, and look for it now?"

He bit his underlip as though he were somewhat unwilling, but arose. I opened the door, and stood on the step, while he stood in the doorway. There was the dangerlight. There was the dismal mouth of the tunnel. There were the high, wet stone

walls of the cutting.

"Do you see it?" I asked him, taking particular note of his face. His eyes were prominent and strained, but not very much more so, perhaps, than my own had been when I had directed them earnestly towards the same spot.

"No," he answered. "It is not there."

"Agreed," said I.

We went in again, shut the door, and resumed our seats. I was thinking how best to improve this advantage, if it might be called one, when he took up the conversation in such a matter-of-course way, so assuming that there could be no serious question of fact between us, that I felt myself placed in the weakest of positions.

"By this time you will fully understand, sir," he said, "that what troubles me so dreadfully is the question, what does the spectre mean?"

I was not sure, I told him, that I did fully understand.

"What is its warning against?" he said, ruminating, with his eyes on the fire, and only by times turning them on me. "What is the danger? Where is the danger? There is danger overhanging somewhere on the line. Some dreadful calamity will happen. It is not to be doubted this third time, after what has gone before. But surely this is a cruel haunting of *me*. What can I do?"

He pulled out his handkerchief and wiped the drops from his heated forehead.

"If I telegraphed danger, on either side of me, or on both, I

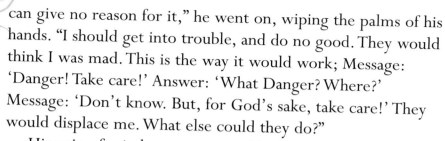

can give no reason for it," he went on, wiping the palms of his hands. "I should get into trouble, and do no good. They would think I was mad. This is the way it would work; Message: 'Danger! Take care!' Answer: 'What Danger? Where?' Message: 'Don't know. But, for God's sake, take care!' They would displace me. What else could they do?"

His pain of mind was most pitiable to see. It was the mental torture of a conscientious man, oppressed beyond endurance by an unintelligible responsibility involving life.

"When it first stood under the dangerlight," he went on, putting his dark hair back from his head, and drawing his hands outward across and across his temples in an extremity of feverish distress, "why not tell me where that accident was to happen, if it must happen? Why not tell me how it could be averted, if it could have been averted? When on its second coming it hid its face, why not tell me, instead, 'She is going to die. Let them keep her at home'? If it came, on those two occasions, only to show me that its warnings were true, and so to prepare me for the third, why not warn me plainly now? And I, Lord help me! A mere poor signal-man on this solitary station! Why not go to somebody with credit to be believed, and power to act?"

When I saw him in this state, I saw that for the poor man's sake, as well as for the public safety, what I had to do for the time was to compose his mind. Therefore, setting aside all question of reality or unreality between us, I represented to him that whoever thoroughly discharged his duty must do

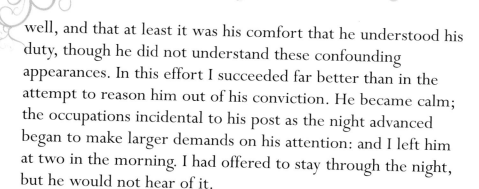

well, and that at least it was his comfort that he understood his duty, though he did not understand these confounding appearances. In this effort I succeeded far better than in the attempt to reason him out of his conviction. He became calm; the occupations incidental to his post as the night advanced began to make larger demands on his attention: and I left him at two in the morning. I had offered to stay through the night, but he would not hear of it.

That I more than once looked back at the red light as I ascended the pathway, that I did not like the red light, and that I should have slept but poorly if my bed had been under it, I see no reason to conceal. Nor did I like the two sequences of the accident and the dead girl. I see no reason to conceal that either.

But what ran most in my thoughts was the consideration how ought I to act, having become the recipient of this disclosure? I had proved the man to be intelligent, vigilant, painstaking, and exact; but how long might he remain so, in his state of mind? Though in a subordinate position, still he held a most important trust, and would I (for instance) like to stake my own life on the chances of his continuing to execute it with precision?

Unable to overcome a feeling that there would be something treacherous in my communicating what he had told me to his superiors in the company, without first being plain with himself and proposing a middle course to him, I ultimately resolved to offer to accompany him (otherwise keeping his secret for the present) to the wisest medical

practitioner we could hear of in those parts, and to take his opinion. A change in his time of duty would come round next night, he had apprized me, and he would be off an hour or two after sunrise, and on again soon after sunset. I had appointed to return accordingly.

Next evening was a lovely evening, and I walked out early to enjoy it. The sun was not yet quite down when I traversed the field path near the top of the deep cutting. I would extend my walk for an hour, I said to myself – half an hour on and half an hour back, and it would then be time to go to my signal-man's box.

Before pursuing my stroll, I stepped to the brink and mechanically looked down, from the point from which I had first seen him. I cannot describe the thrill that seized upon me, when, close at the mouth of the tunnel, I saw the appearance of a man, with his left sleeve across his eyes, passionately waving his right arm.

The nameless horror that oppressed me passed in a moment, for in a moment I saw that this appearance of a man was a man indeed, and that there was a little group of other men, standing at a short distance, to whom he seemed to be rehearsing the gesture he made. The danger light was not yet lighted. Against its shaft, a little low hut, entirely new to me, had been made of some wooden supports and tarpaulin. It looked no bigger than a bed.

With an irresistible sense that something was wrong, with a

flashing self-reproachful fear that fatal mischief had come of my leaving the man there, and causing no one to be sent to overlook or correct what he did, I descended the notched path with all the speed I could make.

"What is the matter?" I asked the men.

"Signal-man killed this morning, sir."

"Not the man belonging to that box?"

"Yes, sir."

"Not the man I know?"

"You will recognize him, sir, if you knew him," said the man who spoke for the others, solemnly uncovering his own head, and raising an end of the tarpaulin, "for his face is quite composed."

"Oh, how did this happen, how did this happen?" I asked, turning from one to another as the hut closed in again.

"He was cut down by an engine, sir. No man in England knew his work better. But somehow he was not clear of the outer rail. It was just at broad day. He had struck the light, and had the lamp in his hand. As the engine came out of the tunnel, his back was towards her, and she cut him down. That man drove her, and was showing how it happened. Show the gentleman, Tom."

The man, who wore rough dark dress, stepped back to his former place at the mouth of the tunnel.

"Coming round the curve in the tunnel, sir," he said, "I saw him at the end, like as if I saw him down a perspective-glass. There was no time to check speed, and I knew him to be very

careful. As he didn't seem to take heed of the whistle, I shut it off when we were running down upon him, and called to him as loud as I could call."

"What did you say?"

"I said, 'Below there! Look out! Look out! For God's sake, clear the way!'"

I started.

"Ah! it was a dreadful time, sir. I never left off calling to him. I put this arm before my eyes not to see, and I waved this arm to the last; but it was no use."

Without prolonging the narrative to dwell on any one of its curious circumstances more than on any other, I may, in closing it, point out the coincidence that the warning of the engine driver included, not only the words which the unfortunate signal-man had repeated to me as haunting him, but also the words which I myself – not he – had attached, and that only in my own mind, to the gesticulation he had imitated.

The Masque of the Red Death

1842

Edgar Allan Poe

The 'Red Death' had long devastated the country. No pestilence had ever been so fatal. Blood was its Avatar and its seal – the redness and the horror of blood. There were sharp pains, and sudden dizziness, and then profuse bleeding at the pores, with dissolution. The scarlet stains upon the body and especially upon the face of the victim, were the pest ban which shut him out from the aid and from the sympathy of his fellow-men. And the whole seizure, progress and termination of the disease, were the incidents of half an hour.

But the Prince Prospero was happy and dauntless and sagacious. When his dominions were half depopulated, he summoned to his presence a thousand hale and light-hearted friends from among the knights and dames of his court, and with these retired to the deep seclusion of one of his

castellated abbeys. This was an extensive and magnificent structure, the creation of the prince's own eccentric yet august taste. A strong and lofty wall girdled it in. This wall had gates of iron. The courtiers, having entered, brought furnaces and massy hammers and welded the bolts. They resolved to leave means neither of ingress or egress to the sudden impulses of despair or of frenzy from within. The abbey was amply provisioned. With such precautions the courtiers might bid defiance to contagion. The external world could take care of itself. In the meantime it was folly to grieve, or to think. The prince had provided all the appliances of pleasure. There were buffoons, there were improvisatori, there were ballet dancers, there were musicians, there was beauty, there was wine. All these and security were within. Without was the 'Red Death.'

It was toward the close of the fifth month of his seclusion, while the pestilence raged furiously, that the Prince Prospero entertained his friends at a masked ball of unusual magnificence.

It was a voluptuous scene, that masquerade. But first let me tell of the rooms in which it was held. There were seven – an imperial suite. The apartments were so irregularly disposed that the vision embraced but little more than one at a time. There was a sharp turn at every twenty or thirty yards, and at each turn a novel effect. To the right and left, in the middle of each wall, a tall and narrow Gothic window looked out upon a closed corridor which pursued the windings of the suite. These windows were of stained glass whose colour varied in accordance with the prevailing hue of the decorations of the chamber into which it opened. That at the eastern extremity was hung, for example, in blue — and vividly blue were its windows. The second chamber was purple in its ornaments and tapestries, and here the panes were purple. The third was green throughout, and so were the casements. The fourth was furnished and lighted with orange — the fifth with white — the sixth with violet. The seventh apartment was closely shrouded in black velvet tapestries that hung all over the ceiling and down the walls, falling in heavy folds upon a carpet of the same material and hue. But in this chamber only, the colour of the windows failed to correspond with the decorations. The panes here were scarlet — a deep blood colour. Now in no one of the seven apartments was there any lamp or candelabrum, amid the profusion of golden ornaments that lay scattered to and fro or depended from the roof. There was no light of any kind emanating from lamp or candle within the suite of chambers. But in the corridors that followed the suite, there stood, opposite to each window, a heavy tripod, bearing a brazier of fire that protected its rays through the tinted glass and so glaringly illumined the room. And thus were produced a multitude of gaudy and fantastic appearances. But in the western or black chamber the effect of the firelight that streamed upon the dark hangings through the blood-tinted panes, was ghastly in the extreme, and produced so wild a look upon the countenances of those who entered, that there were few of the company bold enough to set foot within its precincts at all.

It was in this apartment, also, that there stood against the western wall, a gigantic clock of ebony. Its pendulum swung to and fro with a dull, heavy, monotonous clang; and when the minute-hand made the circuit of the face, and the hour was to be stricken, there came from the brazen lungs of the clock a sound which was clear and loud and deep and exceedingly musical, but of so peculiar a note and emphasis that, at each lapse of an hour, the musicians of the orchestra were constrained to pause, momentarily, in their performance, to hearken to the sound; and thus the waltzers perforce ceased their evolutions; and there was a brief disconcert of the whole merry company. And, while the chimes of the clock yet rang, it was observed that the giddiest grew pale, and the more aged and sedate passed their hands over their brows as if in confused reverie or meditation. But when the echoes had fully ceased, a light laughter at once pervaded the assembly. The musicians looked at each other and smiled as if at their own nervousness and folly, and made whispering vows, each to the other, that the next chiming of the clock should produce in them no similar emotion. And then, after the lapse of sixty minutes, (which embrace three thousand and six hundred seconds of the Time that flies,) there came yet another chiming of the clock, and then were the same disconcert and tremulousness and meditation as before.

But, in spite of these things, it was a magnificent revel. The tastes of the duke were peculiar. He had a fine eye for colours and effects. His plans were bold and fiery, and his conceptions

glowed with barbaric lustre. There are some who would have thought him mad. His followers felt he was not. It was necessary to hear, see and touch him to be sure that he was not.

He had directed, in great part, the moveable embellishments of the seven chambers, upon occasion of this great *fête*; and it was his own guiding taste which had given character to the masqueraders. Be sure they were grotesque. There were much glare and glitter and piquancy and phantasm. There were arabesque figures with unsuited limbs and appointments. There were delirious fancies such as the madman fashions.

There was much of the beautiful, much of the wanton, much of the bizarre, something of the terrible, and not a little of that which might have excited disgust. To and fro in the seven chambers there stalked, in fact, a multitude of dreams. And these – the dreams – writhed in and about, taking hue from the rooms, and causing the wild music of the orchestra to seem as the echo of their steps.

And, anon, there strikes the ebony clock which stands in the hall of the velvet. And then, for a moment, all is still, and all is silent save the voice of the clock. The dreams are stiff-frozen as they stand. But the echoes of the chime die away – they have endured but an instant – and a light, half-subdued laughter floats after them as they depart.

And now again the music swells, and the dreams live, and writhe to and fro more merrily than ever, taking hue from the tinted windows through which stream the rays from the tripods.

But to the chamber which lies most westwardly of the seven, there are now none of the masquers who venture. For the night is waning away; and there flows a ruddier light through the blood-coloured panes; and the blackness of the sable drapery appals. And to him whose foot falls upon the sable carpet, there comes from the near clock of ebony a muffled peal more solemnly emphatic than any which reaches *their* ears who indulge in the more remote gaieties of the other apartments.

But these other apartments were densely crowded, and in them beat feverishly the heart of life. And the revel went whirlingly on, until at length there commenced the sounding of midnight upon the clock. And then the music ceased, as I have told; and the evolutions of the waltzers were quieted; and there was an uneasy cessation of all things as before. But now there were twelve strokes to be sounded by the bell of the clock; and thus it happened, that more of thought crept, with more of time, into the meditations of the thoughtful among those who revelled. And thus, too, it happened, perhaps, that before the last echoes of the last chime had utterly sunk into silence, there were many individuals in the crowd who had found leisure to become aware of the presence of a masked figure that had arrested the attention of no single individual before. And the rumour of this new presence having spread itself whisperingly around, there arose at length from the whole company a buzz, or murmur, expressive of disapprobation and surprise – then, finally, of terror, of horror, and of disgust.

In an assembly of phantasms such as I have painted, it may well be supposed that no ordinary appearance could have excited such sensation. In truth the masquerade license of the night was nearly unlimited; but the figure in question had gone beyond the bounds of even the prince's indefinite decorum. There are chords in the hearts of the most reckless which cannot be touched without emotion. Even with the utterly lost, to whom life and death are equally jests, there are matters of which no jest can be made. The whole company, indeed, seemed now deeply to feel that in the costume and bearing of the stranger neither wit nor propriety existed.

The figure was tall and gaunt, and shrouded from head to foot in the garments of the grave. The mask that concealed the visage was made so nearly to resemble the countenance of a stiffened corpse that the closest scrutiny must have had difficulty in detecting the cheat. And yet all this might have been endured, if not approved, by the mad revellers around. But the mummer had gone so far as to assume the type of the Red Death. His vesture was dabbled in *blood* – and his brow, with the features of the face, was besprinkled with the scarlet horror.

When the eyes of Prince Prospero fell upon this spectral image (which with a slow and solemn movement, as if more fully to sustain its role, stalked to and fro among the waltzers) he was seen to be convulsed, in the first moment with a strong shudder either of terror or distaste; but, in the next, his brow reddened with rage.

"Who dares?" he demanded hoarsely of the courtiers who

stood near him. "Who dares insult us with this blasphemous mockery? Seize him and unmask him, that we may know whom we have to hang at sunrise!"

It was in the eastern or blue chamber in which stood the Prince Prospero as he uttered these words. They rang throughout the seven rooms loudly and clearly – for the prince was a bold and robust man, and the music had become hushed at the waving of his hand.

At first, as he spoke, there was a slight rushing movement of the courtiers in the direction of the intruder, who at the moment was also near at hand, and now, with deliberate and stately step, made closer approach to the speaker. But from a certain nameless awe with which the mad assumptions of the mummer had inspired the whole party, there were found none who put forth hand to seize him; so that, unimpeded, he passed within a yard of the prince's person. And, while the vast assembly, as if with one impulse, shrank from the centres of the rooms to the walls, he made his way uninterruptedly, but with the same solemn and measured step which had distinguished him from the first, through the blue chamber to the purple – through the purple to the green – through the green to the orange – through this again to the white – and even thence to the violet, ere a decided movement had been made to arrest him. It was then, however, that the Prince Prospero, maddening with rage and the shame of his own momentary cowardice, rushed hurriedly through the six chambers – while none followed him on account of a deadly terror that had seized upon all. He bore aloft a drawn dagger, and had approached, to within three or four feet of the retreating figure, when the latter turned suddenly and confronted his pursuer. There was a sharp cry – and the dagger dropped gleaming upon the sable carpet, upon which, instantly afterwards, fell prostrate in death the Prince Prospero. Then, summoning the wild courage of despair, a throng of the revellers at once threw themselves into the black apartment, and, seizing the mummer – whose tall figure stood erect and motionless within the shadow of the ebony clock – gasped in unutterable horror at finding the burial clothes and corpse-like mask which they handled with so violent a rudeness, untenanted by any tangible form.

And now was acknowledged the presence of the Red Death. He had come like a thief in the night. And one by one dropped

the revellers in the blood-bedewed halls of their revel, and died each in the despairing posture of his fall. And the life of the ebony clock went out with that of the last of the merry. And the flames of the tripods expired. And darkness and decay and the Red Death held illimitable dominion over all.